LOST TO DESIRE

Francis pulled her to him again and this time his kiss was hard and demanding. She felt his tongue probing against her teeth, felt his hands move to caress her buttocks, felt the strength of him pressing against her, forcing her backwards toward the bed. Despite her vow to remain unmoved and unresponsive, Morgan struggled in his arms. He was pushing her down, his weight on top of her, his tongue now roving at will inside her mouth, his hands moving to the ties of her blue silk traveling blouse.

Clumsily, he undid the ties with one hand while the other pushed the heavy tawny hair from her forehead. Morgan's heart beat rapidly as he finished unlacing her blouse and parted the fabric to reveal her full, white breasts. As if by reflex, she attempted to shove his hands away.

"Whom do you fight, Morgan?" he inquired with that whimsical grin. "Me—or yourself?"

Other Avon Books by
Mary Daheim

LOVE'S PIRATE

Avon Books are available at special quantity discounts for bulk purchases for sales promotions, premiums, fund raising or educational use. Special books, or book excerpts, can also be created to fit specific needs.

For details write or telephone the office of the Director of Special Markets, Avon Books, Dept. FP, 1790 Broadway, New York, New York 10019, 212-399-1357.

MARY DAHEIM

AVON
PUBLISHERS OF BARD, CAMELOT, DISCUS AND FLARE BOOKS

DESTINY'S PAWN is an original publication of Avon Books. This work has never before appeared in book form.

AVON BOOKS
A division of
The Hearst Corporation
1790 Broadway
New York, New York 10019

Copyright © 1984 by Mary Daheim
Published by arrangement with the author
Library of Congress Catalog Card Number: 84-90792
ISBN: 0-380-86884-9

All rights reserved, which includes the right to
reproduce this book or portions thereof in any form
whatsoever except as provided by the U. S. Copyright Law.
For information address Donald McCampbell, Inc.
12 East 41st Street, New York, New York 10017

First Avon Printing, April, 1984

AVON TRADEMARK REG. U. S. PAT. OFF. AND IN
OTHER COUNTRIES, MARCA REGISTRADA, HECHO
EN U. S. A.

Printed in the U. S. A.

WFH 10 9 8 7 6 5 4 3 2 1

PART ONE

1534–1535

Chapter 1

MORGAN SQUINTED against the April sun and frowned. She couldn't be mistaken. The feet sticking out from under the much-hemmed riding skirt definitely belonged to her cousin Nan, but why was Nan crouched under a huge golden forsythia bush with only her shoes and backside showing?

Picking up her own worn muslin skirt, Morgan hurried noiselessly, stopping behind Nan's motionless form. "Whatever are you doing?" Morgan hissed at her cousin, whose posterior twitched with surprise.

Nan extricated herself as quietly as possible from the bush, yellow blossoms clinging to her wide shoulders and night-black hair. "Hush, Morgan!" whispered Nan, a mischievous twinkle in her dark eyes. "It's Bess and one of the Madden twins. They're—they're . . ." Nan's big eyes grew even wider, and she spread her tapering hands in a helplessly inarticulate gesture. "You know what I mean!" she said in a breathless voice. "See for yourself!"

Morgan looked perplexedly at her younger cousin. Bess, the cook's sly-eyed daughter, was scarcely sixteen, only a year older than Nan and two years younger than Morgan herself. Morgan had a vague idea what Nan was talking about and knew Aunt Margaret had said recently that Bess was "no better than she ought to be." But still . . .

"I've no intention of crawling around in the bushes to peer at Bess and one of the Madden twins," Morgan replied haughtily. "Whatever they are doing, as long as they are not stealing from us, it's their business."

"Ooooh!" Nan was all but jumping up and down with excitement. "You're afraid to look, Morgan Todd; you're too prudish."

Despite the difference in their ages, Nan had always

been the more adventuresome of the two cousins—the first to learn to swim, the first to take her pony over the hurdles, the first to climb to the pinnacles of the manor house's single turret. To make matters worse, Nan had surpassed Morgan in height the previous year and now was a good three inches taller and showed no signs of stopping her rapid growth.

Morgan gave in to the taunt with a toss of her thick tawny hair. "I'm not a prude," she announced with injured pride, and marched resolutely to the forsythia bush, pulling aside two of the more forbidding branches. At least she didn't have to worry about ruining her clothes since she was wearing a very old kirtle and an even older bodice; her good clothes were already packed along with the new items she would need for life at King Henry the Eighth's court in London.

Crawling on her hands and knees along the pathway Nan had already made, Morgan peered through the green-and-yellow maze of flowers and leaves. The stable door was ajar, and sure enough, there was Bess, bare to the waist, her high round breasts exposed, her skirts bunched up to reveal long, slim legs. One of the Madden twins—Davy or Hal? Morgan never could be sure which—was lying naked as a newborn babe on top of her. Bess was giggling in a strange, throaty sort of way, and Davy—or Hal—looked far more serious as he concentrated on whatever he was trying to do between her thighs.

But of course Morgan knew and felt her cheeks turn hot. She knew that men and women did such things. She could not have grown up in the same household with her French grandmother, Isabeau, and not have known. Indeed, she had seen the animals at the manor house mate during their seasons and it all seemed quite natural. But here, before her very eyes, was one of the Madden twins—a boy her own age who, along with his brother, had been a stable hand ever since Morgan could remember—and the shifty-faced, hip-swaying Bess, rutting away like a couple of goats. And Bess was actually giggling! Morgan turned away and plunged back through the forsythia bush, almost poking herself in the eye with a wayward branch.

"They really ought to have closed the door," Morgan declared with what she hoped was an air of disdain and composure.

"Oh, they did!" Nan laughed. "But I opened it!"

"You *what?*" Morgan all but flew at her younger cousin, the tawny hair flying around her slim shoulders.

Nan put up her hands in a reflex of self-defense. "Stay, coz, I didn't do it on purpose! I was going to ride my new mare, the one your father bought me for my birthday last month, and when I opened the stable door, I saw Hal and Bess tussling by the feed sacks. They didn't see me, so I decided I'd better leave the door open or they'd know I was there." Nan blinked twice, looking ingenuous and smug.

"So you spied on them?" Morgan was shocked and incredulous.

"Well, sort of. I *was* curious. Bess spends a lot of time in the stable when she's supposed to be in the kitchens. And I've seen Davy pinch her bottom."

"Davy—or Hal?" Morgan asked in exasperation, at last finding a less embarrassing target for her distress.

Nan waved her hands again. "Oh, I don't know which. Probably both."

Morgan glanced over her shoulder in the direction of the stable. "Probably," she drawled, and now her own topaz eyes glinted with humor. "No wonder she gives herself airs and sneers at both of us. She must fancy herself quite the worldly woman for all that she is just a kitchen wench."

"Well, that's all she ever will be," Nan said, starting to wander along the lime walk which circled Faux Hall. "Not that there's anything wrong in being a servant. Maybe Bess is having a better time than we are."

"Nan!" Morgan paused at the edge of the oval fishpond with its borders of white and pink azaleas. "You'd rather be off in a stable somewhere with the Madden twins than have fine clothes and the chance to serve at court?"

Nan sat down by the pond and took off her shoes. "No," she said in a vague sort of way, "of course not. But people like Bess seem to have more freedom than we do. They may not live in manor houses or palaces or go to balls and supper parties, but they seem to—I don't know, just enjoy themselves more."

Morgan was about to retort that she did not consider rolling around in the hay with Hal—or Davy—a very enjoyable idea, but held her tongue as she gave more thought to Nan's remark. Both girls had been brought up at Faux

Hall at the edge of the Chiltern Hills in Buckinghamshire; both had been only children; both had led sheltered, relatively pampered lives, exposed only to as much of the real world as was seen fit by their doting parents. Nan's father had died four years earlier, and Aunt Margaret had become even more protective. Morgan's parents, Lady Alice and Sir Edmund Todd, had made sure that the two girls were well educated, well mannered, and, except for a trip to London and an occasional visit to Aylesbury or St. Albans, confined to their own little world, which revolved around the family and Faux Hall.

But all that was about to change for Morgan, who was eighteen, marriageable, and ready to leave for London the following day. It was Nan, now dangling her bare feet in the fishpond's cool waters, who brought up this great adventure. "But you will be at court in just two days," she said rather peevishly. It was, after all, a sore point with Nan, who saw the three years' difference in age as no barrier to prevent her from joining Morgan in what would surely be the most momentous event in anyone's life.

"You'll have your chance, too," Morgan said a bit wearily, for she and Nan and the rest of the family had argued this very point into the ground over the past few months. Following Nan's lead, she also took off her shoes and dipped her feet in the pond. "Besides, if you must know, I'm frightened."

"Frightened!" Nan kicked one foot up and splashed them both. "How can you be frightened of anything so exciting?"

Morgan shrugged, gazed up at the dovecote, then turned to watch a pair of barn swallows swoop in the direction of the granary. "King Henry is said to be very fierce when he's angered, Anne Boleyn has a vile temper, and all those great personages with their wealth and wit and power . . ." Morgan shook her head as the swallows disappeared toward the orchard. "I'm just another young girl from the country, trying to be a fine lady. Why wouldn't I be frightened?"

"Well, your Uncle Thomas is there, and he's said to wield influence almost as great as the King's. Surely that ought to make you feel better." Nan pulled her feet out of the pond and stood up, shaking the cold water off onto the new spring grass. "Lord knows he rose from nowhere and is now His Grace's most indispensable accomplice."

"That's the word, 'accomplice,' " Morgan said glumly. "You know perfectly well that nobody here at Faux Hall gives a fig for Thomas Cromwell. In fact, they blame him more than Anne Boleyn for what's happened to the Church since Henry got rid of Catherine of Aragon."

"Oh, Morgan," Nan said, her dark eyes huge, "you won't say things like that at court, will you?"

Morgan lifted her feet from the pond but decided not to put her shoes back on. The grass felt soft and fresh beneath her bare feet, and it occurred to her that it would be a long time before she could go without shoes again. "Of course not," Morgan assured her cousin. "At least I hope not. Lord knows we have always been able to speak freely here. Anyway, Uncle Thomas is only related by marriage."

"But his influence won't harm you any," Nan teased, but got no reaction from Morgan, who seemed deep in thought, staring into the pond, apparently not even seeing the darting movements of the brilliant orange goldfish. "I take it you're not frightened about seeing Sean O'Connor?"

This comment did rouse Morgan, who whirled on her cousin. "Sean! Why do you say that?"

Nan leaped away from Morgan. "Because you're mad with love for him and have been ever since he was here last spring on his way to London. For six months all you said was, 'Don't you think Sean is handsome? Aren't Sean's eyes ever so blue? Doesn't Sean have the most attractive freckles?' I felt like throwing up."

"Oh!" Morgan threw her shoes at her cousin, missed, and watched in horror as they fell into the fishpond and sunk out of sight. Nan laughed, and Morgan started to chase her cousin, but the younger, longer-legged girl had a head start. Morgan watched her disappear down the lime walk and around the corner of the gray-stoned manor house.

Nan was right, of course. Sean O'Connor, now apprenticed to the great court artist Hans Holbein the younger, did have the bluest eyes, the most attractive smattering of freckles, the waviest black hair, and a smile that would have melted an ice sculpture. Morgan had known Sean all her life, since he was distantly related to her father and came from Armagh at least once a year with his own family for weddings, christenings, funerals, or whatever event served to unite the Irish side of the family with its English counterpart.

But it wasn't until the previous spring when Sean had stopped on his way to London that Morgan had realized she felt more for the young Irishman than just familial affection. He had kissed her, gently, lingeringly, and she knew that what she felt for him must be love. Surely he must love her too. Though Morgan was indeed apprehensive about the glitter and glamour of the court, she was also very excited about seeing Sean O'Connor again. She thought suddenly about Bess and the Madden youth. What did their raucous mating have to do with love? Real love wasn't two young bodies crudely rutting in the stable. By Our Lady, Morgan thought, real love was meaningful glances across a crowded supper table, clasped hands under a star-filled sky, tender kisses exchanged under the rose-covered arbor. It was what she felt for Sean O'Connor and had nothing to do with whatever repellent activities went on between Bess and the Madden twins. Buoyed by anticipation, she thrust aside her increasing doubts and fears about her court debut as she wandered off the lime walk toward the orchard. She could almost still feel the touch of his lips on hers and how she all but reeled in his arms. Morgan had been seventeen at the time and, some would say, overripe for her first kiss, but Faux Hall was relatively isolated and young men of her own age did not often come to call. On the rare occasions when they did, both Lady Alice and Aunt Margaret watched their daughters like a pair of mother hens.

A sparrow was pecking for food in the grass, but flew off as Morgan approached. She paused to reach up and break off a cluster of lilacs, savoring the blossoms' heady fragrance. She could still see the old stone granary beyond the flowering fruit trees and could not help but wonder when she would return to Faux Hall again. Suddenly every gray stone, every shining leaf, every scrap of sod seemed touchingly dear. Morgan had entered the world in this very place during a blinding February blizzard. Lady Alice had favored the name Elizabeth for a girl, but Sir Edmund Todd wanted his female child called Jane, after his mother. Neither parent would give in, but Lady Alice finally suggested a compromise.

"Since there are Elizabeths and Janes aplenty, and as I'm very fond of my kin by marriage, Morgan Williams, why—"

Sir Edmund had all but exploded at the very notion. "A daughter called Morgan? You would want her to be a witch such as Morgan le Fay?"

"Scarcely, since Morgan Williams is a man and certainly not a witch!" Lady Alice had laughed. "But it is a distinctive name."

Sir Edmund had to agree with that. "Morgan Williams is also the only connection with your Cromwell kin that you can abide, so I suppose it's only right to honor him somehow."

"My sister showed poor judgment by marrying a Cromwell," Lady Alice had acknowledged, but had added archly, "of course, *her* name is Jane."

Sir Edmund had chuckled in spite of himself, gazed down at his firstborn, and decided that perhaps Morgan wasn't such a peculiar name for a girl after all. And the child was unusual-looking, even as a newborn: Her eyes were not the customary blue but flecked with green and gold; her full head of hair was neither brown nor blond but somewhere in between; the facial features were perfect, yet somehow exaggerated, as if a painter had added a touch here and there for dramatic emphasis.

As she had grown into young womanhood, with her tawny hair, big green-tinged topaz eyes, and the wide, full mouth and high cheekbones, only her small, turned-up nose seemed underemphasized. And while Morgan had never considered herself actually pretty, the adults among her family and friends commented on the drama of her striking looks rather than mere beauty.

But as she grew older, there were no brothers or sisters to join her in the nursery. For some inexplicable reason, Lady Alice never bore another child, and Morgan's only company at Faux Hall was her younger cousin, Nan, whose own mother had lost her other two babes in childbirth. Still, it had been a happy, peaceful existence.

When Morgan was twelve, her parents had taken her to London, some forty miles to the southeast. How awed she had been by the bustle, the throngs of people, the fine houses along The Strand! She had no opportunity to glimpse Henry or his first Queen, Catherine of Aragon, but just passing by their palaces of Whitehall and St. James had thrilled her.

And now she would actually live in London with the court. Of course Catherine was no longer Queen; Henry had forsaken her for Anne Boleyn. It was hard to think of anyone but Catherine as Queen. She had been consort long before Morgan was born. It was especially hard to think of Anne Boleyn in her place, since Morgan's parents neither approved of the new Queen nor of Henry defying the Pope to marry her.

But politics and religion were not uppermost in Morgan's mind as she strolled along the edge of the oval-shaped fishpond. The cloud of anxiety which had fallen upon her so swiftly had departed. Sean awaited her in London; the court awaited her; the whole center of the world seemed to await just a two-day journey away.

From somewhere, a cry broke Morgan's reverie. A cat, an owl—or was it human? Morgan turned slowly, unsure of where the sound had come from. The dovecote, maybe, or the stable. Perhaps one of the servants had been hurt. But she heard the sound again, and, alert this time, she decided it was coming from far out in the orchard and was not human but an animal cry. Picking up her muslin skirts, she ran past the stable and through the tunnel of trees laden with pink and white blossoms. There, not far from the road, was Gambit, the family's aged collie, in obvious pain and tended to by a very tall man dressed in riding clothes. Morgan paused, unable to recognize Gambit's rescuer and faintly bemused that the dog seemed unafraid of a stranger.

The man looked up from under bushy sandy brows as Morgan approached. "A thorn," he said in a deep, vaguely gruff voice. He was in his mid-twenties, with short-cropped hair and slate gray eyes. Gambit gave a brief bark of gratitude, sniffed once at the man's long fingers, brushed past Morgan and limped back toward the manor house.

"How kind of you," said Morgan, smiling pleasantly.

"Indeed." The gray eyes glinted with amusement. "Then it is obviously your turn to be appreciative."

"Why surely," Morgan began, as the stranger unclasped his riding cloak and threw it on the petal-strewn ground.

She blinked once and then stared in frozen astonishment as the man walked purposefully toward her and took Morgan in his arms. "Sir!" Morgan cried, attempting to push him away. But before she could make another sound, his mouth claimed hers in a devouring kiss. Stunned, all Morgan could think of in that moment of shock was that this was certainly not the way Sean had kissed her. But as his tongue forced her mouth open and she felt his teeth on her lips, Morgan began to struggle in his grasp. This was no prank, no fantasy; it was real—and terrifying.

With one desperate wrench, Morgan pulled away a scant two inches. "No! Leave me be. I'll scream!"

The stranger merely laughed in a low, rumbling manner. "Assuming anyone would hear you from this distance—what would they think?"

Morgan stared at him with a mixture of fear and puzzlement. He was very tall. She didn't even come to his shoulder. He was lean, but hard-muscled; Morgan could feel the strength of him as he held her close. And he seemed quite unperturbed by her reaction. She opened her mouth to scream—but no sound came out, and before she could try again he was kissing her even more savagely than the first time. He was also pulling the thin bodice from her shoulders, and Morgan began to kick at his shins and pummel him with her fists. He was easing her onto the soft ground, none too gently, and his weight seemed tremendous. One hand went to her mouth and covered it; he lifted himself off her enough to slide the bodice down, down, down—until her full, firm breasts were almost thrust against his chest.

"Enchanting," he murmured—and winked. "They were right; you are a delightful little morsel."

Morgan's eyes sparked fury, and her cheeks flushed with humiliation. She reached out to claw, to scratch, to slap—but his hand grabbed both of hers, and in one swift motion he had pulled off his finely wrought leather belt. Morgan felt tears of helplessness well up in her eyes as he slipped the belt around her wrists and cinched them fast together.

"They did say you were a bit fractious," he said, frowning slightly. "Though I think you're carrying it too far." He shrugged his slightly sloping shoulders, seemed to consider taking his hand off her mouth, saw the mutinous look in her topaz eyes, and changed his mind. Then his other hand began to stroke her breasts, slowly, appreciatively. The long fingers traced the deep pink around her nipples, and he nodded with satisfaction. "You are not as unwilling as you pretend." He grinned, a wicked yet vaguely whimsical expression. His fingers squeezed each nipple in turn and Morgan suddenly realized what he was talking about; the petal-pink tips had turned hard and seemed to throb at his touch. He was hurting her—not a great deal, yet there was something else besides the slight pain, another ache further down in her body, a sensation she had never felt before. She writhed under him in a vain effort to escape.

But he mistook her movements. "You are *that* eager?" His hand was so large it almost enveloped both of her breasts in a crushing embrace. "Very well, my horse is probably ready by now anyway." He raised one bushy eyebrow and looked at Morgan speculatively. The topaz eyes were pleading with him, she was begging him wordlessly to stop—and yet she herself was confused by that unfamiliar sensation in the very core of her being. The man hesitated, kept his hand over her mouth, and with her legs still pinioned under his weight, he moved just enough to pull down the muslin skirt and leave her naked except for the small undergarment which covered her most intimate self.

Morgan tried to turn away in horror but she couldn't move her head. "Long legs—for your size." He nodded again in approval. "I'm not much good at flimsy stuff such as this," he said in the same conversational tone, his thumb hooked into the undergarment. "You'll have to cooperate from this point on." At last he removed the hand from her mouth and started to lift her up so she could take off the final vestige of clothing. Morgan did scream this time, a piercing shriek which seemed to paralyze the stranger. He kneeled motionless for a brief moment, then hurled himself on top of her, the hand again clamped to her face. "Damn!" He glowered at her from under the bushy brows. "This is not a game!" The other hand tore at the undergarment, shredding it swiftly. Just as rapidly, he undid his own clothing, and Morgan shut her eyes in shock as she caught her first glimpse of hard, firm manhood. Eyes still tightly closed, she felt his hand pry her thighs apart, felt the intensity of him searching her out in the most secret recesses of her flesh—and then shuddered as he penetrated her unwilling body.

His movements seemed harsh but sure. Morgan's head reeled, and she wondered vaguely if she would faint. And then she felt real pain, sudden, searing and totally unexpected. I *will* faint, she thought hazily, as tears rolled down her cheeks. And then the world seemed to come apart in a blinding explosion, and though she still hurt, the unfamiliar ache was gone, to be replaced by something else, another new sensation, which caused her to go completely limp in her assailant's grasp.

It was his turn for shock. He withdrew himself from her slowly, staring at her in astonishment. He took his hand off her mouth and put both arms around her. "Christ," he murmured softly. "They swore you were no virgin." One long finger brushed the tears from her hot cheeks. He grabbed his riding cloak, threw it over Morgan, and quickly got his clothing back in order. "Are you . . . all right?" He looked genuinely concerned, deep furrows on his faintly sunburned forehead.

Morgan was too stunned, too shocked to speak. Of course she was not all right. She had been violated—and her wrists were still bound together. "Untie me!" she demanded in a shrill, hysterical voice. "Oh God," she moaned, as the world stopped spinning and her power of speech returned, "you are a monster!"

The man had clearly forgotten about Morgan's wrists. The cloak had slipped down to her waist but she was too outraged to care. Yet even as he undid the belt, he could not resist grinning at her naked breasts. "You are enchanting just the same."

"Animal!" Morgan snatched her clothes off the ground, turned her back and dressed quickly. The shredded undergarment she hid in the folds of her skirt. "If you think you can get away with such a heinous crime without serious repercussions, you're mad! In fact, I think you *are* mad!"

The man had also stood up after retrieving his riding cloak. "Nonsense. You got precisely what you came for. And you enjoyed it, despite your maidenly protestations." He gazed around, taking in the orchards and the distant stable. "The twins said they would be done in half an hour. I was headed for Woodstock and my horse lost a shoe." He was speaking in the same conversational tone, not even faintly contrite and no longer apologetic. "You have pears, apples, and what else—quince?" He jerked his head in the direction of the stable.

"Quince!" Morgan could hardly keep from flying at him, but it occurred to her that the man was knave enough—and somehow deluded enough—to think she might be offering him her body again. "That's enough! You'll talk no more of apples and quince after I've told—"

"Ah," the man interrupted, brushing a stray leaf from his sandy hair, "here comes my horse—and the twins."

Morgan turned to look over her shoulder. The Madden boys were approaching, leading a gray gelding by the reins. They both looked as good-natured as ever, their identical red-cheeked faces smiling somewhat vacantly at Morgan and the man. The vacant look was not caused so much by lack of intelligence as by extreme shortsightedness, however, and it dawned on Morgan that they probably hadn't yet recognized her—nor did she want them to. She gave one last swift glance at the stranger. "I hated what you did to me. I hate you!" And she ran as fast as she could, deep into the orchard and away from the man who had ravished her and hadn't seemed to care.

It took Morgan almost ten minutes to traverse the long way back to the manor house. As she reached the lime walk, she saw Bess coming from the direction of the stables. Bess cast a wary, petulant look at Morgan and scurried off toward the kitchens. Morgan paused. So that was it, she thought, thunderstruck. She had been mistaken for the promiscuous Bess. One of the Madden twins, whichever one had not been with her in the stable, had no doubt offered the wench to the stranger as a means of passing time. But Bess had been otherwise occupied, giggling under the weight of Hal or Davy. Morgan cursed the slut and clenched her fists. Bess was the wanton creature who had caused this unspeakable, horrendous calamity!

But Morgan already knew she could do nothing about it. As she had walked through the orchard she had realized she could not tell her parents what had happened, no matter how horrible it had been. As Lady Alice had said, Morgan's life at court would determine her whole future. If her parents knew she had been raped, they might not even let her go to court. Worst of all, they might not let her marry Sean O'Connor. And if they did, what would Sean think of taking a bride who was not a virgin? Better to explain away her lack of maidenhood as the result of a riding accident or some other such mishap. Her parents must not know, Sean must not know, no one must ever know.

Except, of course, the stranger. But she had no idea who he was. Going to Woodstock, he had said. That meant nothing. Many people went to Woodstock. His accent was different, but Morgan had no notion of its origins. One thing she did know, however, was that he was a gentleman—at least by rank. He was well-spoken and his clothes were of fine quality. He was, she supposed, even rather handsome in a faintly satyrlike way, with his longish face and wicked, whimsical grin. He was certainly tall and . . . Morgan stopped herself and resumed walking toward Faux Hall. He was also certainly an uncivilized beast, and she prayed to God that she would never see the man again. Indifferent to her pain, uncaring about her loss of virginity, more bemused than concerned by her reaction—and stating that she had enjoyed his animallike attack on her body! She paused at the entrance to the manor house's small gallery; she had felt something like pleasure, a physical excitement as he explored her breasts, the ache that had asked to be assuaged, the sudden blinding relief after pain. Yet it couldn't be so. She didn't even know him. There could be nothing like that without love, the kind of love she felt for Sean O'Connor.

Cautiously, Morgan slipped inside the gallery. She would have to change her rumpled and dirty clothes and dispose of the torn undergarment. She didn't realize she was still trembling until she reached the sanctuary of her bedroom on the second floor and closed the door behind her.

Morgan stripped her kirtle and bodice off quickly, rolled the undergarment inside them, and put the whole bundle at the bottom of a box in which she and Nan had been placing worn, discarded items Morgan would never need again.

There was only a small looking glass in Morgan's bedroom; the one full-length mirror at Faux Hall was in the sewing room where her grandmother and the seamstresses were working. Morgan sat down on the bed and scrutinized her body closely. Her wrists were red and chafed; small bruises were beginning to appear on her breasts, upper arms, and legs; but what shocked her most was the stain of blood between her thighs. Morgan's trembling became more violent as the enormity of what had happened finally struck her with full, terrifying force.

"Oh, sweet Mother of God!" Morgan's fingers shook uncontrollably as she traced the bloody evidence of her shame. Until now, it had seemed unreal, almost as if she had dreamed the incredible episode in the orchard and the blond giant who had so cheerfully ravished her.

She had no idea how long she sat on the edge of the bed, shaking and uttering short, gasping sobs. At last, she became aware of someone pounding at the door. It was Nan, calling for Morgan to come out.

"Grandmother is finished! She says you must try the dress on!"

With enormous effort, Morgan responded in what she hoped was a normal voice, "I'll be there at once. I was—I was taking a nap."

Nan did not reply. Morgan knew that her cousin was probably standing outside the door, dark eyes dubious. Morgan seldom napped; she was too full of youthful energy and good health to need extra sleep. But the strain of leave-taking might explain her sudden tiredness, and apparently that must have been what Nan thought, because within a few moments Morgan heard the younger girl say, "Very well," and walk away.

Morgan bathed herself as best she could with a bowl of scented rose water. She brushed the tawny hair and put on another kirtle and bodice, almost as old and worn as the one she had just discarded. Picking up the looking glass, she stared at her face: I look the same, she thought, but I am not. I was a maid a little over an hour ago; now I am a maid no longer.

"Sweet Jesu, help me," Morgan murmured aloud, and put the looking glass down. Bess had obviously relished her encounter with the Madden youth. But an uneducated, unprincipled wench such as Bess didn't give a fig for her virtue, only for momentary pleasures of the flesh. Bess probably wouldn't know love if she found it, Morgan told herself. Yet the blond giant had taken her not only without love but without even knowing—or caring—who she was. And Morgan could do nothing about what had happened except try to forget. Taking a deep breath, which actually seemed to hurt, she opened the door and walked down the empty hallway to the sewing room.

"By the Saints, child, that neckline is a disgrace!" Lady Alice folded her arms across her own full bosom. "Either wear something under that or have Grandmother Isabeau see that a row of embroidery is added to it."

"There's no time, Mother," Morgan replied, sneaking another look in the full-length mirror. Yes, it was perfect, emphasizing the white shoulders and the high, full breasts. She hoped she would be wearing it the first time she saw Sean O'Connor. She also hoped the bruises would have faded by then.

Lady Alice heaved a sigh born of resignation and the desire to keep peace at the time of parting. "How did you manage to take such a tumble just before you are about to leave? It's fortunate you didn't break or sprain anything!"

Morgan's tale of trying to remove the thorn from Gambit's paw and having the dog leap up in pain and cause her to fall against a tree had not been questioned. Accidents involving dogs, horses, cats, and even an occasional dunking in the fishpond were not new with either Morgan or Nan.

As Morgan removed the ball gown, she tried to shield her bruises from the others. Grandmother Isabeau was chuckling: "Grace, movement, carriage—I have tried to educate both you girls. Yet still you fall down!" She shook her gray head and motioned for Clemence, her aged servingwoman, to take away the pincushion, fabric remnants, and a handful of seed pearls which had been left over. "You will do well, *ma petite.* As will Nan, when her time comes." The old woman looked shrewdly at both Lady Alice and Aunt Margaret. "They are alike in some ways, your girls, yet so different from one another. But that is well, for life takes many paths. Nan is tall, like the larch, hair black as the night bird. Morgan, so tawny, so—what is the word? Leonine?" She saw her daughters-in-law both nod. "Like the cat, eh? But the big cat, the one they keep in the Tower of London."

"They keep lions in the Tower?" Nan had jumped up, astounded by this piece of news.

"Well, they used to," Aunt Margaret said. She had not been to London in twenty years and swore she would never go now—not as long as King Henry rejected the Pope and the Church of Rome.

"Eh?" Grandmother Isabeau looked quizzically at Aunt Margaret. The old woman was quite deaf, but her wit and intelligence only seemed to wax with age. "Lions, night birds, all are handsome creatures given us by the *bon Dieu*. And beauty, human or otherwise, comes in all forms."

Her kinswomen smiled with affection. Morgan knew that her grandmother spoke from sweet experience: Fifty years ago Isabeau d'Esternay had been one of the most beautiful women in France. William Todd had visited the court of Louis XI where he had taken part in the negotiations for Margaret of Anjou's ransom. The frightening stare of the miserly French King had been obliterated by the sight of the blue-eyed creature who stood just a few yards away from the royal chair of state. William Todd returned from France with the ransom in his saddlebags and Isabeau d'Esternay in his arms.

Morgan's gaze shifted from her grandmother to Nan, who was peering out the mullioned window. "Someone's riding up," Nan called, throwing open the casement. "It's Tom Seymour! I'm going down to meet him." She ran out of the room, her long, coltlike legs visible beneath the fluttering hem.

Morgan helped her grandmother walk from the sewing room as Lady Alice and Aunt Margaret preceded them. Like Nan, Morgan was delighted to have Tom Seymour visit. They had always looked up to Tom as the big brother neither had ever had. During Sir Edmund's last years in the Royal Navy, Tom had been his protégé. Although Sir Edmund had been retired for almost two years, he still received vicarious pleasure from listening to Tom relate his own exploits.

Sir Edmund had been the first to greet Seymour. As Morgan descended the curved flight of stairs and gently steered her grandmother toward the entrance hall, she watched Tom as he talked to her father and Nan. Tom was gesturing with a wide eagle-sweep of his big hand. His laugh filled the room.

"Ah, Saint-Maur!" called Grandmother Isabeau, using the ancient origins of Tom's surname as she always did to tease him. If any man ever had a less than saintly reputation, particularly where women were concerned, it was Tom Seymour—and Grandmother Isabeau's Gallic background appreciated his flair.

"La Belle Isabeau!" Tom's bow was as courtly as if the old woman had been the grandest and most beautiful woman in Christendom. Indeed, there was still an aura of beauty about her, akin to the last fading rays of a glorious sunset. "No, I have not found you another husband, alas," Tom said in mock despair. It was an old jest between them, with Tom always reporting that he could never find any man who was match enough for Isabeau.

Morgan's grandmother gave an exaggerated sigh. "Ah, but you must hurry, Saint-Maur! One day I shall be too old to care!"

Lady Alice and Aunt Margaret exchanged swift, familiar glances. Naturally, they had grown used to the older woman's frank tongue. But occasionally they wished she would temper her remarks in front of her two impressionable, innocent granddaughters. And Morgan suddenly regarded her grandmother with something other than the usual amusement; until this very day, she had given little thought as to why the old woman talked about wanting another husband. Lonely, Morgan had always decided, and dismissed the comments from her mind. But now she realized that the undertones of Grandmother Isabeau's repartee with Tom—and occasionally others—had a different, less sentimental origin. Morgan's grandmother didn't want a man just to sit by the fire and talk to on rainy winter nights; she actually wanted a man to love her, to caress her, to do with her what the tall blond stranger had done to Morgan herself that very afternoon. It was a powerful insight, frightening at first, until Morgan realized there was comfort in the revelation. Whatever she had felt, assuming it *had* been a sensation of pleasure or fulfillment or whatever—that was not unnatural in itself. At least for women such as Isabeau d'Esternay. As Morgan half listened to the conversation flowing around her, she wondered how much she was like her grandmother.

Such speculation was interrupted when Tom finally came to take Morgan's hand, his white teeth flashing in his red beard. "By God's eyes, Morgan, I swear you've gotten three inches taller since I last saw you six months ago!"

"Nay, Tom," Morgan laughed, looking up at his own splendid height. "You know I haven't grown a jot since I was thirteen."

"She seems taller because she's suddenly a young lady and leaving for court," Sir Edmund said. He smiled at Tom and then at Morgan, who put an arm through her father's.

"Court?" Tom cocked his head at Morgan. "When?"

"Tomorrow. Isn't that exciting?" Morgan was almost dancing with anticipation. Her fears, her anxieties, even the blond stranger were momentarily forgotten.

"Tomorrow! Why, muffet, even now I'm headed for court. Might I have the honor of escorting you to Whitehall?" He grinned at Morgan and then turned to Sir Edmund. "If I may, sir."

Sir Edmund rubbed at his graying temples and glanced at his wife. He and his brother's widow had at least one thing in common—neither cared for London, and Sir Edmund positively loathed court life. "Well—I don't see why not. If Morgan doesn't mind that I don't take her myself . . ."

"Oh, Edmund, I'm not sure if we should presume upon Tom," Lady Alice protested.

But her husband's puckish smile silenced her. "You're not sure my absence won't offend the King—and that odious Cromwell relation of yours who has assumed such almighty powers." He squeezed his wife's plump shoulder and looked directly at Tom from clear, keen eyes not unlike his daughter's. "Nay, they won't miss me, any of them. I've not been too popular in royal circles since I told King Henry to scrap all that decoration he insisted on putting on the fleet's flagship. And that damned gold telescope he carries around. I don't think he can see farther than his foot with the bloody thing!"

"Now, Edmund," said Lady Alice in a soothing voice, knowing that once her husband was launched on a favorite opinion he would lecture them all until suppertime.

"Well," Sir Edmund declared, glancing at Tom as if for masculine reassurance, "you know they like me as little as

I like them. It's only a two-day ride, and one of the Madden twins can follow with Morgan's belongings."

Lady Alice flicked her tongue over her lips. There was no use arguing with her husband once his mind was made up. In fact, Lady Alice half suspected that her husband had asked Tom to take his place in escorting Morgan to London. Tom's reputation as a womanizer didn't perturb either Lady Alice or Sir Edmund; his demeanor within the Todd family circle had always been above reproach. His own particular code of honor, his outgoing nature, and his generosity of spirit had won him firm favor in the hearts of both Sir Edmund and Lady Alice. They would entrust their only child's safekeeping to Tom without the slightest qualm.

So it was decided: Morgan and Tom would leave for London early the next morning. Meanwhile, there was still packing to be done, supper to be served, and last-minute lectures from both parents, Aunt Margaret, and Grandmother Isabeau. Morgan listened dutifully to the first three, but it was her grandmother whose words captured her real attention:

"Half a century ago, a lifetime in truth, I was young and at court, a different court, Paris, King Louis, Queen Anne of Brittany . . ." The faded blue eyes held a far-off look as the old woman paused. "But pay no heed, 'tis all the same. *La même chose, n'est-ce pas?* So I was young and comely, not in the same way you are, though there is a likeness of spirit if not of features." Grandmother Isabeau had paused again, this time to nod as if in approval. "Many men paid me suit, some were rich, some were handsome. Of course some were ugly and some were poor." She shrugged in that still-graceful manner and laughed. "But they all swore they loved me greatly—and maybe some of them did. Yet young as I was, I knew what love was not. When I met your grandfather, my Sweet William as I came to call him after we went to England, when I met that man I *knew*. I see you smiling, *ma petite*, but you are smiling for the wrong reason. You think you will know, too. But you may not. I was fortunate, very fortunate, and why I cannot say. It is not always easy to know love, real love, when you find it. I give you no other advice, no words on manners or modesty or even to remind you to walk with your head held high. I give you only this—and my blessing."

21

Morgan and her grandmother had embraced for a long, silent time. And that night, as she lay sleepless, Morgan pondered her grandmother's words, tried to conjure up the image of Sean O'Connor once more, failed, and instead saw the tall, lanky outline of the sandy-haired stranger in the orchard.

Chapter 2

MORGAN HAD EXPECTED loneliness, tension, excitement, delight—but not boredom and disappointment. She had been at court a week, and except for Tom and his gentle sister, Jane, Morgan had seen no one of importance. The King and Queen were on a royal progress throughout the Midlands, and virtually all the courtiers except Morgan's ever-diligent uncle, Thomas Cromwell, had accompanied the royal couple. Morgan had not yet met her uncle, but that was of small importance compared to the fact that Sean O'Connor was not at court.

No, Jane had told Morgan, he was not on progress, either. He was not even in England, but had fled to France after speaking out too freely against King Henry's rejection of Catherine of Aragon.

"It was not just that," Jane explained patiently for at least the third time since Morgan's arrival. "Sean is such an ardent adherent of the Pope that he could not hold his tongue about our sovereign's quarrel with Rome."

Morgan sighed; all this political and religious turmoil confused her. It was one thing to hear such matters discussed in the relative sanctuary of Faux Hall. It was quite different to be in London where the intricacies of state affairs were acted out on a daily basis. Morgan knew that Henry and Catherine's marriage had been annulled, not by the Pope, but by Bishop Cranmer. When the Pope refused Henry an annulment, the thwarted, impassioned monarch had defied papal edict and set himself up as the head of the Church of England.

"Somehow these things never mattered much at home," Morgan remarked as the two young women strolled through the almost-empty corridors of Whitehall. "But here, it seems—menacing." Indeed, Morgan noted, there were reminders of Henry's iron will everywhere, even on the bay windows of Whitehall. The palace had belonged to the once-powerful Cardinal Wolsey. York Place it had been called then, but Wolsey had failed to secure a papal annulment and had fallen from favor. Henry had confiscated York Place, and now his badge and the King's arms under the crowns imperial adorned every window, gate, and fireplace mantel.

Jane shrugged her slim shoulders. She was somewhat older than Morgan, fair-haired, and if not pretty, had a pleasant, composed countenance. "Life at court is only menacing if one opposes His Grace's will." The words were spoken matter-of-factly, as if such opposition were so mad as to be unthinkable.

"But Sean wasn't formally banished," Morgan hurried to point out. "He could come back if some influential person were to put in a kind word for him."

A slight smile lifted the corners of Jane's thin mouth. The two young women were heading out into the courtyard, toward the cockpit. It was a late April day, with sun and rain fighting for dominance. At present, the sun had won out and the young women needed no cloaks to stroll the palace precincts. "If you refer to your uncle, think again. He's a man who takes no chances."

Morgan's long, gold-tipped lashes drooped in renewed disappointment. No Sean, no courtiers, no banquets or balls—Faux Hall seemed exciting by comparison. "I wish I'd never come," she grumbled, and kicked angrily at a small stone that lay in her path.

"Nay, Morgan," Jane chided with a little laugh. "You'll change your mind when the court is back in residence tomorrow. Change is the byword here these days." She looked back at the palace and gestured with a tapering hand. "When His Grace moved into Whitehall, Anne Boleyn's father, the Earl of Wiltshire, was given the first suite of rooms. If Cardinal Wolsey knew how the King had set the Boleyns up in such grand style, he would turn in his grave."

Morgan was surprised at Jane's candor. "Aren't you afraid of being overheard?"

Jane shrugged again. "There is scarcely anyone around, not even the Queen's spies. And," she added, leading them through the cockpit entrance, "it's not as dangerous as it once was to criticize the Boleyns."

Morgan had stopped at the top tier of wooden benches. "Jane—you think the King no longer dotes on Anne?"

The older girl's glance was enigmatic. She pulled her simple gray skirt up to reveal white-stockinged ankles. "I think a great many things. Come, see where the cocks tear each other to pieces, here in this ring." She put a hand on Morgan's shoulder. "It's a savage sport—not unlike the court itself. The most spectacularly colored cocks are always chosen to compete in killing each other." Jane paused to smooth her somber skirts. "Sometimes I think only the birds of muted plumage survive."

Morgan would be presented to the King and Queen at the May Eve ball the following night. She sat alone on a marble bench in the palace gardens, brooding over the introduction, hoping she would do and say the proper things. The courtiers had ridden into Whitehall before noon; Morgan had glimpsed the tall, imposing King and his dark-haired, graceful consort. But when Morgan had called Jane to join her at the window, the other girl had merely smiled in a kindly but disinterested manner.

Now, several hours later, Morgan could hear the sound of masculine voices raised in high spirits from another part of the garden. Some contest or other, she thought vaguely, knowing that sports, games, and all types of competition were very much a part of court life. Jane had been teaching her some of the newer card games, and Morgan already played shuttlecock and tennis. She rode well enough and was a passable dancer, but had scant knowledge of musical instruments, and even her mother admitted that Morgan could not sing a note.

She was dwelling on her successes and failures when an object hurtled just inches away from her head and landed with a loud thud only a scant distance from her hem. She jumped up and whirled around but saw only a small grove of ornamental yews. Suddenly a head poked out through the evergreen branches.

"Perhaps you've seen my bowling ball?"

"Bowling ball!" Morgan exploded. "More like a cannonball! It nearly decapitated me!"

A broad-shouldered young man who moved with assured

masculine grace came through the yews. Though his mouth was solemn, the twinkling green eyes betrayed him. "I am sorry, mistress. I had no idea anyone was sitting here." He made an unnecessarily low bow. "And I'm doubly sorry that I've not had the pleasure of meeting the fair lady I almost decapitated."

Morgan's initial fright had been replaced by anger. "I'm Morgan Todd of Faux Hall and you're extremely careless!"

"Don't scold me, Morgan Todd." He took her hand and raised it to his lips. "I'm Richard Griffin and you are lovely."

Morgan snatched her hand away. "Nonsense. You're trying to disconcert me."

The twinkle in the green eyes faded. "See here, Morgan, I *am* sorry. It was an accident; it *was* careless. Will Brereton and Francis Weston and I were practicing at bowls and I tossed my ball up in the air and Will batted it with a very big board and . . . well, at least now we've met." Richard grinned again and Morgan thought he looked very pleased with himself.

"Very well." Morgan tucked her hands up her long oversleeves, lest Richard make another grab for them. Her ire had cooled; there was something infectiously good-humored about Richard Griffin. "But it sounds like foolishness for men of your age."

"Twenty-four is a good age to be foolish. Besides, we've just returned from a progress. Such royal sojourns are very confining." Richard turned as voices from behind the yews called out his name. "I must take my ball and run. Just to make sure I'm forgiven, will you dance the first measure with me at the May Eve festivities?"

Morgan wasn't looking directly at Richard; her topaz eyes were fastened on the narrow band of lace trim at the cuffs of her undersleeves. Would he think her too eager if she accepted? But except for Tom, who would doubtless be pursued by half the court ladies, she knew no other men at Whitehall. "Yes," she said at last, and now her eyes were turned up to meet his smiling gaze. "Forgiveness, after all, is our Christian duty."

The solemn words made Richard smile even wider. Morgan noted that he seemed to have a great many teeth and there was a slight gap between the two in front. But instead of detracting from his appearance, the minute flaw

"Richard Griffin? God's blood, Morgan, he's a perfect example of what I'm talking about. That wild Welshman has absolutely no restraint. The man's a rake, and an unprincipled one at that."

Tom's sudden attack of moral indignation struck Morgan as both funny and annoying. But this was no time for anger; the ball would be starting in just a few minutes. She put a hand on his shoulder and tried to look dignified. "Tom, I know you promised my parents that you would watch over me, and I'm grateful. But I'm eighteen years old, I'm at court, and I don't intend to be seduced by every charming man who comes along." Though the words sounded sincere, Morgan winced inwardly, once again remembering the bold, blond stranger.

Tom put a finger on her turned-up nose. "I know, muffet, you're as virtuous as you are dazzling. It's just an unfortunate combination."

Morgan burst out laughing. Somehow, they began to talk of other things, mainly Tom's efforts with the fleet during the past week. The daughter of a seafaring man, Morgan listened attentively and asked pertinent questions. As the French clock on the dressing table chimed nine, Tom announced that they must leave for the ball. If he couldn't be the first to dance with her, then he and Jane and their older brother, Ned, must introduce her to the King and Queen.

Anne Boleyn had made all the arrangements for the evening's entertainment before leaving on progress, carefully picking each course, supervising the musicians, and planning each detail of the decorations. A fully dressed roasted swan pulled a barge of condiments. Suckling pigs wore flowers of marchpane, the delicate paste buds garlanded around their necks. Great slabs of beef swam in their own juices and bouquets of garden herbs. Each course was announced with a flare of trumpets. Purslane and cucumbers, artichokes and cabbage lettuces came first, accompanied by capons in lemon, trout in a fine sauce, and stewed sparrows. Fresh sturgeon, quail basted a golden brown, and a pasty of venison followed. Morgan had balked at the roasted stork, only sampled the gannet, and gave up entirely when the servants brought blancmange, apples with pistachios, and clotted cream with sugar.

"We don't eat like this at Faux Hall," Morgan murmured to Tom, whose appetite seemed infinite. "Would anyone notice if I fell asleep?"

Tom laughed. "Richard Griffin would. He's been ogling you throughout the banquet."

Morgan cast a discreet glance in Richard's direction. She had been aware of his unguarded stare from first course to last, but had averted her own eyes out of confusion and embarrassment. It was one thing to speak boldly to Richard Griffin in anger, but to flirt across the banquet table was another matter entirely. Morgan was unskilled in such arts, and Tom's warning about Richard had disconcerted her more than she had realized.

So Morgan let her gaze wander around the banquet hall itself, admiring the garlands of spring flowers, the mass of purple and gold iris which banked the wall behind the royal dais, and the enormous Tudor rose at the opposite end of the hall, which was made from green leaves and white blossoms. Tom had told her it had taken a dozen pages nearly all day to assemble.

But Morgan found the royal couple the most intriguing sight of all. King Henry seemed larger than life, his big body swathed from head to toe in cloth-of-silver. The red-gold beard seemed to shimmer in the light of a thousand candles, and his small eyes appeared to miss nothing. Queen Anne sat edgily beside him, a tall, slim figure more elegant than beautiful. The famous almond-shaped eyes were set in an oval face which would have been sallow if she hadn't known how to use color in both her clothes and cosmetics. She, too, wore cloth-of-silver, but her underskirt was a brilliant scarlet and the big oversleeves glittered with rubies. Morgan recalled that Grandmother Isabeau had once told her Queen Anne had imported the oversleeve fashion from France. It had not merely been a concession to French couture, but a clever means of concealing a defect in Anne's left hand, a sixth finger, in fact, which only the Queen's most intimate friends ever glimpsed.

King Henry was rising from his elaborately carved armchair. His long arms spread out to take in the entire gathering as silence quickly fell around the hall. "We have come here tonight to eat and dance in such a manner as to welcome in the merry month of May," he announced in his big, booming voice. "We have eaten. Now let us dance."

The royal hand signaled to the musicians; Queen Anne started to rise, but her husband's glance was raking the ladies arrayed before him, as if he were considering his choice of partner. At last he turned back to Anne and extended his hand. She gave him a dazzling smile, but he merely stared straight ahead as he strode out onto the dance floor.

"The whore looks well tonight, but I don't think His Grace has noticed," Tom remarked over the rim of his wine goblet. "It seems that possession for our monarch might be equated with tedium."

"Tom!" Morgan was genuinely shocked. "He pursued Anne for seven years; it's scarcely been two since they wed. . . . You mustn't say such things!"

The blue eyes glinted with something Morgan could not fathom. Malice? Anger? Or mere cynicism? But there was no opportunity to probe further, for Richard Griffin stood before them, bowing low.

"I regret intruding upon your dalliance, Thomas, but the lady's first dance was promised to me." Richard's smile was as audacious as it was charming. He offered Morgan his hand while Tom watched with guarded amusement. But by the time Morgan and Richard reached the dance floor, the music had stopped. "I tarried too long," Richard said, bestowing his smile on Anne Boleyn's pretty cousin, Madge Shelton, who was being partnered by the King's brother-in-law, the Duke of Suffolk.

"They will start another dance soon, won't they?" said Morgan, and recoiled at her lack of witty banter.

"Ah, yes," agreed Richard, "even now, the gay lavolta." He put his arm around Morgan's waist as the lively tune filled the hall. Couples whirled around them, each man trying to swing his partner higher in the air than the others. On the last boisterous measure, Richard whisked Morgan off her feet and practically over his head. She cried out in fright but he only laughed.

The King, who had not taken part in the second dance, applauded heartily. "Ho, good Richard, don't hide your pretty partner. Bring her forward. I've yet to meet that honey-haired maid."

Richard kept Morgan's hand firmly in his. She hoped that neither he nor King Henry would notice that she was trembling. She also hoped Tom would not be annoyed because he was not the one to introduce her to their sovereign.

"Your Grace," Richard said, "Mistress Morgan Todd."

Morgan made a deep curtsey, hoping that her nod toward the Queen would be noticed; she did not wish to exclude Anne Boleyn from her obeisance. "I am deeply honored," she murmured, her tawny lashes lowered to hide the fright she knew must be showing in her eyes.

"Arise, arise," the King said airily. He was unabashedly peering down the front of her gown. Morgan got up quickly, grateful for Richard's steadying hand. Henry was fingering his red-gold beard. He suddenly seemed to remember his consort who sat rigidly at his side, the almond-shaped eyes flashing from Morgan to her husband and back again. "We are pleased to welcome you to court. I assume you will be attending Her Grace now that we have returned from progress."

Morgan glanced at Anne Boleyn for confirmation; the Queen gave a curt nod as Henry began speaking again. "Todd . . . Sir Edmund's daughter, eh?" As Morgan affirmed that she was, the King's small eyes grew speculative. "Ah, yes, Sir Edmund Todd—the man who does not approve of the way I run the Royal Navy. Is he still trying to convert Tom Seymour to his manner of thinking?"

Morgan swallowed hard, wishing Tom were at her side for reassurance. "My father has never wanted to force his beliefs on those who think otherwise," Morgan said at last. Her voice had not trembled; the statement was succinct and true. For one brief instant Morgan felt proud of herself—until she realized that several people had all but gasped, Ned Seymour was frowning from his place near the throne, the Queen had turned pale, and Henry's eyes seemed to glint with anger.

Seemingly from out of nowhere, Tom had moved to stand by his brother and the King. "That's why I admire Sir Edmund so much," Tom interjected in a casual tone. "He has his own ideas about seamanship, yet is always willing to listen to others. As you know well, Your Grace, seafaring men must be flexible, for wind and weather are unpredictable foes."

The King had given Tom a sidelong glance. A small growl rumbled in the royal throat as he considered Tom's words. "True," Henry allowed at last, and, apparently mollified, turned back to Morgan. "God knows I've sailed enough myself to have respect for nature's vagaries. Well, Mistress Todd, you are certainly a more decorative addition to court than your father. I hope you will also prove less obstinate." The merest hint of a smile played around Henry's mouth.

Morgan's composure had been shattered. She wasn't quite certain how she had offended the King and shocked the courtiers, but though her legs had turned weak as water and her mind seemed a total blank, Morgan knew she had to extricate herself as gracefully as possible from this awkward, even frightening exchange. Summoning all the courage and wit she could command, Morgan took a deep breath, vaguely aware that in doing so her full breasts almost burst over the bodice of the apple green gown. "The obstinate one in my family is Grandmother Isabeau. She is still determined to find another husband."

Henry stared at Morgan, looked from Richard to Tom and back again. "Isabeau? William Todd's widow?" The King's fleshy face screwed up in puzzlement. "And just how old is Grandmother Isabeau?" demanded His Grace as the small eyes flickered once more with amusement.

"Seventy-two," Morgan answered, and almost felt faint with relief as Henry slapped his thigh and roared with laughter. The rest of the courtiers followed suit, and finally, when Henry's rich guffaws had subsided, he shook a forefinger at Morgan.

"You are a crafty wench, Morgan Todd. So you would have your sovereign play Cupid for your grandmother? And from what I remember of Isabeau when I was a lad, she might well wear a younger man out. Perhaps," he went on, leaning forward in a loud whisper and managing a much closer look at the cleft between Morgan's breasts, "I ought to visit the lady myself." He roared again with laughter, and though the Queen looked tense, she was the first to join him this time. At last Henry reached out and pinched Morgan's cheek. "I do believe I'm glad you've joined us, Mistress Morgan. Let this mad Welshman resume his pursuit of you—or is it your grandmother he really desires?"

Richard had clasped Morgan's hand firmly in his and she made no attempt to move away. The physical contact was reassuring, and for the moment, Morgan was too elated over her small triumph to worry about Richard's reputation. Nor did she even hear his response to the King, who was now on his feet, motioning for the musicians to resume playing. She acknowledged the King's parting sally with a deep curtsey and a second obeisance for Anne, who was strained but smiling. The music resounded throughout the hall, couples were once again whirling across the floor in a dizzying blaze of color, and people were talking and laughing everywhere. Dazed, heart still pounding and limbs not quite yet steady, Morgan let Richard lead her from the hall and into the gardens of Whitehall.

He said nothing until they had passed by the bowling alley, the great open tennis court, and the stairway that led to the smaller, enclosed tennis area on the first floor of the palace. It was a gentle night, befitting May Eve, with only a few wispy clouds trailing across the star-specked sky. Here, in the formal privy garden, the spring flowers seemed more sculpted than planted. Such symmetry and design seemed foreign to Morgan, who was used to the lush, untrammeled flora at Faux Hall. Her composure was coming back, and even in the dark, she could not help but note the carefully spaced rows of tulips, the borders of lobelia, the tall iris which stood like sentinels against the box hedges.

Richard seemed to be reading her mind. "It's the first garden of its sort in England," he said, leaning against a young oak whose mate stood precisely a hundred feet away. "The concept comes from Italy."

"It seems unnatural," Morgan remarked, watching a slight breeze send a circular bed of narcissus swaying in unison. She paused and then looked up at Richard. "Please—whatever did I say wrong?"

Richard smiled, the white, slightly gapped teeth flashing in the moonlight. "You mentioned people forcing others to believe what they believe. That is precisely what Henry intends for all of us to do. The Act of Succession, which your worthy uncle has helped draft, is a first step in that direction."

Morgan frowned. "I know little of such things. Is that why Uncle Thomas has just been named the King's official secretary?"

"One reason. But do you know what the act is?" Richard's green eyes were unusually serious, and Morgan noted that he glanced in all directions to make sure they could not be overheard.

"It's something to do with whoever succeeds His Grace as sovereign. My father has talked of it but I never paid much attention." Morgan recalled lively discussions at supper between her father, mother, and Aunt Margaret, but neither she nor Nan had ever listened closely and Grandmother Isabeau had usually managed to end the exchanges with one of her brief but eloquent French phrases. Argument at mealtime, Grandmother Isabeau always said, was bad for the digestion.

"I'm afraid you had better pay attention now." Richard rubbed at his upper lip and appeared to be trying to form his words with care. "The Act of Succession is quite simple. It states that the heirs of the King's body by Anne Boleyn are first in line for the throne. Though Anne's baby is many years younger than Catherine of Aragon's daughter, the little Elizabeth takes precedence. Princess Mary, meanwhile, is declared a bastard, since Henry's marriage to her mother was never valid."

Morgan was silent for a few moments, absorbing Richard's words. "Of course the King says that since Catherine was married first to his brother, Arthur, their own marriage was unlawful," Morgan said. "But Catherine has sworn that the marriage was never consummated. Arthur was so young and sickly."

"Yet Henry swears Catherine was no virgin when he came to her, and because he took his brother's widow to wife—against the dictates of the Old Testament—child after child has died or miscarried and the King says it is because the marriage was accursed by God."

"He and Catherine did have great misfortune begetting children," Morgan allowed. "Yet it's difficult not to believe Queen Catherine—she has always sounded like such a saintly woman."

Richard put a finger over Morgan's lips. "She is not to be called Queen, but Dowager Princess of Wales as befits Arthur's widow." Richard's hand strayed to Morgan's shoulder. "See here, sweet Morgan, you mustn't say such things, you mustn't trust anyone, not even me. Catherine is not Queen, Henry was never married to her, their daughter is illegitimate. Only Anne's children matter. You, along with the rest of us, will be asked to accept the

Act of Succession. Before long, we will all have to pledge ourselves to Henry and the church he has created out of this marriage muddle."

Morgan could not help but laugh. "Oh, Richard, that sounds ridiculous! To break from Rome and start a new church just because Catherine may or may not have consummated her marriage to Arthur! No wonder Grandmother Isabeau finds the English so funny!"

Richard squeezed Morgan's shoulder gently and sighed. "It's not funny. And Henry Tudor is almost as Welsh as I am." He stared into the darkness for a moment, the green eyes in shadow. Then he turned to Morgan and pulled her into his arms. "No more talk of politics, Morgan Todd. Just be careful what you say and do."

"Being in your arms isn't being careful," Morgan asserted, trying to disengage herself. "I've been warned about the likes of you."

Richard grinned down at her. "Good, then you know exactly what delights you will find in my bed."

"Richard! I have no intention of ending up in your bed! Now let me go; everyone will wonder where we are." She grasped his upper arms and tried to pry herself loose, but he merely laughed.

"They'll just think I'm taking care of you after your ordeal with His Grace. Which I am. They'll also think I'm trying to seduce you. Which I am." He lowered his face to hers but she turned abruptly away. "Oh, Morgan, don't be a goose. This isn't the rigid court it used to be when Catherine was Queen. Love rules all—and we can rule love."

"No!" The word came out loud but trembled on the night air. "You've been kind—but I won't repay such gestures with my body! Now let me go or I'll never speak to you again!"

Morgan felt Richard's grasp slacken almost imperceptibly. At last he chuckled and shook his head. "All right, Morgan Todd. I'll be content with just a kiss—this time. Is that not fair?"

Morgan considered the alternatives. A kiss did not seem too outrageous a demand. She hesitated, then lifted her face to his; Richard gathered her close and bent down to kiss her lips. It was a long, sensuous kiss, and Morgan marveled at the difference between men: It was not tender like Sean's, yet it lacked the animal fervor of the stranger's in the orchard. And as Morgan leaned against Richard's chest, she was alarmed at her own reaction. Richard was the one who finally pulled away and gazed down at her with bemused astonishment.

"I'm not sure that's adequate compensation, but it's a delicious taste of future delicacies." Richard put his hands on her shoulders again and moved just a few inches away. The green eyes rested on her bosom and he shook his head. "Oh, Morgan, you are as enticing as you are stubborn. But," he added as the green eyes flashed in the moonlight, "you will belong to me some day."

His arrogance obliterated the pleasure Morgan had found in his kiss. "You are too sure of yourself, Richard Griffin. I will never belong to you. I will only belong to the man I love. And that choice will be my own." Morgan made a sudden, sure move and darted out of his arms. She began to run back toward the palace, and tried not to hear Richard's laughter as it floated after her on the soft, spring night air.

Chapter 3

DESPITE HIS ADVANCING AGE, the Duke of Norfolk was still one of the finest warriors in England. Attired in battle armor, Norfolk was hoisted onto his black stallion and handed his blunted lance. He tested the weight and feel of his weapon, and announced himself ready to meet his opponent, the Duke of Suffolk.

Norfolk was a proud Howard, with Plantagenet blood in his veins. Though Anne Boleyn was his niece, there was no love between them; despite Henry's flagrant disobedience to the Church of Rome, the Howards remained fiercely Catholic.

Suffolk, however, remained himself—ambitious, opportunistic, and charming. A commoner born Charles Brandon, he had eloped with Henry's youngest sister, Mary, after the death of her first husband, King Louis XII of France. Mary was dead now, but Suffolk retained his royal brother-in-law's affection.

Morgan sat in a corner of the royal box in the new tiltyard at Whitehall and silently prayed that the dukes would make short work of their joust. She had enjoyed the earlier meets of the day, the pageant carriage drawn by mock unicorns, the colorful trappings of the horses, the crash of lance on shield, the byplay between the combatants and their ladies. But it had grown unusually warm for May and Morgan could feel her dress clinging to her back.

She glanced down to the front of the royal box where the King sat with Anne Boleyn. Henry was to have taken part in the jousting but a stiff neck had forced him to sit on the sidelines. He called out a greeting to Norfolk and Suffolk as they cantered onto the field.

Morgan fanned herself with her hand and fingered the

pomander which hung from her waist. There was dust everywhere, and even the royal box was beginning to smell fetid from a combination of human sweat and horse dung. Madge Shelton poked Morgan in the ribs and giggled.

"It's not fair to look bored, Morgan," said Madge, whose red curls were beginning to peek out in damp coils from under her coif. "These are the two most important dukes in all England—and it is the last competition."

"Praise St. George for that," Morgan answered dryly. Morgan was beginning to learn the names and faces of various court personages. Tom Seymour had defeated Will Brereton earlier on, and Tom's brother, Ned, had been victorious over Norfolk's son, the Earl of Surrey. Richard Griffin, however, had lost a very close contest to Anne Boleyn's brother, George. Both Anne and her sister Mary had cheered their brother lustily.

Morgan stifled a yawn as Suffolk and Norfolk thundered toward each other—and missed. "I should think they'd both die of heat stroke," she said to Madge. "That armor must weigh twenty stone."

"Not quite," Madge replied, waving at Thomas Wyatt, who had just entered the royal box. Wyatt was a poet, not a warrior, and his amorous verses directed at Anne Boleyn had once earned him exile from court. He sat down next to his sister, Margaret, who was said to be Anne's closest confidante. She was also said to be in love with George Boleyn, who returned her passion but was married to a shrewish wife. Morgan was casting her gaze about the overcrowded royal box, speculating on the intricacies of court romance, political alliances, and family relationships, when she was startled by a diffident tug at her flowing oversleeve. She looked down to see a young page not more than eleven or twelve bowing awkwardly.

"Mistress Todd?" he asked in an uncertain, piping voice. Morgan nodded and had to lean over the edge of the box to catch his next words as the dukes' lances clattered together just a few yards away. "Your uncle, Master Secretary Cromwell, wishes to see you."

"Jesu," Morgan whispered to herself, and got up at once. She pushed past Madge, Thomas and Margaret Wyatt, and half a dozen others to reach the center aisle, which led out of the box. She was not unhappy about leaving the overwarm tiltyard but somewhat disconcerted by the sudden summons from her powerful uncle. As she followed the page through one of the palace's smaller tennis courts toward the ground floor lodgings, Morgan adjusted her coif, smoothed her wrinkled skirts, and wondered if Thomas Cromwell was quite the ogre he was often made out to be. Halfway down the long drain yard, the page halted in front of a finely carved oak door. He made another clumsy bow, mumbled something Morgan couldn't understand, and scurried away.

Her gaze followed him in puzzlement for a few moments; then Morgan took a deep breath and knocked firmly three times. When the door opened it was not Thomas Cromwell who greeted her but Tom Seymour. Morgan stared at him in wide-eyed amazement. "Tom! I wasn't told you would be here!"

"Come in, muffet," he said quickly, taking her arm and half dragging her inside. As he closed the door behind them, Morgan noticed that someone else was also in the room—but it was not her uncle, either; it was the young Earl of Surrey, sitting in his shirt sleeves and drinking a glass of red wine.

"You know Surrey," Tom said as Morgan bobbed a curtsey. The young Earl smiled indolently and reached for the decanter on the table beside him. "These are not your uncle's apartments but Surrey's. I don't have much time, but Harry and I have a surprise for you. Get your doublet on, man, you've had enough wine already to sink half the royal fleet."

Surrey shrugged and set the decanter down. He was scarcely older than Morgan, but had already been married for two years to the Earl of Oxford's daughter. "I'm not drunk, good Thomas, it's just that jousting makes me uncommonly thirsty."

Morgan was looking from one to the other with increasing perplexity. "Where's the surprise? Please, Tom, you're mystifying me!"

He reached out and brushed her cheek with his big, bronzed hand. "We can't spoil it. But we must make haste; we don't want undue attention called to our absence."

Surrey had pulled on his doublet and drained the last of his wine. Morgan allowed Tom to propel her back into the drain yard and out toward the east gate of the palace. It passed through her mind as they hurried under the two-story structure that directly above them Hans Holbein had his quarters. Sean had lived there briefly in a small apartment adjacent to the master artist.

Whatever the surprise was, it must be outside the palace. Surrey was humming. Some of his own verse, Morgan decided, which he had set to music. The Earl was not as tall as Tom, but both men's strides made Morgan all but run to keep up with them. They were walking north from the palace toward The Strand, a reviving breeze coming off the Thames to ruffle the plane trees which lined the paved roadway.

"It's not far now," Tom said as they reached Charing Cross. Several hawkers stood talking among themselves, apparently having concluded their business for the day. A horse-drawn litter carried a middle-aged, well-dressed couple who were both extremely obese. Their chins bobbed up and down as they moved over the cobbles while a feisty terrier barked its disapproval.

"But where, Tom? We're halfway to the Fleet River," Morgan finally noted as they passed the medieval walls of the Palace of Savoy.

Tom waved his arm in the direction of a grandiose four-story red-brick house with the Howard arms displayed above the elegantly carved lintel. "His Grace of Norfolk's residence. Harry, you may have the honor of admitting us to your sire's handsome house."

Surrey sketched a mocking bow, opened the front door, and found himself confronted by a frail, elderly retainer. "Away, good man," said Surrey, "we need no attendance this day." The old servant backed off, disappearing into a narrow corridor just off the entry hall. "The library, I believe," Surrey called, leading the way past a banquet room with a table that seemed to go on forever. Next was a music room where Morgan glimpsed lutes, virginals, and an exquisite harp.

The library door was closed; Surrey rapped once, then, without waiting for a response, opened the door. Morgan peered inside. Unlike the other rooms they had passed, this one was comparatively small and the draperies were drawn against the late-afternoon sun. Standing in front of one of the tall bookcases was a slender, masculine figure in riding clothes. Morgan froze in the doorway, unable to believe her eyes.

"Sean?" she finally breathed, taking a tentative step forward.

Sean O'Connor moved quickly across the tiled floor. He was smiling at her, that boyish, delightful smile she remembered so well. "Morgan!" He took her hand and raised it to his lips. Morgan vaguely heard Tom and Surrey chuckling behind her. Morgan and Sean were staring at each other as if in a trance, his hand still holding hers, her gaze absorbing each detail of his wavy black hair, the faint smattering of freckles, the blue eyes, the well-defined chin.

"You came back from France," Morgan breathed at last—and felt foolish at the inadequacy of her remark.

"That I did." Sean released her hand and shook his head. "Oh, Morgan, I am very glad to see you."

Morgan was about to reply but Tom put a hand on their shoulders. "Surrey and I will discreetly withdraw. But first I must explain that we should all exert the utmost discretion. I had to ride down to Deptford this morning where I discovered that a ship had just arrived from France. Who should be disembarking but this young Irishman?" Tom clapped Sean on the shoulder and grinned at Morgan. "He was determined to head straight for Ireland, but I convinced him he ought to bide for a few hours in London. Surrey and his father agreed to let him stay here, since they adhere as stubbornly to Popish ways as Sean."

"I think you're boring them, Tom. Let's be gone; I'm still thirsty." Surrey waved a hand at Morgan and Sean, grabbed Tom by the arm, and all but hauled the bigger man out of the library.

Even after Surrey and Tom had left, Morgan could not take her eyes off Sean. When she finally spoke it was with a voice filled with regret. "You are not staying in London?"

Sean shook his dark head. "It's best I don't. I much mislike the appointment of your uncle as the King's secretary. He intends to destroy the Church of Rome in more ways than one. Since the poor likes of me can't stop him, I'd rather not watch such blasphemy and heresy."

"Then why come back at all?" Morgan stood with her

palms pressed together, as if she were pleading for answers she wanted to hear.

But Sean merely shook his head. "I can't stomach France. The court is dissolute, worse than here. No one will acknowledge that an Irishman can paint and even the food is disagreeable." He sighed deeply, turning to look at the Italian painting of Madonna and Child that hung over the fireplace. "I'm better off back in my own country, where a man's art—and his faith—are not mocked." Sean was moving around the room, pausing to finger the golden clasp of a damask-covered breviary. Abruptly, his fist slammed against the oak paneling of the library's wall. "What choice have I? To serve a King who flaunts the authority of St. Peter and Christ himself? Or end up in the Tower as Sir Thomas More and Bishop Fisher have done?" The blue eyes blazed with anger. "Those men are veritable saints, yet King Henry will butcher them both because they refuse to sign the Act of Succession!"

Morgan's hands pressed the flowing linen skirts against her thighs. She had heard the talk about More, the former chancellor, and Fisher, Bishop of Rochester, but had not paid a great deal of attention. Fisher was old and much revered; More, however, was said to be a brilliant, witty, and extremely kind man who had been a close friend to the King. "But isn't it just some sort of misunderstanding?" Morgan asked in a voice that sounded unusually meek.

"Oh . . ." He stared at her for a moment, as if he couldn't quite remember her name. "Oh, Morgan," he went on in a tone that was tainted with exasperation, "of course not! You've been here a very short time and you're listening to the wrong people. This is a matter which imperils not just lives but souls. Sir Thomas More, God help him, had no quarrel with signing the act itself. But the preamble disclaims papal authority. More couldn't stomach that. Nor can I."

Morgan rubbed her hand between her brows in agitation. It was an unconscious, characteristic gesture, as if she were trying to erase the problems which troubled her. "I'm sorry, I was never much good at politics and such. I came to court not for intrigue but for—" She stopped speaking abruptly and stared at Sean. For *you*, she thought fiercely, and *you* don't even care that I am here! "So why did you stop in London?" she demanded, trying to control her sudden anger with his rantings and ravings about religion and preambles and ex-chancellors.

He lifted his slim shoulders in an eloquent gesture. "Why, to visit Sir Thomas More in the Tower, of course. To seek counsel and inspiration from him. He is a most remarkable man."

"Oh." Morgan nodded several times, trying to rein in her temper and absorb Sean's explanation. "Well. It sounds foolhardy to me, but I imagine your mind is quite made up."

"Indeed it is. Surrey has arranged it, and by the time anyone finds out I've been there, I'll be well on my way to Ireland." Sean was smiling now, looking well pleased with himself and pausing again to admire the breviary's workmanship.

Morgan toyed with the chain around her waist, which held the pomander. "If you should pass by Faux Hall, give my parents my love." She paused for his reply but he said nothing. "I write to them, of course," she went on a bit too rapidly, "but I don't have a great deal of time for letters. How is your father?"

The blue eyes turned shadowy. "I have not heard for some time. He was unwell this past winter, though."

"I'm sorry." Morgan's fingers worked at the silver chain until she realized she was in danger of breaking it apart. "I should go now. I'll be needed by the—" Again she stopped abruptly. She did not dare call Anne Queen in front of Sean.

But Sean had taken three quick strides and stood directly in front of her. "I've not forgotten what happened last spring," he declared, and his face softened, the blue eyes no longer angry or troubled. "Thomas Seymour told me you would be here, but I would rather you had not come." Seeing Morgan flinch at his candor, he touched her face. "Nay, Morgan, it's not that I didn't want to see you—but I can offer you nothing. I'm an outcast, an exile, a man with no future."

Morgan put her own hands on his. "Oh, Sean, I don't care! I have no desire for riches or lands or—or any of those things! I would rather live with you in an Irish bog than with the finest lord in a palace!" She saw his look of astonishment at her frank declaration, watched his disarming smile twist wryly, marveled at the faint flush which all but obliterated the smattering of freckles. She was as surprised as he, for she had all but proposed to him.

He was laughing very softly. His arms went around her and he kissed her gently, lingeringly. She held him close and felt her heart race in her breast. "I would marry you tomorrow, Morgan, if the world were otherwise," he sighed at last. Her head was against his shoulder, and he stroked her back with his hand. "Last spring I'd thought to go to court and make a name for myself as an artist, then ask your parents' permission for us to wed. But now . . ." He put his hands on her upper arms and held her away just enough so that he could look into her face. "We must see how events move along. Dare I ask you to wait?"

Her answer was to hurl herself back into his arms and hold him tight. "Of course I'll wait! Why would I not? I love you!"

"I love you, too, Morgan." He kissed the thick tawny hair that was not covered by her coif. "I probably always have, though I was never certain until last year. You are so fair, so alive, so good."

Morgan felt something twist inside of her. What would Sean think if he suspected she had been ravished and was no longer a virgin? It occurred to her that perhaps she should tell him the truth, now, before she had spent time at court and he would think she had dallied with all sorts of importunate suitors. But she could not mention that unspeakable afternoon in the orchard.

A knock at the door startled them both. Sean let go of Morgan and backed away toward the fireplace. Morgan adjusted her coif as Tom Seymour entered the library, his big grin wide in the red beard. "I hate being the meddlesome chaperone," Tom said, "but Morgan must get back to Whitehall before someone finds out her uncle never summoned her in the first place—and you, Sean, must go with Surrey to the Tower as soon as it begins to get dark."

Sean agreed. He took Morgan's hand and again raised it to his lips. The blue eyes sought hers and their glances locked for a moment. "I will write, I swear," he said.

"I, too," Morgan answered in a voice that was barely above a whisper. "Take care. Please."

He relinquished her hand. "And you." He gazed past Morgan to Tom. "You will watch over her?"

Tom put an arm around Morgan. "I've already promised

her parents that I would. God's teeth, I'm beginning to feel like a doddering old nursemaid!" His big laugh resounded against the library walls while Morgan and Sean smiled at each other. Then Surrey was in the room too, and after a flurry of farewells, Morgan found herself outside Norfolk's great house and heading back along The Strand toward Charing Cross and Whitehall. She and Tom walked swiftly and silently until they reached the palace gates. Morgan stopped suddenly and looked up at Tom.

"Thank you. I can't tell you how much I appreciate what you did for me—for us—this day."

Tom touched her chin with his forefinger. "You two might make a most happy match some day. But for now, Sean's better off in Ireland." He looked around to make sure the palace guards could not overhear them. "Whatever you do, don't encourage him to come back too soon."

"I won't, I promise." Morgan tried to match Tom's solemn expression. But, she told herself, the silly squabbles over religion and succession should end before long—and Sean would be hers forever.

Morgan spent the next few days in a haze of happiness. Sean did love her as she'd been certain he must. They would wed some day, perhaps within the year. Spring, of course, since that was when they had first discovered they loved each other and again when they had been reunited, however briefly. She was still dwelling on her future when someone poked her in the ribs as she sat at supper, idly rearranging the first strawberries of the season in a porcelain bowl.

"The Queen," Margaret Wyatt whispered rather frantically. "She is calling you!"

Morgan whirled around so fast she almost knocked over a wine goblet. Sure enough, Anne Boleyn was glaring at her, the almond eyes narrowed. Morgan got up rather awkwardly and hurried to the Queen's chair. The King was not supping with his consort on this early June evening, but that was not unusual of late. Morgan dropped a deep curtsey and felt her cheeks grow warm.

"You will attend me tonight," Anne said without preamble. Two footmen helped the Queen rise from her chair as Morgan stood aside and followed her mistress toward the royal chambers.

No words were exchanged as Morgan helped Anne out of her rust-colored gown. Three maids scurried about the bedchamber, pulling back the coverlet, adjusting the hangings of the elaborately carved bed, opening a window to let in the soft spring air.

When Morgan began brushing the Queen's long black hair, the maids each bobbed a curtsey and departed. Morgan tried to grip the brush firmly but her hands were shaking.

"You needn't be nervous, Morgan," Anne said at last, and there was a glimmer of amusement in the almond eyes. "I've been watching you since you came to court; you've performed your duties well thus far. You comport yourself respectably, too, and contrary to what my enemies say about me, I do not encourage licentiousness."

Morgan was dumbfounded by the Queen's candor. Though she knew Anne spoke freely among her circle of friends, it came as a surprise that the Queen of England would converse in such a manner to a lady-in-waiting she scarcely knew.

Anne seemed to sense Morgan's reaction. "Come, come, Morgan. I was only fourteen when I went to France as an attendant to Queen Claude. I was terrified, but I never let anyone know that. You seem quite young for your age—eighteen, isn't it?—and I'd advise you to develop a tougher exterior. Women must have their own armor, you know."

"I appreciate your advice," Morgan said rather lamely.

Anne laughed, the high-pitched sound that sometimes seemed to verge on hysteria. "That's what I mean. You haven't the remotest notion what I'm talking about." Anne turned around so abruptly that Morgan almost dropped the silver-edged hairbrush. "You are a dazzling young woman, Morgan. You haven't any idea of how men watch you or react to you. I can't imagine why you haven't been seduced at least six times already—except that I suspect most of our jaded courtiers aren't quite certain what approach to take. But eventually they will, and you'd best be prepared."

"But . . ." Morgan felt ridiculously tongue-tied and wondered if Anne was making sport of her. "I've never learned how to flirt," she declared at last.

Anne made one of her eloquent French gestures with both tapering hands. "My dear child, I'm not talking about

47

flirtation! I'm talking about lovers, real lovers. Unless your uncle finds a husband for you soon, you *will* take one."

Morgan gripped the hairbrush more tightly and resumed untangling the royal mane. "I don't want a lover," she said at last in a low, firm voice.

Anne rolled her dark eyes. "Nonsense. You not only want a lover, you need a lover. Or would you prefer to end up at twenty-five like that sheep, Jane Seymour, with her dried-up little mouth and drab clothes?"

"I should hope to have a husband long before then," Morgan retorted, and this time there was fire in her voice. Queen or not, no one was going to dictate Morgan's future. "I would also insist that he be of my own choosing and not my uncle's."

"Hmmm." Anne signaled for Morgan to stop brushing her hair. The Queen stood up and pulled her deep blue nightdress more closely around her slim figure. "*I* wished to choose my husband, too. And I did—Harry Percy of Northumberland. We were very much in love." Anne paused, stared down at her hands, as if to make sure that the flawed finger was concealed. "But Cardinal Wolsey intervened. I was to marry the Irish Earl of Ormond, and Harry was to wed Mary Talbot, the Earl of Shrewsbury's daughter. I was heartbroken; so was Harry. But we had no choice." Anne began to move about the room, her nightdress floating across the new Persian carpets like a soft blue tide. Morgan also stood up, but the Queen motioned for her to sit on a footstool by the dressing table. "We are alone. I don't demand ceremony at such times."

Anne stopped, her back to Morgan, her right hand clutching the damask bed hangings. "I vowed vengeance on Wolsey then. When the King fell in love with me and prevented my marriage to Ormond, I finally reaped my reward. Wolsey failed to get the annulment for His Grace. Wolsey fell and would have been executed had he not died first. And I ended up with a crown." Anne's fingers brushed at the top of her head, as if a diadem actually sat upon her heavy black hair. "It took seven long years but I prevailed." The almond-shaped eyes seemed to bore into Morgan's very being. For the first time, Morgan saw Anne Boleyn not as the ambitious, selfish jade her detractors called her, but as a woman who had been thwarted in love, manipulated by powerful men, set on a lifelong course she had not charted for herself—and had not only vanquished her enemies, but had become Queen in the process. How cleverly, how shrewdly, how brilliantly Anne must have played her hand! And how naive and unaware Morgan felt by comparison. In that moment of insight, Morgan silently pledged her allegiance to Anne and prayed that she might be as strong and clever as her Queen.

The court never remained in London during the summer. As the weather grew warmer, the air became fetid, the water turned foul, the sun hung over the city like a burning spectre, reminding Londoners that the plague, the sweating sickness, and pestilence of every kind were close at hand.

During the third week of June, carts, wagons, and litters formed a caravan headed west to Hampton Court Palace. Another of Wolsey's properties, the Cardinal had actually presented this great house to King Henry almost a decade earlier. As lavish as the gesture—and the edifice—had been, it had not helped save Wolsey. Nor was Henry satisfied with the splendor of Wolsey's design: The King had added a great hall which had taken five years to complete. The chapel was renovated and a magnificent fan-vaulted ceiling had been installed. A second kitchen was built, a tiltyard was laid out, and an indoor tennis court had been erected.

Fragments of cloud spattered the blue sky as the royal barge pulled up to the pier at Hampton. Morgan had counted herself fortunate that she had been able to make the journey by water, but her pleasure had diminished when she learned why there was room for such a relative newcomer: "I'm going home to Wolf Hall for a few months," Jane Seymour had told her on the eve of the court's departure. "I find this life stifling after a time."

Morgan had been surprised by Jane's casual, sudden announcement. But Jane was closemouthed. And though she felt no real intimacy with Jane, Morgan would miss her. She was also less than enthusiastic about Jane's replacement to share her quarters: Madge Shelton, the Queen's cousin, was pretty, red-haired—and as promiscuous as she was empty-headed. As the air turned heavy and the clouds gathered more closely together, Morgan and Madge began unpacking in their room overlooking the great maze of clipped hedges.

"I love Hampton Court," Madge twittered as she shook out a great bundle of petticoats. "See the maze?" Madge giggled as Morgan glanced through the leaded glass window. "If ever you have an opportunity to lose yourself—and whoever you are with—it's wonderful! You can wander for hours before—"

But Madge was mercifully cut short by a rap on the door. Morgan hurried to answer it and found Tom Seymour on the threshold. He gave her a perfunctory hug and winked at Madge. "Muffet, your uncle wishes to see you. Would you like time to change from your traveling clothes?"

Morgan looked dubiously at Tom. "My uncle?"

"Yes. He arrived yesterday, to get a head start on state affairs."

In the wake of Tom's previous ruse, Morgan remained vaguely skeptical. But Tom seemed sincere, and Morgan looked down at her plum-colored skirt and jerkin. They were wrinkled, but clean. If she took time to change, she'd only become more nervous. "I'll go at once," she declared, and nodded at Madge, who was openly ogling Tom.

"This way," Tom said, steering her to the left in the passageway. "Listen, Morgan, I'm almost certain Cromwell will ask you to sign the Act of Succession. Almost everyone at court has—save those who have refused straight out and gone to the Tower for their trouble. I assume you have not let Sean—or anyone else—influence you against the act?"

Morgan slowed her step. "I truly haven't thought about it," she said as they stopped outside a formidable oak door. "Are you coming with me?" She looked up at Tom with big pleading eyes.

Tom cuffed her chin. "Nay, muffet. You'll do well; he *is* kin, you know."

Morgan shook her head. "I hope I make a favorable impression." She let Tom knock on the door and gave a weak smile of gratitude.

An adolescent boy, somewhat younger than Morgan herself, greeted her. He was dressed somberly and looked unusually austere for his age. Morgan announced herself and the youth made a brief bow, then wordlessly ushered her into an almost barren anteroom and through another door.

Sir Thomas Cromwell, soldier, merchant, lawyer, banker, the late Cardinal Wolsey's henchman, the Putney Blacksmith and presently the King's secretary, was seated behind his oak desk. It was a consciously tidy desk, considering the mound of work that crossed it every day.

The man in the chair behind the desk stood up to greet his niece as she entered the room. He was dressed in black. His nose was long, his lips narrow, his eyes of no color at all. The face was slightly sallow, evidencing the hours its owner spent indoors. He seemed short, but his shoulders were broad and his body stocky. As Morgan hesitated, he put a hand across the desk and smiled.

"You were seven, I believe, when last I saw you," Cromwell said amiably enough. "Pray sit, Morgan, and give your poor old uncle some surcease from his work."

"I've heard how hard you work," Morgan said in a small voice. "I'm told you shoulder heavy responsibilities."

Cromwell waited until Morgan sat down before he dropped back into his own chair. "It's a time-consuming position, I confess, but worthwhile if one does it well. Serving the King, serving England—it's an honor as well as a duty." He paused, absorbing every detail of Morgan's appearance, and noted that she had no ready response. "But you are young. You needn't listen to my wearisome tribulations."

To Morgan's surprise, Cromwell was smiling. Indeed, there were crinkles around his eyes, which indicated he smiled often. "It's not so much wearisome as awesome," she finally said, beginning to pluck up her courage. "How is my lady aunt, Elizabeth?"

"Fine and fit as ever," Cromwell replied. "She and your mother used to bear quite a resemblance to each other. You must sup with us some evening. You can see for yourself how time has changed them."

Morgan and Cromwell began to talk of family matters, of his own offspring, of Morgan's parents and Grandmother Isabeau, of Aunt Margaret and Nan and life at Faux Hall. Morgan relaxed in her uncle's company, but remained guarded in her comments. She was especially circumspect when Cromwell asked how she reacted to serving Queen Anne: "The Queen is quite kind to her attendants," Morgan said. "She has made me feel welcome."

Cromwell nodded in an avuncular manner. "It's quite a change from the serenity of Faux Hall. But it's good that you get on well with your mistress. It's always very important to have a satisfactory relationship with those whom you serve." He paused again, but this time he put one blunt finger on a piece of parchment. "Which reminds me. . . . As long as you are here and we have been discussing Her Grace, it's an excellent opportunity to have you sign the Act of Succession. I assume you have not yet done so?"

Morgan swallowed hard. "No. I've not yet been asked."

"Oh, such matters ought to be left between kinfolk," Cromwell chuckled. "So much fuss has been made over this act. If only it could be always administered thusly, with pleasant talk and congenial surroundings." He pushed the parchment across the desk toward Morgan and handed her a quill. "There, at the bottom—just sign your name, my dear."

The words on the parchment blurred before Morgan's eyes. "Sign," Tom Seymour had counseled. Then she thought of Sean, the burning blue eyes decrying the act and its evil implications. But what if Sean was wrong? She felt faintly dizzy; she could not have read the words if she had wanted to. The room seemed to become very small, and Morgan was vaguely aware of how stark, how Spartan it all was: no elaborate decor for Thomas Cromwell, no finely wrought trappings, only a small portrait of the King behind her uncle's chair, and the simplest of wall hangings and draperies.

Morgan wrote her name very carefully. She allowed Cromwell to sand the signature and sat motionless as he rolled up the parchment, affixed it with sealing wax, and slipped it inside a drawer. "Well done," Cromwell asserted amiably, and sat down again. "Now tell me, what did you think of your first trip on the Thames by royal barge?"

They continued chatting thus for another quarter of an hour. Morgan was somewhat amazed at the time her uncle had taken out of his busy day to visit with a niece he hadn't seen in over ten years. But when she finally left his chambers she felt pleased—and relieved. The powerful King's private secretary had seemed friendly, pleasant, even concerned for her welfare. Surely Thomas Cromwell was not the ogre so many people, including her own parents, had pictured him to be.

* * *

It was very close inside the enclosed royal tennis courts. Morgan pushed at a damp strand of hair which had escaped from under her coif as she moved closer to one of the open windows. Though she was not in official attendance on the Queen that day, she didn't dare leave the tennis enclosure since the King himself was playing a doubles match. Will Brereton and the Duke of Suffolk were paired against Henry and Ned Seymour. Ned was a year or two older than Tom, not quite as tall, darker of complexion, and far less good-natured. But he was a fine tennis player, though not as expert as the King. Indeed, Morgan was amazed at how agile Henry was despite his increasing girth and encroaching age. Hard muscles rippled under the thin lawn shirt, and the King's legs were sturdy as twin oaks.

"It's an equal pairing," Richard Griffin commented as the King smashed a ball just out of Will Brereton's range. "Suffolk and the King are of an age, but His Grace is much the better player. Brereton is more athletic than Ned, but Ned has more natural cunning. Will you wager with me, Morgan?"

"Is it treason to wager against the King?" Morgan asked with a smile.

Richard waved across the court to Margaret Wyatt and the Queen's young musician, Mark Smeaton, who had just come in with the Earl of Surrey. "Nay," Richard laughed. "The King encourages wagering; he loves to see his courtiers lose their money on his behalf either way."

"Are you going to compete?" Morgan asked, for she knew Richard was a keen tennis player.

But Richard didn't reply at once. His gaze was fixed on Mary, Duchess of Richmond and wife of Henry's only surviving—but illegitimate—son. "What? Oh—no, I imagine the royal match will be the last. It usually is." He sketched a bow in Mary's direction and she dimpled prettily. "Such irony," he murmured, "that our sovereign liege could only sire a son by the likes of Bessie Blount. Yet Richmond doesn't seem to have inherited the royal robust health of his father."

"Hush, Richard," warned Morgan as Ned Seymour made a near-impossible return off Suffolk's serve. "You should not say such things, even to me."

Richard turned his full attention to Morgan, the green

eyes mischievous. "There are other things I'd like to say to you, Morgan. I believe I will, as soon as this infernal competition is done with."

Morgan shifted uneasily and felt warmer than ever. A long volley ensued between the foursome and ended suddenly with Will Brereton misjudging his swing and sending the ball into the net. It also ended the match and Henry roared with pleasure, slapping Ned on the back and congratulating Will and Suffolk for their fine, if futile, efforts. Several of the courtiers had begun to mill around the King and the other players, but Richard was drawing Morgan away from the group and out into the gardens.

"Have you been into the maze yet?" he asked.

"No," said Morgan, and took a deep breath of fresh air. "I'm overwarm. I'd prefer to sit."

"Well enough. Let's walk down by the river." He took Morgan's hand and led her through the gardens, heavy with the scent of marigolds and verbena and roses and lilies. There was a slight breeze coming up from the Thames, and in the distance, two fishermen were calling to each other. On the opposite bank several cows grazed as their tails flicked at pesky flies. It was a pleasant vista, making Morgan feel suddenly far away from the glitter and bustle of the court. She sat down a few yards above the river, under an old maple tree whose branches had harbored countless generations of birds' nests.

"I think I'm homesick," Morgan said suddenly. "I've been gone almost three months, you know."

Richard stretched out on the grass beside her, plucking at some weeds that had dared take root on the royal grounds. "That's natural. But you'll have a change of scenery soon; we're moving on to Windsor."

"Yes. I'm told we should begin packing tomorrow." She pulled off her coif and shook out the heavy tawny hair. She had not seen a great deal of Richard since their arrival at Hampton Court. He had been busy, it seemed, involved in certain political matters Morgan knew nothing about but which kept him occupied—and within notice of the King.

"That hair," Richard said, taking a thick strand in his hands. "It's like copper and gold and sable all entwined together."

Morgan shrugged. "My cousin Nan used to make fun of

it. She said I looked like a dirty tabby cat. Her hair is very black, like the Queen's."

Richard seemed to pay no heed. His hand moved through her hair until he touched the back of her neck and made her face him squarely. "Kiss me, Morgan."

Morgan pulled back but his grip was firm. "Nonsense, those fishermen can see us."

"Fishermen never see anything but fish. Besides, you ought to feel safe with them nearby. I'm not asking for anything but a kiss."

The green eyes still danced but his smile was friendly, encouraging—and very attractive. Morgan looked down at the ground, then back to Richard. He pulled her into his arms and his mouth came down on hers, a long, breath-devouring kiss that stirred Morgan's senses. He kissed her again and again, and then she was on the ground next to him and his hands were on her breasts.

"No," she cried between kisses, "you promised—no more than a kiss!"

"That's a very hard promise to keep, under the circumstances," Richard breathed, his fingers searching through the silken bodice for her nipples. "You are quite irresistible, you know."

"Richard!" Morgan pushed with her hands against his chest and managed just enough leverage to keep him momentarily at bay. "You are not to trifle with me!"

" 'Trifle'!" Richard burst out laughing. "That's not quite what I call it. Pleasure you, make you deliciously happy, give us both a few moments of joy. That's not 'trifling,' Morgan."

"It is to me, no matter what honeyed words you use to describe it." Morgan started to sit up, but Richard pulled her back down beside him. He kissed her again, and this time his hands were working at the ties of her bodice. Morgan pushed and pummeled, but without much effect. Without much determination either, she noted somewhere in the back of her mind, for Richard's kisses were not unpleasant. In fact, they were making her dizzy. Then her bodice was undone, the ties trailing to her waist in silent surrender, and he had pulled her bodice down to expose her full, white breasts.

"Ah, sweet heaven, you are bewitching!" Richard bent over her, kissing each breast in turn, then gently tonguing the nipples until Morgan felt herself gripping his back tight and pressing him down on top of her. She saw something in her mind's eye, something hazy and yet distressing, another man, another place, another time—the tall blond stranger in the orchard at Faux Hall . . .

"Stop!" she cried. "Please! You cannot!"

"I can," he breathed, and held a breast in each hand, his thumbs provoking the pink tips into rigid, burning mounds of sensual pleasure. "You see, you want me; you will not be satisfied unless you let me take you here and now."

"No . . ." Morgan groaned and made a feeble attempt to pull his hands away. But she was fascinated by the sight of those strong fingers plying her flesh, and she absorbed the physical contact with a curious sense of detachment. She did not love this man, she was certain of that, and yet . . .

From several yards away, a voice was calling Richard's name. He paused, his hands still on her breasts, his eyes suddenly alert. "Damn!" he breathed, and got to his knees. "A moment, Ned, I'll be right there!"

"Ned?" Morgan clutched her gown over her bosom and hurriedly began to lace her bodice back up. "Ned Seymour?"

"Aye. Spoilsport," Richard murmured and grinned at Morgan. "Ned is damned near as diligent as your uncle."

Morgan's fingers weren't working properly, and she glanced over her shoulder to see if Ned were close enough to recognize her. Sure enough, he was now a mere twenty feet away, still dressed in his tennis clothes, hands on hips and the perpetual frown deeper than ever. "A pox on the man!" Morgan cursed angrily but low—and then realized what she had said. Richard was offering her his hand as he stood up, and he winked.

"You see, I knew you would find 'trifling' a pleasant pastime."

"A pox on you, too!" Morgan exploded, and cared not if Ned heard her this time. "This is most embarrassing. Tom Seymour has promised to watch—"

Richard put a finger over her lips. "Hush, Morgan, let's not make a mildly awkward scene worse. I must go. Dream of me this night!" He kissed her hand, bowed deep, and turned away to join Ned Seymour, who nodded curtly at

Morgan. Her rage building to explosive proportions, Morgan watched the two men hurry away and then uttered one of her father's foulest seaman's oaths so loudly that the two fishermen looked up in astonishment.

Tom Seymour was pacing Morgan's chamber and frowning as deeply as ever his older brother had. "You find favor with your uncle—and the King—by signing the Act of Succession, and then put a blot on your reputation with that wild Welshman! God's teeth, Morgan, Jane and I warned you about him!"

"Oh, stop, Tom," Morgan shouted back, as angry as he. They were both dressed in riding clothes and ready to set out for Windsor within the hour. "Ned has doubtlessly exaggerated. You've said yourself he's a dreadful prig. . . ."

Tom whirled around and grabbed her by the shoulders. "Ned has many faults, but exaggerating the truth is not one of them. He saw you, half-naked, lying in Richard's arms and enjoying every moment of it." His strong fingers dug into her flesh and she flinched. "And in full view of anyone who came along—as my brother did!" The blue eyes flashed under the red brows; the wide mouth was set in a grim line.

"Stop lecturing me!" Morgan wrenched away from him in one swift motion and tried to assume some dignity as she met his gaze head on. "You, of all people, peddling moral rectitude! Meanwhile, most of the courtiers are doing far worse—and I'm reprimanded for letting Richard Griffin try to make love to me when you know perfectly well he would never have succeeded!"

"He seemed to be succeeding extremely well," Tom drawled. "He had sufficient cooperation, it seems. He just needed a bit more time."

"Ohhh!" Morgan flew at him, striking out with her fists, but Tom grabbed her arms to stave off the blows. "Whoreson! How dare you accuse me of such a thing!"

"I dare because you . . ." Tom stopped abruptly and the anger began to fade from his tanned face. "Because I'm in charge of your conduct, as you know perfectly well. You can imagine what Ned said to me about my responsibilities!"

"Ned, Ned, Ned!" Morgan's own temper began to sputter out even as she repeated the name. She started to laugh and collapsed against Tom's chest. "Oh, Tom, I would never have let Richard do anything else! I would have called to the fishermen for help or somehow made him stop."

Tom held her close, bending down so his chin touched the top of her head. "Perhaps, muffet. But I mislike the idea of you sporting in such a way with Richard Griffin. It's not . . . it's not like you, it's . . . uncharacteristic."

Morgan shook her head and moved out of his arms. "So it is. But I'm a woman now, Tom; such things happen."

He grinned and cuffed her chin. "I *know* you're a woman—at least I do now. I'm just having trouble getting used to the idea. I still see you as—" This time Tom was interrupted by a knock at the door. "God's teeth, they can't be ready to leave this soon." He turned away, the short miniver-trimmed riding cape swinging from his broad shoulders. But the messenger who stood in the doorway bore no summons to assemble in the courtyard; instead, he had a letter for Mistress Todd.

"It must be from my parents," Morgan said, snatching the letter from Tom's hand. "How fortunate this arrived before we left! I've only heard twice from Mother and Father since I came to court." Morgan pried off the seal and unfolded the slim packet of parchment. Tom watched with curiosity as her eyes widened and her mouth opened in surprise. "It's not from home, it's from Sean!"

Morgan all but ran to the window to catch the morning sunlight. "To My Lady Mistress Todd," the letter began on a conventionally formal note. "I was in Armagh less than a month before I realized I could not leave you in London." Morgan had been reading aloud but she stopped and saw Tom grin.

"Save the words for yourself, muffet; they're not meant for me."

Morgan was flushing from excitement as much as embarrassment. She turned back to the letter and read the rest in silence.

"My good sire is improved in health but still frail," Sean continued in his beautifully wrought handwriting. "I must stay to help tend the fall harvest and the horses. Yet I cannot bear to think of you far away at court. My love is true and strong; so is my conscience, which demands that I must see to your removal from that hellish place. I have prayed daily to Our Lady to defend you from those who would lead you into heresy, mayhap even attempt to force you to sign the damnable Act of Succession." Morgan paused and frowned. Sean's prayers had been in vain. What would he say when he found out she had already signed the act? But what was done was done, and she was anxious to finish the letter. "Therefore, it is my Christian duty to marry you as soon as possible and take you hence. I wish to make you my wife and, in so doing, save your immortal soul from perdition. If you will accept my heartfelt proposal, I shall write to your parents and ask for your hand. Yours in Christ, Sean O'Connor."

Morgan rubbed at the place between her eyebrows and frowned. Her heart was beating very fast, yet she was unsettled by the wording of the letter and Sean's potential reaction to what she had done at the urging of both Tom and her uncle.

"Well?" Tom stood, arms folded across his chest. "Does true love run smooth?"

"Does true love run at all?" Morgan retorted, and looked chagrined. "I'm sorry, I shouldn't be flippant. Maybe I've read too many love poems." She waved the letter at Tom. "This sounds more like a sermon than a proposal."

Tom tipped his head to one side, the single earring catching the sunlight. "Will your parents approve?"

Morgan was refolding the letter and looking for some place to put it. Everything was packed. She'd have to keep it on her person. There was a pocket on the left-hand side of her riding skirt and she carefully tucked it away. "They've always been very fond of Sean. He is distant kin, and while he is not wealthy or a great landowner, his family has done well enough."

"But do you truly fancy raising horseflesh and barley?" Tom asked.

Morgan had turned away, ostensibly to make certain her belongings were all in order. "I assume we'll raise children as well." She looked over her shoulder at Tom and smiled brightly. "It's love that matters most, isn't it?"

Tom shrugged. "I wouldn't know. I've never been in love. At least not the kind that leads to wedded bliss."

His reply disappointed Morgan. She had expected reassurance; she sensed that she needed it. But there was no time for that now, as Madge returned to announce that the servants were ready to load the baggage carts. Morgan left the chamber with Tom and Madge but paid no heed to their flirtatious banter. She was too confused, too muddled to think of anything except Sean's letter and why she was not as ecstatic as she ought to be at having her heart's desire within reach.

Windsor Castle sat on the site of a fortress dating from William the Conqueror's era. The vista of the imposing round keep built by Henry II and the Long Walk down through the great park revived Morgan's spirits. She had no sooner finished changing her clothes and unpacking than she sat down in her chamber overlooking the Thames and began her reply to Sean.

"My love," she wrote, dispensing with formalities, "I accept your proposal with all my heart. Pray write my good parents at once. Give my greetings to your dear father with wishes for a full recovery." She paused, tapping the quill against her cheek. Should she say anything about dowry or trousseau? Would the wedding be at her parish church adjacent to Faux Hall? Morgan needed a few moments to think. She got up to retrieve Sean's letter from her riding skirt, which she had already hung in the wardrobe. Should she say something about the Act of Succession or let the matter lie for the time being? His wording had been quite adamant. She must reread it and then perhaps she could devise some tactful explanation. . . .

But the letter was not there. She shook out the skirt, turned the pocket inside out, knelt down to see if it had fallen on the wardrobe floor. Panicky, she searched through the rest of the clothes, scoured the rushes strewn across the chamber, even looked into the corridor to see if she had dropped it before entering her new quarters.

"Sweet Jesu," she murmured, knowing she must find the letter. It was incriminating, dangerous to Sean, perhaps even to herself. She walked out of the castle, past St. George's Chapel, under the massive gateway and around the battlements.

She was at the head of the tree-lined Long Walk when she saw a familiar figure coming toward her: Thomas Cromwell, arms tucked inside his plain black sleeves. He called her name. Morgan stood stock-still, but managed a weak smile as he drew near. "Are you exploring Windsor already, Niece?" Cromwell asked, touching his somber black cap in greeting.

"Oh—yes. The castle is most impressive, like a fairy-tale place. I thought I'd walk a bit. I got stiff riding so much today."

"Hmmm. One does. I arrived yesterday." He chuckled. "To get a head start, you know."

Morgan forced a laugh. "Very wise, Uncle. Are you, too, taking the air?"

He nodded. "I get stiff too, sitting so much. In my younger years I became accustomed to considerable physical exercise. But now . . ." He lifted the palms of his blunt-fingered hands upwards. "Now I try to walk some every evening before suppertime. You are going down the Long Walk?"

"For a bit," Morgan allowed.

"I'll join you then," Cromwell said as they fell in step together. The shadows of the trees were beginning to lengthen and meet across the drive. There was no breeze, but it was cooler at Windsor than it had been at Hampton Court. Morgan kept a watchful eye and wondered what she would do if she found the letter while in the company of her uncle.

"This is rather fortuitous, actually," Cromwell said as their feet crunched on the gravel. "I had planned to speak with you before we left Hampton Court but I had no time, no spare time at all." He sighed. "A pity to have to put family matters after other responsibilities."

Morgan shot him a wary glance but didn't break the pace. "Oh? Is aught wrong?"

"Oh, no!" Cromwell chuckled again. "It's something very right—for you." Now he paused and Morgan had to stop and turn to face him. "I am requesting your parents' permission to arrange your betrothal to a most impressive young man—James Sinclair, heir to the earldom of Belford."

The shadows seemed to surround Morgan; the night seemed to steal over her all at once. Surely she had not heard right. Certainly her parents would never force her into marriage with a man she didn't know. "Who?" The question was barely audible, and Morgan didn't even realize she had placed both hands over her breast.

"Of course you're surprised!" Cromwell put a strong

hand on her shoulder. "This is an excellent match, better than you might have expected, though I must say I exerted as much influence as this humble servant of the King could. James is said to be a fine-looking fellow, in his late twenties, and his father has considerable holdings in Northumberland."

Northumberland, thought Morgan, as far north as one could go and still remain in England . . . a fine-looking man she'd never laid eyes on . . . But of course she could not marry him. Her parents would understand. As soon as they learned that Sean had asked for her hand they would nullify Thomas Cromwell's mad plan.

"Naturally, it will take time to absorb this." Cromwell was gazing up through the heavily leafed trees. "James will come to court soon for the betrothal ceremonies, and the wedding will be at Belford next spring. Yes, you will have ample time to make your plans, ready your trousseau, even visit your family at Faux Hall, if you like."

Morgan was tempted to state simply that she would have nothing to do with James Sinclair and his future earldom and his castle at Belford. But that would be open rebellion and she had the feeling it would suit her purposes better to appear docile for the time being. But as Morgan and Cromwell exchanged glances, his colorless eyes seemed to harden ever so slightly. "You do appreciate what this means for your future?"

"I'm sure I will, once I've had—as you say—some time to think on it," Morgan replied in a calm, reasonable tone. "I had not anticipated anything like this so soon."

"Hmmm. Of course." Cromwell gave her shoulder a pat. "It's almost dark. Perhaps we had better head back." They turned and began walking toward the massive bulk of Windsor Castle. Cromwell, however, was turning toward a side entrance in the Norman Gate. "I must leave you now, Niece," he said, and once again touched his black cap. "You will be very busy, planning your wedding gown, the nuptials and such." He paused and looked directly at her. "Along with your other duties, you'll have little time for incidental matters—such as writing letters." He smiled, a benign, pleasant smile, and turned into the castle.

Morgan remained where she was for several minutes: He knows. He has Sean's letter. If I refuse to marry this unknown man from Belford, my uncle will use the letter against Sean. . . . And though Sean might be safe in Ireland for now, Morgan knew the danger to him was real. While he might worry about saving her soul, she was now engaged in a battle to save his life.

Chapter 4

MORGAN'S LETTER to Sean was destroyed, of course, burned late that night while Tom Seymour stirred the ashes in the grate.

"Absolutely anyone could have picked up Sean's letter to you," Tom said for the sixth time. "And all too many people at court would see it as a tool in winning Cromwell's—and thus the King's—favor."

"But neither Sean nor I are of any importance," Morgan argued, also for the sixth time.

Tom made a slashing gesture with his big hand. "That's not the point. Anyone who opposes the King in this matter, whether peer or peasant, will suffer. And anyone who seeks advancement knows the value evidence such as this has in the King's eyes."

Morgan sat tapping her fingernails on the armchair and staring into the darkened room. A single taper burned on the mantel and there was only the cleft of a moon in the summer sky. "What if Sean never comes back? What if I go to Ireland?"

Tom sighed. "I don't know. I can't tell you how lethal this business will get. More is the barometer there. If the King executes Sir Thomas for treason, then any man—or woman—who defies Henry is as good as dead already." Tom came to kneel by Morgan's chair. He took her chin between his thumb and forefinger and smiled gently. "See here, muffet, you are very young, and so is Sean. This Sinclair marriage may never happen. Often such arrangements fall through. My advice is to play for time, go along with your uncle's schemes for the moment. The wedding itself is still a long way off."

"I think I'd rather elope with Richard Griffin than

marry this whoever-he-is from Northumberland," Morgan said grimly. "Where *is* Richard, by the way?"

Tom stood up, stretching his long arms. "He didn't come to Windsor. I heard he'd left for London."

Morgan stared at Tom. "Not because of—of what happened when Ned found us?"

"Nay," Tom laughed, "that's a hobby of Richard's no one thinks twice about. Except when it's you." He bent down and brushed her nose with his finger. "That is, your uncle will not want you dallying with Richard or anyone else while these marriage arrangements are being made. The future Earl of Belford will no doubt insist upon a virgin bride."

Morgan felt her supper of poached salmon and roasted partridge turn over in her stomach. *That* problem had not yet occurred to her in all the other turmoil which had raged around her during the day. Even in the ill-lighted room, Tom saw her pale and his brow furrowed.

"You haven't given in to Richard?" he asked rather harshly.

"Oh! No, of course not! I was just . . . I was just thinking about what James might be like."

"In bed?" Tom was grinning again.

"No. Well, maybe." Morgan got up and clung to Tom's arm. "I'm sure there's a way, Tom. I know I can get out of this and still marry Sean."

"It's possible." Tom squeezed her hand. "But you will not write to Sean?"

"Not now. I heard tonight the King is going on a short progress next month. In fact, he will visit Ned's new estates in Hampshire. I thought I might go to Faux Hall for a while. I'll write from there."

Tom considered this idea for a moment and then nodded. "That ought to be safe enough." He let go of her arm and started for the door. "I'd better leave before Madge comes back and decides we've been doing something scandalous." He winked at Morgan before stepping into the hallway.

All the windows in Anne Boleyn's apartments stood open, letting the cool evening breeze blow up from the Thames. Servants passed platters of cold meat, fresh green salads, and bowls of fruit among the courtiers who had assembled in the Queen's chambers after a day of hunting in the Great Park. The King was expected to join them later but was said to be in conference with the Portuguese ambassador.

Anne was determinedly gay that night, encouraging Mark Smeaton to improvise on his lute, demanding new verses from both Wyatt and Surrey, insisting that Francis Weston and Will Brereton partner her in a series of dances.

When the door burst open, the music ceased and the laughter stopped. All present thought it was the King—but instead, Richard Griffin came striding into the chamber, dropping on one knee before the Queen.

Anne greeted him with a gay laugh. "Welcome, good Richard, you've been gone a fortnight or more. Was she fair and willing or dark and tempestuous?"

But for once Richard seemed in no mood for banter. He bowed low. "Neither, Your Grace. I have just returned from London where the Earl of Northumberland has had Lord Dacre indicted for treason. The trial is set for next week."

A gasp went up around the room. Lord Dacre was one of the staunchest Catholic lords in the kingdom. He and Northumberland had quarreled for obscure personal reasons some time ago. The Earl had waited for the right moment to strike back; with his old love, Anne Boleyn, on the throne, the time was ripe.

Thomas Wyatt wiped his mouth with a linen napkin. "If Lord Dacre is found guilty a great victory will be yours," he told Anne.

She smiled confidently at Wyatt. "The religious tides pull in my favor. He will be proven guilty."

Morgan shifted uneasily in her chair. Her own situation dictated that she favor Lord Dacre, even though she hadn't the remotest notion who the man was. Yet, she served the Queen. Her ambivalent feelings reflected the disquiet of the times. But she shoved such thoughts aside and looked at Richard Griffin. He seemed as dashing as ever, if somewhat rumpled from his London ride.

He was again speaking to the Queen. "There is someone else here to see you, Your Grace, a spokesman for the Earl of Northumberland."

Anne nodded. "Of course. Send him in."

Richard motioned to the page at the door which the youth opened promptly. A lean, blond young man in his late twenties stepped into the room. There was something faintly austere about him—the thin, purposeful mouth, the cool gray-blue eyes, the faintly hawklike nose. His clothes were conservative, yet modish. He moved in quick, decisive steps toward the Queen and dropped to one knee.

Richard Griffin stepped aside, saying, "Your Grace, may I present James Sinclair."

All movement in the room seemed to cease for Morgan as the name pierced her brain. She half fell against Will Brereton, who looked startled but managed to support her with one arm. James Sinclair was speaking to the Queen but Morgan heard only the sound of his voice and none of the words. Gradually, she became aware of her surroundings. Will Brereton leaned down and asked if she were all right. She nodded, making a weak attempt to laugh off the incident. The concluding phrase of James Sinclair's speech floated across the room to her: ". . . to which end my brother, Francis, and I will be honored to serve you."

Anne Boleyn bestowed a glowing smile on James Sinclair. "Well spoken, my good man. Your loyalty and support have put me in the mood for celebration." She signaled to Mark Smeaton. "Come, Mark, let us have more music. James, you shall lead the dancing. Do you know any of the ladies here?" He replied he did not. "Then I will choose for you," said the Queen. Fate marched to the end of Anne Boleyn's fingertips as she beckoned to Morgan.

Morgan moved stiffly across the floor. All she could think of was that at least he wasn't three feet tall and covered with warts. Somehow, it seemed little enough consolation.

"My dear," said the Queen, taking Morgan by the hand, "this is James Sinclair." She was still smiling. "As I'm sure you know by now."

Anne must know about the betrothal, Morgan thought. Did everyone else at court know, too? She glanced quickly about the room, noting that several courtiers were whispering to one another and a few seemed to wear interested, knowing smiles.

Anne had turned to James. "This is one of our more recent and most delightful additions to court, Mistress Morgan Todd."

The muscles of James's face tightened slightly but his eyes remained impassive. It occurred to Morgan that his lack of enthusiasm matched her own. She forgot to offer him her hand, and he didn't seek it. He merely bowed and murmured that he was honored to make her acquaintance.

Anne put a hand on each of their arms. "Lead the way to joy, good friends. Start the music!" Smeaton brought his fingers down across the lute strings.

Morgan and James stepped out onto the impromptu dance floor. Their bodies and feet moved in accompaniment with the rhythm but not with each other. Morgan couldn't raise her eyes to meet his. They did not exchange a word throughout the dance.

The first tune ended. Morgan stood uncertainly in front of James, suddenly wishing he would say something, anything. But Francis Weston called for la ronde, and James Sinclair began to swirl Morgan about in time to the rapid beat of the music. In accordance with the dictates of the dance, they changed partners. She was whisked into the arms of Ned Seymour and then Will Brereton and on to Francis Weston, and finally, as Mark Smeaton strummed the last notes, she was in the grasp of Richard Griffin.

The dancers paused to catch their breath. "You don't favor North Country nobles, I see," Richard chided, inclining his head toward James, who was escorting Margaret Wyatt from the dance floor.

"No concern of yours," Morgan retorted. "He's a stranger, you know."

"But will not be for long, I hear." His voice was very low.

Morgan gave him a sharp look. "Did he tell you that?"

Richard was evasive. "I make a point of keeping my ears open. It's necessary in making one's way at court." The music had started again, but neither Morgan nor Richard made any move to join in. "Is it his religion which makes him so unpalatable?" he asked, smoothing his brown hair into place.

"Hardly. He could be a supporter of the Grand Turk, for all I care. What happens between Northumberland and Lord Dacre matters not to me." But she avoided Richard's eyes as she spoke.

"You ought to be concerned. It will set a precedent for what constitutes treason."

Morgan's patience was running out. They had been conversing in low, dogged tones while their companions laughed and chattered and danced around them. Morgan glanced quickly about the room. She was fed up with Richard Griffin's irritating remarks, annoyed by James Sinclair's rigid demeanor, digusted with Thomas Cromwell's meddlesome politicking, no longer grateful for Tom Seymour's well-meant interference, and angered by Sean O'Connor's intransigent religious views. There were too many men in Morgan's life and none of them seemed to care about her feelings or her happiness. The Queen's chambers were abustle with chattering people, but Morgan felt very much alone.

Lord Dacre's trial was to be held in St. George's Hall at Windsor. Ordinarily it would have taken place in the Tower of London, but none of the nobles wanted to suffer the city heat of late August.

In her apartments, Anne Boleyn exuded self-confidence. "This will be a quick and clear victory," she told her brother, George, on the morning of the trial. "Lord Dacre's criticism of my marriage to His Grace is blatant treason. A verdict of guilty will be an obvious reproof to those fanatical adherents of Catherine of Aragon and her mulish daughter."

Morgan, ostensibly practicing her lute, wondered what Anne would do if she knew one of her own ladies-in-waiting did not wholeheartedly hope for Lord Dacre's conviction. She also considered that her unspoken support for Dacre might not be so strong if James Sinclair had not taken Percy of Northumberland's side. James had been at court for over a week, but Morgan hadn't seen him since the night he arrived. She kept expecting him to seek her out so that they might get to know one another. Not that she wanted to see him—but surely it would be the thing to do.

"It is time for Lord Dacre's peers to assemble," George Boleyn commented. "I will join them so that I may give you an eyewitness report, Sister."

"Go as my talisman," said Anne, giving her hand to her brother. "And give my best wishes to Harry Percy."

George started for the door but someone else was already coming in. It was the Earl of Surrey, accompanied by a very tall, sandy-haired man with a long loping stride.

Morgan could have sworn that she had screamed aloud, but as no one looked her way, the sound apparently had strangled and died in her throat. Indeed, she thought she might faint, for the tall blond man was the stranger from the orchard, and Surrey was introducing him to the Queen as Francis Sinclair, Sir James's younger brother.

Francis was nodding, acknowledging the others as if all but the Queen and perhaps Thomas Wyatt were negligible. "Francis was delayed by business in Woodstock," Surrey was explaining, "or else he would have come here directly with his brother."

Morgan was hiding behind Wyatt. Anne Boleyn and Surrey had introduced everyone but her. Morgan fervently prayed that the Queen would not notice the omission, but while Anne and the other courtiers resumed their chatter, Francis headed straight for Wyatt.

"You are a fine poet, sir," Francis declared, and put out his big hand with the long fingers Morgan remembered so well. "I have attempted poetry myself. I know it is a difficult art form."

Wyatt seemed to sense that Francis was not the sort to engage in idle flattery. "That's kind of you. It is always satisfying to have one's poor efforts applauded by someone knowledgeable."

"Indeed. Surrey over there is quite good, too, but I prefer your verse." Francis stopped and peered over Wyatt's shoulder. "Are you hiding someone or do you have an appendage?"

"What?" Wyatt turned around and laughed. "Oh! No, no, this is Mistress Morgan Todd. I don't believe you've met."

The gray eyes seemed transfixed; Morgan could have sworn there was no sound in the room at all, no motion, nothing but the two of them staring at each other. But that was not so. The other courtiers were gossiping and laughing, the Queen was teasing Mark Smeaton about his lute, and Margaret Wyatt was showing a new dance step to Surrey.

"A pleasure, Mistress Todd," Francis said at last in that deep drawl, and put out his hand. "I believe you're going to be my sister-in-law."

Morgan felt his fingers on hers, felt the obligatory kiss, felt as if this could not really be happening. "Yes," she replied, and was amazed that she could speak at all.

"Though I did not realize an announcement had yet been made."

Francis shrugged his slightly sloping shoulders. "Well, it has now." He still stared at her, but his surprise and shock had turned to something Morgan could only assess as amusement. "Since I came here not so much for Lord Dacre's trial but to assist my brother in the formalities of the betrothal, I presume your news is no secret. As future kin, why don't you show me St. George's Chapel? I've wanted to see it for years."

Now Morgan did find it impossible to reply. She just stood there, with Francis Sinclair towering over her, wishing that Wyatt, the Queen, anyone would rescue her from this giant beast of a man who was asking her to show him the splendors of Windsor Castle.

"Go ahead, Morgan," Thomas Wyatt said to break the awkward silence. "The Queen is too absorbed with the Dacre affair to mind your leave-taking." He smiled kindly and unexpectedly kissed her cheek. "I had heard rumors about your betrothal. I must congratulate you."

Dazed, Morgan left the royal apartments and headed in the direction of the courtyard and the chapel. Francis walked beside her, making an obvious effort to curtail his long stride.

"You can't say that life isn't full of ironies," he remarked as they walked down the wide, winding staircase.

"I can't say anything," Morgan snapped, and realized that her temper was returning along with some semblance of composure. She stopped abruptly halfway down the stairs and almost tripped both of them. "You! Of all people in the world, *you* turn out to be my future brother-in-law! I don't believe it!"

Francis gave her a faintly sheepish, crooked grin. "It certainly is a coincidence. I thought you were the cook's daughter."

"So I gathered. You might have asked first!"

Francis considered this suggestion for a moment. "Yes, I might have, now that you mention it. But I was told that a winsome and willing wench with ripe breasts and long, slim legs would meet me. You certainly fit the description."

"Except for being willing, you blackguard. I was not willing!"

"You are also shouting," Francis commented dryly, and took her by the arm. "Come, come, we can't stand here on the stairway and argue. Besides, I just thought you were being playful and coquettish."

Morgan had fallen in step with him as they got to the bottom of the stairs and crossed a short hallway to an outside door. "Playful! I was defending my honor, and now your brother will discover I'm no virgin and God himself only knows what will happen then!"

"James? Oh, he won't know the difference," Francis said airily, as they walked out into the heavy late-summer air.

It suddenly occurred to Morgan that she had gone the wrong way. They would have to walk clear around Windsor and back under the great archway entrance to get to the chapel. She cursed inwardly and then realized what Francis had said.

"Do you mean James is simpleminded? He didn't seem so to me." Morgan looked up at Francis's profile—the strong-willed mouth, the heavy brows, the high forehead.

"No, not that," Francis said, and stopped, hands on hips, to admire the towers of Eton College across the river and the rolling Berkshire fields beyond. "He's never had a woman, you see. I was the first to marry."

"You're married!" Morgan made the statement sound blasphemous.

"Umm. This is a splendid place. How I'd like to visit Eton. What? Oh, yes, I've been married since I was twenty. You'll like Lucy; she is a wonderful woman."

Morgan had a terrible desire to smash Francis with something very hard. She also knew that it probably would make little impression. And she suddenly realized that she and Francis were discussing her future life as if it were an accomplished fact instead of the impossible probability she knew it had to be.

"I'm not married yet," Morgan declared, but Francis seemed to pay no heed. He still appeared to be admiring the view. "I said, I'm not—"

"I know, you're not married yet." Francis began walking again and Morgan joined him since he was at least headed in the right direction. "But you will be. The Sinclairs usually get their way, and for some reason I don't fathom, James seems set on marrying Cromwell's niece. I

72

suppose it's politics and religion, though I'm not overly keen on the directions either are going right now."

"Then let me tell you something, Francis Sinclair," Morgan said in an angry tone. "You had better not say so in front of anyone here."

"That's true," Francis allowed as he paused to glance up at the Curfew Tower and the adjacent Horseshoe Cloisters. "You and I have our secrets and I trust we'll be able to keep them."

Morgan didn't respond. Francis was right about that, at least. She was also vaguely pleased that Francis did not condone the current trends in court circles. Yet James must, or he would not have come to court to support Northumberland. Obviously, there was disagreement in the family, though apparently not serious.

"Ah, the castle gateway," Francis remarked as they walked into the courtyard. "Henry's one great change. It's well done."

"I'm glad you like it," Morgan said, and could not stifle the sarcasm.

But Francis had stopped again, this time to observe the exterior of the chapel. It appeared like a miniature cathedral, its stained-glass windows dazzling in the sunlight, the carved King's beasts surmounting the roof, a perfect example of late Gothic genius. "Magnificent," breathed Francis, and he began walking rapidly toward the entrance.

It was cool inside, the choir stalls empty, the elaborately wrought altar set off like a treasure chest. From the entry they could see the banners of the Knights of the Garter, and the Royal Closet where the Queen and her guests could watch the ceremonies in discreet privacy.

Francis had genuflected upon entering and Morgan did the same. It seemed a mockery under the circumstances, but Morgan had to admit that Francis was behaving more like an avid connoisseur of church architecture than an importunate ravisher.

Francis, in fact, was now kneeling at the altar, hands clasped, head bowed. Morgan stood behind him in the aisle, confused and disturbed. The shock of seeing this man again had been tremendous; the discovery that he was to be her future brother-in-law was overwhelming. But now incredulity had given way to more rational thought. Of course she had no intention of marrying the aloof, reticent James Sinclair. Yet she still found herself puzzling over Francis, who seemed to be a complex, unusual—and infuriating—sort of man.

Crossing himself, Francis stood up and began examining the carving on the choir stalls, the fan-vaulted ceiling with its delicate tracery, and the side chapels. "Very impressive," Francis said at last as they returned to the entrance. "Some day I'll show you York Minster. It's the grandest piece of architecture in England." He squinted up at the afternoon sun. "I suppose the Dacre trial will drag on. Maybe I ought to go into the town and explore for a while."

Morgan stared in perplexity at the tall, indolent figure. He was dressed much as he had been that day in the orchard, in a white cambric shirt, dark brown hose, leather boots, and the riding cape thrown over one arm. She realized that she was waiting for an apology, an explanation, anything that alluded to the terrible wrong he had done her at Faux Hall.

But Francis was already striding toward the great archway. "I'll see you later, I imagine," he called over his shoulder, and the sound of his heavy tread on the gravel walkway faded in the distance.

"I don't believe it, I don't believe it," Morgan breathed aloud. "I don't believe *him!*"

"Don't tell me the Sinclair brothers have already got you talking to yourself," said an amused voice behind Morgan.

She turned and saw Richard Griffin standing on the courtyard green, looking amused and yet weary. "Well, why not?" she demanded, and to conceal her confusion, stooped to pick up a young gray cat which had wandered out from the castle precincts.

"I should think you'd be elated," said Richard, taking out a kerchief and wiping his damp forehead. "I'm told you are some day to be Countess of Belford."

"Rot." Morgan scratched the cat behind its ears and was rewarded by a shrill howl of displeasure. She dumped the animal back on the grass and looked at Richard. "You've met James, of course. Have you met his loathsome brother?"

"No, he went from Belford to Woodstock. He has some

property there, I gather. But I assume that was him. There's a resemblance in coloring, if nothing else." Richard put a hand on Morgan's upper arm. "From what I've seen of James he's not man enough for you. You might have been better off with the other one."

"Oh!" Morgan jerked away from Richard and could hardly keep from shrieking. "He's married, and God knows I pity his wife already! James may be a stick but at least he's not . . ." She clamped her mouth shut, realizing she had almost said too much.

Richard raised both eyebrows. "But I thought you just met Francis. I gather he doesn't make a favorable first impression."

"Oh, Richard, I'm just upset! I hadn't counted on an arranged marriage, especially not so soon—I've only been at court four months."

Richard sighed and turned serious. "I know, it's unsettling. We'll talk about it later. I must get back to the trial. I had to get outside for a moment. It's very warm in there—in more ways than one." He wiped his forehead again and tucked the kerchief away. "Before you're carried away kicking and screaming to Northumberland, you and I have some unfinished business."

His green eyes flashed and one hand brushed the bodice of her gown. But Morgan was in no mood for romantic allusions. "I'll be tending my own business in the future," she asserted. "From here on I take fate in my own hands."

Richard started to laugh but stopped. Morgan's topaz eyes had hardened, her wide mouth was set grimly, even her stance seemed immovable. And though he was not of a mind to give up his pursuit, he realized this was the wrong time. He saluted her with a deep bow and went back toward the castle, unaware that Morgan didn't seem to notice his departure.

"It can't be! It can't be!" Anne Boleyn was almost screaming, her almond-slanted eyes blazing fury. "Lord Dacre acquitted! The King will be enraged!"

George Boleyn tried to soothe his sister. "The lot of them should be clapped in the Tower," he said, trying to get Anne to sit down. "Everyone was so sure—I was myself. But they changed their minds."

"A fine time for petty sympathy and maudlin good fellowship," Anne rasped. "Good God, is there no end to my troubles?" At last she sank into a chair, her head in her hands. "Percy had him indicted for treason not so much because of their quarrel but because he thought it would help my cause. And now Dacre is freed!" Her fingers twisted at her pearl-and-ruby necklace. "A strange kind of help it has been, adding more grief where there is already a surfeit!"

Though Morgan felt great pity for the Queen, she was secretly relieved over Lord Dacre's acquittal. She stood with Margaret Wyatt at the far end of the room, noting that neither Tom nor Ned was present. She hadn't seen Tom for several days and understood he had taken dispatches to the Low Countries. She missed him and needed his counsel. Somehow, Anne's distress seemed no greater than her own. A commoner, Morgan thought bitterly, could suffer as much as a Queen.

Late in the day, Morgan was summoned to her uncle's chambers. This time she went without any sense of nervousness or apprehension. She didn't even bother to change from her red-and-white gown into something less frivolous.

Thomas Cromwell's desk was as orderly as it had been on the day of Morgan's first visit. He, however, seemed less composed. He sat behind his desk garbed in the inevitable black, his fingers clasped together.

"Do sit, my dear," he said with a faint smile. "I have to make this brief. Today has been most difficult. His Grace is highly distressed over the acquittal of Lord Dacre, as are all of us."

Morgan shifted in her chair, hoping she didn't betray her own reaction. Cromwell apparently didn't notice anything amiss. He cleared his throat and continued speaking. "James Sinclair leaves with his brother tomorrow for Belford. I have prepared a contract for you to sign—it's been accepted by your parents. But I think you two young people should spend a few moments alone before James returns north."

Morgan looked at Cromwell from under her thick lashes; for just a second the topaz eyes sparked fire. But she recovered control and merely nodded.

Cromwell pulled a bell cord behind his chair. "I would like to spend more time with the two of you myself, but events pile up these days . . ." His words were interrupted by the arrival of a page who ushered in James Sinclair. He greeted the King's secretary cordially and bowed to Morgan. It crossed her mind that so far their courtship had consisted of more bows than words.

Cromwell opened a drawer and pulled out a long sheet of white paper. "I'll give you both the contract to read. That door leads to an anteroom where you can have some privacy." He handed the contract to James. "Take your time, young friends."

Sinclair looked as uncomfortable as Morgan felt. He paused and coughed slightly. "As you wish, Master Secretary." Opening the door for Morgan, he followed her into the adjoining room. For the first time, they were alone together.

Neither of them looked directly at the other. James stared at the seal on the prenuptial contract; Morgan kept her gaze riveted on the pattern of the dark wood in the floorboards. Out of the corner of her eye she could see one of his boots, highly polished and tooled in the finest leather. Her mind was hurtling in several directions at once. He's very neat about his person, she told herself. He's about the same size as Sean but fair, while Sean is dark. Sean . . . oh, what would he think? She couldn't wait to get to Faux Hall and write him.

She jerked up her head and looked him straight in the eye. "Do you want this marriage?"

Dumbfounded, he stared at her. "That's not the issue," he said at last in a calm, reasonable tone. "It's what the King wants, what Master Cromwell wants, apparently what both our families want."

"Why?"

James scowled and ran his fingers over the contract several times. He seemed to be very self-controlled, yet Morgan detected an inner distress and an enormous amount of self-discipline. "Because northern England, so distant from court and the center of politics, is a natural hotbed for rebellion. Lord Dacre is a prime example. If the King can link his secretary's kin with my family, such an alliance will help counter the dissident elements."

Morgan stabbed at the contract so hard that her fingernail actually made a small tear. "You mean we are but two tiny links in a political piece of chain mail?" She stared fiercely at James, who looked extremely uncomfortable, even distraught. "Are you willing to be used thus? Have *you* no feelings, no desires about your future?"

James Sinclair was not accustomed to women who spoke with candor or vehemence. James, in fact, wasn't used to women, save for his mother, the Countess, and his sweet-natured sister-in-law, Lucy. While the Countess had a mind of her own, she was the family matriarch; James had no idea how to deal with his future bride and Morgan sensed his uncertainty.

"You are a future earl and would content yourself with being a pawn?" Morgan demanded. "See here, James Sinclair, I bring no vast dowry, only my family's holdings in Buckinghamshire. We have a modest manor house, some cows and pigs and chickens and horses and sheep. We also have a large orchard but . . ." Morgan stopped and turned away. The orchard conjured up a most unpleasant picture, and James's presence only reinforced her discomfiture.

"Your dowry has been itemized for me," James said tersely. "Twenty acres, forty cows, twelve horses, and the like. Plus one-sixth of the fifteen tenant farmers' holdings and the right to purchase cloth at tuppence above cost per yard from the local wool merchant. A right, I believe, your grandmother negotiated many years ago and which continues through the fourth generation."

It was clear that James could have gone on at length, but Morgan was gaping at him in astonishment. It was also clear that in matters of business, James stood on very firm ground. "You certainly know more about me than I do about you. What do you raise," she snapped, "puffins?"

James straightened his shoulders with dignity and pursed his thin lips. "Puffins have been sighted off the Holy Isle from time to time. But we do not raise them as such."

Obstinacy was getting Morgan nowhere. More and more, she realized that her sheltered, pampered upbringing had not prepared her for dealing with the real world. But she would learn; she had already learned quite a lot since that April day at Faux Hall.

"What you really wish is an alliance with the King's secretary. Why not choose one of Cromwell's daughters rather than me?" Morgan now sounded logical and composed. She carefully folded her hands in her lap.

"I was not offered Cromwell's daughters. I was offered you."

"I see." Morgan was silent for a moment, considering outright refusal. But Cromwell had Sean's letter. She had promised herself to play for time. "Very well, let's sign this and be done with it."

James picked up the parchment in his thin hands. "Would you like me to read it to you?"

"I can read," Morgan retorted. "I can even write—and count beyond ten."

James looked faintly apologetic. "I've been told you are well educated. I only meant that we should save time that way."

"True." She moved her chair closer to his and noted that he stiffened slightly. "Here," she said, trying to sound agreeable, "we'll read it together."

Morgan raced through the elaborate wording, determined to finish before James did. She then sat back and waited; he read with great care and concentration, occasionally stopping to consider a fine point. At last he put the parchment aside and nodded. "Yes, it seems to be in good order."

"Naturally, since my uncle drew it up." But James failed to notice the irony in her voice.

"We had best have Master Cromwell and my brother witness our signatures," he said, as they both stood up. He fingered the parchment, which bound them reluctantly, inalterably together. For the first time he seemed actually to see her, the topaz eyes, the wide sensual mouth, the thick tawny hair, the slender yet wonderfully female body. He turned abruptly, the fingers of one hand drumming on the back of the chair. "You'll like Belford, I'm sure. We'll go to court sometimes, of course." He spoke very rapidly, his eyes fixed on the Italian clock in one corner of the room.

"I've never been north," Morgan said. Silence followed, a stifling silence that made Morgan want to shout. Instead, she suggested that they return to Uncle Thomas. James readily agreed.

Thomas Cromwell was behind his desk, his quill scraping noisily across a piece of paper. He looked up when Morgan and James came into the room.

"Ah. You've settled everything?" he asked with a smile.

"Yes, sir," answered James, sounding much relieved.

"We're both prepared to sign and leave you to your duties."

"Oh," said Cromwell with a wave of his blunt hand, "I can still find time for family matters on the busiest of days." He tugged at the bell cord. "I believe Francis is waiting to be the other witness."

Morgan's fingers began to pleat the folds of her red-and-white gown in an almost frenetic manner. Somehow, she had hoped she would not have to see Francis Sinclair again. But the door opened and there he was, looming over all of them. He made a brief bow, which included Morgan and Cromwell, and pulled up an armchair before the King's secretary could say a word. Morgan eyed her uncle and was surprised that he seemed more amused than annoyed by Francis's presumptuous behavior. She noted for the first time that Francis wore courtier's clothes, but the dark blue doublet was slightly rumpled and there were mud stains on his cloak. North Country dolt, she thought savagely, and was startled when he put out his big hand.

"Congratulations," he said, and only Morgan saw the mockery in his gray eyes.

"Thank you," she replied stiffly, and thought her fingers would break in his grasp.

James was smoothing out the prenuptial contract on the oak desk. Cromwell offered the quill to Morgan, who realized that her hands had begun to tremble. Hastily, she scrawled her name across the bottom of the paper. James took the quill from her and carefully affixed his own signature. Cromwell and Francis then each wrote their own names and the deed was done: Morgan and James were sworn to each other in the sight of God and man. And only Morgan knew that she had also sworn herself to a document she would never honor.

James thanked Cromwell for his efforts and concern. Then he turned to Morgan and took her hand. "Good-bye, Morgan." He paused. "Until the spring."

She felt his lips lightly press her fingertips. "Safe journey to you," she said noncommittally.

Francis was already at the door. He merely waved his hand and said good-bye in that deep, almost gruff voice. And then the Sinclair brothers were gone and Morgan was left alone with her uncle.

"This is a deed well done," Cromwell declared, and began rolling up the contract. "As you can see, James is a most decent man and his properties are considerable. Your future is well secured, my dear."

If Cromwell expected gushes of gratitude, he was doomed to disappointment. Morgan merely nodded. Yet she knew her uncle was secretly exulting in his triumph and that this would be a propitious moment to inquire about visiting Faux Hall. "I should like to see my parents," she said, and was surprised at how flat her voice sounded.

Cromwell was putting the contract into a drawer. The same one where he had placed the act she had signed? Morgan wondered. Perhaps even Sean's letter was there; her whole life seemed to be piling up in Cromwell's desk.

"A reasonable request," he said amiably. "If you can secure the Queen's permission, I won't hinder you."

"Thank you." Morgan forced a smile and made as if to stand up. Cromwell got to his feet at once and put out his hand. Uncle and niece exchanged polite farewells, hers carefully masking the wildly divergent futures each had in mind for Morgan Todd.

Chapter 5

BY MID-SEPTEMBER, all but the apple trees had yielded their fruit in the orchard at Faux Hall. The sheep had been shorn, the three foals birthed that spring were already a good size, and the half-dozen pigs that had been chosen for butchering were so fat they could hardly move.

Morgan's first reaction to her old home was that it seemed smaller. After Whitehall and Hampton Court and Windsor, Faux Hall was dwarfed by comparison. But it was no less dear than it had ever been, and even the orchard, with its leaves turning from green to gold, did not distress Morgan as she feared it might.

But she was otherwise upset and made her feelings known to her parents soon after her arrival. "I could not imagine either of you letting me wed a man I'd never met," she told them as they sat in her father's study after supper. "When Uncle Thomas said you had given your consent, I almost didn't believe him."

Sir Edmund and Lady Alice did not answer right away but exchanged pained glances before turning back to their daughter. "It was not an easy decision," Sir Edmund allowed at last. "We would both have preferred that you choose your own husband, if possible." Her father stopped and again looked at his wife. "But there were other matters to consider, you see."

"Such as what?" Morgan leaned forward on the footstool, the topaz eyes darting from father to mother.

"Oh, tell her, Edmund," Lady Alice said at last, and there was an uncharacteristic bitterness in her voice.

Sir Edmund sighed and pushed away the glass of port he'd been sipping. "Cromwell sent a special messenger this summer. The man was no mere lackey, but Richard Rich—you know him?"

82

Morgan frowned, trying to conjure up a face to match the name. "I'm not sure. He works for Cromwell, of course. Hasn't he had something to do with indicting Sir Thomas More and Bishop Fisher?"

"Precisely." Sir Edmund's mouth twisted with distaste. "Richard Rich is Cromwell's henchman. The letter he brought informed us that you planned to wed Sean O'Connor." Seeing that Morgan was about to interrupt, Sir Edmund put up a hand to stop her. "You know that your mother and I are very fond of Sean, and all things being equal, it would be an acceptable match. But they are not equal. Sean wrote you a letter which smacks of high treason, at least as interpreted by Cromwell—and the King."

This time Morgan could not hold her tongue. "I lost that letter! It's all my fault! I ruined it for both of us!" She began to sob, the tears she had held in check for over a month spilling down her cheeks.

"Sweeting," Lady Alice comforted, getting up from her chair and putting her arms around her daughter. "It was an unfortunate accident; you mustn't blame yourself. In any event, Sean had already stated his position about the Act of Succession. He could never have returned to court nor received permission to marry you."

"But we don't need permission!" Morgan gulped between sobs. "We could have run away to Ireland, or even the Continent!"

Lady Alice sighed, her big bosom rising majestically under the muslin gown. "I don't think so. As kin to Cromwell—and God only knows I despise the thought as much as you do—your actions could bring retribution down on all of us. Especially Sean."

But Morgan wasn't convinced. The family relationship was tenuous. What one young niece-by-marriage did was hardly important. She was about to argue this point when her father resumed speaking:

"Richard Rich told us some other disturbing news." Sir Edmund ran a hand through his graying hair and lowered his voice. "Your mother and I realize that gossip is rampant at court. But he told us you were . . . dallying with a young Welshman named Griffin."

Morgan wiped at her tears and all but choked. "Dallying! The swine! How dare he bring you such tales!"

"Now, now," soothed her father. "It would be unnatural

if you did not allow young men to court you. I'm sure Rich's stories were exaggerated. Still, they can be damaging, and given all these factors, your mother and I finally agreed that your marriage to James Sinclair would not be a bad thing. He is wealthy, a future earl, a pleasant-looking young man, and of good character."

"We do wish his home weren't so far away," Lady Alice put in, and her own eyes misted over. "Still, Morgan, we have honestly tried to do our best for you."

Morgan reflected for a moment on her parents' words. No doubt they had—yet she still felt a sense of betrayal. But she could imagine Rich's persuasive arguments, perhaps even a detailed account of how Ned Seymour had found her in Richard Griffin's arms by the river at Hampton Court. That alone would have convinced Sir Edmund and Lady Alice that it was high time for their daughter to have a husband.

Nor was there any use in arguing further with her parents. Once again it seemed prudent to appear docile and obedient. "At least you will permit me to reply to Sean's letter?" she asked in a meek voice.

"Certainly," her father agreed. "It would be ill-mannered not to. The O'Connors are also kin and we must not ignore Sean's honorable request."

Morgan rose and hugged her parents. They spoke for some time about wedding arrangements, the dowry, whether or not they themselves would make the long journey to Belford for the nuptials. Morgan joined in with apparent enthusiasm, but her mind was far away. Her body was there in the study of Faux Hall, but her heart was across the Irish Sea, in Armagh, with Sean O'Connor.

The Madden twins were thrilled to be undertaking such a long and exciting journey. Morgan and her parents waved them off on a crisp, sunny morning that heralded the first day of autumn. And as they disappeared down the road headed west, Morgan prayed fervently that they and their precious letter would reach Ireland safely.

"My love," she had written, "forgive my long delay, but the most calamitous events have prevented me from writing." She had hesitated a long time about whether or not to tell him his letter had fallen into Cromwell's hands. How could she explain her carelessness? But he had to know why she appeared to be submitting to Cromwell's will; even more important, she had to tell him he was in danger.

"So I shall play their game," she continued, "but meanwhile, play for time. While I fear for you and for the safety of my family, we both know how frequently betrothals are broken. James Sinclair is no more eager to marry me than I am to wed with him. If at all possible, come to Faux Hall. I am certain we are not being spied upon and no one need know of your visit." Morgan reread the last sentence and shook her head sadly. Less than six months ago the idea of anyone spying on her home or its inhabitants would have been ludicrous. Now, however, the possibility was not only realistic but frightening.

Morgan spent the golden days of early autumn telling Grandmother Isabeau about the latest court fashions and the current amours. She and Nan spent hours riding their favorite mounts in the nearby forest while her cousin asked interminable questions about life at court. She helped her mother and Aunt Margaret make soap and candles and apple preserves and a new counterpane for Grandmother Isabeau's French bed. It was a happy if anxious time, and after the first three weeks, Morgan could not refrain from going down to the road almost every hour to see if the Madden twins had returned.

By mid-October, the weather had changed and rain began to pelt Faux Hall while the leaves dropped off the fruit trees in the orchard. A week later, a letter arrived at Faux Hall for Morgan but it was not from Sean O'Connor. Thomas Cromwell had written to ask when his niece was returning to court. "By the end of the month," he had written in his cramped style, "we will be assembled at St. James, the King having by then finished his progress. I entreat you to resume your duties with Her Grace at that time."

Of course it was no entreaty at all, but a command. Morgan angrily crumpled the letter and threw it onto the fire.

"I thought you'd be happy to go back," Nan said in surprise. "You keep telling me what fun it is."

"I keep telling you how busy it is, you mean," Morgan said petulantly. She picked up her bone embroidery needle and thrust it into the outline of a chrysanthemum on her section of the counterpane.

"Still, it sounds more enjoyable than this," Nan declared, shaking out a tangle of thread. "And now you'll be planning your wedding! Oh, I do hope we can all travel to Belford!"

"Don't be too hopeful, *ma petite*," said Grandmother Isabeau from her place by the fire. She had been supervising her granddaughters' needlework carefully, noting that both of them tended to be too impatient and haphazard. "It's a long journey from here, and even if the rest of you go, I will not."

Morgan paused in midstitch. "It's not fair. The wedding should be here. And I could hardly get married without you, Gran'mère."

"Ah, such sentiment warms my heart—but the cold North would not warm my old bones." She smiled fondly at Morgan. "As for being married there, he is the son of an earl and you are but the daughter of a knight. His people, tenants, whatever they are called in such a place, will want to witness this momentous event. You must do your duty as a future Countess." The smile faded and she gazed closely at Nan's handiwork. "Too far apart, those eyes. You are stitching a peacock, not an owl." As Nan made a wry face, Grandmother Isabeau turned back to Morgan. "And it *is* your duty, of course. I am sorry for that. In truth, I am more sorry for James than for you."

Morgan stared at her grandmother. "How can you say such a thing? You don't even know James!"

But Grandmother Isabeau merely smiled enigmatically. "But I do know *you*."

Two days later a very bedraggled pair of Maddens walked their weary mounts up to the main entrance of Faux Hall. Hal was coughing badly and Davy looked very pale. Or maybe it was the other way 'round; Morgan could never be quite sure. Still, they were basically robust young lads and their health was not Morgan's primary concern. She all but shouted at them, demanding Sean's response.

"We've no letter," answered the one Morgan thought to be Davy. "Master O'Connor was unable to write."

Morgan had to hold her hands rigidly at her sides to

keep from shaking the lad. "What do you mean? Is something wrong with him?"

But Sir Edmund had joined the trio in the entryway. "Come, come, Morgan, let the lads change and then they can tell you." He motioned the Madden twins to head for the kitchens. "Warm yourselves and eat before you come back."

Morgan tried to conceal the exasperation she felt with her father. Nor was her temper improved by the sight of Bess, skittering after the Madden twins, hips swaying, breasts jiggling in her homespun gown. Since Morgan's return home, Bess's presence was more of an irritation than ever, serving to remind her over and over of the odious Francis Sinclair.

An hour passed before the Maddens were dried out, changed, and fed. Morgan feared her father might insist on sitting in on the interview, but he did not.

"Well?" Morgan demanded, impatiently gesturing for the twins to sit on the inglenook in the parlor. "What has happened to Sean?"

"Nothing," replied Hal, who began to cough again.

"Nothing? Then why didn't he send a letter?" Morgan was trying to keep a check on her raging emotions but it was not easy.

"His father died," Davy said. "He was dying when we got there. It took him more than a fortnight."

"Jesu." Morgan crossed herself and felt callous. Liam O'Connor no doubt had suffered terribly, with his anguished son at his side—and all Morgan had been thinking about was herself. "I'll have Masses said for his soul at St. Michael's," she asserted, and noted that Hal and Davy were looking at her questioningly. "But," she asked at last, "did Sean send any sort of message?"

"Oh, aye," answered Davy. "He begged you to forgive him, but he had time neither to write nor to come to England. The burden of the land rests with him now."

Morgan paced the small carpeted area in front of the fireplace. Within a very short time, a month even, travel conditions between Ireland and England would be all but impossible. And by spring, it might be too late. . . .

"Did he say anything else?" Morgan's voice held a desperate note as she looked from one Madden twin to the other.

Davy scratched his head and Hal coughed again. "Oh—aye, he said he would pray for you," Davy finally replied.

Morgan clenched her fists and bit her lip. Prayers were well enough, but certainly not what she had in mind. Surely Sean did not intend to abandon her without even a protest over her betrothal to James Sinclair.

Remembering her manners and the hardships the Madden twins had suffered on her behalf, Morgan thanked them profusely and said she would see to it that they were generously recompensed. But except for the colds and chills they had caught in the last two days, the twins seemed well pleased with their adventure over the Irish Sea. It struck Morgan that if they had withstood the journey, so might she. But the shadow of Thomas Cromwell could follow her even to Armagh.

The holiday season of 1534 was one of the least festive in recent memory at court. Though Henry and his Queen appeared on better terms than when Morgan had last seen them, Anne was more high-strung than ever. But she seemed pleased to have Morgan back in her service. Late one evening a few days after Twelfth Night, the Queen dismissed her other ladies so that she and Morgan could speak privately.

After a few pleasantries, Anne lay down on a satin-covered settee and bade Morgan pull over an armchair. "I was neglectful of you last summer," the Queen said as she tucked the folds of her sable-trimmed peignoir more closely around her. "Your uncle arranged a marriage for you, much as Wolsey did for me. I assume you are not overjoyed at the prospect."

"You saw James," Morgan commented dryly. "Would he seem to promise great joy?"

Anne raised her fine eyebrows and laughed. "You have changed since I last saw you, Morgan Todd. Your tongue has grown bolder." Noting that Morgan looked abashed, she held up her tapering right hand. "Nay, nay, I prefer having my attendants speak out. Is it that James is distasteful—or that you love another?"

Morgan avoided the almond eyes. She dared not mention Sean's name. Or did she? "I do love someone else. We had plans to wed," she conceded, deciding to test the waters of Anne's unpredictable emotions.

"Ah. I suspected as much." The Queen took a deep draught from a glass of wine which had been sitting next to her on a tiny inlaid table. "Is it someone I know?"

"I'm not sure." It was true. Morgan really had no idea if the Queen had ever come into contact with a mere artist's apprentice.

But Anne Boleyn was not easily put off. "His name?" The dark eyes skimmed the edge of the crystal goblet and forced Morgan to return her gaze.

If Cromwell knew, perhaps the Queen knew, Morgan reasoned. Perhaps the entire court knew. "His name is Sean O'Connor," she said, and her glance did not waver.

"Ah!" Anne seemed surprised. She lay back among the pillows and shook her head. "Such irony—I loved a North Country man and Wolsey wished me to wed an Irishman. You love an Irishman and Cromwell would have you marry a North Country man. But Sean O'Connor has been gone for months. Wasn't he the artist with the prickly conscience?"

"He finds some of the changes in the Church difficult to accept," Morgan allowed. "He also must tend his land in Armagh, since his father died this past autumn."

But Anne did not appear to be listening. She was staring into the darkened corner of the chamber, her high forehead lined in concentration. "I have sympathy for you," she said at last, and sat up straight. "Cromwell was my friend once. But now . . ." She let the words trail off and frowned again. "Henry has broken off with the mysterious lady whose favors he enjoyed for most of this last year. Doubtless he is already on the scent of another to take her place in his bed." She stopped, her sallow skin darkening, apparently unconcerned about speaking so candidly. "Oh, by the Saints, Henry's amours are no secret. He still comes to me. He always will, at least if I can give him a son." She ran an unsteady hand through the long black hair and licked her dry lips. "But as he will also go on pursuing other women, I would prefer his infatuation directed at someone I can trust. You, for example."

Morgan gasped. "Oh, no! I could never dare. . . . He wouldn't want me; I'm not skilled in the arts of . . ." Morgan's hands waved tremulously as she tried to describe whatever it was the Queen expected of her.

"I've seen him watch you; he's intrigued enough. But

the point is, no one knows better than I how to hold Henry at bay. God knows I managed it for seven years. I can school you in that art, and meanwhile, Henry will remain fascinated but unsatisfied and turn to me so that I can become pregnant again. You, on the other hand, will certainly not be permitted to marry James Sinclair since the King will insist that you remain at court." Anne lay back against the pillows, suddenly looking well pleased with her scheme.

"Oh, Jesu." Morgan rubbed at the place between her eyebrows. "Truly, I don't think I can manage it."

Anne leaned forward and grasped Morgan by the wrist. The almond-slanted eyes burned, as if she were imposing her own will on Morgan's. "You will. You must. For both of us."

Morgan did not like falcons. The hooded creature that sat on her wrist did not seem to like her much either. It was a clear, cold February day, the ground still hard from the heavy frost of the previous night. The horses were skittish and the courtiers were lighthearted as the King led the way through the park at St. James.

Morgan found herself riding close to the King and Queen. Anne Boleyn had used every opportunity in the last month to see that Henry should take notice of her tawny-haired lady-in-waiting.

"We will release the falcons just before we reach that copse," Henry declared, pointing with a pudgy finger toward a stand of larch trees. He turned to Morgan. "Do you know how to remove the hood?"

"I think so. Francis Weston taught me," she replied, and tried to remember to flutter her eyelashes demurely.

"Yours is a falcon-gentle," the King said, "though the name does not necessarily describe her temperament." He regarded the bird with amusement. "I would like to know, however, if it describes the lady?"

"I am not a hunter, Your Grace," Morgan answered, "but I can be gentle."

He patted her shoulder with his gloved hand. "Charming. But gentleness is only one facet of a lady's personality. Indeed, one might equate 'gentle' with 'tame.' "

"One might," Morgan said, and attempted looking enigmatic. She caught Richard Griffin's eye and saw him watching her with a puzzled expression. At that moment, Henry signaled for the falcons to be let loose. Morgan fumbled with the hood, jerked back as the bird flapped her wings, and felt her horse paw nervously at the ground. She finally got the hood off, but the ill-tempered falcon did not seem inclined to fly. The King had taken notice of her difficulties and was about to come to the rescue when the bird finally soared into the air—but not before Morgan's horse shied and took off at a gallop for the copse.

"Jesu!" Morgan cried, and could not remember her horse's name. Valiant—Valor—Victory—it was all a terrifying daze as Morgan desperately tried to slow the animal. But the horse had his head now and was into the trees, still heedless of Morgan's frantic sawing on the reins. It seemed very dark among the stand of evergreens, and Morgan felt branches slap at her face and tear at her rust-colored riding habit. She prayed, she cursed, she cried out in fright as she narrowly missed riding headlong into a large limb. Still the animal did not slacken its pace and Morgan clung to his neck for her very life.

She did not remember how the accident actually happened. Possibly the horse stumbled over a fallen branch or stepped in a rabbit hole. All Morgan knew for certain was that she was lying on a thick pile of larch needles, the horse was nowhere in sight, and she hurt all over.

For several minutes, she stayed as she was, trying to get her mind functioning properly. She must have been knocked unconscious at least briefly. Sure enough, already a large swelling was appearing just at the hairline. Her riding hat was several feet away, upside down but unscathed. Gingerly, she tested her arms and legs—they ached but she could move them. She was just attempting to stand when she heard a noise nearby.

Mounted on a black stallion, Richard Griffin appeared between the trees and looked enormously relieved to see Morgan. "Good Christ, I was sure your neck would be broken!" He jumped from his horse and hurried to her side. "The King's Master of the Horse should never have given you Viking," he said angrily. "Is anything broken?"

"The horse apparently wasn't," Morgan replied testily. "I'm just bruised and sore. And frightened." She made a tentative attempt to get up but Richard's firm hand kept her on the larch-strewn ground.

"Give yourself a chance to recover your nerves," Richard insisted. He was sitting beside her, heedless of what the larch needles and dirt might do to his modish dark green hunting costume. "Here," he said, taking her hand, "let's be absolutely certain nothing is seriously damaged." Gingerly he fingered her right arm, then her left. "Well enough. Can you move your head from side to side?"

Morgan did so with only minimal pain between her shoulders. But Richard's solemn, conscientious manner amused her. "You should have been a physician. You actually seem to know what you're doing."

He was watching the topaz eyes very closely. "Hmmmmm. I would have been had I not been born a gentleman. What we call medicine is mainly superstitious rot. A tragedy, since there was a time when man knew far more about disease and cures than we do now. Perhaps one day . . ." He stopped and grinned, the gap-tooth grin that suddenly looked both charming and sheepish. "I'm fulsome with opinion, while you freeze your delightful backside on the February frost. Let's see your legs."

Morgan looked at him questioningly, but his intentions seemed strictly honorable. She lifted the hem of her riding skirt to her knees, revealing long, slim legs encased in dainty Moroccan-tooled boots which came to her ankles.

Richard was still grinning. "Offhand, I'd say there was nothing wrong with your legs. But it won't hurt to make certain."

As he started to remove one of the boots, Morgan sensed rather than heard something move behind them. Her horse, she decided, and obeyed when Richard asked her to wiggle her toes for him. He was taking off the other boot when she heard her name cut across the brisk winter air like an icicle. Whirling around, she saw Sean O'Connor just a few yards away, a stunned, disbelieving look on his face.

"Sean!" She breathed his name in fear, knowing at once what he must be thinking, and wondering how in God's name he had so magically appeared in the park at St. James. Richard had looked up too, and a quiet oath escaped from his lips.

Dark head held high, Sean was astride Morgan's horse, his furious gaze fixed on Richard: "I pray to the Virgin that you have no dishonorable intentions toward Mistress

Todd," Sean said, his brogue never more pronounced than at that moment. "So, Richard Griffin of Carmarthen, you must swear you have never touched her in an impure manner. Tell me you are not a despoiler of maidens."

Richard got resignedly to his feet, brushing the larch needles from his hunting costume. "Dismount, Sean O'Connor, and ask me once more." He spoke evenly, but the green eyes were menacing.

Sean got down from his horse. "Once is enough. Defend yourself, if you will not answer." His jaw set as he planted his feet firmly on the ground. Irishman and Welshman faced each other with savage stares.

Morgan, at last getting shakily to her feet, spoke sharply through her rising terror. "Hold, Sean. It's not what you think. I fell from my horse . . ."

Sean signaled her to be silent. Neither man even looked at her. They faced each other as the tension cut through the clean winter air. Richard was three inches taller and four stone heavier than Sean. He had an oft-repeated reputation for being an excellent wrestler in bouts at court.

But it was Sean who made the first move, lunging at Richard, who kept his balance as they grappled. Sean when down but his knees came up, catching Richard in the stomach. He rolled onto the ground, momentarily out of breath. They both stood up. Sean landed a hard fist on Richard's jaw. A second blow glanced off Richard's shoulder as he ducked and caught Sean in the face with his left fist. A thin trickle of blood crept from Sean's mouth. He staggered slightly. Richard hit him again, this time catching him square on the jaw.

"Stop it!" Morgan screamed, flying at Richard. She grabbed at his arm but he pushed her away. Stumbling, she fell back against a tree.

The distraction had given Sean time to steady himself. Now he leaped on Griffin, his fury reinforcing his strength. Again the two men toppled to the ground. First Sean was on top, then Richard, then Sean again.

Morgan watched helplessly, one hand against her mouth. She had nearly bitten through her kidskin riding glove. Suddenly she looked beyond the two struggling men and saw three riders cantering into the clearing.

"God's body!" cried Harry Norris, who quickly dismounted. "No more! You'll kill each other."

Ned Seymour and the Earl of Surrey followed him. The three of them managed at last to pull Sean and Richard apart. Mud, dirt, and blood covered them both.

"What is all this?" asked Ned Seymour, more angry than worried.

The two combatants were too breathless to speak. Morgan tried to answer for them, appealing directly to Ned. "Truly, it was all a misunderstanding. I fell from my horse and Richard came along to see if I was hurt. Then Sean rode into the clearing and he thought . . ."

Ned was neither willing nor able to keep up with the tumble of words. He waved his hand at Morgan. "I'm sure your excuse is excellent." He ignored her wince. "But we must take these men some place where they can get some clean clothes and a bit of ale."

Surrey offered to share his horse with Sean, who needed help mounting the animal; Richard managed alone, but it was obvious that it cost him something to sit erect on his black stallion. Norris asked Morgan if she wanted to ride her own horse back to the palace. Reluctantly, she said she would; it hardly seemed the time to complain of her own pains. Biting her lip to keep from crying out, she let Norris hand her into the saddle. The little group started out of the thicket, riding in silence until they reached the postern gate.

King Henry presided over a gay supper that evening, but Sean O'Connor was not among the guests. Morgan, trying to avoid the swollen face and laughing eyes of Richard Griffin, kept watching the door. Now it all seemed a great joke to Richard—she could tell that from his attitude. Occasionally she would see Will Brereton or George Boleyn or some other courtier stop by Richard's chair to make a witty remark and then glance in her direction. She sat tight-faced between Francis Weston and Surrey, scarcely exchanging a word with either of them during the long meal.

Finally the last plates were removed and Morgan got up to ask the Queen's permission to leave. Anne, pleased that Henry seemed in a good mood again, granted Morgan's request with a wave of the hand. Morgan left the hall as inconspicuously as possible. She headed for the west end of the palace, to the improvised studio where intuition told her she would find Sean.

She entered without knocking. He was there, his back to the door, working with fierce concentration on a sketch which appeared to be Sir Thomas More.

"Sean?" She called his name softly, tremulously.

His head came up slowly as the muscles in his shoulders seemed to tense under the brown smock. He did not turn around.

Morgan took a deep breath. "I love you, Sean." She closed her eyes, as if afraid of his reaction.

He came across the room in an instant and took her in his arms. "Oh, Morgan—what a fool I was! I didn't realize until today how much I love you! I went mad with jealousy—and love!" He held her even closer, his lips seeking hers with an uncharacteristic hunger. She felt him straining against her, and the studio seemed to whirl about them. At last he released her and smiled in a forlorn, apologetic manner. "I'll get paint on your gown," he said.

"I don't care. But, Sean, please tell me how you happen to be here in the first place!" Morgan was out of breath, leaning against an empty easel, one hand on her heart.

Sean picked up a rag and wiped his hands. "I thought you might tell *me* that." He looked at her quizzically, but when he saw her blank expression, he went on. "I received a message, borne by two seamen from the Royal Navy who had sailed into Dundalk. It invited me back to court, at the Queen's command, to resume my duties as 'prentice to Master Holbein. I wanted to tear it up at first, spit in the men's faces, send them away." He put the rag down, examined his hands with the fine, sensitive artist's fingers, and smiled again at Morgan. "But I thought of you, and the letter you had sent when my sire lay dying. If ever I were to see you before your marriage with that man from Northumberland, this was my chance. So I took ship at the end of the month and arrived in Portsmouth two days ago. The journey up to London was not difficult though it was very late when I got here last night. Too late, in fact, to see you or anyone else, save Surrey."

Morgan was frowning. "The Queen sent for you?"

"Aye, I thought it might be trickery. I was sure of it this morning when I found you with Richard Griffin in the copse. I had gone out walking until the royal hunting party returned. I found a riderless horse by a stream and knew someone had had an accident. I know horseflesh well," he continued diffidently, "so I quieted the animal down and let him lead me back to you."

"I see." Morgan was beginning to see more than Sean realized. The Queen had sent for him—her reward to Morgan for leading the King on. But Morgan dared not allude to Anne Boleyn's scheme. She went to Sean and put her hands on his shoulders. "I'm just so glad you're here—though I hope your presence will not bring you to grief."

Sean held her close for a moment before he spoke. "Yet I am aggrieved. First, the Act of Succession; now the Oath of Supremacy, which makes Henry head of the Church in England. That's diabolical heresy."

Morgan searched in vain for some argument to soften Sean's indictment. But he was right, the King was indeed putting himself above the Pope's jurisdiction. Henry had formed his own church, and it was not the Church of Rome. "If only we dared flee to Ireland and were married, would the King's acts and oaths and such matter?" she asked, wishing he would look at her instead of turning away to fidget with his paintbrushes.

"It would be disobedient. Disloyal." He rearranged a half-dozen brushes and turned to gaze at Morgan. "But to the King—not to the Pope, who is more important in God's eyes."

"Sir Thomas More agrees—and he lies in the Tower."

His dark brows drew close together. "So he does. And Fisher, too." Sean abruptly pushed the brushes away and began to pull the brown smock over his head. "Come, Morgan," he urged, taking her arm, "let's walk as far from this place as we can. Everyone at court is mad."

Morgan gave him a sidelong glance as they started out into the darkened corridor. "Like ourselves?"

He gave a short laugh. "Aye. Like ourselves."

The following week Morgan and Sean planned to visit Moorfields and watch the Londoners gather for gossip and recreation on the partially drained area at the city walls. But despite several days of mild weather presaging an early spring, it rained that afternoon and they postponed their outing. Morgan spent an hour or more watching Sean touch up a portrait of a wealthy burgher. They had not talked much, since Sean didn't like to be distracted from his work, but now and then they exchanged a few words, mostly about the shadings in the painting and if the eyes looked sufficiently shrewd, but not insultingly avaricious.

By noon, Sean had all but finished the portrait and wanted to seek Master Holbein's counsel. Morgan left the studio to return to her own rooms. She had no duties with the Queen that day and thought perhaps she might write a letter home. To her surprise, there was a note on her dressing table from Madge Shelton, written in a very unpracticed hand. Madge had moved to other quarters, it said; Morgan would now share her chambers with Margaret Howard, a cousin of Surrey's. She was a tall, willowy blonde with perfect features and little wit. Neither Madge nor Margaret were ideal companions, but at least the Howard girl would be more quiet. Morgan reread the note and started to throw it into the fireplace when she noticed that Madge had scrawled another message on the back of the page. It was difficult to read at first, but finally Morgan got the gist of it and sank down on the bed in horror: Francis Sinclair was at St. James Palace.

Morgan was still sitting on the bed with the note clutched in her hand when someone knocked loudly on the door. The sound was so demanding and importunate that Morgan knew instantly it must be Francis. She considered ignoring the knock but knew he would eventually seek her out.

"Well," he said in greeting, almost filling the door with his great height and heavy riding cape. "You aren't sparkling with welcome, I see."

"You're all wet," Morgan countered, standing aside to let him in.

"So I am. When I discovered you were with your artist friend I went for a canter in the park." He took off his cloak and shook it out, the droplets of water falling onto the rushes.

"Did you just arrive?" Morgan eyed him with distaste as he put one muddy boot on a damask footstool.

"Last night. It was too late to call on you." He was eyeing her speculatively, the bushy blond brows drawn together, the gray eyes missing nothing. "I rode hard this morning. I certainly would like a drink. Whiskey, if you have it. I'm no ale man."

Morgan gestured toward a chair near the sputtering fire. She went to the cabinet and got down two pewter cups and the bottle of whiskey Madge had kept for her male visitors. She poured red wine for herself, gave Francis his whiskey, and sat down in the armchair opposite him.

"Your efforts at hospitality are improving," he remarked, taking a deep draught of whiskey. "You haven't screamed at me once so far."

"I'm not even sure I want to talk to you," Morgan retorted. "As for hospitality, you certainly repaid my family poorly when our stable boys took care of your horse."

Francis drained the cup and handed it back to Morgan. "I'll have more. It's not as wretched as most of the stuff one finds this far south."

Feeling her temper rise, Morgan clattered the cup and the bottle together on purpose, then thrust the whiskey at Francis in such a way that some of it sloshed onto his sleeve. He scowled for a split second at the stain, and took another drink.

"You don't forgive and forget, I see," Francis drawled, resting one high-booted leg on his knee.

Morgan had not yet sat down again and all but jumped up and down at his comment. "Oh! How could I? You were an animal! You even tied me up!" She looked at her wrists as if she could still see the belt wrapped 'round them.

"Some wenches like that," Francis said equably. "It's a sort of game."

"A game!" Morgan looked aghast. "You have some peculiar playmates, if you ask me, Francis Sinclair!"

"Good God, I wouldn't dream of asking you!" Francis sounded impatient and a bit gruff. He finished off his second cup of whiskey but did not ask for more. "See here, I made an honest mistake, which surely even you could understand considering the circumstances. If we're going to live in each other's pockets at Belford, we can't spend the rest of our lives arguing about whether or not I thought you were Meg or Moll or whoever in hell you were supposed to be."

"Bess." Morgan was pouting, her fingers tracing the outline of the whiskey decanter in jerky little motions. She wanted to cry but would not give Francis the satisfaction.

"Bess, then." Francis had stood up, looking awkward as well as angry. "Well? Can't we let the past rest?"

It occurred to Morgan that his words about Belford were only his own opinion. She had no intention of going there, nor of marrying his brother. At the moment, all she wanted was to be rid of Francis Sinclair, who made her extremely nervous.

She tried to muster as much dignity as possible with her head held high and the topaz eyes looking up into his scowling countenance. Obviously, if she expected a formal apology she was not going to get it. "Since it can't be undone, I suppose I can at least say that I will not harangue you further."

The slightly sloping shoulders seemed to slump even more with apparent relief. "All right." The scowl faded as he ambled to the fireplace and poked at the wood, which appeared not to have been completely dried out. "I'm in London to do some buying—household goods and cloth. I also came to take you back to Belford."

Morgan clutched the arm of her chair and wondered how she should react. Submissive, of course; she must stall for time. "There is so much to do—I have no trousseau, and it's only the second week of March. I did not think you—or James—would come until April, at the earliest."

"We had an early spring; the roads became passable before February was over." He continued working with the poker but without much success. "James would have come but our sire has not been well this winter." Francis finally replaced the poker on the hearth and dusted off his hands. "I plan to be here at least a month and you can shop with me. James has planned the wedding for early May."

"He might have consulted with me on the date," Morgan said irritably. A month or so did not give her much time. "I would have liked to have been informed of these details since I planned on visiting my parents before going north."

Francis had paused to admire the few volumes that Morgan carted from palace to palace. "That should still be possible," Francis allowed. "Faux Hall is not that far away. You should be able to stay there for a week or more." He paused and looked at her closely, his sandy brows drawing close together. "How old are you, Morgan?"

"I was nineteen last month. Why?"

"You look younger." He shrugged. "Not that it matters. I'm twenty-six and James is twenty-eight. Lucy is but a year younger than I."

"Lucy?" Morgan pretended puzzlement at the name.

"My wife. You'll like her, I'm sure. Everyone does. You'll like our children, too." He had extracted one of the books and was flipping through the pages, apparently quite at ease.

"You have children?" Morgan's question was low and faintly incredulous.

"Of course. Two, a boy and a girl. They're amusing little creatures, if I do say so myself." Francis put the book back and actually smiled, that whimsical, crooked smile Morgan was beginning to know quite well.

He seemed so sure of himself, so sure of her future, so sure that she would trot off to Belford with him come April that her courage faltered and unbidden tears surfaced in the topaz eyes. With growing discomfiture, Francis watched her and sighed deeply. "Oh, come, come," he said almost roughly, looking away from her to the cuff of his boot. "This isn't life's end. Few people marry for love, yet many arranged matches work out in a way that defies romantic daydreaming such as you cherish."

Morgan brushed at the tears with her hand and steadied her voice. "Did you marry for love?"

He looked up at her with some surprise, then smoothed out his rumpled doublet. "No," he answered candidly. "But I love my wife now. Very much."

Morgan could not resist an outraged gibe: "So much that you tumble any willing—or unwilling—wench who falls across your path?"

Francis waved a big hand in exasperation. "God's teeth, I don't have to explain my most intimate behavior to you!" He snatched up his cloak and stomped off toward the door, scowling up at the lintel. "See here," he said, turning back and speaking in a more ameliorating tone, "my brother, James, is basically a good, gentle man. Don't judge him by me; we're very different."

For some inexplicable reason, Morgan did not find this statement at all reassuring. She was shaken and upset: Marriage to James Sinclair was impossible; a long, drawn-out unconsummated flirtation with the King of England would surely snap her nerves; but worst of all, the prospect of becoming Sean O'Connor's wife seemed as dangerous as it was unlikely. Her only hope was to keep the King dangling just long enough to make James so angry that he would change his mind and seek another bride. Morgan had to clutch at this slender straw, even as she watched Francis Sinclair shuffle his booted feet in the rushes and look impatiently around the room.

"I must be going," Francis said at last when he realized that Morgan was not going to comment further on himself or his brother. "Do you like clothes?"

The question caught Morgan off guard. "I—yes, very much."

He nodded. "I thought so. I like what you have on; it's a comely shade of turquoise. But the sleeves aren't right. You need a longer oversleeve to add height. You're rather small, you know."

Morgan's brow crinkled. Francis Sinclair hardly struck her as a connoisseur of women's fashion. But then, he hadn't seemed like a husband, a father, or an expert on architecture and poetry, either. This tall, gruff man had a great many facets that Morgan had not readily recognized, and she could not help but respond with a mixture of annoyance and mirth. "And you? Surely that doublet is slashed to make you seem even taller than you already are."

"Mmmmmm?" Francis looked down at his attire. "Oh, perhaps so. But I have a very short tailor." Only his eyes betrayed his amusement.

Morgan was so surprised that she had to bite her lips to keep from laughing. His hand rested on the latch, but as she held out her fingertips for the customary kiss of leave-taking, he shook his head. "It's not necessary," Francis asserted. "Courtly manners go down ill with me."

Morgan felt like telling Francis Sinclair that manners of any kind seemed to go down ill with him, but merely let her hand fall to her side. "Then good day to you, sir," she said stiffly.

"Good day," said Francis, and loped out of the room.

"Of course Jane is well," Tom Seymour assured Morgan as they discreetly withdrew from the gaming tables at Whitehall where the court had moved just three days after Francis Sinclair had arrived in London. "She becomes caught up in the quiet routine of Wolf Hall, especially our brother Harry and his children. He needs another wife," Tom explained as they watched the usually dispassionate

Harry Norris cry out over a trick he had lost by mistake to Madge Shelton. "He's not interested in politics or the court, and prefers the life of a country squire. A good thing, since our father has not been well lately."

"Everyone's father seems unwell," Morgan remarked, thinking of Liam O'Connor's recent demise and the Earl of Belford's reported ill health. "I begin to wonder if it isn't the times which make our parents' generation ill."

Tom cuffed Morgan's shoulder with a gentle fist. "Now, Morgan, you mustn't say that sort of thing. Nor is it like you. I've noticed your tongue has honed itself to a fine point since you came to court."

"Isn't that part of being at court?" Morgan retorted as Anne Boleyn clapped her hands in glee over her victory at Dame Chance.

Tom shrugged his broad shoulders. "I suppose." He was watching the sleekly beautiful Margaret Howard puzzle over a newly dealt hand. "How do you get on with the fair Margaret?"

"Well enough. She's placid, if dull. But I still haven't found out why Madge moved."

Tom moved back a few paces farther from the tables laden with cards, coins, delicacies, and drink. "You don't really know?" he asked, a red eyebrow raised at Morgan.

"No," she replied, frowning quizzically. "I take it you do."

"Some of us do." He glanced about to make sure no one could overhear them. But the richly dressed assembly of gamblers were engrossed in their games. "Let us say that Madge is now in more accessible and commodious quarters."

Morgan still looked puzzled until his meaning dawned upon her. "The King?" She breathed the words and saw Tom nod once. Her first reaction was to laugh—until she realized the implications for herself. If Madge Shelton had surrendered her body to Henry, he might abandon his fruitless pursuit of her own virtue. If he did, Morgan's ploy would have failed and she would be headed for Belford within just a few short weeks. Panicky, she scanned the royal chamber for Sean, though she knew he was not among those who were gaming small fortunes away with no apparent heed of the consequences. She had to get away; she had to find Sean; she had to think of some reason for leaving Tom so abruptly. The excuse appeared unexpectedly in the form of Francis Sinclair, who had just entered the royal apartments and was surveying the courtiers with a mixture of disdain and bemusement.

"Don't think me rude, Tom," Morgan said in a forced voice, "but I must speak to Francis—about my trousseau."

Tom glanced at Francis and grinned. "That big bumpkin? What would he know of trousseaus?"

"More than you might think," Morgan replied tartly, and she was astonished to find herself defending Francis Sinclair.

So was Tom, who stopped grinning at once and looked perplexed as he watched Morgan hurry to the side of her future brother-in-law.

But Francis proved no help in aiding Morgan's search for Sean. He had come looking for her, insisting upon a shopping trip to Cheapside despite the drizzle which fell on the city. "You'll have to get used to foul weather," Francis declared as he propelled her out of the Queen's apartments. "It's much worse in Northumberland."

Morgan wanted to remark that no doubt everything was worse in Northumberland, but held her tongue. She was depressed and apprehensive. At that moment, as she pulled her heavy gray wool cloak around her and put the hood up over her hair, Morgan fervently wished she could throttle the promiscuous Madge, whose lax morals might well wreak unwitting havoc with Morgan's future. First Bess, now Madge; Morgan cursed all women of blemished virtue.

"You *are* quiet," said Francis as they headed out of Whitehall and toward The Strand. Despite the rain, Londoners were going about their business, and the usual unending parade of drays, carts, barrows, and litters jostled the horses and foot traffic along the route to Cheapside.

"You expect me to be elated at the prospect of life in Northumberland with your brother?" Morgan demanded sharply as a young boy carrying two buckets of milk pushed past them.

It was Francis's turn to remain silent. He grimaced when two roistering 'prentices all but ran into him as they chased each other through the busy street. Nearing Temple Bar with its wall and chains proclaiming the boundary of the city's jurisdiction, Morgan realized that her feet were wet. She also realized that Cheapside was a great deal farther than she had thought.

"I'm not fond of walking great distances," she announced as they passed the Temple itself, which housed one of London's four great Inns of Court.

"It's good for you." Francis glanced down at Morgan's unsuitable court footwear, dainty green suede slippers embroidered with saffron-colored lilies. "I think we'd best buy you some sensible boots. You'll be ankle-deep in mud half the year at Belford."

Morgan did not catch the twinkle in his gray eyes and she was not amused. The more she heard of Belford and the North Country, the less she liked it. "We must have walked a mile already," she declared peevishly as they sighted Ludgate Hill and the great spires of St. Paul's Cathedral. "Oh!" she exclaimed, and stopped in her tracks. "I've never seen St. Paul's so close before."

"A handsome church," Francis said, gazing up at the imposing structure with unconcealed admiration. "The aesthetic effect is sullied inside by the hawkers and concessionaires."

"That shouldn't be permitted," Morgan declared, making way for a towheaded yeoman driving a team of oxen in the direction of the Fleet River.

"What's happening to our churches and monasteries and convents shouldn't be allowed in general," Francis said with a frown. "Just two years ago London was not as congested as it is now. But since your uncle, with the King's sanction, began closing the holy houses all over England, not only have the religious orders been displaced but so have the people who depended upon them for employment and charity."

Morgan felt the need to defend Cromwell in some token manner. "The monasteries and convents spawned much licentious behavior; everyone knows that."

Francis actually snorted. "Some did. What would you expect, with the tradition of sending second sons and unmarriageable daughters off to the Church when they had no vocations? But generally, they have been godly places, doing more good than harm."

It struck Morgan that Francis sounded a bit like Sean. Yet Francis seemed to state his case in a more rational manner. "Francis, I'm confused. James follows the new religion, but I gather you don't."

"That's right." Francis steered her around the north side of St. Paul's. "But thus far, our differences of opinion are no cause for serious concern." He held out a big hand and noted that the rain had all but stopped. Overhead, above the spires of the cathedral, a patch of blue emerged among the heavy gray rain clouds. "So far," he repeated, almost to himself.

They visited the mercer's, the silk merchant's, the leather-maker's, the shoe-maker's, the hat-maker's, and even the perfumer's. Depite herself, Morgan was fascinated; the noise, the haggling, the arguments, the volatile bustle of commerce both excited and exhausted her. Francis, however, did not barter; he stated what he was willing to pay, waited for the merchant's reply, and either made the purchase or left, depending upon the answer. Money seemed no object, and Morgan suddenly realized that the Sinclairs must be a very wealthy family. It was only at their last stop, the furrier's just off Chancery Lane, that she and Francis engaged in out-and-out conflict. Morgan wanted a tan cape trimmed in dark brown fox. Francis favored a deep blue model lined with sable.

"The fox feels more lush," Morgan declared, wrapping the cape around her and turning full circle in front of Francis.

"You look like a small bear," Francis said.

"Nonsense. The tan and brown suits my hair and eyes."

"It makes you look all of the same color. You need contrast, not camouflage."

"I know what I need. I've always worn tan and brown!"

"And looked like a tabby cat most of the time, no doubt."

Though Morgan's shoes had begun to dry out, her feet hurt and she was very tired. Francis's obstinacy was making her furious. "I want *this* one," she asserted, clutching the tan cape close to her body.

"You shan't have it. I'm paying for it!" Francis's gray eyes were cold with anger. "You're a spoiled chit, Morgan Todd, and you'll take the blue or none at all!"

Morgan pulled the tan cape from her shoulders and flung it at Francis. "Then it's none! I'll freeze in your northern wasteland first!"

Francis loomed over her, both capes clutched in his

hands. The furrier had kept his distance throughout this exchange and now had disappeared altogether. His only other customers, a Flemish burgher and his portly wife, had left as soon as Morgan and Francis had begun to quarrel.

Morgan was fumbling at her own gray cloak, unsteady hands trying to fasten the small silver clasp which held it together. Francis carefully laid the hotly disputed capes down on a table and then abruptly grabbed Morgan by the shoulders. She thought he was going to shake her but instead he kissed her, hard, almost violently, and she reeled against him, stunned and off-balance. Morgan tried to push him away but her efforts were as vain as they had been in the orchard. His mouth continued to plunder hers and her feet were actually off the floor. She felt dizzy in his embrace and knew if he let go of her without warning she would fall; her arms went around him—to prevent a nasty tumble, she told herself hazily—and she was further shocked to feel that odd sensation begin to burn in the pit of her stomach. She was even more stunned to discover that she was kissing Francis back, letting his tongue explore her mouth, allowing his hands to roam at will down the curve of her back and to her buttocks. At last he released her lips and set her on her feet, though his arms were still around her.

"Christ," he growled, his sandy hair disheveled, the thick brows drawn together, "you make a man want to either strangle you or make love to you. Why couldn't you have been—*bland?*"

His choice of words made Morgan laugh, a choked, shaken little sound that was almost a hiccough. "All I wanted was the fox-trimmed cape," she said in a voice that shook.

"Mmmmmm." He started to release her, then pulled her back against his chest. "You will cause me more problems than fox and sable, Morgan Todd," he said in his gruffest voice over the top of her head. "Why don't you run away with that Irishman?"

She wondered if he were serious. If only he were, he could help her and Sean . . . Morgan looked up at him, attempting an innocent gaze through her tawny lashes. "It might be all for the best, you know. I don't think your brother likes me."

Francis broke away and stomped about the furrier's shop, his riding cloak billowing behind him like a huge banner of war. "It's not my brother I'm thinking of." He continued storming about the shop for at least another full minute, knocking over a bolt of cloth, cursing at a mouse that crept out from its hiding place, and visibly frightening two young men who made a very tentative entrance through the door just as the furrier emerged from the recesses of his establishment.

"Here," Francis called to the man, "we'll take these." With one swooping gesture he scooped up both capes and all but threw them in the furrier's face. Francis did not even question the amount, which was exorbitant, but merely dumped a large pile of gold sovereigns on the counter. "Send them to Whitehall," he called over his shoulder as he grasped Morgan by the arm and dragged her out of the shop.

Chapter 6

MORGAN DID NOT SEE Francis Sinclair during the next few days. They had returned to Whitehall in virtual silence, Francis scowling and Morgan disturbed. Obviously, Francis had not been serious about her marriage to Sean. But she herself was confused by Francis's behavior; until that moment in the furrier's he had seemed not only unconcerned about his ravishment of her at Faux Hall, but indifferent to the episode and herself as well. She could not understand what had made him act so strangely. Nor could she determine the cause of her reaction to him. Why on earth did she experience that throbbing ache in the core of her being when she was with Francis Sinclair? Sean's embrace made her feel cherished and happy; Richard Griffin's caresses had been exciting. What was it then, Morgan wondered, about that gruff, infuriating giant with his rumpled clothes and disregard for etiquette of any sort that made her feel so . . . what? She could not even describe her reaction except that it was pleasurable in a mysterious, unfamiliar way.

She was anxious to talk to someone about it, but the only person she felt free to confide in was Grandmother Isabeau. Still, if Morgan's plans worked out she would be at Faux Hall within a fortnight.

Meanwhile, she and Sean spent as much time as they could together and she longed to tell him about her dilemma. His reaction to Francis Sinclair's arrival at court had struck Morgan as odd: Sean appeared upset, even angry, but had made no overt attempt of his own to forestall her marriage plans. On the other hand, he was very much absorbed in his painting since Master Holbein had lavished praise on the burgher's portrait, and the burgher himself had offered even more money for it than the original amount.

But there were other matters to consider as well. After only ten days at Whitehall, Henry ordered the royal barges to move the court to Greenwich. The King was very restless, and the Lenten season put a damper on much of the court's usual activities.

Despite the seasonal ban on undue ostentation and revelry, Anne Boleyn decided to stage a masque just three days after their arrival at Greenwich. To placate those who might criticize her, the Queen ordered that decorations should be kept to a minimum, the costumes would be plain if elegant, the spectacle itself comparatively brief. Privately, she confided to her ladies that if she did not think of new ways to divert the King, great troubles might fall upon them all.

The theme was Orpheus, and the setting was simple enough by court standards—a miniature River Styx, which flowed from one side of the banquet hall to the other. Had it not been Lent, no doubt a giant shimmering cavern would have been erected and the river would have flowed with wine instead of water. George Boleyn portrayed Orpheus and Anne was Euridice. The Queen cast Morgan as Amor, clad in thin, clinging flesh-colored silk, an ingeniously contrived costume all of a piece with the undergarments stitched into the dress and of a slightly darker, heavier silk.

The performance, despite Morgan's nervous portrayal, was a great success. Henry led the applause himself as Orpheus and Euridice embraced and began their journey from the dark realm of Pluto into the outer world.

After taking her bow with the others, Morgan joined Tom Seymour, Margaret Howard and Will Brereton. They complimented her lavishly, but Morgan only laughed in relief that the performance was over.

"I marveled at how you spoke your lines," Margaret Howard said with awe. The sleekly beautiful blonde rarely said much at all, though so far Morgan had found her kindhearted and gentle.

"I forgot once, but George Boleyn prompted me. Now I must change into another gown," she told them. "It's chilly away from the fire and there's not much substance to this costume."

"I've noticed," drawled Tom. "I've always had a lively imagination, but I don't need to tax it tonight."

Morgan blushed, started to glare at Tom, and then burst out laughing. "Oh, you're outrageous! I don't know who's worse—you or Richard Griffin."

"There's a decided difference between us," Tom said, the blue eyes suddenly serious. "I'd never seduce you and walk away without giving a damn. Richard Griffin would."

Morgan frowned, but of course Tom was right; Richard was just a shallow if charming rake. As the musicians struck up a cheery tune, she glanced around the room, looking in vain for Sean. Morgan was relieved that he was not present, for she was certain he would have disapproved of the role she had taken in the festivities—and, of course, of her revealing costume. No doubt he disapproved of such joyousness during the solemn Lenten season.

Perhaps she should excuse herself to change her dress and seek out Sean. But before she could slip away, the King was at her side.

"Lovely, utterly lovely," murmured Henry, taking in every detail of her face and body. "You made young men sigh and old men cry tonight, Morgan Todd. And those of us in between . . ." He held up his hands and let his eyes roll back. "Ah! That I could exchange the Thames for the River Styx!"

Morgan edged a little closer to Tom, who was grinning at Henry. "You didn't know that Mistress Todd had such hidden talents, Your Grace?" he asked.

"I suspected as much, Tom," Henry answered, looking straight at the generous curve of Morgan's breasts, "but not so hidden tonight, either. Won't you dance with me, lovely Amor?"

"I'd be honored," Morgan replied, struggling for composure. The voice sounded like her own, but she hadn't been sure that she could speak. She let the King take her hand as he led her onto the dance floor. Morgan was vaguely aware of a murmuring among the courtiers. She mustered a smile for her royal partner as they stepped together in time to the music.

Henry danced very well, with masculine grace and an innate sense of rhythm. He seemed quite absorbed by the music as he hummed softly to himself. His hold on Morgan was firm but scarcely improper. She tried to relax, tried to concentrate not on the King but the dance itself. Surely if Henry were bedding Madge Shelton he would not be interested in pursuing Morgan at the same time. Yet only his continued interest could forestall her marriage to James Sinclair. Morgan felt as trapped by her dilemma as she was by the King's arms.

The musicians ended their tune. Henry bowed his thanks to Morgan, then took her arm and guided her back in the direction of Tom Seymour, who was talking to Thomas Wyatt.

At least she could *say* something, she thought desperately, her sense of inadequacy rising. "Your Grace dances wonderfully well," she declared. True as it was, the statement sounded vapid.

Henry seemed not to hear. He walked straight ahead, looking neither right nor left. A whisper came from lips that never moved: "I want to show you the gardens—join me by the sundial in a few minutes."

Morgan's step faltered but she kept her face composed. Tom Seymour grinned broadly at them.

"Dancing with Mistress Todd is a pleasure," Henry said aloud. Kissing Morgan's hand and nodding to Tom, he moved back into the circle of courtiers gathered near the royal dais.

More than ever, Morgan wanted to seek the sanctuary of Sean's arms. But she dared not. She danced next with Tom, barely hearing his teasing remarks about her captivation of the King. Somehow, Tom seemed to understand her preoccupation and offered to bring her a glass of wine. She waited for him by the fire, trying to warm herself.

"The Griffins are as Welsh as the Tudors," said Richard, coming to stand beside her. "Won't you dance with me, too?"

Morgan looked up into Richard's taunting green eyes. "I think not," she replied, but couldn't hold back a smile.

Richard shook his head in feigned sadness. "So I'm still to be rejected, eh, Morgan? I must be losing my charm. Surely you aren't saving that delectable body of yours for a man you hardly know? Or is it reserved only for that wild-eyed Irishman?"

"Whoever it's for is no concern of yours," Morgan snapped, her amusement with him fading fast.

Richard shrugged. "Perhaps. But remember one thing:

What you give to a knave you can't save for a King—and the reverse is just as true." He strode off, his broad-shouldered shadow cast by the fire disappearing rapidly across the stone floor.

The King stood alone, half-hidden by the shrubbery which encircled the arbor. An impatient man, he had spent almost five minutes restlessly pacing the ground around the sundial. A noise on the path made him turn quickly, his short fur-trimmed coat swinging. She had come. Finally.

"I was afraid you'd lost your way," Henry said by way of greeting. His tone was jovial but it did nothing to dispel Morgan's fear. "Sit here—on this bench with me." He patted the marble and sat down. Morgan joined him obediently, but her apprehension, coupled with the chilly night, made her shiver.

"Poor sweetheart," said Henry. "That dress does justice to your charms but not to your health." He took off his coat and put it over Morgan's shoulders. "Better?" he asked, moving closer.

Morgan answered the ambiguous question with an undecipherable murmur. She felt the royal arm slip around her back. He leaned closer, the red beard brushing her cheek.

"Forgive my impulsiveness, Morgan," he said softly, "but I'm only a man, after all. And you are a woman—a very desirable one. You mustn't be afraid of me."

"But I *am* afraid of you," Morgan confessed. "More as a man than as a King." She tried to avoid the hungry look in his small eyes but it was difficult. Was it just his size that made him so overwhelming? No, it was not his big body nor his great strength that demanded submission; rather, it was the sense of sheer will which he exuded, overpowering men and devastating women.

"No, no fears," murmured Henry, his mouth coming down on hers. Morgan remained motionless, neither resisting nor responding. She felt as if she were playing a part in another masque, a farce this time. He held her close, his hands fondling her body. Despite his nearness and the warmth from his coat, she began to tremble violently.

His lips claimed hers again as his embrace grew so tight that her ribs and breasts ached. She moved away slightly but his arms pulled her back. One hand caressed her buttocks while the other imprisoned her against his chest.

"Don't fret so, sweetheart," Henry whispered hoarsely. "I want you, as any man wants a maid. That shouldn't frighten you."

A sound close by stopped Morgan's answer. She craned her head over her shoulder; there was someone just outside the arbor.

"Your Grace, somebody is spying on us," she whispered.

Henry quickly loosened his grasp. He was the King of England and not about to be discovered like some peasant making illicit love to a dairymaid. "There'll be another time, sweetheart," he said, his voice very low. But Morgan had already gotten up and was racing out of the arbor.

Whoever had made the noise was no longer in sight. Morgan started back for the palace at a run. She paused only when the gallery doors were just ahead, trying to get her wind back. She was looking behind her to see if Henry was anywhere in sight when a big hand went over her mouth and a strong arm pulled her off the path. Terrified, Morgan struggled impotently. She was aware that her assailant was using only a small portion of his strength to hold her.

Her feet scraped along the ground as he dragged her behind a row of tall hedges. Morgan could no longer see the lights of the palace. She squirmed around, trying to catch a glimpse of her captor's face, but the hand he had clamped over her mouth kept her head turned away.

"You'd entice a King to thwart my brother, you silly slut!" The words were gruff and fierce, and she recognized the voice of Francis Sinclair.

"You! You, who ravished me in the first place! How dare you meddle with the King's business!" Morgan had broken free, her hair streaming around her face, the King's short cape lying in a crumpled heap on the ground.

Francis waved a long finger in her face. "We agreed to talk no more of what happened last spring! That is our secret. But what happens between you and Henry will be fodder for every tongue in England!"

Morgan was shivering from anger as much as from the chill night air. "Were you following me?"

"I came to meet a certain young lady," Francis said defensively. "She seemed willing enough, but I must have been too rough. That's beside the point. I have my family name to protect."

"Oh!" Morgan flew at him, fingers reaching out to rake his face. "I hate you! I hate your brother! Pox on your family name!" She spat at Francis as her nails just missed his skin. He grabbed her wrists and growled out an angry, vile curse. With one swift motion, he scooped Morgan off her feet and threw her over his shoulder. She hung with her head down, the long hair almost trailing in the dirt as he stalked back toward the palace. Morgan kicked with her feet and pounded at his back with her fists. The silver sandals fell off and her bracelet became unfastened, clattering onto a stepping-stone. Francis seemed not even to notice her feeble efforts and angrily kicked open a side door which led into a narrow hallway. A single torch illuminated the passageway, and compared to the laughter and chatter of the banquet hall, the silence seemed eerie.

They had gone about fifty yards when Francis kicked open another door, slammed it shut, and dumped Morgan onto a bed in a completely darkened room. Stunned, she lay as if paralyzed and suddenly blinked as Francis struck a piece of flint and lighted a short, stubby candle.

"You even *look* like a whore in that God-awful gown," he growled, standing by the bed with his tall figure casting a shadow which reached the farthest corners of the room. It was a small room, Morgan noted somewhere in the recesses of her befuddled mind, with few but finely wrought furnishings. Obviously, judging from the disarray of boots, cloaks, and other articles of clothing strewn about, it was Francis's private chamber.

Morgan started to get up, but one rough hand pushed her back on the bed. "Women who play the whore should be treated as such," he declared fiercely, and with one swift motion bent down to rip the thin silk from shoulder to hem. Morgan shrieked in horror and vainly tried to cover herself with her hands. Francis, however, had not moved to touch her again. He still loomed over her, unfastening his short, undecorated cape of serge and removing the doublet with its subdued silver slashings. "You can yell your empty head off," he said in a more amicable tone as he sat down on a wooden bench to pull off his boots. "Only a handful of visitors to the court reside in this wing and I'm quite certain they are all still drinking themselves into a Lenten stupor."

Morgan felt utterly helpless and totally terrified. She rolled over onto her stomach and whimpered into the counterpane as she heard the rest of Francis's clothes fall to the floor.

"You have a charming backside, too," he remarked in a voice that was now downright agreeable. "I didn't get much of a look before."

"Oh, don't!" she cried in a muffled voice. "Just leave me be!" His response was to put a heavy hand on her buttocks and squeeze hard. Morgan's reaction was to jerk her legs up under her, unconscious of the fact that she was revealing even more of herself than before. Francis was sitting on the bed now, and his hand slipped into the crevice of her buttocks, the long fingers finding the intimate recesses and exploring them with a sure, probing touch. She pulled away furiously and banged her forehead on the bedpost. Francis laughed; Morgan reached out for the candle on the nightstand and flung it at him. The pewter holder grazed his temple and he cursed. As the candle fell against a chest of drawers, it sputtered out, plunging the room into darkness once more.

Morgan took advantage of his momentary surprise by leaping off the bed, praying frantically that she could remember where she had seen one of the two long cloaks. If only she could snatch it up and run to the door . . .

But Francis grabbed her, catching her around the waist and hurling her facedown onto the wooden bench. Morgan cried out in pain and shock, feeling the breath go out of her. The edge of the bench had hit her just below her breasts and she hung with half her torso dangling toward the floor. Francis sat on her thighs, imprisoning her in that awkward position, and now his tone had changed again: "You damned near brained me with that candle holder and might have set the place afire," he said angrily. "I warned you, Morgan, you have a lesson to learn." He grabbed her arms and pulled them behind her, moving just enough so that he could entrap them under his legs. She writhed beneath him but knew her movements were completely futile. His hands reached 'round to grasp her breasts, kneading them roughly, tugging at the nipples, bruising the tender flesh. She begged him to stop—he was hurting her, he was crushing her, causing her almost unbearable physical and mental anguish.

Then his hands were between her legs, again seeking out the most sensitive parts of her, thrusting his long fingers inside her body. She cried out again but this time with a moaning sound as the pain became more of an ache, that same strange sensation she had felt with Francis in the orchard at Faux Hall. His fingers plied and probed and set her flesh throbbing. She felt dizzy from lying in that awkward position for so long, and when one arm went around her neck and held her head up, Morgan felt as if she were a drowning swimmer who had suddenly come up for air.

She was taking deep breaths of relief when she felt Francis move again and part her legs wider still—and pull her to her knees. Then he was inside her, thrusting fiercely, forcing her to move with him in a rhythm of passion which took her breath away once more. His hands were on her breasts again and she experienced both pleasure and pain; the hard presence of his manhood inside her plunged deeper and deeper until they both cried out as the darkness seemed to explode in a blaze of blinding light.

For a few seconds, he continued holding her tight, steadying them both lest they fall off the wooden bench. At last he withdrew from her, picked her up around the waist, once again dumped her on the bed, and collapsed beside her.

Neither spoke for several moments, and it was Morgan who finally broke the silence. "You are an animal," she said in a small, shaky voice.

"What?" His eyes had been closed, and now that Morgan had become accustomed to the darkness she could just make out his face next to hers. "Oh—yes, I am." He seemed totally unapologetic.

"I hate you." The voice was still shaky but stronger.

"Hmmm. Perhaps." He sat up and tugged at the counterpane. "I'm freezing. Move over a minute."

She obeyed without thinking, letting him pull down the counterpane and a thick woolen blanket. He covered them both up and lay down again, this time with one arm over Morgan's shoulder.

"That was disgusting, unnatural," she hissed. "Why are you so bestial?"

Francis let out an impatient sigh. "It was *not* unnatural.

Unconventional to some, perhaps, but scarcely disgusting. Nor did you find it so."

"You've raped me twice!" She pulled away from him and sat up on one elbow.

"Good. You can count. Now go to sleep."

"I can't sleep here! I must go back to my room." She started to get out of bed but a strong arm hauled her back.

"Not now. I'll see you get back before dawn. I'm usually an early riser."

Morgan made a face at his conversational tone and then realized he was smiling faintly, even though his eyes were closed again. He looked almost boyish, and she suddenly realized something: "You never even kissed me!"

"Oh, God!" He sat up and scowled at her, then pulled her into his arms and gave her a short, fierce kiss. "Now consider all the ritualistic trappings of romantic love completed. And go to sleep!"

Morgan sighed and lay down again. How could she sleep peacefully beside this rude beast of a ravisher? If she'd been armed, she would have killed him and avenged her honor. But Francis looked quite relaxed and even harmless with his head resting on one outflung arm and the sandy lashes against his tanned skin. I hate him, Morgan told herself, and frowned. She wasn't sure she hated him. She only hated what he had done to her. At least, she lectured herself, she ought to hate his dishonorable, ungallant assault on her body. But if she weren't going to avenge herself, the least she could do was make certain he got no peace. "What if you get me pregnant?" she demanded, thumping on his shoulder with her fist.

He shrugged under the covers. "You'll be married in a month. First babies come when they will."

"But your brother!"

"Well, at least we're related." He pulled her back into his arms and put a hand over her mouth. "Now be quiet or I'll lose my temper again."

Morgan didn't doubt that he meant it. He might even become more violent, and God only knew what physical pain he could inflict upon her in a full-blown rage. She turned away from him, tugging the blanket up around her shoulders. The man was a conscienceless beast, she told herself, probably the most selfish, unfeeling person she had ever met. But the mental tirade was wearying her brain and the physical onslaught had exhausted her body. She was extremely tired, and despite the agony of the last hour, she felt strangely warm and contented inside. Francis was already asleep, his deep, rhythmic breathing lulling her into drowsiness, too.

The first glimpse of dawn filtered through the mullioned window, scattering pale diamonds of light across the rushes. Francis was already up, partially dressed, and splashing water on his face from a pewter basin.

"How would I look with a beard?" he inquired, turning to glance at Morgan, who had sat up but kept the blanket clutched to her chin.

"Like a billy goat," she replied, and yawned widely.

"Mmmm. No, I think I'd look—very mature, scholarly, perhaps."

"Scholarly!" Morgan could not suppress a derisive hoot. "It's cold in here. Please let me have one of your cloaks."

"Fetch it yourself," shrugged Francis, running his hands through his sandy hair and reaching for a shirt, which was hanging on a peg.

Morgan glared at him. "I'm naked," she declared.

"I know." Francis pulled the shirt over his head and grinned wickedly.

"Oh . . . !" There was nothing at hand to hurl at him; she jerked the blanket free and clutched it around herself, then marched across the room to snatch up one of the two cloaks that had been dumped on the floor. She turned her back on Francis as she quickly exchanged the blanket for the cloak. "Now get me out of here," she commanded.

"Very well, but first I must put on my boots." He did so, taking his time and pausing to examine a callus on his heel. Morgan waited impatiently at the door but said nothing until he joined her.

"There's a back stairs out of this wing, so our chances of being undetected are good. Here, this way."

The cold stone floor of the corridor spurred Morgan to walk fast enough to keep up with Francis's long, loping strides. They passed only a disinterested halberdier, tired from his long night's watch, and a sleepy-eyed pot boy as they made their way through the palace. Outside her door, Francis paused. "You will pack today and go to Faux Hall for a month. I will not have scandal about you and the King following us all the way to Belford."

Morgan stared at Francis and tried not to shiver under the cloak. "You're m-m-mad! You ravish me and then send me home! And just because I let the King kiss me!"

"True. But it's useless to argue. And," Francis went on, waving a long finger in her face, "don't consider going to the King with your dilemma. He may find you fetching, but with Anne as his Queen and Madge Shelton in his bed, he won't go to great lengths to upset his very helpful private secretary's plans for a marriage alliance with the North."

Before Morgan could reply, he was already walking swiftly down the corridor and had turned the corner toward the back stairs. Sputtering to herself, Morgan lifted the latch. The room she shared with Margaret Howard was bathed in the pale light of dawn. Margaret was asleep, her blond hair splashed across the pillow, one white arm flung out over the counterpane. Morgan quietly took off Francis's cloak and hid it in the wardrobe, hurriedly put on her bedgown, considered lying down and pretending to be asleep, but decided instead to sit at the dressing table and simply tell Margaret she had risen early.

But Morgan's entrance had roused Margaret slightly. She turned over, flung a hand across her face, and let out a small frightened cry. "No, I cannot . . . you are too rough!" Margaret rolled over again, whimpering softly. Morgan frowned, wondering why Margaret's words stirred something in her memory. Then she saw the red bruises on Margaret's arm and remembered that Francis had said he'd come outside last night to join a lady but that he'd been too rough . . .

It was all Morgan could do to keep from smashing a cosmetic jar against the wall. Francis Sinclair was a philandering brute who treated all women like whores. He spoke lovingly of his wife and children, deplored any scandal attached to the Sinclair name, fell on his knees to worship in church—and apparently all but raped every woman he met. He raped *me,* Morgan thought savagely, twice against my will and in the most unromantic, ferocious ways imaginable. A more courageous woman would have killed him—or at least tried. Morgan didn't know if she was more angry at Francis for his repulsive behavior or at herself for not being able to stop him. She glared at her image in the mirror: For someone who had vowed to steer her own course, to find true love and hold on to it, Morgan had failed dismally. The plot to enthrall the King had been foiled by Francis; the plan to avoid marriage to James Sinclair and wed Sean O'Connor instead had been ruined—also by Francis; and her ideals about romantic love as the only possible reason for physical intimacy had been totally shattered by Francis. Indeed, Francis Sinclair seemed to have recharted her course as successfully—if not more so—than her damnable uncle, Thomas Cromwell.

Once again, Margaret Howard thrashed in her sleep and cried out. Morgan set her mouth in a grim, straight line. Francis Sinclair, James Sinclair, Thomas Cromwell, and all those who would thwart her would not be the ultimate victors, Morgan vowed. Perhaps they had taken a few tricks, but Morgan was still determined that she would win the game.

Chapter 7

THE DAYS AND WEEKS at Faux Hall had gone by slowly and quietly. Her parents were delighted to have her home and readily accepted her explanation of a lengthy visit before going north to be wed.

Easter Sunday fell in mid-April that year. It was a cloudy day, with no promise of sun. Morgan tried to rally her spirits to meet the joy of the Resurrection, but her heart seemed to sag. Now it would only be a question of days before she would leave Faux Hall.

There was no word from Sean, no indication that he missed her, and Morgan wondered if he'd heard gossip about herself and the King. Nor did Morgan write to him, since she was certain her letter would be intercepted by Cromwell's henchmen. Still, she had not given up hope entirely. Indeed, she was already plotting to get them both away from London when she returned and, perhaps with Tom Seymour's help, flee to the Continent.

There was little talk at Faux Hall of Morgan's marriage. Her parents understood and accepted the necessity of their daughter's match with James Sinclair, but they loved her too much to dwell on the subject in front of her. Indeed, as during her previous visit from court, conversation reverted to its old pattern: local farming, the weather, ships, prices at the market in Aylesbury, the neighbors' doings. For the Todds, life went on unexcitingly but with comfort and reasonable security.

Nan did her best to conceal her enthusiasm for going to London. Often she would start to say something about the trip and then catch herself in midsentence. Morgan usually pretended she hadn't noticed. But one day—the first real spring day—the two girls were sitting on the rolling lawn in front of the house when Nan glanced up at the clear sky and sighed:

"Finally the weather is turning warm. Look, there's someone riding up the road. Maybe whoever it is will have news from London."

Morgan's first thought was that it was a messenger from Thomas Cromwell. She remained seated on the grass, her chin resting on her fist.

Nan jumped up, running toward the road. "Come on, Morgan, let's see who it is. We haven't had a visitor for days."

"That's well enough with me. I'm quite content to sit here." She stretched her legs out on the grass. The earth still felt damp. Was it only a year since she had left Faux Hall the first time? Impossible. But it was so. Yet how could it be that her life, after changing so little in eighteen years, could change so much in one?

Morgan watched Nan as she reached the road's edge. The rider had slowed his horse to a walk. He was waving at Nan. For the first time, Morgan looked closely at him. Incredulously, she looked again, then leaped to her feet. She grabbed her skirts in her hand and raced across the grass.

"Sean! Sean!" called Morgan, long hair streaming behind her.

Sean had dismounted. Now he began to run, too, until the two of them met, falling into each other's arms. Neither could speak as they clung together, savoring the moment of reunion.

"I can't believe you're here," Morgan said at last, taking Sean's face between her hands. "I thought you'd forgotten me!"

Sean smiled sheepishly. "I tried—it all seemed so futile. I was angry, too, that you had left without a word. But I dared not write. So finally I decided to see you, no matter what the consequences."

Morgan hugged him close. "Oh, dear Sean, you'll never know how happy I am to have you here!"

Nan, who was watching the reunion uneasily, took the reins of Sean's horse and patted the big roan's nose. She wondered how she could artfully disappear. Instead, she finally called out, "I think your horse needs a drink, Sean."

Sean released Morgan and turned to the younger girl. "You're right," he laughed, suddenly embarrassed by

Nan's presence. "Poor Turlough—I've ridden him very hard these last miles." He took the reins from Nan. "Come, we'll walk him around back. By heaven, I hope your parents won't be too upset to see me," he told Morgan.

She took his free hand. "Of course not! They'll be delighted you're here. Wait and see."

But it was not delight that greeted Sean at Faux Hall. Although the Todds were both too polite and too fond of Sean to reveal their true feelings, Morgan sensed at once that her parents were dismayed and alarmed by the Irishman's visit. Even as Lady Alice called for food and Sir Edmund ordered ale, the atmosphere at Faux Hall suddenly seemed disturbed.

After the hurried meal, Morgan sought a moment alone with her father. They went into his library, where she sat on a stool at his feet.

"Something is wrong, Father. Was it so terrible of Sean to have come?"

Sir Edmund leaned back in his carved armchair, unable to avoid his daughter's searching eyes. "Often, in youth, love overcomes reason. The things which seem so right at the time are not, in the long run, right at all." He straightened out one of the sails on the *Sea Serpent* model in front of him. "Think, Morgan, what will happen if Cromwell finds out that Sean is here."

Morgan bit her lower lip. "Must he find out?"

"Probably. He usually does."

"Even so, he knows we are kin, and at court we were often seen in each other's company."

A pained expression crossed Sir Edmund's face. "True. But I know why you were sent from court," he said quietly, opening his top desk drawer and pulling out a folded sheet of parchment. "Cromwell sent a letter with all the . . . unsavory details."

Morgan stared in horror at her father. "Oh, no! But you don't know why I did it. . . . It wasn't what you think at all. Nothing really happened with the King. I only let him . . ."

He again looked directly at her, the passionate, intense gaze so like his daughter's. "I know. It was a clever plan, but dangerous. And that is why Sean should not be here.

He may stay a day or two, but then he must return to Armagh."

"Does Mother know? About the letter from Uncle Thomas, I mean."

"No. And I won't tell her." He put the parchment back in the drawer and the lock clicked shut. It seemed to Morgan as if her father were closing a door in her life forever.

The following afternoon Sean and Morgan took a long walk by the river. They scarcely spoke but went hand in hand, keeping a steady, determined pace. At last they came to a landing where a small skiff was tied.

"That's Will Covey's boat," said Morgan. "He only has one arm, but you should see the way he gets around the river. I daresay he's near seventy now."

Sean stared at the little craft for a long minute. He released Morgan's hand and moved to the water's edge. "Do you think he'd mind if we borrowed it?" he asked, closely inspecting the inside of the skiff.

"Borrowed it?" Morgan frowned. "I don't know. I suppose not. He probably wouldn't know if we did. I don't think he comes down here unless somebody has to cross the river."

Sean stepped gingerly into the boat. "Come," he said, extending his hand to Morgan. "We're going on a little voyage."

Morgan gathered up her skirts and climbed in. Sean untied the skiff and pushed off from the bank. He took hold of the oars but made no effort to row, letting the current carry them downstream.

A slight breeze ruffled the new foliage along the river's edge. Morgan trailed her hand in the water as Sean pulled at the oars, steering them around a slight bend in the river. On the far bank was a meadow, a stable, and several cows who were lazily cropping on the young grass. Morgan tried to concentrate on the pastoral scene, but they had gone a good distance and the current had grown quite swift. "The river is high, Sean. I don't think we should venture much farther, do you hear?" Anxiety surfaced in her voice.

He made no reply. And when at last he did speak, he put a question to Morgan: "How far is it to the village of Thame?"

"Thame?" Morgan's brow furrowed in puzzlement. "Oh, at least ten miles. Why, it's practically halfway to Oxford."

"Do you know the Convent of St. Ursula?"

"I've seen it. It's a mile or so this side of Thame."

"That's where we're going." Sean kept looking straight ahead, his body moving rhythmically as he began to pull on the oars.

Morgan leaned forward. "Why? Why are we going there?"

"I'm taking you to the Convent of St. Ursula while I go on to London. I have an urgent task there—something which I can't disclose even to you. I'll be back in a few days to get you and then we'll flee—to Ireland, to France, maybe Scotland. You must promise to wait for me at the convent."

"But, Sean, why couldn't I have waited at Faux Hall?" She clasped her hand over his.

"Your uncle's men may be watching Faux Hall this very minute. You see, I refused to take the Oath of Supremacy, declaring Henry head of the Church. I had not planned on staying at Faux Hall for more than a day or two anyway"—he made a wry face—"regardless of your father's limited hospitality. I can't be seen again in London, either. But most of all, I can't give you up to a Northumberland heretic."

"Oh, Sean, this is too dangerous! What of my parents? What if you're caught in London?" She half stood up, setting the skiff rocking dangerously. Sean spoke sharply and Morgan sat down again on the seat board. She was on the verge of tears. "Dear God, Sean, this is insane!"

Again he let the oars go slack as he leaned forward. "Do you love me?" He saw her give a shaky nod. "Then," he went on, "I want to hear no more arguments. Not another word until we reach the convent. Very well?"

She nodded again, even more meekly than before. Composing her trembling hands in her lap, she tried to keep her mind on the peaceful countryside as the skiff moved steadily toward Thame.

It was dark when Morgan and Sean pulled onto the bank at the Convent of St. Ursula. The only part of the original building was the chapel, which had been built in the early thirteenth century to commemorate the British princess who had marched on Rome with eleven thousand virgins. Ursula, together with her followers, had been put to death by the Huns. The present convent had been built some hundred and fifty years later with, some said, contributions from Henry the Sixth's Queen, Margaret of Anjou.

Sean quickly but carefully tied the skiff near some stone steps which led up from the river to a heavy wooden door. He gave Morgan his hand and spoke for the first time since his demand for silence. "The mother superior is a cousin of my mother's. I haven't seen her since I was a child, but she'll know my name."

Morgan still said nothing. She was very cold and her foot slipped once as they climbed the damp steps. Sean tightened his grip on her arm, releasing it only when they got to the door. He grasped the iron knocker but Morgan suddenly protested:

"Sean—you must promise—before you go back to London, send word to my parents. Not where I am, perhaps, but at least that I'm with you and that . . . that all is well. If you don't, they'll come looking for me, and that could be disastrous, too."

He bent his dark head and considered her statement. Finally, he nodded. "Yes, you may be right. I shall tell the mother superior to send a message." He banged the door three times.

It was a full minute before anyone appeared. Then a little hole opened above the knocker and Morgan saw an eye looking out at them. She jumped and grabbed Sean's arm. The voice that belonged to the eye asked the visitor's identities.

"I am Sean O'Connor of Armagh, seeking the help of the Lord and the mother superior. She knew me as a child in Ireland. I bring with me a pious young lady who seeks your protection."

There was no reply from the other side of the door as the eye disappeared and the peephole closed. Morgan asked Sean if he thought they would be admitted.

"I am sure of it," he answered. "They are still saying prayers for my father's soul." He crossed himself, then noticed that Morgan was shivering. "My poor love." He put both arms around her and held her close. "I know how hard it is for you—not knowing what I plan to do. You will love me, no matter what?"

126

"Yes," sighed Morgan, barely able to conceal the apprehension and the weariness in her voice. "I will love you always."

The door swung open and before them stood a tall, heavy woman in her late fifties. Her white robes made her seem even larger than she was, but the kindness in her face contrasted with the formidability of her size. Sean released Morgan and went down on his knees to kiss the mother superior's hand.

"Enough of that," she said with the trace of a smile. "Come inside quickly; the spring air is chilly at night." She led them down a long corridor and into a small room, which was bare except for two candles, a small desk and prie-dieu, and a magnificent gold crucifix.

"My son," she said in her low voice, "it has been fifteen years since I saw you. What brings you here?"

Sean put his hand on Morgan's wrist and brought her forward. "This is Mistress Morgan Todd, Thomas Cromwell's niece by marriage. She is a follower of the true faith and needs your protection for a few days—until I come back to fetch her."

At Cromwell's name the mother superior's face tightened visibly and her eyes grew wary. When the nun spoke again, her voice seemed to have lost some of its kindness. "You live at Faux Hall?"

"Yes, Reverend Mother," replied Morgan, attempting to lower her gaze with what she hoped the older woman would take for maidenly modesty.

Sean intervened quickly. "She is hiding neither from her uncle nor her parents. This is all my doing. I must attend to important business in London, the nature of which I can't disclose. I want Morgan to be assured of safety while I'm gone."

The mother superior fingered her rosary—Morgan thought the beads looked like real pearls—and glanced away from the young couple. She was obviously loath to get embroiled in what was surely a dangerous court intrigue. "I fear for this sad, sin-filled world of ours." Her eyes traveled to the crucifix. "Within walls such as these is the only peace this side of heaven. But when disturbing elements from the outside world creep inside our doors, even that peace comes to an end."

Sean glanced away from the reluctant nun to his exhausted love. Suddenly he went down on his knees. "I beg you, Reverend Mother, in the name of my father's soul and for the sake of my mother's memory, help us! I swear that what I must do, I do in the name of Christ, the savior of us all!"

The nun seemed moved by Sean's fervent plea. She rested her hand on his head for a moment before she spoke, and the kindness returned to her voice. "Very well. Mistress Todd may stay. I must trust any son of Mary O'Connor's. It is only that fear walks with us all these days. Sir Thomas More and Bishop Fisher languish in the Tower and they are the two finest men in England. Sometimes I grow weak with the thought of what will happen to us lesser mortals."

Sean rose and took the mother superior's hand. "You speak truly, Reverend Mother. I shall remember you in my prayers until I die." He turned to Morgan. "I must be on my way now."

The nun protested. "Surely you won't be starting out so late?"

"Yes," said Sean, "I must. I will need a horse, though. Do you have one to spare or know of where I could get one? I'll pay for it, of course."

The mother superior told Sean of a farmer just down the road who would lend him a mount. She also insisted that he have some supper before he left. He finally agreed and they adjourned to the refectory, where a young nun brought food for Sean and Morgan. During the meal Sean made arrangements for a message to be sent to Morgan's parents by a trustworthy village boy. And then the mother superior left Morgan and Sean alone for their good-byes.

It was a brief but tender parting. Sean kissed Morgan only once, very gently, and then held her against his chest and said nothing for at least a minute. An almost desperate fear clutched at Morgan, as if he were already parted from her, even though she could still feel him in her arms.

"If only I knew . . . It all seems so dangerous . . ." she ventured when at last he released her.

He shook his head. "You cannot. Just pray for me . . . and wait." And he held her close again and then he was gone.

It started to rain the next day, and kept up until the river had risen half a foot. Morgan spent much of her time at the windows, glumly looking out at the wet spring weather. Prayer was some source of consolation. The mother superior was kind but the other nuns kept their distance, and it was a lonely, anguished week for Morgan.

The messenger had returned the day after Morgan's arrival. All he had told her parents was that she had gone away with Sean and that she was safe. She knew they would worry, but for the time being her fate seemed completely out of her hands. But it usually did, she thought vexedly, despite her vows to the contrary.

Seven days, thought Morgan, and then she recounted. It suddenly occurred to her that it was the first day of May—the month her wedding was supposed to take place. She shuddered and said another quick prayer for Sean. She was standing in the small cell the mother superior had assigned her; it was barren except for a chair, a desk, a priedieu, and a lumpy pallet.

A bell from the village tolled the noon hour—time for the Angelus, followed by dinner. Morgan adjusted her coif, wishing she had a mirror like the one from Venice she used at court. She considered joining the nuns for their prayers but decided to stay in her cell until mealtime. Just as the dinner bell rang and Morgan turned to leave for the dining hall, she heard hoofbeats in the distance. Her heart fluttered. Sean? But that was the sound of several horses. Had he come with friends? It was possible, but not likely. Unable to contain her curiosity or maintain her decorum, she fled from the cell, racing along the narrow corridor and up the stairs to the main floor.

Down the hall near the main entrance she saw one of the younger nuns heading toward the door. Out of breath, Morgan stopped and tried to hide herself in a narrow wall recess. She could barely hear the nun's voice and the closed door muffled the sound of whoever was on the other side. Apparently some sort of exchange was going on between the nun and the visitors. Anxiety was turning to disappointment for Morgan—surely if it were Sean, the nun would have let him in at once. . . .

At last the nun stepped aside to admit the callers. Morgan gathered her skirts around her tightly and tried to peek out into the hall. The day was still dark and only one window admitted any light into the corridor. Morgan peered at the men—three of them, she counted—but all she could make out were forms. From the other end of the hall came the mother superior, who joined the little group. Her voice, though low, carried better than the others, and Morgan strained to hear. She picked up only a fragment of the sentence but it was enough:

"Of course, if it is the King's wish that Mistress Todd be brought back . . ."

Escape—it was the only thought, completely blanking out fear or discretion. Morgan raced back down the steps. She could reach the door to the river by crossing to the other end of the convent. Once outside, she would head for the woods. No, she countermanded herself, they might have dogs with them. The river was the only answer—yes, the river, for Sean had left the boat there. It would be the last place they would look since the mother superior had no inkling how she and Sean had arrived at the convent.

Gasping for breath, she reached the little door, thankful that the nuns were in the refectory. With effort, she pushed open the heavy door, ran down the steps, and untied the skiff. Removing the oars from the oarlocks, she began to row back toward Faux Hall. It was hard going. Morgan hadn't rowed a boat for years and she was fighting the current and the high waters. Her muscles strained in protest as she struggled with the oars, trying desperately to hold her course.

It was only after she had battled half a mile upstream that her mind began to function normally again. How had she been found? What had happened to Sean? Who had told the King's Men where she was? Panic overcame her and her hands trembled on the oars. She stopped rowing and attempted to calm herself. Maybe her parents had asked for help in finding her. They could have sent word to Cromwell. And they would have known she might still be in the vicinity . . .

She gripped the oars again and began to pull away, now conscious that it was raining once more. Another half mile; the rain had turned into a spring downpour. The little skiff was beginning to fill with water. Morgan stopped for a second time. Could she bail out the boat with only her hands? Or should she go ashore and risk hiding in the woods? Her dress was soaked, the rain was cold, and her arms ached. But she was still only a mile from the convent. She decided to keep rowing until she was forced to abandon the boat.

Each pull on the oars tired her more. Oblivious to everything but her physical effort, she never heard the riders along the bank. It wasn't until a man jumped into the water that she looked up. Her sharp scream pierced the rainfall as she recognized Richard Griffin swimming toward her.

"Pull in, you little fool!" he cried. "Pull in, or I'll tip you over!"

Morgan's eyes flashed; there was just enough strength left for a final defiance. "No! Whoreson!" She plunged the oars back into the river.

Richard was an excellent swimmer and he had only a few yards to go. He reached the skiff in seconds and grabbed the prow with his hands. Morgan lashed out with an oar, just missing the top of his head. With one heave, Richard threw the little skiff over and Morgan splashed into the river. Richard dove under and pulled her to the surface. Morgan limply let him fight the current, hauling her to the riverbank where she slumped onto the ground. She was vaguely aware of Will Brereton and Francis Weston standing by their horses.

Morgan coughed and spat water. The men watched her closely, not speaking until she spoke to them. "How did you find me?" she asked wearily, attempting to stand. It was so miserably cold and wet on the ground that she had to get up.

Richard helped her to her feet. "Your lover told us," he replied abruptly.

A spark returned to her eyes. "Sean? He didn't! You lie! Where is he?"

Richard's voice was low, even, and faintly malicious. "He's dead. He died on the rack two days ago."

"No! It's not true . . ." Morgan whispered. "No . . ." She screamed once, a piercing shriek that cut through the damp air.

Her shocked reaction disconcerted Richard more than he'd expected. He didn't reply, and Francis Weston intervened. "Sean didn't betray you, Morgan. I know that. He was told that if he didn't tell where you were hiding, you'd be tried for treason. He only talked because he was afraid for you."

Morgan stood very still, her eyes unseeing, unblinking. "No . . ."

"You've been a fool, Morgan," said Richard, his composure regained. "You stand a fine chance of going to the Tower. Your uncle is in a rare fury over this insane plot."

Morgan's stare broke. "Plot? Plot for what?"

Weston spoke gently. "Sean was trying to get Sir Thomas More out of the Tower. He was caught and put on the rack. They . . . they tortured him to find out who his accomplices were. He revealed no names at first, but apparently your parents had already sent a message to your Uncle Thomas asking him if he knew where you were. In their own innocence, they finally admitted that you had fled Faux Hall with Sean. At any rate, the inquisitors asked Sean where you were, he said he didn't know, and that's when they told him it would be best for you if you were found at once, to prove you knew nothing of the plot."

Morgan scarcely heard the last sentence. Her eyes glazed over again and she wandered dazedly toward an oak tree. "Madness . . . madness . . . I should have guessed . . ." Suddenly she cried out, wildly pounding her fists against the weathered tree trunk. "Why didn't he tell me? I might have stopped him! I could have saved him! Oh, God, dear God, oh, God!"

Weston took a cautious step toward her, waiting for the cries to die out. "Morgan, did you truly not know of this wild plan?"

She was convulsed by sobs; all she could do was shake her head.

"Then," Weston went on, "you must convince your uncle. I'm sure he doesn't want to put his own niece in the Tower."

"I don't care!" she shouted at him. "Sean's dead! I don't care what happens to me!" She had a sudden urge to race back to the river and plunge into the deepest waters. Sean had chosen martyrdom over her love. What was left except long years of lonely remorse?

Richard spoke out sharply. "God's eyes! Maybe you don't care what happens, but I'm like to die of a chill. Come along. We've got to head back to the village and get some dry clothes."

Morgan hesitated, trying to control her sobs. Her entire body was convulsed with shock, grief, and terror. Stumbling blindly she went to Francis Weston, who helped her onto his horse and then climbed up behind her. Exhausted, she slumped back against him, and the little party headed back to Thame.

PART TWO

1535–1540

Chapter 8

THOMAS CROMWELL'S BURDENS grew by the day. Law, taxes, trade, church and state, foreign affairs, domestic politics, dynastic considerations, all claimed his attention and required the full concentration of his inexhaustible mental energies. He worked harder than ever, longer than usual, those spring days of 1535. And now one more matter was thrust upon him, and a family concern at that.

Morgan, he thought, silently cursing his sister-in-law and her husband for ever letting the little chit stray from the confines of Faux Hall. Here she was, his own niece, involved in a brazen attempt to thwart the King's justice.

He barely gave a thought to Sean O'Connor. That foolish young man had met a fitting end. But implicating Morgan was a different matter. True, Francis Weston had convinced him that Morgan seemed to know nothing of O'Connor's intentions. And O'Connor, even in agony on the rack, had denied that she knew anything about his singlehanded effort to free Sir Thomas More.

Shoving some papers distractedly around his desk, Cromwell considered his next move. He was a practical man who understood people very well; Morgan's guilt was not for political treachery but for love, a love which Cromwell himself had tried to snuff out. More important, it was Morgan's family that had given him the respectability he had needed so desperately to make his way in the world. To have any of his kin locked in the Tower—or worse—would surely not reflect well.

And then there was the Sinclair marriage. Belford was an important link in the chain Cromwell was drawing around the Catholic Church. The North was predominantly of the old faith—Lord Dacre had been evidence of that. Cromwell and his King might one day need a loyal lord upon whom to rely in time of trouble, especially since the Earl of Northumberland seemed to grow more weak-kneed all the time. What better man to bind to the crown than one married to Cromwell's own niece?

He drummed his fingers on the desk, then nodded slowly to himself. Yes, personal and political matters both weighed in favor of mercy. Morgan was definitely a useful pawn. He could present a fine argument to the King in support of his decision. At last satisfied, he looked up as a page entered, announcing that Morgan Todd was waiting outside the door.

She came slowly into the room, a subdued, dispirited version of the Morgan Todd her uncle had come to know.

"Good morning, niece," greeted Cromwell, trying to be kind. He motioned for her to be seated. "Now," he began, "you must realize the deep shock I feel over the O'Connor affair. I cannot understand how you could have been witless enough to get involved. This is a matter of the utmost seriousness. . . ."

Morgan barely heard her uncle drone on. The sunshine through the leaded windowpanes made her feel sleepy; besides, her mind hadn't seemed to function properly since Richard Griffin had dragged her from the river five days earlier. Still, Sean's image beat like a death drum on her heart, and there was no help, no succor for it.

At last Cromwell seemed to be drawing to a conclusion. Morgan forced herself to focus on his words.

"So tomorrow morning you will leave for Belford. It's best that you go before any more scandal is spread. And it's most fortuitous that Francis Sinclair returned from Woodstock only a few days ago. At the moment, I am seeing to it that as little information as possible about your part in this affair is mentioned . . ."

Morgan again lost track of what Cromwell was saying. Belford . . . tomorrow . . . Sean . . . dead . . . murder . . . my uncle is a murderer . . . Yet somehow her mind could not accept that awful, horrendous fact—that the man who sat before her spewing endless familial advice had actually sent her love to his death.

"Morgan!" Cromwell spoke sharply, then checked his temper. "I know you're distraught. But I'm saying something very important to you." He pushed a sheet of paper across the desk. "This is the Oath of Supremacy. Will you sign?"

Somewhere on the fuzzy edges of her mind she heard Sean warning her about how the Act of Succession would lead to further destruction of the Church, how even Francis Sinclair had foretold a dire fate for the old ways. She gave herself a shake, ignoring Cromwell's questioning gaze. What difference did it make, all this religious controversy and ghastly violence? What had the Pope done to save Sean? What had God himself done to spare a young man's life? She had signed the act. Now she would affix her signature to the oath as well. A pox on Popes and Kings and all their minions.

She picked up the quill Cromwell proffered her. With swift, almost reckless strokes, she signed her name.

"You've shown great wisdom," Cromwell said with a smile. "I will tell the King that you have learned your lesson."

Morgan looked out at him from bitter, ironic eyes. She dared not speak. Cromwell stood up, his shrewd mind plumbing her thoughts. "You'd best start packing. I believe Francis Sinclair has made some purchases for you."

Morgan stood up, too. She stared dumbly at the wall as Cromwell awkwardly cleared his throat. "Godspeed, Morgan," he said at last. She didn't look at him but turned and left the room without having said a single word.

Wrapped in her riding cloak, Morgan sat by the window as the first rays of morning sun challenged the darkness. She concentrated on the details of her leave-taking, rather than on what lay ahead or had gone before. Everything was in order—the trunks and two extra boxes, which the serving people had already removed to the courtyard.

She had been waiting for almost ten minutes when a heavy knock sounded at the door. Francis. She sighed and got up to let him in.

But it was Tom Seymour, not Francis Sinclair, who came through the door. Morgan cried out his name and flew into his arms.

"Muffet, my poor muffet," soothed Tom, as he felt Morgan's body begin to shake with convulsive sobs. "I am so very, very sorry."

She clung desperately to him, the pent-up grief released

in a terrible torrent. Tom held her close, saying nothing. He knew that she must let her tears assuage her sorrow or her heart would surely break. He had returned from the Low Countries only the night before; Ned, one of the few people at court who knew the whole story about Sean, had recounted it to Tom.

When at last the tears stopped flowing and the shaking ceased, Tom took her face in his hands. "Morgan, you won't believe or accept what I'm going to say—at least not now. But you are young, so very young. You have many years ahead of you. A girl, a woman like you will fall in love again." He shook his head, aware that his words were in vain, that Morgan would have to live that lesson to learn it.

Morgan tried to speak but the tears started again. Tom pulled her against his chest and kissed her forehead. "The sun is up, muffet. Sinclair will be here any moment." He released her and moved toward the door but stopped with his hand on the latch. "One other thing, Morgan—Sean O'Connor didn't die on the rack. He died the day King Henry defied the Pope. The man you loved—the real man— could never have survived in this new world his monarch has created. I swear to you, Sean must have welcomed his second death."

The Great North Road, England's main artery, was still muddy from the spring rains. The wagon carrying Morgan's belongings bumped along precariously at the end of the little caravan. Still, the travelers maintained a steady pace, for Francis Sinclair was anxious to reach Belford lest more rain cause flooding.

The party included two Sinclair retainers, and two serving women sent by James Sinclair for his bride-to-be. Francis led the way, with Morgan following; the two scarcely spoke the first day. They reached Kettering that night, where Morgan, her spirit more weary than her body, toyed with her food and wished she had insisted upon eating alone in her room.

"I know you don't want to discuss it with me," Francis said without preamble as he cut a huge chunk from a leg of mutton, "but I'm sorry about what happened to Sean O'Connor."

Morgan stared at him, wondering at first if he was being

sarcastic. But Francis was regarding her with an open, candid expression. He knew more than she wished he did, but her ties with Sean had been no secret at court. Cromwell would play down her involvement, of course, but Francis was not easily deceived.

"Sean's dead. It's over." Morgan dropped a chunk of dark bread into the congealing gravy. It wasn't over for her, it never would be, but she had vowed that no one ever again would guess what was in her heart.

"On the contrary," Francis contradicted, piling boiled potatoes into his trencher, "it's just begun." He saw the question form on her lips and waved his empty whiskey cup at her. "I don't mean O'Connor, I mean the entire religious issue."

"You were right from the start," Morgan commented in a peevish voice. "But I don't want to discuss it."

Francis nodded. "Indeed. Yet it's only fitting that I tell you I have no intention of bringing tales home to James."

In her desolation, that possibility had never occurred to Morgan. If her future husband knew his betrothed had been even remotely implicated in a Papist plot to free Sir Thomas More, he might denounce her and try to extricate himself from the marriage contract. Not that she would care—but she found it curious that Francis Sinclair, so concerned about his family's honor, had not taken it upon himself at least to delay the wedding until he had more time to consult with his brother.

She would not pose such a question, however. Instead, she remained silent, her own food growing cold while Francis ate with gusto. Now that he had said his piece, he seemed to have forgotten about Morgan's presence. She studied him covertly, noting the big, rather bony hands; the long, clean-shaven face; the broad, slightly sloping shoulders; and the fine lines of laughter around his gray eyes. He must laugh more than I realize, she thought idly. But then, they had hardly found themselves in mirth-provoking situations; maybe at Belford he would be different. More to the point, James might be different, too, the kind and gentle man Francis had described.

For some reason her gaze kept straying back to Francis's hands. It's because I'm avoiding his eyes, she told herself, and watched him skewer one last piece of mutton with his dagger.

* * *

The next day was the warmest of the spring thus far. Morgan's dark blue riding costume grew uncomfortable and the silk blouse stuck to her back. But she made no mention of her discomfort to Francis. She kept silent, watching his broad back in front of her as he doggedly pointed his gray gelding toward their second stop, Nottingham.

On the third day the weather turned cool again, with a hint of rain. They moved now out of the rolling hills and quiet forests into the flat farm country. The fields were scenes of activity, with whole families working on the spring crops. Morgan was beginning to take notice of her surroundings, suddenly realizing that London and Faux Hall had been left far behind. Events had moved too swiftly during the last few days for her to know how she really felt. Now it occurred to her that she would miss her family, that she would miss Tom Seymour, that she would even miss life at court—though all its intrigues seemed unbearable to her now.

They entered York through one of the ancient Roman gates. The walls seemed remarkably intact, causing Morgan to marvel at the conquerors' building prowess. Inside the city, tradesmen, farmers, and merchants were busily engaged in making the last profits for the day.

The little party wound through the narrow streets, slowly making its way among the hawkers and housewives, beggars and strumpets, priests and yeomen. Francis finally reined in at The Cock and Kettle, a small but respectable inn.

Francis helped Morgan dismount, and the retainers led the animals away. "Do you want to go to the minster now?" Francis asked.

"I'd rather eat supper first," Morgan answered, genuinely hungry for the first time since Sean had left her at the Convent of St. Ursula.

Francis shrugged. "It makes no difference. It should still be light by then." He led the way into the inn, the serving women following Morgan at a respectful distance.

Morgan ate in her room, as she had done since the first night out. After Kettering she had wondered why Francis seemed so unconcerned about leaving her alone. But one glance at Peg and Polly, the sturdy serving wenches, made her realize that they were her keepers as well as her servants. Still, they seemed pleasant enough, especially Polly, the older of the two. Morgan felt no resentment toward either of them and decided she might eventually try to win them over. Loyal servants, she had learned at court, often were more valuable than pure gold.

She began to grow impatient when Francis hadn't appeared after over an hour. It was beginning to get dark, although the rain had stopped. She paced the length of the room, stopping every so often to glance out the small window. Finally, as the church bells struck seven, a loud knock sounded on the door. Polly hurried to answer it.

"Ready?" was Francis's only greeting.

Morgan looked at him swiftly, noting that he nearly filled the door. She nodded and picked up her cloak, which Peg helped put over her shoulders. Francis held the door open as she swept past him into the passageway.

"How was your supper?" Francis asked amiably, as they made their way through the crooked street leading to the minster's east entrance.

"Well enough," Morgan answered, wondering if Francis's good humor had been caused by her effort to break the barrier of silence between them.

They reached the outside of the great church, stopping to stare up at the three great towers. Morgan peered upwards for a long time, awed by the minster's massive beauty.

"The tower to the west is over two hundred feet high," Francis told her. "See the great window? There are two thousand square feet of glass in it." He watched Morgan's eyes widen with amazement. "Still," he went on, "the Five Sisters window on the other side is even more beautiful."

They went inside where Morgan gasped with wonder. The vaulted ceiling soared heavenward, with both the length and width of the church contributing to a spiritual and temporal vastness. Then Morgan saw the Five Sisters, an immense but infinitely delicate window of rainbow colors. Each of the five panes, Francis explained, represented a different saint. Morgan kept staring upwards, her dark eyes marveling at the intricate craftsmanship.

"You told me how lovely it was," she murmured, "but I don't believe anyone could truly describe it."

Francis moved away toward the choir stalls. "The needlework is superb, too. Come see the intricacy of design here."

Morgan followed obediently and marveled at the even stitches, the use of color, and, most of all, the hours of dedication it must have taken to create such masterworks. Her own efforts seemed more than just amateurish, they seemed pathetic.

At last they left the minster, heading back for The Cock and Kettle in a very fine mist. Francis was now the one who was silent, though Morgan tried to ask him questions about the ancient city, particularly the narrow street called The Shambles. But he answered tersely: Yes, the original walls had been built by Romans; yes, it was still one of the most strongly fortified cities in England; yes, The Shambles, so narrow that the roofs almost abutted across the lane, had originally been the local butchering area.

Back at the inn, Francis bade Morgan a curt goodevening and headed for his own room. Morgan sat by the fire in virtual silence, though Peg and Polly exchanged scraps of conversation. Just as a buck-toothed serving wench arrived with hot water for bathing, Francis appeared again in the doorway.

With an abrupt motion of his hand, Francis gestured for Peg and Polly to leave. Morgan frowned at him after the serving women left; he was standing with his back to the door, the bushy brows drawn together.

"We are only two days' ride from Belford now," he declared, moving more slowly than usual to the roughhewn table where Morgan still sat. "Once we are at the castle you and I must not engage in physical contact."

"I should think not!" Morgan all but shrieked. "I never wanted to—what did you just say?—'engage in physical contact' with you in the first place!"

Francis impatiently waved a big hand at her. "You haven't the remotest notion what you really want. You want a knight in shining armor to praise your charms with well-measured verse."

Morgan was on her feet, glaring up at Francis. "That's not what I wanted; I wanted Sean O'Connor!"

"You did not *want* Sean O'Connor, you merely wanted to be in love with Sean O'Connor." His tone suddenly turned softer: "Oh, you may well have been in love with him, though I doubt it. Never mind. You are ready to argue that forever, but at this late date, it scarcely matters. What does matter is that you and I have wasted our opportunities until now. Of course, I knew you would not be ready to bed with me right away, but our time together is almost over and soon you will be married to James."

Morgan was so astounded and angry that she could hardly speak. "You're talking rot, Francis Sinclair," she spat out at last. "I want no time with you. I never have!"

"Hmmm." There was a twinkle in the gray eyes, which Morgan could not believe she had actually seen. "I've just taken a too-hasty approach with you before, that's all. You wish to be wooed? Very well, I can woo as well as the next one."

"Don't woo me; don't touch me!" Morgan backed away from him, colliding with a chair.

Francis put his hands on her shoulders, a firm but painless grip. Now he was smiling, that whimsical, satyrlike expression that made him seem strangely guileless. His mouth brushed hers, and then he paused, waiting for her reaction. "What? No clawing, biting, kicking? Have you so lost your spirit that you will not even try to defend your honor?"

"I left my honor in the orchard at Faux Hall—and my heart on the bank of the Thames," Morgan replied faintly. "Have your way. You will, no matter what I do."

Francis searched her face for a long moment. "That isn't what I intended this time."

"Oh. Well, it doesn't matter. Though it ought to matter to you. What will Peg and Polly think?"

He shrugged. "Our servants are as loyal as they are discreet, even—perhaps especially—within the family circle. They are well treated and well imbursed."

Morgan did not reply. Francis continued studying her, his hands still on her shoulders. She knew that he was arguing with himself, trying to calculate whether or not a totally unresponsive female was worth the trouble. She also knew that he would have preferred that she respond with either ardor or anger—but that her inanimate, indifferent attitude must dampen his desire considerably. It was an instinctive reaction on her part and she was suddenly very pleased with her innate sense of what would thwart Francis Sinclair's unwelcome advances.

But she was wrong. Francis pulled her to him again and this time his kiss was hard and demanding. She felt his tongue probing against her teeth, felt his hands move to caress her buttocks, felt the strength of him pressing against her, forcing her backwards toward the bed. Despite her vow to remain unmoved and unresponsive, Morgan struggled in his arms. He was pushing her down, his weight on top of her, his tongue now roving at will inside her mouth, his hands moving to the ties of her blue silk traveling blouse.

"Whoever invented these damnable lacings?" he growled, but there was a humorous undertone in his voice. Clumsily, he undid the ties with one hand while the other pushed the heavy tawny hair from her forehead. Morgan felt her heart beating very rapidly and wondered if she ought to renew her struggles. But he had finished unlacing her blouse and parted the fabric to reveal her full, white breasts. As if by reflex she attempted to shove his hands away; her gesture was futile, and he took a nipple between each thumb and forefinger, grinning at the almost instantaneous rigidity.

"Who do you fight, Morgan?" he inquired with that whimsical grin. "Me—or yourself?"

Morgan's topaz eyes regarded him with confusion, but she refused to answer. He was kissing her again, over and over, while his fingers plied the pink tips which seemed to throb and take fire. Then his mouth covered her right breast, his tongue wreaking new havoc with her senses, while his hands reached down to pull up the skirts of her riding habit. This time he did not rip the undergarment but merely tugged it down over her hips.

"Francis . . ." It was more moan than protest. He undid the fastening of her skirt and pulled that, too, from her body. At last he stopped kissing her breasts and moved his mouth to the triangle of tawny hair between her thighs. And there was the ache again, the yearning, burning sensation which demanded fulfillment. Involuntarily, Morgan reached out and blindly pulled Francis's head even deeper into the cavern of her most intimate self. "Jesu . . ." she gasped as his tongue seared the tender flesh. She writhed with pleasure, arching her back, her fingers all but clawing him.

"I told you . . . you were born to be pleasured, one way or another."

"You're a blackguard," she murmured, and watched with only vague embarrassment as he stood up beside her, taking off his own clothes. And though she flinched slightly when she saw the hard, firm manhood thrust so close to her, she could not resist reaching out to touch him. For one fleeting moment, she glanced up, as if to ask if she had done the right thing.

"Yes, you goose, do what you will. I don't always have everything my way."

To Morgan's astonishment, he bent down and kissed the fingertips that had just caressed him. It was her turn to smile. In fact, she felt almost like laughing for the first time in weeks. Her fingers now moved eagerly along his hardened member, and as he knelt above her, she captured him between her breasts and actually shivered with delight.

He again explored the flesh between her thighs, then fondled her breasts, covering himself with her bosom, and at last she relinquished him so that he might satisfy them both. Together they rocked back and forth on the creaky bed, both gasping, sighing, convulsing with ecstasy. Then the ultimate explosion roared in their ears and made their bodies shudder—and they lay in each other's arms, replete, exhausted, and silent.

Francis spoke first, cradling Morgan against his chest. "You will be quite splendid in bed someday," he declared. "What a shame to waste it all on James."

Morgan pulled away just enough to look up at him. "You make James sound so dreary. Isn't there any attribute you share besides your coloring?"

Francis seemed to consider this question for some time. "We both like to ride," he said at last, and seeing the bemused expression on Morgan's face, burst into the first real guffaw Morgan had ever heard from him. "Oh, Morgan, I don't mean to disparage James. We are just—different."

"Perhaps I should take consolation in that," Morgan said with some asperity. "I don't think I would take well to a philandering husband—as some wives apparently do."

Francis's expression turned grim. "There are things about me you don't understand, Morgan. Nor is there any reason why you should. It's sufficient that Lucy not only understands me, but loves me anyway."

"She must be a saint," Morgan snapped, and then, seeing the very real pain in Francis's gray eyes, diffidently reached out to touch his cheek. "I'm sorry, Francis, I'm just confused. I don't understand myself, you see."

"No. I know you don't." He sighed and gave her a quick hug. "But understanding oneself is part of life's journey. The only problem is, most of us reach the end of life before we achieve the understanding."

Morgan did not respond to this unexpected profundity. She was very tired, not just from the hard day of traveling and the visit to the minster, but from the emotional drain of letting Francis make love to her. She closed her eyes and, with her head against his chest, listened to the beat of his heart and the steady breathing. "Making love" seemed an inappropriate term as far as she and Francis were concerned; their encounters were more like those of Bess and the Madden twins, mere animal mating, with no ties of affection or commitment. Not only did she not love Francis, she wasn't even sure she liked him very well. In fact, most of the time she was convinced she hated the man. But why did she find such pleasure in his arms? Yes, she finally had to admit to herself that it was pleasure she had experienced, at least this time when he wasn't treating her like a slut. Perhaps it was just a natural response which any man could arouse. If so, then she would be equally pleasured by James and maybe their marriage would not be so miserable after all. Grandmother Isabeau had told Morgan she might not know love when she found it; Morgan had been certain she loved Sean, yet he had aroused no great physical desire within her. But Richard Griffin had, and she knew she didn't love him. He was charming, he was likable, he was experienced in the ways of making a woman want him; but if she never saw Richard again—especially after his callous behavior on the banks of the river—Morgan wouldn't care one whit.

Perplexed and exhausted, Morgan snuggled even closer to Francis and felt drowsy. But Francis was not yet asleep. "We will have to behave very carefully at Belford, you know," he said in a deep, low voice. "It will not be as easy as you may think."

Morgan was about to ask him why not—and then it occurred to her that perhaps she didn't want to know the answer. So she merely said, "Of course," and fell into a deep, dreamless sleep.

On the road to Newcastle the following day, Morgan and Francis were both very quiet. That evening they supped in their separate rooms after exchanging polite but brief good-nights.

The following morning, on the last day of their journey, Morgan began to feel an overpowering sense of depression come upon her. How far she was from Faux Hall, how long ago her life at court seemed, how dim Sean's freckled face already had grown in her memory! Could he really be dead and she on her way to her marriage ceremony? Nothing seemed quite real, and the unfamiliar terrain only contributed to the strange atmosphere in which she was riding. More like a nightmare, she told herself, gazing hostilely at the rolling banks of sand and scrubby clumps of heather. This was not at all like the soft, lush green farm country she had known since her birth; it was desolate, lonely land with only an occasional shepherd's hut giving evidence of human habitation.

At last she glimpsed the sea in the distance. Would Belford itself be like this? she wondered. "The North" had always sounded faintly forbidding, but she knew little about it except that these borderlands were famous for raids between English and Scot. She shivered as the wind picked up, blowing sand in her eyes. This was a wild land, as foreign as China or Peru. No wonder the people who dwelled here were said to be wild, too, wild and stormy like Francis Sinclair himself. Yet, Morgan told herself, Francis also seemed vaguely indolent and occasionally even kind. As for James, he had been despairingly formal.

She sighed unhappily, flicking at her gelding's reins. Her mount was growing as weary as its rider, yet the day was not half-done. Morgan patted the horse's neck, then looked up to see an old dead tree standing by the road ahead of them with a form dangling from its withered branches.

"Dear God!" she cried. "What's that?"

Francis looked at her over his shoulder, a vaguely amused expression on his face. "Oh, some miscreant. Our

Warden of the Marches deals out justice swiftly in these parts."

Morgan kept her eyes averted until they had passed the tree and its gruesome burden. But when they stopped to eat their noon meal at Alnwick, she could barely touch her food.

"A pity we can't linger here for a bit," Francis said, stuffing a piece of rye bread into his mouth. "This is the seat of the Percys of Northumberland, and Alnwick Castle is most interesting."

Morgan said nothing, but kept her eyes fixed on her plate. But Francis ignored her silence and went on talking, now about the many wondrous mineral springs and wells in the vicinity.

After they started out again, the wind began to blow even more gustily, sending gray clouds tumbling across the sky. The sea could be seen almost constantly now. Morgan wanted to ask Francis if Belford Castle was on the coast, but for some inexplicable reason she could not bring herself to speak to him.

Late in the afternoon they passed the road that turned east to Bamburgh. Just beyond the crossroads Morgan sighted some strange, shaggy animals clustered in a small patch of grass. They were large, white, and ugly. Morgan's horse shied and she gripped the reins hard.

"What are those?" she called out, unable to keep silent.

Francis turned and grinned at her. "Wild cows. They're descendants of the ancient wild ox. If you touch a calf, the rest of the herd will kill it."

Morgan shuddered. Even the cows were wild in this strange land. But the animals paid no heed to the travelers and continued to graze on the coarse grass beside the road.

An hour later they arrived in the town of Belford, which seemed to Morgan a forlorn little place, gray and dreary in the pale light of early evening. Most of the inhabitants were fishermen and tradesmen, and there were several inns, kept busy by travelers on the Great North Road. As the little group rode through the main street, men doffed their caps and women made curtseys to Francis. Although some of the townsfolk eyed Morgan with curiosity, none of them smiled or waved a greeting.

Outside of Belford, the road sloped gradually upward until Morgan at last saw a castle keep outlined against the darkening sky. Soon the castle itself came into view, perched atop a crag overlooking the sea. Trees grew along the outer confines of the castle, and even in the twilight Morgan recognized the blossoms of apple and cherry. Somehow, the thought of the fruit trees, daring to flourish in this unencouraging ground, lifted her spirits slightly.

They were approaching the drawbridge, which was set off on each side by big round towers. Francis shouted over his shoulder into the wind: "Parts of the keep date back to Roman times." He grappled with his cloak to keep it from flying into his face. "It was one of the prime coastal fortifications—for the Normans, too."

A fortress, thought Morgan, that's what it looks like, fruit trees or no. She took a deep breath as they clattered across the bridge and into the courtyard. Francis dismounted quickly, his eyes scanning the castle entrances.

"Where in God's name is everyone?" he yelled. "What kind of welcome is this for the bride of Belford?"

"Maybe," Morgan said dryly, "they're no happier to have me than I am to be here."

Francis shot her a reproving look. Two servants came through the main door, hurrying toward them. To Francis's astonishment, they both fell on their knees at his feet.

"Master Francis!" cried Malcolm, the older of the two. "Thank the good Lord you've come!"

Francis lifted them both up, but his hands froze on their arms when he saw the mourning bands. "Jesu! What's happened?"

Again the older servant spoke, the words tumbling out. "Your father, the good Earl. Last Sunday . . . he was going riding . . . he seemed quite fit and came out here into the courtyard . . . just about where you're standing, Master Francis . . . and he fell to the ground. He was dead before the Countess could be brought to him."

Francis's hand clutched at his forehead; he turned away from the little group. Morgan watched him stumble toward the far end of the courtyard, his big shoulders slumped. Pity touched her, and she turned away just as two women came out of the castle. The younger one, a tall brunette, was obviously Francis's wife. The other, short and gray-haired, apparently was the Countess. Both wore mourning and both were pale and sad-eyed.

Morgan got down from her horse without help. She

curtsied to the Countess, not knowing exactly what to say. "My lady, I'm so sorry about your loss . . ."

The Countess motioned for her to rise. "God's will," the older woman said simply, with surprising strength in her voice. "It is most unfortunate that your introduction to Belford should come at this sad time." Her long, blue-veined hand beckoned to the dark-haired girl. "Mistress Todd, this is Francis's wife, Lucy."

To Morgan's astonishment, Lucy Sinclair rushed forward and embraced her future sister-in-law warmly. "I'm so glad you've come. Perhaps you can bring some joy to assuage our sorrow."

Morgan winced inwardly, the sudden memory of Francis Sinclair's passion coming back to her. His wife was some five or six years older than Morgan and would have been pretty if her face hadn't been so drawn by grief. Lucy's eyes were following her husband, who still stood alone at the end of the courtyard. Apparently, thought Morgan, she knows better than to intrude upon him at a moment like this.

The Countess was speaking again, her voice strong: "James is in the town. A pity he didn't see you ride through, but he'll return shortly. He's had so much to do since his father died. Of course, he and Francis will discuss the wedding plans at once. The decision is in their hands."

Morgan's eyebrows rose almost imperceptibly. A few months ago, even weeks ago, she would have asserted angrily that it was her future, too. But now she only nodded and drew her cloak more closely around her to keep out the chilling wind. She saw Lucy watching Francis, and as he turned to face the others, his wife picked up her skirts and ran toward him, almost falling into his arms. Morgan turned away from them; it was a very awkward moment.

"You missed something in not knowing my husband," the Countess was saying. "He was a good, wise man. You would have benefited from the acquaintance."

"Yes," said Morgan, trying to keep the sudden weariness she felt out of her voice. "I'm sure I would."

James Sinclair, the new Earl of Belford, returned to the castle just before supper. Morgan didn't see him until she entered the family dining room, a small but comfortable area off the kitchen. His greeting was polite, and the only change in his appearance was the new sadness around his eyes. No mention of the marriage was made during supper and Morgan exchanged only a few words with James throughout the entire meal. The family conversation centered upon the late Earl: James explained to Francis that they wished he could have been at Belford for the funeral but they weren't sure when he'd arrive so the services had been held two days before. Francis had nodded abruptly and looked away. A short time later, Morgan saw him striding toward the chapel.

After supper, Lucy accompanied Morgan to the room that had been readied for her arrival. It was small but well furnished. Indeed, the interior of the castle belied the exterior. From what Morgan had observed so far, there was a handsome gallery, a large banquet room, and, of course, the comfortable dining room. A terrace ran along the east end of the castle, giving a magnificent view of the sea. It was in this direction that Morgan's room faced, though the terrace was a floor below her.

"Is everything all right?" Lucy inquired. She was already at the windows, making sure they could be opened.

Morgan replied that all was quite satisfactory. She noted that the servingwomen had unpacked her belongings while she'd been at supper.

"You may think it a bit dreary here at first," Lucy went on, as she gave a push at the third and last window, "but in the summer, especially, it's very pleasant. There's riding and hunting and trips to Berwick—that's where my family is. I keep busy with the children. I suppose Francis told you we have a boy and a girl and"—she smiled, looking younger and prettier than she had so far—"we'll have another child in the fall."

Morgan avoided the other girl's eyes and smoothed her skirts with a nervous gesture, but Lucy didn't seem to notice and continued talking. "The Countess isn't Francis and James's mother, you know. The first Countess was a Percy. She died when Francis was nine and James eleven. Two years later, the Earl married Elizabeth Armstrong from Bamburgh. Her first husband was killed long ago at Flodden Field. He left her childless. She's really very kind. I'm so sad for her now, for she loved the Earl, though she tries to keep her grief to herself."

Morgan nodded sympathetically, thinking that Lucy

seemed to need someone to talk to. She realized Lucy might be a good friend and companion, but the image of Francis kept cropping up to make Morgan feel guilt-ridden and embarrassed.

Lucy talked on about the countryside, about her children, about her relatives in Berwick. She recalled a trip to Edinburgh she'd made with her parents when she was sixteen. She asked Morgan about London, for Lucy herself had never been beyond Woodstock. At last she rose, saying she knew Morgan must be tired from her long journey.

"You'll grow fond of James, Morgan," she said gently, as she stood by the door. "He's quiet but he's kind—more like the Earl than Francis is. I suppose that's why their father favored James . . ." Her voice trailed off. She smiled then and said, "Rest well. The sea will lull you to sleep."

It was decided by the Sinclair brothers that the wedding should take place without delay. Because of the too-recent bereavement, the service would be held in the castle chapel, with only the family and servants in attendance.

On a sunny Tuesday morning a week after Morgan had arrived at the castle, she was wed to James Sinclair, sixth Earl of Belford. A small but elegant wedding feast was laid out in the banquet room and a few neighboring families paid their respects. Some of the townspeople came up to the castle and James saw that food and ale were dispensed.

Morgan scarcely remembered the ceremony at all. It had been conducted by a clergyman of the new faith, of course, but his name and face were already a blur. The chapel was small and dark, for the narrow windows let in only slits of sunlight, and the candles on the altar gave little illumination.

The banquet droned on into the late afternoon. About four o'clock one of the servants came to James and said the townspeople wished to see the bridal couple. They also wanted to dance outside the castle—would permission be granted? James considered both requests for a full minute. Yes, he told the servingman, he and his new Countess would appear on the west balcony. And there could be dancing, as long as there was no drunkenness or unseemly behavior. James had confidence in the villagers' decorum for they had respected and, in some cases, had loved his father. Morgan realized now that their indifferent attitude upon her arrival had been caused not by lack of interest but by their sorrow over the Earl's death.

Half an hour later James led Morgan through the gallery and onto the balcony overlooking the main entrance to the castle. The townsfolk sent up a cheer at the sight of their young lord and his tawny-haired bride. The accolade brought a little thrill to Morgan's spine; she had her first taste of what it meant to be a Countess. She smiled widely and waved at the people below as they cheered more loudly. Impulsively, Morgan removed the lace and silk handkerchief from her sleeve, tossing it to the crowd. Several younger women tussled after the prize and a buxom redhead emerged victorious, waving her trophy in the evening breeze. The crowd cheered lustily again.

The hint of a smile on his lips, James took his bride's arm and steered her back inside the castle. "You've won their hearts," he told her.

Morgan shrugged and avoided his eyes. "Little enough—the lace tickled my nose," she said to conceal her embarrassment at his words of praise.

Back in the banquet hall there was another round of toasts, led by Francis. Although he had drunk more than anyone, he still seemed in control. He appeared to be having a fine time, making frequent jests about finally getting his older brother married off.

At last the wedding guests escorted the bridal couple to their nuptial chamber. Morgan was grateful that James had been most emphatic about allowing the guests only as far as the door—the old custom of actually putting the newlyweds to bed had always been repugnant to her.

When at last they were alone, James offered to leave the bedchamber while Morgan's servingwomen undressed her. She agreed, and when he was gone, a sudden tremor overtook her. She could hardly stand up while Polly and Peg helped her out of the white satin gown and the lace underskirts.

"Never saw a bride who wasn't fair fit to swoon on her wedding night," Polly clucked reprovingly. "An hour or so from now you'll think you were crazy to be so wrought up."

Morgan was too nervous to reprimand Polly, and she wondered if Polly knew what had happened with Francis at York. But if the servingwoman had guessed the truth, she obviously was going to ignore it. So Morgan concentrated instead on trying to keep her limbs from shaking as she settled into a chair while Peg brushed her long hair.

Morgan leaned forward to catch her reflection in the mirror. Were those the eyes that had looked so lovingly at Sean O'Connor? Were those the lips that had touched his? Were those the arms that had held him so close? And was it only weeks ago that Sean was alive and by her side? She shook her head so violently that she almost knocked the hairbrush from Peg's hand.

"I'm sorry," Morgan apologized quickly, and tried to still the images of her mind's eye.

After the servingwomen had gone, Morgan lay naked between the cool sheets, her trembling somewhat abated. Outside she could hear the sea. The room was almost dark except for a fluttering taper on James's side of the bed. Then the antechamber door opened and James stepped inside.

"You must be very tired," he said, his hands stuffed far into the pockets of his night-robe.

Morgan sat up, keeping the sheet high around her neck. "Yes, I am," she answered.

James walked around the room, pausing to glance out at the sea, to adjust the drapes, to check the contents of the washbasin on the nightstand. "See here," he said, clearing his throat in the same nervous way Morgan had remembered from the day they had signed their prenuptial contract, "if you'd rather wait until tomorrow night when you are more rested . . ."

Morgan suddenly realized that he was as frightened as she. Moreover, it occurred to her that he must still be ridden with grief from losing his father. She felt pity, if not affection, overcoming her. "Waiting would only make me more nervous," she admitted. "But if you'd rather just talk for a bit—we've still not had much chance to get acquainted. Here," she said, smoothing the counterpane next to her, "why don't you sit?"

Hesitantly, he did so, but his slender frame still seemed tense. There was another long pause before he spoke again. "You must find Belford very different from Faux Hall," he said at last.

"Oh, yes—but I'm sure I'll get used to the changes. Francis tells me there is much to see nearby, even miraculous mineral springs. We have nothing like that around the Chiltern Hills."

"Some are credited with miracles," James replied, "though I don't know that I believe it myself. What's more important and beneficial is the coal which comes from the rich veins around Newcastle. We own some of the mining lands, and our coal is even sold in London—and at a much higher price than locally."

Morgan bit her lip to keep from smiling. Talking about springs and coal on her wedding night! It seemed absurdly comic, so unlike the rhapsodic, romantic accounts she'd heard ladies whisper about at court.

James sensed her amusement and flushed. "You find my conversation humorous?"

On impulse, she reached out and touched his hand. "No, no. It's just that I'm a trifle . . . giddy after everything that happened today. Please forgive me."

He took her hand in his and studied it for a long time. "Might it not be, too, that you find it disconcerting that I'm not the eager bridegroom?"

"Oh, no!" Morgan exclaimed, all amusement fleeing as she recognized the genuine distress on his face. "I know how you feel about me, that you wish I were someone else."

He released her hand and looked directly at her for the first time since he had come into the room. "It's not just that," he said with difficulty. "I've never had a woman before."

"You should be proud, not ashamed," she admonished. "So many men pride themselves on their conquests; they think any woman would tumble willingly into bed with them." She looked away, quickly regretting having spoken so freely, and unable to blot out the image of Francis and his importunate lovemaking. It was clear that talk was not going to bring them any closer at the moment, that she herself would have to take the initiative. Deliberately, she let the sheet fall to her waist.

But James, staring at the flickering taper, seemed not to have noticed. He looked quite miserable and very young.

"James," she said quietly, "do you want me to take a chill?"

He looked at her then and flushed very dark. Morgan held out her arms to him as he moved slowly toward her.

His kiss was tentative; the arms that held her seemed stiff. Morgan forced herself to press against him, trying to rub her naked breasts against his chest. James glanced down to the lush flesh which glowed like rich cream in the candlelight. Experimentally he touched each breast in turn and, as if more embarrassed by his actions than aroused, buried his lips against her throat.

Morgan held him tight, running her fingers through his fair hair, attempting to wrap her legs around his hips. His arms encircled her waist, and his mouth moved down to the hollow between her breasts. She fell back among the pillows, spreading her legs in the hope that he would become more impassioned; but James paused and looked up into the topaz eyes.

"I think we are both too weary, Morgan," he said stiffly, but the misery of his gaze betrayed him. "We'll wait until tomorrow night."

Morgan suppressed a sigh. Although she had felt no response to him thus far, postponement might make it more difficult for them both. Besides, she was anxious to get the consummation over with; despite her bridegroom's inexperience, she was still afraid he might realize she was not a virgin.

But she meekly agreed, and watched James blow out the single taper by the bed. He lay down beside her, keeping his distance in the big bed and leaving his dressing gown on. Morgan heard him say, "Good night," replied in kind, and tried to go to sleep. But her body remained tense and her mind alert. She honestly could not fault James, unschooled in lovemaking and burdened with sorrow as he must be. Still, Morgan was disconcerted by his apparent lack of fervor, and when she did sleep, she dreamed of Francis and the ferocity of his passion—and the pleasure he had given her.

The next night was no different, however: James had complained all day of an upset stomach, a result of the rich food at the wedding banquet.

On the third night, Morgan demurred. She had not felt well herself most of the day, and the following morning she retched several times, causing James to display what appeared to be genuine concern.

"It's nothing," she insisted after Polly had taken the basin away. "Often, when I was younger, my stomach would become unsettled if I got too nervous. I'm sure the trip north and the shock of your father's death—even though I didn't know him—and then the haste of the wedding all distressed me more than I realized." She did not add that Sean's death had disturbed her far more than the other events combined.

That night James did not attempt to make love to Morgan, asserting that he wanted to be certain she was completely well. Morgan started to protest, thought better of it, resigned herself to sleeping side by side with her husband while still not touching one another, and wondered if James ever really intended to consummate their union.

But the next morning, Morgan was ill again. James had already left to make his rounds of the tenant farms, and only Polly knew of her mistress's poor health.

"It must be something in the food here," Morgan declared vexedly as she finally fell back onto the bed after retching for the sixth time. "Are there local herbs or crops I might not be accustomed to?"

For some reason, Polly's ruddy cheeks grew even more flushed. "That might be," she replied, but there was a lack of conviction in her tone.

Morgan dozed for a while after Polly left, but was soon jarred into consciousness by a loud rap on the door. Before she could ask who was there, Francis loped into the room, a deep frown etched between his bushy brows. "Polly tells me you are unwell," he said without preamble. It was the first time they had spoken since Morgan's wedding day; Francis had been away from the castle most of the time, in Newcastle, Lucy had said.

"Something here at Belford doesn't agree with me," Morgan asserted crossly, pulling up the counterpane to cover her bare shoulders.

"Hmmm." Francis paced the room in silence, glancing occasionally out toward the North Sea. At last he came to the bed and sat down, the frown still creasing his forehead. "Morgan, I could be wrong, but I think you're pregnant."

The topaz eyes widened as one hand flew to Morgan's mouth in shocked dismay. "No! I can't be!"

"Oh, but you can—probably from the night of the masque." The frown slowly faded as he drummed his fingers on the counterpane. "I'd say you are probably almost two months along. If you carry the child to term, James will not be particularly suspicious. He himself was almost six weeks premature."

Morgan lay back among the pillows, too upset to care that the counterpane had slipped down to her waist and that her bosom was clearly outlined in the thin bedgown. "Oh, sweet Mother of God!" She rubbed her fist against her forehead, as if she could blot out the dilemma which faced her. And then she sat up straight, clutching Francis's arm. "It's—it's worse than you think, Francis! James hasn't yet bedded me!"

It was Francis's turn to look astounded. "Oh, good God!" he groaned—and then laughed and shook his head in incredulity. "Even James could hardly resist you!" But seeing the horrified expression on Morgan's face, he sobered at once and clumsily patted the hand that still clung to his arm. "Well, it's been less than a week since you wed. I suggest you do your best to seduce him tonight."

"He won't touch me if he finds out I've been ill again," Morgan all but wailed.

"Don't tell him. Polly won't," he added, and Morgan suddenly realized that Polly knew a great deal more than she ever told—except to Francis.

"I'll try to—arouse him," Morgan said wearily, and again slumped back into the pillows. "Francis, he doesn't want me, I'm sure of it."

"He's mad," Francis stated in his deep growl, and suddenly looked very stormy. Abruptly, he got up from the bed and started for the door. "Good luck," he called over his shoulder in a terse voice. "I fear you'll need it." Before Morgan could respond, he had banged the heavy oak door behind him.

James was more talkative than usual that evening as he prepared for bed: The crops had been especially good this spring, despite generally poor weather throughout the rest of England. Part of the reason for his tenants' success, he told Morgan diffidently, was some of the innovations he had implemented the previous fall. "It seemed to me that if one crop didn't do well in certain soil, another might," he explained as he snuffed out the candles on the bureau. "Consequently, I suggested to my farmers that they try something new when they planted. Oh, some were reluctant, but most agreed, and I daresay the idea has worked well."

"That was very clever of you, James," Morgan said as he eased into bed beside her. He still wore his dressing gown and she had yet to see him naked.

"It just made sense," he went on, blowing out the last taper by the bed. "The ground here is quite sandy, yet I'd noticed that vegetable marrows and beans and even corn seemed to thrive, while wheat did not. At least when it was planted close to the sea."

In the darkness, Morgan couldn't help but roll her eyes. Miraculous springs, coal mining, and crop harvests seemed to be James's favorite topics for nocturnal conversation. Morgan took a deep, silent breath and rolled over to snuggle against her husband. "You must plant seeds of your own, James," she murmured, and grabbed at his hand, moving it to her breast. "We have our duty, after all, to ensure that Belford's prosperity continues through your sons."

James had gone quite rigid at the intimate contact. He said nothing for a long moment and Morgan was certain that he was debating with himself between the necessity of propagating heirs for his beloved land and the apparent repugnance—or fear—he had of attempting to beget them.

"Well, Morgan," he began rather formally, "I have not wished to appear unwilling to seal our union in the—the physical sense." He paused to clear his throat rather loudly. "But circumstances have dictated that we put off doing so, and perhaps, since it is quite late and I've had a tiring day, we might wait until tomorrow night."

Morgan hesitated and then decided that a direct attack was her best weapon. "You don't want me!" she cried, darting away from him. "You find me uncomely! You admitted you'd rather not wed me! I shall write to my uncle tomorrow and ask for an annulment!"

Again James did not reply at once, and it occurred to Morgan that her threat actually sounded like a blessed way out for both of them. And then she realized that Francis was probably right about her condition; a pregnant bride could hardly get an annulment on grounds of an unconsummated marriage.

But James was already attempting to put an arm

around her. "Please, Morgan, I don't find you uncomely at all. You are—very, um, lovely."

"I'm not lovely!" Morgan was trying to work up real tears but without success. She pounded the pillow with her fists and tried to gulp convincingly.

"Well, perhaps 'lovely' isn't quite the right word," James conceded, trying to haul Morgan closer to him. "But I'm well pleased with your appearance, it's just that . . ." His voice trailed off and Morgan finally managed to squeeze out a genuine teardrop. She put her face against his cheek to make certain he knew she was crying, and her arms went around him in a clinging embrace.

"You must show me then, James," she declared in a trembling voice. "If you don't, I'll die of despair!"

Morgan felt perhaps she had overstepped his credulity, but James actually began to kiss her ear, her throat, and the curve of her shoulder. "Poor wife," he said sadly, "I hadn't intended to shirk my duty."

Duty! thought Morgan, and clamped her mouth shut tight lest she make an angry retort. But James was awkwardly fumbling at her breasts, trying to free them from the bedgown. Morgan helped him, then reached for the ties of his dressing gown and pulled the garment from his narrow shoulders. She could see only his silhouette in the darkness, but he seemed fit, if slim in stature. James's hands now seemed more eager as he plied her nipples and paused to kiss her lips. But Morgan felt no particular sensation from his touch except that her breasts were quite sore already, and it dawned on her that this was the result of her pregnancy.

He was now kissing her again, over and over, with more intensity, and his hands hesitantly touched her buttocks, then moved back to her waist. Growing impatient, not for satisfaction but to be done with what Morgan was beginning to find tiring if not downright dull, she gritted her teeth and forced herself to reach between her husband's legs. James's manhood had not yet grown very firm—certainly not like Francis, Morgan thought, and mentally reviled herself for making such comparisons. Uncertainly but with determination, she began to stroke him with her fingers and was surprised when he let out a series of low moans. At last she lay back and opened her thighs, guiding him with her hands. It was difficult, despite James's newly found eagerness, and Morgan was astonished to discover that she didn't have to pretend the pain when he finally penetrated her body. His inexperience had served her well.

But they seemed to be locked together for an eternity, rocking back and forth until Morgan actually became dizzy and feared she might retch again. Just before she was certain she would be ill, James erupted within her and let out a great groan of satisfaction. Morgan lay very still beneath him, exhausted but triumphant. And, she suddenly realized, unmoved. Not only had she received no pleasure from James's lovemaking, she had not even been aware of desiring fulfillment. As he withdrew from her and murmured something Morgan didn't hear, real tears began to trickle down her cheeks. Oh, dear God, she thought, as James held her in his arms and bade her a drowsy good-night, why couldn't he have been his brother?

If James ever wondered how his innocent bride was so adept at arousing him and had gone about it so boldly, he never let on. Morgan was puzzled by this at first, but it occurred to her after a few days that in his pride at finally having taken possession of a woman, he was far less concerned about how she had behaved than how he had performed. And her pained reaction had told him all he needed to know about her virginity. Morgan blessed all the saints, fates, and whomever else she could think of that James was not only inexperienced but self-absorbed as well.

Yet in the weeks that followed, his demands upon her body were not frequent; he made love to her every four or five nights, and though he became somewhat more imaginative in the exploration of his bride, he did not seem to notice that she was less responsive than she might have been.

If Morgan had to force herself to let James touch her, she also had to be fair. She now felt queasy a great deal of the time and it was a strain on her nerves to conceal the bouts of nausea from her husband. Wordlessly, Polly conspired to help Morgan with her deception. Virtually every morning the servingwoman would rouse them early, and as James preferred to begin his daily rounds as soon as possible, he was always gone before Morgan had to cry out for the basin.

Her first private conversation with the Dowager Countess had gone well, however, and that exchange was one of the brighter sides of Morgan's new life thus far. The older woman confided that she was not in good health and that her husband's death had made her less inclined than ever to play out her role as chatelaine.

"In truth," she had said, with a wan smile, "I'm relieved that you are here. Lucy is wonderful with our people, but her pregnancies are quite difficult and before long she will be able to do very little. So it's a blessing that you can act in my stead and hers as well."

Morgan had been pleased at the Dowager Countess's kindly words, though she wondered how long she herself would be able to keep up any heavy burden of responsibilities. Still, she would do her best, and began by visiting each tenant farmer and his family, nervously making conversation at first, then growing more at ease as she discovered the men and women of Belford had more in common with their Countess than she had expected.

"I never really *talked* to our people at Faux Hall," she confessed to Lucy one late-June afternoon as they sat out on the terrace, watching the tide come in to completely cut off the Holy Isle and its abandoned monastery. "I'd greet them and exchange a few words, but even though I had known most of our people since I was a child, I never really learned what they were like."

Lucy reached down to pat the mastiff, who had been roused from his nap by a pesky bee. "They are not so different, really," Lucy remarked with her gentle smile. "They have their happy times and their sorrows, just as we do. They love and they hate, they beget children and live and die." She paused, staring out at the breakers. "We are, after all, human beings, each with his or her own weaknesses and virtues."

Morgan was about to remark that she could not imagine Lucy having any weaknesses or ever hating anyone, but saw her sister-in-law suddenly give a start, put her hand to her curving abdomen, and look at Morgan with an expression of surprised delight. "Oh," she cried, "I felt the baby move! It's the first time!"

"How wonderful!" exclaimed Morgan, and she wondered why the words sounded so hollow. Her own nausea had lessened, and so far she had not begun to show except for a general ripening of her body. But she actually felt vaguely ill at the thought of both her and Lucy carrying Francis's babes. Indeed, she had avoided Lucy the last few weeks, since the other woman could talk of little but her expected child and the conversations overwhelmed Morgan with guilt. Luckily, she had managed to keep away from Francis almost entirely, since he was gone a great deal, sometimes with James, but more often alone.

Yet it was Francis who now came through the open terrace doors, his son and daughter at his side. Morgan still found the sight of the arrogant giant of a man with his two small children quite incongruous, but he appeared to be an extremely patient and even indulgent father. "We've just come from the village," he announced, kissing Lucy's cheek and nodding abruptly to Morgan. "Mary wants a certain necklace for her birthday and Geoffrey got into a squabble with the smithy's son."

"Why, he's twice Geoffrey's age!" Lucy cried, but seeing that her son bore no visible signs of being mishandled, she glanced up at her husband. "Who won?"

"*I* did," said Francis with a grin, patting the boy's fair head. "They're both a pair of scamps."

"Francis, guess what?" Lucy got to her feet and put a hand on her husband's shoulder. Her hazel eyes glowed as she looked up into his face, and Morgan averted her gaze, watching Mary pull the mastiff's ears. "I just felt life! Perhaps the baby will come sooner than we thought!"

Francis ruffled her brown hair and bestowed an affectionate smile on his wife. "I'm pleased. But you know what that means, wife. You must rest more or Dr. Wimble will start his lectures."

"Oh, I will, I will. In fact, I think I'll go lie down now. It's warm out here in spite of the breeze, and the children should nap, too." Lucy picked up her sewing basket and told the children to follow her back into the castle. Mary balked, but a single word from her father sent her trudging behind her mother and brother. The mastiff seemed to sigh with relief as he settled back down to sleep in peace.

Francis stood by the railing of the terrace, his gaze apparently transfixed by the Holy Isle. "There are relics of St. Aidan and St. Cuthbert there, you know," he said at last, turning to face Morgan, who was trying to concentrate on her volume of French sonnets. "At one time the island was actually connected to the mainland."

"Yes. James told me." She cleared her throat and had to squint at Francis for the sun was very bright. "He said we would go there some fine day when the tide was low enough to walk."

"It's still very damp going," said Francis. "You'd best wear boots." Neither spoke for several moments, Morgan fidgeting with the thin gold chain she wore at her waist, Francis examining one of the two stone lions which guarded the terrace doors. "You are feeling better now?" he asked at last.

"A bit." Morgan still avoided his gaze.

"You will have to tell James soon," he said, moving to stand by her chair.

"Yes. Another fortnight, I should think." Suddenly her composure broke, and all the tension of the past few weeks seemed to explode at once. "Oh, Francis," she gasped, trying to keep her voice low, "he'll know! If the baby comes in December and I'm already showing in a few weeks, he can't help but realize the truth!"

Francis stood with his hands clasped behind his back, his sandy brows drawn together. "No—I told you, he himself was premature. He'll be so delighted to have produced an heir to Belford, he won't be able to think of more than his own virility."

But Morgan was not appeased. It was well and good for Francis to be so certain of his brother's reaction; he would not have to bear the brunt of James's wrath should the ruse fail. "I'm frightened," she said in a voice that verged on tears. "It's terrifying enough to bear a babe, but to carry the burden of deceit along with the child . . ." She broke off, too distraught to continue.

"Oh, paugh," snorted Francis. "You wouldn't have thought twice about deceiving my family by dallying with the King or marrying Sean O'Connor instead. You would gladly have hoodwinked Henry Tudor, Thomas Cromwell, and half of England to have your way. Now quit whimpering about what is essentially a trivial matter."

"Trivial!" Morgan leapt to her feet, all but shouted, and clamped her mouth shut tight lest someone overhear her. "You're not the one having this baby! Or Lucy's! What do you do, just lope about, getting women pregnant?"

Francis's attempt at looking puzzled did not faze Morgan, and before he could reply, she spoke again in anger though in whispered tones: "Perhaps you intended this all along. Perhaps you are sure I'll bear a boy and your son will inherit Belford!"

Francis froze; the gray eyes turned chilly as the North Sea itself. For one instant, Morgan thought he would strike her, but the hand he had half raised dropped stiffly to his side. "You fool," he growled, and turned on his heel to stride rapidly down the terrace toward the path which led to the sea.

The fair weather of June changed abruptly the first week of July. James had taken Morgan on an extensive tour of the Sinclair lands, pointing with pride to the fields of rye, beans, and farther inland, wheat. Great flocks of geese roamed among the crops, pecking for insects and growing fat for the markets of Alnwick.

But in the late afternoon, as they returned to the castle through the village, rain began to pelt down from a glowering gray sky. Morgan thought perhaps they would spend a cozy hour by the fire and she could tell him about the babe at last. But James had gone directly to make his rounds of the castle and she did not see him again until evening. Even then, he was still hard at work.

James had opened the ledger and set it down on the dressing table. "I'm perplexed over the amount we spent on casks this spring. The cooper is an honest man, yet the dozen we purchased for the new wine come to at least one-sixth more than we paid last year."

In her role as wife and Countess, Morgan had tried very hard to take an interest in all matters pertaining to Belford and the Sinclair properties. However, it was often an effort to exude enthusiasm over details that bored her. "How many did you purchase last year?" she asked patiently.

"Only six," James answered, frowning down at the precisely written figures. "But based upon that number and the price then as opposed to what we paid this time, there's definitely an increase of two shillings per cask."

Morgan vainly tried to think of some plausible explanation, failed, and climbed into bed. James continued to mull over the columns until his face suddenly lit up. "I remember! Francis suggested that the cooper use a new type of stave, which was more expensive. I'd forgotten. I suppose it was because the casks were delivered about the time my father died."

"No doubt," Morgan remarked, hoping she didn't sound sarcastic; since the Earl had passed on while James was awaiting his new bride, it occurred to Morgan that her husband just might have been equally distracted by that event as well.

James closed the ledger and smiled with satisfaction. "That's a great relief," he declared, snuffing out the candles and coming to join Morgan in bed. "It's very trying work to keep the accounts straight, but fortunately my father made certain I knew how from the time I was sixteen."

"How wise of him," Morgan murmured against her husband's shoulder. "James, I'm going to have a baby."

James neither moved nor spoke for some time. At last, he took Morgan's hand and squeezed it gently. "I'm—very glad, Morgan," he declared. "Our efforts have been rewarded."

Morgan was glad that the stormy night made the bedchamber so dark that James could not see the resentful expression which crossed her face. She held her tongue for a few moments, lest she say something tactless, even angry. Efforts, indeed! She had thought that at least he seemed to enjoy making love to her, even if she found no fulfillment in his embrace.

"The child will probably arrive early in the new year," she finally said, hoping the statement would be sufficiently ambiguous.

"Dr. Wimble must visit you at once," James said, suddenly sounding very businesslike. "He's very competent and has taken excellent care of Lucy, despite her delicacy. I would think, in fact, that we ought to follow Lucy and Francis's example and refrain from, uh, our conjugal duties until after the child is born."

Morgan's eyes widened in the darkness. To be honest, she didn't really care if James ever laid a hand on her again. But his decision had enlightened her about several things: James did not desire her so much as he wanted an heir; Lucy's health was apparently more fragile than Morgan realized; and Francis's enforced abstinence might explain his adulterous conduct. But it didn't excuse him, she thought savagely, feeling far more sorry for Lucy than for Francis. But most of all, as the rain pummeled the windowpanes and James bade her a rather formal good-night, Morgan felt sorry for herself.

Chapter 9

THE PROMISE of a fine harvest was dimmed considerably by the relentless rains. Both James and Francis cursed the foul weather and bemoaned the probable failure while trying to buoy up their tenants' drooping spirits. It was a miserable summer for Morgan, pent up in the castle, drawing comfort only from her visits with the Dowager Countess and Lucy and occasional romps with the children. But her depression plunged into despair when she received a letter from Faux Hall informing her that Sir Thomas More and Bishop Fisher had both been executed. "Sir Thomas went bravely to his death," Sir Edmund wrote, "making jests all the way. His head was placed on London Bridge, but his poor daughter, Meg, came in the night to take it away and bury it decently."

Morgan had cried for an hour when she learned this terrible news; she cried not just for Sir Thomas More, but for Sean and Bishop Fisher—and for herself. While they ate their noonday meal, she told James what had happened, but he merely shook his head.

"It was most unwise of More and Fisher to blatantly defy their King. Fisher was old, of course, but More could have given many more years of great service to this realm."

Morgan was too appalled to reply; while she had mixed feelings about the religious controversy which had taken Sean's life, she could not understand her husband's cold, practical view of More's martyrdom. She was still wrought up later in the day, and on impulse, sought out Francis in his library.

She had only been inside the little room once, when Lucy had taken her through the castle the day after Morgan had arrived at Belford. Every available space was taken up with books, and while Francis might be untidy about other things, he seemed to maintain a certain order where his reading materials were concerned.

The gray eyes looked up in surprise when Morgan entered the room. Except in the presence of others, they had not spoken since that afternoon on the terrace in June. "Well?" was Francis's greeting, and his tone was brusque.

Morgan was unsettled as it was, and the glowering stare made her knees feel weak. Unbidden, she collapsed in the armchair across from his desk. "My father has some wonderful books and maps and nautical charts," she babbled, and didn't wonder that Francis was looking faintly bewildered.

"I'm sure he does. What's the next topic, crop failure?"

Morgan twisted her hands nervously in her lap, touching the growing mound of her abdomen with trembling fingers. "Well, I know that's very serious. Is it true that if there is famine in Scotland, the borderers may attack?"

Francis closed the volume he had been reading with an impatient gesture. "They used to. But if we have nothing to offer, they'll stay on their side of the Tweed." He looked at her more closely, noted the tears which were brimming in the topaz eyes, and let out a resigned sigh. "All right, you've not come here to discuss nautical charts and rain-soaked rye. What is it, then?"

"It's Sir Thomas More," she said in a gulp. "Have you heard?"

Francis's shoulders seemed to slump in relief. "Of course, James told me. Good God, I thought from the look of you he'd managed to figure out your little game after all."

"Oh!" Morgan rubbed at her forehead in an anguished motion and shook her head. "No, no, I'm just so upset—and James is not."

"I know." Francis's tone softened. "I was greatly distressed myself. Somehow, I could not quite believe that Henry would actually have More killed. Fisher, perhaps, but not Sir Thomas. It's a horrendous tragedy."

Morgan suddenly relaxed and felt herself go limp. For one long, dizzy moment she thought she was falling into space and was only aware of reality when she realized Francis was kneeling next to her with his arms around her shoulders. "What happened?" she whispered faintly.

"Not much. You just had a mild reaction to the shock you received. It's all right. Here, I'll get you some brandy."

"No—I mean, please wait. I—I just want to stay still for a bit." Their faces were almost touching and Morgan felt strangely safe in Francis's arms. He held her in silence for some time and then put a big hand on her stomach.

"Whether you believe it or not," he said in his deep voice, "I try to think this is James's child. But I don't succeed."

"Oh, Francis." Morgan let her head fall against his chest. "Of course not. It *is* your child and perhaps it's just as well."

He lifted her chin and stared at her, a puzzled, almost angry expression on his long face. "No, you mustn't think that. At least you shouldn't."

"I can't help what I think," Morgan said, her voice muffled against Francis's white cambric shirt.

He sighed on a long, deep note, which seemed to cause him pain. His hands fell away from her and he stood up, looming so tall that Morgan had to crane her neck to look at him from her place in the armchair. "I'll get us both some brandy," he said, and turned to a small inlaid cabinet where he found a decanter and two unmatched silver wine cups. Francis managed to spill a bit as he poured, frowned at the spots on the worn carpet from Araby, shrugged, and handed Morgan her cup.

She had never tasted brandy before and choked on the first draught. "You sip it," Francis informed her, looking half-vexed, half-amused. "You also sniff it. Like this." He demonstrated, and Morgan followed his example but gave a sudden start.

"It's very strong," she murmured, but was surprised to note that she felt somewhat restored already.

"It's also very expensive, being newly imported from France. I first discovered it in a small monastery outside of Paris when I was on the Continent two years ago." Francis sniffed at the cup again, sipped at the brandy, and seemed to let it roll around in his mouth before swallowing.

Morgan tried to imitate him and this time only emitted a slight gasp. "You have been to France?" she inquired, wondering if her stomach was going to catch fire and if the conflagration would roast the small being she carried within her.

"Twice. Once when I was seventeen and then again in '33. The first time I was sent away to spare the family name." He made a dour face and gazed into his brandy. "A certain dilemma involving the daughter of a country squire near Warkworth. It seems I have always been the black sheep, and James, the golden boy." He paused, his expression darkening for a fleeting moment, then crossed his long legs and resumed speaking. "The other trip was a commercial venture, to see if we could make a profit selling wool abroad. But the market was already glutted in France and we decided to continue raising sheep only for our own needs."

"Strange," remarked Morgan, now able to drink the brandy without more than a faintly warm sensation coursing down her throat, "I lived all my life in a manor house and yet I've learned more about the maintenance of an estate in just a few months here than I ever did at home. Of course," she added quickly, "Belford is much larger than Faux Hall."

"True. But it's much the same. Indeed," Francis said dryly, "you have probably learned more than you wanted to know, with James as your tutor."

Morgan looked away from Francis, her gaze wandering to the manuscript that lay on his desk. "You are composing something?" she asked to change the subject.

He looked over his shoulder. "Oh, that? Yes, sometimes I express my opinions on paper to mark time until I feel it's right to speak out."

Morgan laughed outright. "I can't imagine you not speaking your piece at any time, Francis."

He stared at her for a moment, irony in his gray eyes. "I can hold my tongue when I must. I'm impatient in small matters but not in great ones."

She wanted to ask him what he was writing about, but had a feeling he might not wish to tell her. Instead, she took another sip of brandy and commented that she wished he would recommend a book from his library. "I've read all mine over and over," she said, "and James does not have many volumes of his own, as you know."

"James reads only for information, never for pleasure," Francis said, getting up and perusing the crammed shelves. "Hmmmm, I think I put Robert of Gloucester here some place the other day. Ah, there he is." Francis proffered a much-worn volume to Morgan. "Robert was one of the last chroniclers to write in Old English. His histories are all in the form of rhymed couplets, and some are very clever."

"I've never read him," said Morgan, examining the book, which had notations in Francis's sprawling hand. "Thank you, I'm sure I'll enjoy this." She took one last sip of brandy and stood up, surprised to discover that she felt faintly giddy.

Francis waved a long forefinger in her face. "Don't ever be sure you'll enjoy a book until you've read it. Reading, like anything else, should be a matter of individual taste and judgment. You may find Robert dull as dog's dander and don't be afraid to say so."

"I—I won't," Morgan replied somewhat uncertainly, and even in her brandy-befogged state, she couldn't help but think what a very complex, unusual man Francis Sinclair really was. She felt bold enough to tell him so, but Francis was already seated behind his desk again, gazing at his manuscript. She paused, hugged Robert of Gloucester's chronicles to her bosom, and merely said, "Thank you."

Francis glanced up, replied, "You're welcome," picked up his quill, and seemed to pay no attention as Morgan moved quietly out of the library.

Francis and Lucy's third child was another boy, named George after the late Earl. Lucy's labor had been long and painful, and at one point Dr. Wimble had whispered to James that it might be wise to summon a priest. But the baby had arrived a half hour later and Lucy had rallied. Morgan, however, was almost as frightened for herself as for Lucy. Was childbirth always so dangerous? she asked the Dowager Countess the following day.

"For some," the older woman answered, painfully reaching for a dish of marchpane. "Lucy is not made for bearing babes, I fear, but she keeps having them anyway. Perhaps now that she has given Francis two sons and a daughter, she will be content to have no more."

Morgan, whose own movements were now difficult because of the unborn child's bulk, stirred up the dying fire in the bedroom grate. It was a chilly October evening, and a sleet storm had blown in that afternoon from the North Sea. "That would be an agonizing decision," Morgan commented, wondering how Francis and Lucy could endure a marriage in which the greatest of restraint must be exercised in their conjugal bed.

"Life itself can be agonizing," the Dowager Countess replied, nibbling daintily on the marchpane. As always, she was dressed impeccably, her silver hair piled high in plaits atop her head, her ever-present luminous pearls hanging to her waist, the blue eyes clear and sharp, the finely molded features betraying more character than age. Only the blue-veined hands and swollen joints showed the fullness of her years. Morgan had learned that she was basically a kind, though seemingly austere, if proud, woman who still grieved silently, but deeply, for her dead husband.

"It is one way or the other," the Dowager Countess went on, allowing Morgan to adjust the lacy woolen shawl around her thin shoulders. "Either a woman is able to produce child after child or is barren—as I was." She smiled faintly at Morgan's own evidence of fruitfulness and shook her head. "You may be one of the fortunate ones, my dear. Lucy has had no trouble conceiving, but the bearing of the babes has been very, very hard on her. As is the case with such women, she will have to make her own decision—whether to continue risking her life, or desist in allowing Francis to presume upon her body."

Morgan shuddered suddenly and was glad that her mother-in-law was once again engaged in selecting a piece of marchpane. Francis had already proven himself unable to cope with abstinence. That was scarcely unnatural for any man—except James, perhaps—but the thought frightened Morgan. She herself had not really minded her own husband's lack of physical attention during her pregnancy. His lovemaking had never aroused her, and as she grew increasingly awkward and uncomfortable, passion was the furthest thought from her mind. But after her own child was born, she thought, James no doubt would resume his marital duties to ensure another heir for Belford. Lucy, however, might be forced to keep Francis from her bed . . . Morgan moved clumsily out of the Dowager Countess's view and gazed into the storm-tossed night. She was suddenly very much afraid—and didn't understand why.

A fortnight after Lucy's delivery, the new mother was on

her feet again and seemed to have staged an almost miraculous recovery. Rocking tiny George in her lap while the two older children watched with a mixture of curiosity and envy, Lucy looked out the window and informed Morgan that it had started to snow.

"You're right," Morgan said, moving slowly to glance down into the courtyard. "Such huge, thick flakes, too. Do you always have snow in November?"

"Often as not," Lucy replied, pausing to admonish Mary about touching the baby's soft spot. "But it doesn't usually stay on the ground until December."

"It is wet snow," Morgan noted, and saw a lone rider canter through the castle entrance. Although he was muffled in a heavy cloak, there was something familiar about the way he sat his horse. "Oh, Holy Mother," Morgan cried as she flung open the casement in delighted surprise. "It's Tom Seymour!"

"Who?" Lucy swiveled in the rocking chair. "Morgan, close that window, the babe will catch a chill!"

Morgan obeyed at once, but was already moving as fast as her girth would permit. "Tom Seymour," she repeated, already at the nursery door. "I've mentioned him; he's an old family friend."

"Of course, he has a brother and a sister . . ." But Lucy's words were cut off as Morgan disappeared from the room and awkwardly made her way along the corridor, down the winding staircase, and across the entry hall into the courtyard.

A servant was helping Tom with his horse, which was shivering from the cold, hard ride. "Morgan!" Tom called out, racing to meet her.

She all but fell into his arms and they both laughed as her bulky body came between them. "I'm such a sow! Did you know I was with child? What are you doing here? Oh, Tom, I'm so glad to see you!"

"Inside with you, muffet," Tom ordered, still chuckling as he guided her back toward the castle. "Yes, your parents told me the happy news when I was at Faux Hall in September. As for how I happen to be in this northern fastness of yours, I've been on another trade mission to the Low Countries. Not a very successful one, either," he added, shaking out his snow-soaked riding cloak and handing it to a manservant who had appeared as if by magic. "The storm is much worse at sea than it is on land," he continued, sitting down on a carved oak bench and pulling off his boots. He wore a leather doublet over a white shirt, and Morgan noted that the more casual garb of a sailor suited him even better than the elegant attire of a courtier.

"The wind blew us in this direction," Tom explained, as the ubiquitous manservant reappeared with mugs of mulled wine and bread and beef. "I was afraid we might be forced to land in Scotland, but luckily we were able to steer for Bamburgh. We need some repairs before we can head south. My men are quartered in the town." Tom paused to swallow a mouthful of meat and take a drink of the hot, spiced wine. "Where are your menfolk, muffet, on such an inclement day?"

"They left before it began snowing," Morgan replied. "They've gone into the village to see about provisions for winter."

"Then I'll be able to see them." Tom grinned and daubed his thick bread in the meat's juices. "That is, if your ladyship will grant me hospitality. I keep forgetting you're a Countess."

"So do I," Morgan laughed. "Tell me, Tom, what's been happening at court? I hear the important news secondhand from my family but nothing else, no gossip and such."

"I haven't been at court for a while myself," Tom replied. "You heard about More and Fisher, I'm sure." His keen blue eyes gave her a swift, sympathetic glance.

Morgan nodded. "The news made me . . . very sad." She could say no more, and knew that Tom, better than anyone else, must realize that More's execution had served only as a painful reminder of Sean's death.

"Ironically," Tom went on, making his tone conversational, "the King seemed as distraught as More's own supporters. He reviled Anne after the execution and blamed her for having forced him to carry it out."

"That hardly seems fair," Morgan said, remembering high-strung Anne with her wary almond-shaped eyes—and their conspiracy to entice the King and thwart Cromwell's marriage plans.

"Perhaps not." Tom finished off the last chunk of bread and wiped his hands on a linen napkin. "But because of the executions Henry's prestige on the Continent has sunk to a terrible low. Nor have political and military events there gone in his favor. Even this season's poor harvest at home has been blamed on the King—and Queen."

"I feel sorry for Anne." Morgan sighed and took a drink from her goblet. "She was kind to me. Is there any hope that she will ever bear Henry a son?"

Tom's gaze moved about the small sitting room with its heavy oak furniture and the tapestries depicting the labors of Hercules. "That I cannot say." He finished his own wine and allowed Morgan to refill the goblet. "Tell me about your life here—are you and James getting on well? I would assume so, judging from your condition." He winked at Morgan, but she thought she discerned a certain tension in his query.

"He's a very considerate, gentle man," Morgan replied carefully. "My sister-in-law is a wonderful woman and the Dowager Countess is kindness itself. Lucy just had another baby, a boy, and though I've been confined to the castle of late, I did enjoy visiting the tenants and villagers when I could get about more."

"I see." He paused and stretched his stockinged feet toward the fire. "And Francis? How do you fare with that big bumpkin?"

"Well enough," Morgan retorted, and was astonished that she sounded angry and was actually blushing. "He's not a bumpkin, Tom, he's very well read and has many interests and responsibilities."

Tom raised an eyebrow over the rim of his wine goblet. "Oh? I'm sorry, I only spoke with him once or twice. He seemed like a rather rude North Country sort to me. Apparently, I misjudged him."

Morgan chose to ignore the faint irony in Tom's tone. "He gives that impression. But it's inaccurate. Actually," she continued rather hastily, "I rarely see him. He and Lucy keep to their own quarters most of the time and he's gone a lot." She hesitated, waiting for Tom's reaction. But he merely sat there, looking agreeable and apparently expecting her to go on talking. "What of Ned? And Jane?" Morgan inquired to change the subject.

Tom shrugged. "Ned is the same. He hosted the royal progress at his estate in Hampshire this summer and handled the event with his usual aplomb. Jane returned to court just before I left England."

"I missed her after she went away," Morgan said. "She always seemed to be chiding me—kindly, of course—but perhaps I needed her guidance more than I realized."

He was about to respond when a movement outside the window caught his eye. "Hold, Morgan, I believe your husband and his brother are riding in. They must be as chilled as I was. Shall we greet them?"

Morgan let Tom lead her from the sitting room into the entry hall where she stood at his side while the servants hurried to the door to let their masters in.

James greeted Tom with solemn formality, while Francis was offhand but apparently good-humored about the unexpected visitor's arrival. Lucy joined the four of them for supper, but while the Dowager Countess granted Tom a short but pleasant audience, she did not come down to the dining hall.

Supper was congenial, with James relaxing somewhat under the spell of Tom's gregarious nature and the great quantity of wine which Francis insisted the servants keep pouring. Lucy was obviously enchanted with the red-haired, seafaring courtier and his infectious charm, while Francis seemed unusually quiet. He's jealous, Morgan thought, and wanted to laugh aloud.

It was quite late when Tom had spun out his final anecdote about an unsuccessful bartering encounter with a merchant in Liege. Lucy looked peaked and excused herself, insisting that she had not enjoyed such an evening as this in some time but that childbirth had made her tire easily. Tom kissed her fingertips, and paid her a compliment which Morgan didn't catch but which made Lucy's dimples deepen and caused Francis to frown into his wine cup.

Morgan was weary too, but not having seen Tom for so long, she was reluctant to leave his company. James, however, suggested that as Lucy had already withdrawn, no doubt she, too, would prefer to retire. Morgan balked mentally, but knew it would be best not to display any sort of obstinacy and embarrass her husband in front of their guest. She bade them all good night and smiled up at Tom when he hugged her as tightly as he could, considering the bulging barrier between them.

"Pray excuse me, Lord James," Tom said, grinning. "Since Morgan has been like a sister to me, this is one of my prerogatives." James smiled rather rigidly as Tom kissed Morgan's cheek. Then she sketched the faintest of curtseys and headed slowly toward her bedchamber.

But Morgan did not sleep well that night. James had come to bed more than an hour later; although she was still awake, she did not let him know. He seemed to fall asleep at once and even snored a bit off and on. The wine, Morgan thought, and wished her body were not so unwieldly. Finding a comfortable position was hard enough these nights, but her mind was troubled as well. As happy as she was to see Tom again, his presence had served as a sorrowful reminder of Sean and all that had happened during those tumultuous, tragic months before her marriage.

By early December it was an effort for Morgan just to get up and down the stairs. Her interest in outside affairs shrank as she grew more concerned about her own body and the small creature which grew there. She heard James and Francis discussing the visitation of monasteries by Cromwell's agents. The investigation had been going on since summer. Cromwell was determined to discredit the clergy and, in truth, had found some grounds on which to base his charges. At Whitby Abbey, not far from Belford, the abbot was accused of taking profits from piracy while his servants brawled with fishermen in town. At Lichfield two nuns were reported with child. At Cerne Abbas the abbot kept concubines and used church funds to support his bastards. The tales ran on and on, but Morgan was too absorbed in the child's imminent arrival to dwell on such matters, which seemed so unrelated to her small world at Belford Castle.

Ten days before Christmas, James told Morgan he and Francis were going to Newcastle for a few days. The castle provisions were low again and this time there wasn't enough food left in Belford without depriving the townspeople. The third day after James and Francis's departure, there was still snow on the ground but the sun had appeared off and on during the day. With the improvement in the weather, Morgan turned her attention to Christmas preparations. She consulted both Lucy and the Dowager Countess, who outlined the traditions that had been handed down from generation to generation at Belford.

There were gifts for each tenant on Twelfth Night, and always the same, dating back to the first Earl, who had based his munificence on need. One hundred and fifty years later it mattered not that Mistress Langley didn't need a new iron pot or that the Greene family had firewood aplenty or that Will Pentworth's loss of an arm made a pair of gloves superfluous. The customs must be observed, along with the Christmas Eve carols, the spiced wine served on Christmas night in the castle courtyard, and the offering of a ha'penny by each child in the village to the crèche in the Church of St. Bartholomew.

"As Countess, you accept the children's offerings to symbolize our Holy Mother receiving the gifts of the Magi. Hopefully, the babe will come soon enough so that you can participate," said Lucy as she rummaged through a storeroom in the castle's upper story. It was actually a large square tower and housed a great assortment of items, from discarded toys to moth-eaten furs to a huge suit of ancient armor, which Morgan decided must have been made for a very corpulent Earl.

"Here," Lucy exclaimed at last, extracting a frayed wicker basket from a large trunk, "this is what they put the coins in." She handed the basket to Morgan, who was sitting on a small window seat in a narrow embrasure.

"This must be a hundred years old, too," Morgan said, still worn out from her climb up the three flights of stairs. "The lining is torn—shouldn't we mend it?"

"Heavens, no, that's part of the tradition!" Lucy giggled. "And it's two hundred years old. The first Earl inherited it from his grandfather."

Morgan was about to ask who would take her place if she were unable to attend the ceremonies, but something in the distance caught her eye. "Lucy!" she cried, twisting around to get a better view. "Look, something's on fire!"

Lucy slammed the lid of the trunk shut and hurried to join Morgan. "By the Saints," she gasped. "There are three fires, all on the edge of the village!"

"What's the occasion?" Morgan asked. "An Advent tradition?"

But Lucy had turned white as new linen. One hand was on her breast and she was chewing anxiously on her lower lip. "I fear not," she whispered shakily. "It's a border raid."

"Sweet Jesu!" Morgan leaned closer to watch the fires spark upwards into the encroaching darkness of the late afternoon. She felt the babe turn heavily in her womb and looked at Lucy for comfort.

But Lucy had lived long enough in the North to know exactly what was happening at the farmhouses outside the town. "Come, Morgan," she said in a tightly controlled voice, "we must tell the others."

"But I thought the borderers never came this way," Morgan said, trying in vain to keep up with her sister-in-law.

"They don't usually," Lucy called over her shoulder. "But if they're hungry enough, they'll go anywhere they think they might find food." She was already at the head of the first stairway. "I'll go on without you—but please mind your step!"

Morgan had little choice since she could manage no more than a clumsy shuffle. Her mind, however, moved faster. Surely the raiders wouldn't come to the village—and if they did get that far, would they try to get into the castle? The Sinclairs had no soldiers. In times of battle they gathered the men from the village and the fields to join up with the Percys. The only protection for the castle were the twenty or so servingmen, and several of them were too old to put up much of a fight.

By the time Morgan joined Lucy in the Dowager Countess's chambers, the bell cord to summon Matthew, the steward, had already been pulled. The older woman seemed as composed as ever:

"I believe flight would be unwise. There is only one direction to go—south. And one would have to follow the coast—too dangerous, especially in your condition, Morgan."

Morgan started to protest, but Matthew appeared in the door. The Dowager Countess told him briefly about the raiders and asked him to assemble all the servants in the banquet hall at once.

"Do we have any arms?" asked Morgan when Matthew was gone.

The Dowager Countess shrugged. "A few swords and pikes and whatever household items can serve for defense purposes." At last she seemed to consider the anxiety etched on Morgan's pale face, and Lucy's as well. "Now, my daughters, I've lived through a great many of these raids. You've seen them, too, Lucy. They can be terrible things—rape and theft and fire and pillage. But there's only one way into this castle, and by the time the borderers get here—if indeed they do—a few buckets of boiling water may dampen their enthusiasm. In the meantime," she said, calmly folding her swollen blue-veined hands in her lap, "there's nothing we can do but wait."

But the afternoon of waiting proved excruciating. Morgan and Lucy watched from the windows, distracted occasionally by the noises of the servants who were rummaging through the castle to find makeshift weapons. Morgan had suggested that some men from the village be brought up to help guard the castle, but Lucy replied they would be needed more in the town.

"Not that they wouldn't come—they're loyal—but it's better to leave them where they are and hope the raiders can be turned away from the village," Lucy explained.

By nightfall, the trail of smoldering farmhouses could be traced to the edge of town. The wild border cries could be heard even in the castle, making Morgan shudder with every yell.

"My nerves are shredded," Morgan declared, lying down on Lucy and Francis's bed.

"I'll give you something to make you sleep," said Lucy, still watching from the window.

"No!" asserted Morgan. "What if they come and you can't wake me?"

Lucy turned away from her sister-in-law, still trying to keep her own fears hidden. She couldn't tell Morgan that it would be better for her if she were asleep when the raiders came. . . .

Morgan did sleep, finally; and Lucy herself, slumped in a chair by the window, dozed for a while before dawn. The three children slept in the next room, quieted by their mother's words of reassurance. Indeed, there had been a lull outside just before midnight and it continued for several hours; apparently even the borderers had to rest.

But before the first light of dawn appeared, new cries broke the morning calm. The yells of the raiders mingled with the shrieks of their victims. Morgan awoke with a start, for an instant forgetting the danger, which grew constantly closer. Though it was hard to see what was happening in town, Lucy had little doubt but that the raiders were in the village, ransacking houses and stealing food.

Her agitation no longer concealed, Lucy moved quickly to the bed where Morgan still lay. "We must go down and get the Countess," she said unsteadily. "I think it best we take refuge in the keep. If all they want is food, perhaps they'll be content not to search for us."

Morgan sat up slowly, one hand on her stomach. She said a quick silent prayer, suddenly realizing how seldom she had prayed since her marriage. Shakily, she slipped off the bed, allowing Lucy to steady her. The two young women moved slowly along the corridor and down the stairs.

"Can they get in?" Morgan asked, as they headed for their mother-in-law's room. "The Countess said the boiling water would put them to flight."

"We don't know how desperate they are," answered Lucy. To herself, she reasoned that if the borderers had even considered entering the castle they must be very desperate indeed. Also, they must have come in large numbers, or else the villagers would have routed them quickly.

The Dowager Countess was sitting by the fire, reading her book of hours. She was completely dressed and seemed unsurprised to see her daughters-in-law.

"My lady, we're going to the keep. You must come with us," Lucy said.

The Dowager Countess shook her head. "No, I cannot walk so far. I prefer to stay here, in my own place. Regardless of what happens, it's fitting that I do so."

Morgan put her hand on her mother-in-law's thin shoulder. "That is foolish! We'll get the servants to carry you in a chair. You must not stay here!"

The Dowager Countess covered Morgan's hand with her own, a faint smile on her lips. "No, my child. They'll expect at least one member of the family to be here. If they find me, perhaps they won't look for you. Lucy, with your three young ones, and Morgan, with the babe still in your womb . . . It must be this way, you see."

Morgan stepped back, looking at Lucy. Apparently the other girl knew argument was futile. At that moment the door opened unceremoniously and Malcolm, the servant who had told Francis of his father's death on a day that seemed so long ago, came rushing in, his eyes bulging with fright.

"M'lady!" he addressed the Dowager Countess. "They've crossed the moat and are at the gates! A horde of 'em!"

The merest flicker of fear passed briefly over the Dowager Countess's face. "What about the boiling water? Is no one at the walls?" There was calm reproof in her voice.

"Aye, but there are so many, must be a hundred. They have a battering ram!"

"Get back to your post, Malcolm," the Dowager Countess ordered quietly. The servant obeyed without another word, leaving the room as fast as he'd entered it. The Dowager Countess looked at Morgan and Lucy. "Go to the keep with the children at once. And no protests!"

Both girls hesitated only momentarily, then fled into the hall. At the foot of the stairs Morgan stumbled, a sharp pain stabbing at her back and engulfing her stomach.

Lucy turned. "Morgan! Are you all right?"

She didn't dare tell Lucy about the pain, not now. "Yes, yes—let me stop to get my breath. Get the children. I'll be right behind you."

Lucy looked at her sister-in-law anxiously, then heard the wild cries outside grow louder. Fear for her young ones overcame everything else and she raced up the stairs and out of sight.

Morgan leaned against the wall at the foot of the stairs for several minutes. It occurred to her now that this wasn't the first pain she'd felt. In fact, she realized, it had been a similar but less severe one that had awakened her. Dazedly, she looked up at the staircase; it seemed insurmountable. Clinging to the wall, she started up, a step at a time. She had reached the first landing when another, more searing pain struck her. Stifling a scream, she fell fainting to the floor.

When she regained consciousness she had no idea where she lay. Slowly, she remembered what had happened and tried to pull herself upright. The shouts and clatter seemed so close now—or was it just the roaring in her ears? She sat up at last, peering down the stairs and into the corridor. She screamed then, a hideous, piercing shriek. A red-headed giant of a man, clad more in rags than clothes, was running down the hall, the Dowager Countess's pearls in his left hand. He looked up at Morgan and broke into a toothless grin.

"A *young* lassie! I've had my due with crones for the day!"

He bounded up the stairs, seeming to grow larger with every step. Morgan huddled in the corner, her teeth chattering, another pain ripping through her body.

He fell on her with such a shock that she could only gasp. He smelled of ale and filth. The pearl necklace tumbled down the stairs behind him.

"What's this?" One hand clutched at her stomach, the other at her breasts. "A bairn in there? What sport!" His hands now ripped at her skirts and Morgan moaned piteously. He pulled her legs apart just as another sharp, racking pain enveloped her body.

"Christ," the borderer muttered, "your belly's so big I'll have to take you sideways." The idea suddenly seemed to amuse him and he chuckled hoarsely. Grunting with effort as well as desire, he began pushing Morgan onto her side. Weak from the pains and terrified for herself and the babe, she made one last, feeble attempt to plead with her assailant.

"I'm having my child—now!"

"Ye be having me—now!" chortled the borderer, as he stood up to undo his breeks.

Morgan saw the lust-crazed glint in the man's small eyes and knew she could not stop him. His exposed member looked more menacing than any dagger. She was sure that his thrust would kill her—and perhaps the babe as well. She wanted to close her eyes, to faint again, to become oblivious to the fate that was about to befall her—but she lay as if paralyzed and the borderer moved toward her.

His deliberate movement turned into a lunging lurch as a look of shock and pain spread across his dirty, bearded face. And then he toppled over and crashed down the stairs. The last thing Morgan remembered was the grim look on Francis Sinclair's face as he stood on the landing, his right hand still drawn back from the dagger's thrust.

Chapter 10

MORGAN'S FINGER MOVED gently down her son's tiny face, tracing the outline of his features. He was to be called Robert, after James's grandfather, the fourth Earl of Belford. Smiling faintly, Morgan held her baby close. James sat beside the bed watching them both, a new softness in his eyes. Lucy and Polly were busying themselves around the room.

Morgan recalled little from the time she had fallen unconscious on the stairs until she awoke to hear James tell her she had given birth to a fine son. Now, a day later, she still felt too weak to talk much, but she had heard a great deal—and what she had been told had filled her with sorrow.

The Dowager Countess was dead, her neck broken by the redheaded borderer. She had been buried the following morning next to her husband in the chapel. Her death struck Morgan as so unnecessary, so wanton. Yet perhaps she had found eternal peace, joined again with her beloved Earl.

Two of the servingmen had also died while fighting the raiders. One of them was Malcolm, poor frightened Malcolm, who had shown his mettle at the last minute trying to defend the Dowager Countess. And three of the serving wenches in the kitchen had been brutally raped, although Dr. Wimble assured James they would recover.

Fortunately the castle itself had not been severely damaged. James and Francis had already noted the needed repairs. The castle entrance had taken the brunt of the assault, but inside, only a few dishes and some of the crystal had been smashed, the hangings on the main floor had been torn, and some of the furniture was ruined.

All but a handful of the borderers had escaped capture.

The others were dealt with swiftly and mercilessly: They were hanged that same day in the market square at Belford, with James supervising the executions. He and Francis had also set out to help the townspeople repair their homes and try to replace or retrieve at least some of the food.

Morgan learned, too, how the Sinclair men had arrived at the castle so quickly. They had finished their business sooner than expected in Newcastle. Even there not a great deal of supplies were available. James and Francis had bargained hastily and shrewdly to make sure they could get anything at all. They had started back early for Belford, and when they got to Morpeth, they went into an inn for some drink. Two travelers who were coming from the North were talking excitedly about a band of borderers who were ravaging their way southward. Alarmed, the Sinclair brothers left the provisions in the care of their retainers and hurried to seek help among the men loyal to their family and to the Percys. With about fifty men accompanying them they raced north for Belford—and arrived too late to save the Countess but soon enough to rescue their wives.

Two days passed before Francis came to visit Morgan and the babe. He entered the bedchamber in the early evening as the winter wind blew down the chimney and rattled the windowpanes. Morgan was dozing at the time, the child asleep in the cradle next to her bed.

For several moments Francis stood looking down at the tiny creature who slept with one small fist thrust out from under the blankets. Little Robert's fuzzy hair was blond, and while Lucy had debated whether he took after Morgan or James, the truth was that despite his fair coloring, he most resembled Sir Edmund Todd.

"He's sturdy," Francis said at last, and started to sit down in an armchair, apparently thought better of it, and loped toward the fireplace. "Dr. Wimble has told James you delivered early because of the border raid," Francis said without inflection.

"That's true," Morgan asserted, speaking for the first time since Francis had entered the room.

"Perhaps." Francis picked up a porcelain nymph from the mantel, almost dropped it, and replaced the little figurine next to a miniature of the late Earl.

The baby squirmed under the blankets and let out a series of squeaking cries. Morgan sat up to see if he was all right, but Robbie had merely turned his head and was already asleep again.

"He's dreaming," Francis said.

"Of what?" Morgan felt a smile tug at the corners of her mouth.

"Oh, food, I suppose. You have a wet-nurse?"

"Yes. A village girl named Agnes, a cousin to the one Lucy has employed for George."

Again the room grew silent, save for the wind battering the castle walls. Francis paced from the fireplace to the window overlooking the sea and then to the bed. "He's a fine babe, Morgan. You did well." Francis's tone was faintly gruff but the gray eyes turned soft as he stared down at the sleeping infant.

"It was you who did well, Francis," Morgan said, and as she saw him raise both sandy eyebrows, she hastened to make sure he understood her meaning. "You saved my life—and his. I will be forever grateful."

Francis's gaze seemed fixed on the brocade bed hangings. There was yet another pause until he spoke. "I never killed a man before."

"You had no choice." Morgan riveted her topaz eyes on his face, willing him to look at her.

And he did, but his expression was pained. "True. I could not let him harm my son. Or you." He saluted Morgan abruptly, glanced once more at the babe, and strode quickly from the room.

Morgan was still abed by Christmas and James had ordered the festivities curtailed. Tradition would have to be broken for once—the customary gifts would be dispensed with, to be replaced instead by whatever the people of Belford needed most to repair their homes and properties.

By Twelfth Night, however, Morgan was able to attend the ceremonies in St. Bartholomew's Church. The previous two days had been mild and Morgan had had an inspiration: Not only would she play her part in the children's homage to the Christ Child, she would have her own babe christened before the little pageant began.

The small Saxon church was crammed with villagers, tenants, and even a few visitors from the neighboring countryside. The same clergyman who had married James and Morgan presided; fortunately, he was swift-spoken and the service was concluded just as the new mother felt her knees grow wobbly.

"Are you able to remain for the offerings?" James whispered as Lucy rocked a now-fractious Robbie in her arms. But Morgan assured her husband that since she would be seated for the children's homage, all would be well. And then another idea came to her:

"James, let's put Robbie in the crèche. The straw is clean, he's well wrapped, and the children will enjoy that very much."

Her husband hesitated; he had not been overly keen on bringing the babe out in the evening air, but when the weather had held, he had given in to Morgan's pleas. "Very well," he agreed, and watched Lucy lay the infant in the makeshift manger.

Morgan smiled with pleasure as she held out the old wicker basket and observed each child look faintly awed by the sight of the tiny Belford heir wriggling in the straw. The grown-ups murmured among themselves and nodded in approval; their Countess was as kind as she was fair.

When Morgan and James finally got into bed late that night, they were both weary but pleased. "You gladdened our people's hearts, Morgan," James said with noticeable warmth. "My father would have been proud of you."

"Babies win hearts easily," Morgan said, adjusting the pillow behind her head. "Our good folk needed something special after the horror they endured from the raid."

James went through his ritual of adjusting the bed hangings and snuffing out the last candle. "True. And our son *is* a handsome child," he asserted with pride. "He is good sized, too, for coming so soon."

Morgan stiffened and forced herself to speak casually. "Babies in my family are usually large. Both Nan and I were, at least for girls." It was true, and Morgan was glad she hadn't had to lie. Somehow, on this one night, she had almost been able to believe that the child she had borne truly belonged to her husband.

"We have been blessed," James said in a voice that had suddenly grown sleepy. He reached out and patted Morgan's shoulder. "We must pray that next time we will be equally fortunate."

"Of course." Morgan spoke as if by reflex. Only now did it occur to her that within a few short weeks James might want to make love to her again. And now that her body was freed of its burden, she wanted to make love—but not, she realized with a sudden sense of despair, with her husband.

Gifts for the new baby arrived along with letters from Faux Hall in mid-February. Morgan and Lucy had a fine time opening the packages and exclaiming over Grandmother Isabeau's exquisitely stitched infant's cap, the quilt Nan had laboriously pieced, the silver cup from Lady Alice and Sir Edmund, and the crocheted lap robe made by Aunt Margaret.

The letters, however, contained sad tidings: Catherine of Aragon had died in January. Rumors flew that Catherine had been poisoned. "I fear it is more likely her sad demise was brought about by a broken heart," Lady Alice wrote. "Yet His Grace and Anne Boleyn"—Morgan noted that her mother still would not refer to Anne as Queen—"dressed in bright yellow and celebrated openly. The court is in a festive mood of late in any event, since Anne is with child again. Your dear cousin, however, has used this change of mood as a weapon in waging her own small war against Aunt Margaret; Nan is determined to go to court this spring."

Morgan smiled at the vision of Nan and Aunt Margaret going head to head over the court venture. Nan would win eventually, as she would be seventeen in March and her mother could not hold her back much longer.

But the second letter, written by her father and dated almost a week later, contained news which changed Nan's fate—and many another's in England. A joust had been held in late January to further mark Catherine's passing. Indeed, it was the same day that the former Queen was buried with little pomp or ceremony at Peterborough Cathedral. But fate dealt both Henry and Anne a cruel if, as some might say, well-deserved blow: The King had been unseated from his mount and lay unconscious for some time. Anne had not attended the tournament, but her uncle, the Duke of Norfolk, was only too pleased to bring his despised niece bad news. He had told her that Henry was dead. The shock made Anne miscarry, and the unborn child had been well-enough formed for the court physicians to determine without any doubt that it was a boy.

"His Grace recovered and told Anne tersely that she would get no more children by him. His rage is said to have been terrible indeed, and Anne's state is most precarious." Morgan puzzled over that sentence. She knew her parents could not be openly critical or specific since letters might be intercepted. Did her father refer to the Queen's health or to her position as consort? Of course, Morgan suddenly realized, now that Catherine was dead, Henry could rid himself of Anne. If he had tried to do so while his first Queen lived, even his most ardent supporters would have insisted he take Catherine back; two discarded consorts would be more than even Henry Tudor's staunchest adherents could stomach.

"In consequence," her father continued, "Aunt Margaret does not feel the time is right for Nan's presentation at court. Nor is Nan certain she wishes to go while matters remain unresolved."

Again, a veiled reference to Anne's future, Morgan thought as she finished the rest of the letter, which dealt with news of Faux Hall and some of the neighboring families. As Morgan put the letters away in her silver casket, she said a silent prayer for each Queen: for the repose of Catherine's soul, and that Anne would persevere.

Still, the events at court seemed very far away and life at Belford continued in its set pattern as the Sinclairs and their tenants made ready for the spring sowing. Then, unexpectedly, the happenings in and around London reached out to touch the castle's inhabitants in a surprising manner.

At the end of March, Harry Percy, the Earl of Northumberland, rode into the castle courtyard with two retainers. Morgan, holding Robbie in her arms, watched Percy from the nursery window. It was a sunny day, promising that winter was over and commonfolks' troubles might be eased. A half-dozen servants were greeting the Earl, and Morgan summoned Agnes to take the babe.

By the time Morgan arrived in the entry hall, James was already welcoming Percy. Morgan recognized him from court and was shocked to see how he had aged in the past year. She always thought of him as Anne Boleyn's lost love rather than as the most powerful peer in the North, but as she dropped a deep curtsey, she felt pity rather than awe. He was stoop-shouldered, with no vigor in his movements, and his brown eyes seemed old and empty. Yet he could not be more than thirty-five, Morgan realized, and wondered if losing Anne had destroyed him.

But Percy was courteous to Morgan and readily accepted James's invitation to go into the study and partake of food and wine. After the three of them had exchanged pleasantries as well as compliments from the Earl on the birth of an heir to Belford, Morgan suggested that she excuse herself so that the two men could speak privately. But Northumberland bade her stay, saying that the message he had brought would be of as much interest to her as to her husband.

Morgan could not suppress a look of curiosity but said nothing. The Earl munched without a great deal of appetite on poached plover's eggs and oatmeal cakes before he addressed his host and hostess: "I'm going to court next month. The weather turns for the better—while events in London turn for the worse." Percy's lips closed over the edge of his wineglass. His sad eyes surveyed James closely. "Will you and your wife join my Countess and me on our journey?"

The hesitancy on James's face gave Morgan time to think about her own reaction to Percy's invitation. She had been dismayed at going to Belford at the time, but on the other hand, she had wished never to see Greenwich or Windsor or St. James or any of the other royal residences again. They held too many unhappy memories and she would see Sean's ghost in nearly all of them. Yet after almost a year in the North, spent mostly within a five-mile radius of the castle precincts, Morgan suddenly realized she would like to renew her acquaintanceship with the courtiers, to see Tom Seymour and Jane and even Ned. Perhaps she would be able to visit her family at Faux Hall. Eagerly, she waited for James's reply.

"I don't know, Harry, it seems that court is not a very agreeable place these days." James looked into his empty wineglass, picked up the decanter, and refilled all three goblets. "I must give your gracious offer some thought. May I send a message in a week's time?"

Percy frowned and dabbed butter on an oatmeal cake. "The court may be troubled—but that's why I think men such as you and I should be there. You've heard the stories about the King, about the bad winter, the poor harvests, the hostile feelings on the Continent, the people's . . ." He paused, stretching his spindly legs out under the table, and searched for the right word. "They're discontent. His Grace needs those who support him at his side. I'm certain he will appreciate our . . . loyalty."

James rubbed at his sharp chin thoughtfully. "Yes, that's so. I've never been caught up in the courtier's role, yet I realize it's never wise to stay away too long." He glanced at Morgan; she knew what was going through his cautious mind, knew that he was thinking his reluctance to be at the King's side in a time of crisis might jeopardize his position as Earl of Belford, might even be cause for suspicion. Yet Percy's attitude perturbed her. He had been Anne's great love, as ardent for her as she had been for him. And now he talked of supporting the King who might be considering ways to rid himself of Percy's former beloved. Or, Morgan wondered, taking a swift look at Percy from under her tawny lashes, did the Earl actually hope Henry would divorce Anne and he could finally claim her as his own? But he had mentioned his wife, and Morgan recalled that Percy had—at Wolsey's insistence—married the Earl of Shrewsbury's daughter. And somehow Morgan perceived that there was no more fight left in the Earl of Northumberland; Harry Percy would go the way the winds blew him and no longer cared from which direction they came.

"Well?" It was James, who had obviously had to repeat himself. Morgan realized she had been lost in her reverie, and she actually jumped in her chair.

"Forgive me, I was thinking—about the choices, I mean," she lied unconvincingly. "In truth," she said, seeing a flicker of anger in James's pale blue eyes, "I was wondering whether we are safer at court or at Belford."

"Safer?" James looked at her questioningly. "An odd choice of words." But he was clearly undecided. "Let me think on it, at least overnight, Harry. You will bide with us until tomorrow, I presume?"

Percy nodded. "Of course. In the meantime, I know

you'll make the right decision, James. The King needs his true and honest men. And," he added, in a tone which suddenly sounded very far away, "you and I are numbered among them."

Morgan woke early the next morning, noted that James was still asleep, heard Polly in the antechamber call for Agnes to feed Robbie, and considered dozing a bit longer. But she could not settle down again; she was anxious to hear James's decision. They had not discussed it before going to bed as James had surprised Morgan by making love to her. It was only the third time he had taken her since Robbie's birth: Morgan had put him off as long as she could, at first pleading the natural consequences of childbearing, then fatigue, and finally, a mild indisposition. But she could see that James was growing impatient, not so much for her own charms, perhaps, as for the prospect of begetting another child. James stirred beside her, slowly opened his eyes and yawned.

"Are you awake?" he asked, propping himself up on one elbow.

"Yes. I've been fretting over going to court." Morgan smiled a bit wanly and forced herself to touch James's thin fingers.

He patted her hand and got out of bed, the dressing gown securely tied in place. "I've made up my mind," he said, opening the draperies to let in the early-morning light. Morgan held her breath while James looked out as the North Sea churned toward the shore and the sun rose behind the ruined abbey on the Holy Isle. "Will Robbie be able to travel?"

"Of course!" Morgan leaped out of bed, amazed at herself for being so pleased. She rushed to James's side and gave him an impulsive hug. Her enthusiastic response startled him, too; he smiled broadly and his eyes stayed fixed on the curve of her bosom, which rose and fell in excitement under the thin nightgown.

"Then it's settled," James declared, clearing his throat and turning away with apparent reluctance. "I'll dress and tell Percy at once."

The day before Morgan and James were to leave, Francis and Lucy returned to Belford from a month-long visit to

Lucy's relatives in Carlisle. They were both surprised to learn about the decision to go to court. Lucy asked Francis if they couldn't go, too.

"I've never been to London. This would be the perfect opportunity," she pleaded as the four Sinclairs sat in James's study.

But Francis was adamant. Percy had invited only James and Morgan; court life did not appeal to Francis; if the weather turned warm as the early spring had promised, London could become a pestilential place. "And," Francis added cryptically, "you know this is not the proper time, Lucy."

Lucy said nothing more, merely looking disappointed and sad. After supper, Morgan sought Lucy out but it was Francis she found in their rooms instead of his wife.

"Lucy went to pray in the chapel," he told her, rummaging through an as yet unpacked trunk. "This would have been the Dowager Countess's birthday."

"I didn't know that. I wasn't here at this time last year." Impossible, thought Morgan. It seemed as if she had been at Belford forever. But Francis was correct—she was just a week away from the day she had arrived at the castle.

"You thought me cruel to deny Lucy the trip to court?" Francis asked, not looking at Morgan but examining a worn jerkin he had taken out of the trunk.

"Well—a little. You ought to take her to London some day, Francis."

"So I shall." Francis sighed, rolled up the jerkin, and tossed it onto a pile of discarded clothing by the bed. "But not now. Lucy thinks she is with child again."

"Oh! Congratulations!" She started toward him, saw the storm gathering in the gray eyes, and stopped.

"She should not have risked it," he said gruffly. "She insisted it was not the time for her to get pregnant. I've children enough, but only one wife."

Morgan plaited the folds of her pale blue overskirt and tried to think of some comforting words. "I'm sure if she takes good care of herself and Dr. Wimble watches her well . . ."

"Paugh!" snorted Francis, beginning to pace the bedchamber. "It's the birth that worries me. I told her no more, I insisted she . . ." This time he interrupted himself, glowering at Morgan. "As for you—isn't it about time you considered giving James his own child?"

Morgan was too astonished to speak. Francis had impregnated her against her will and now he was berating her for not fulfilling her duties to the brother he had betrayed. Was there no end to the man's effrontery? "Don't you dare meddle in my life again, Francis Sinclair!" She was all but screaming. "It's too soon to bear another child!"

The angry gray eyes flickered as Francis grabbed Morgan's arm. "Do you reject his lovemaking or is James indifferent to your charms?"

"Neither!" Morgan snapped, trying to shake off Francis's grip.

"Both, I'd say. I know James—and I know you." He pulled her to him so roughly that her coif fell off, tumbling into the half-filled trunk. His mouth captured hers in a devouring kiss and his hands moved searchingly from her back to her buttocks. Morgan tried to pull away, but it was a token gesture at best, and when Francis began kissing the curve of her throat, her own arms wrapped around him, the nails digging into the fabric of his shirt.

"Francis . . ." she moaned, feeling the fire she had tried to forget begin to well up in the deepest recesses of her being. "Francis, we mustn't . . ."

He picked her up in his arms and looked down at the parted lips, the huge topaz eyes, the thick hair which fell in waves of tawny splendor.

"You want me," he said, and his deep voice growled with emotion. "And God knows, I want you."

Morgan knew she ought to deny his words, knew she ought to fight off the desire that made her body throb, knew that if they were discovered Lucy's heart would break and James might kill them both. But she could only gaze up at Francis and wait for the fulfillment he could offer her.

But Francis was now looking not at her but at the bed. Without warning, he unceremoniously set her back on her feet. "Oh, Christ! I've got to finish unpacking. Go about your business and leave me to mine."

Stunned, Morgan could only stare at Francis's back as he began sorting items of clothing from the trunk. She stood motionless for what seemed a very long time, and at last Francis turned to look at her, a fierce, angry gaze that almost made her gasp.

"Well?" he demanded. When Morgan made no reply, he started to turn away again, then picked something up and hurled it at her. "Your coif, madam. You seem to have lost it. Good night."

Morgan bent to retrieve the coif. Tears brimmed in her eyes as she surveyed a very preoccupied Francis Sinclair—and the bed. Francis and Lucy's bed, Morgan suddenly realized, and with trembling fingers, she put the coif back on and all but ran from the room.

On the second day of their journey south, the little group from Belford Castle stopped at Alnwick, where Percy, his wife, and a dozen retainers joined them. Mary Talbot Percy was blond, with angular features and wide-set hazel eyes. She would have been pretty, Morgan thought, if she did not wear the same look of defeat that her husband did. Married life had not dealt kindly with the Percys of Northumberland.

Mary sat in the coach with Morgan and Robbie and Agnes, while the two earls rode ahead on horseback and several of the retainers moved slowly at the rear of the caravan on mules. Spring, damp and fragrant, had come again to England. Beech, aspen, and birch trees flaunted new greenery. Wood violets and early columbine made festive splurges of color in the woods. Though it had rained off and on for the past few days, the roads were good, and if the travelers hadn't been burdened with the heavy baggage carts and the mules, they might have been able to reach London by May Day.

"The tournament, that's what I would enjoy," Mary Percy was saying in her singsong voice. Though she had at first appeared shy and quiet, Morgan had quickly discovered that by showing the other woman even the slightest hint of warmth, Mary opened up like a spring brook running full spate. Lonely, no doubt, Morgan had decided with compassion, and obviously not much cherished by her husband. So Morgan listened with half an ear, making occasional comments and watching Robbie nap in his place between herself and Agnes.

"... A masque where the Muses and the Furies got their parts confused and . . ." Mary was still babbling on, but Morgan's attention was caught not by her loquacious companion but by a slowing down of the coach and James's voice from outside:

"King's Men? Are you certain, Harry?"

The coach came to a complete halt as Morgan poked her head out of the small window. "What's happening?"

James jerked his hand to the right. "See that monastery? The King's Men are stripping it."

Morgan hesitated as Robbie began to cry. She picked him up and opened the coach door. "Dear heaven! Are those monks by the gate?" she asked as she carefully descended to the ground.

James nodded. "At least they aren't being foolish enough to resist." But even as he spoke, a small, thin, elderly monk stepped away from his brothers and said something to one of the soldiers. The soldier gave him a shove, nearly toppling the old man.

Outside the gates, near the road, a group of villagers had gathered. They seemed to take one step forward as a body in protest but went no farther. The soldiers were husky and well-armed; the townsfolk were empty-handed.

Percy tried to quiet his rambunctious gelding. "They've found many a religious house here in Yorkshire teeming with vice," he said.

"This one among them?" asked Morgan.

Percy shrugged. "Does it matter? It seems they are all dens of iniquity, one way or another."

"In the eyes of the King at least . . ." said Morgan in a low voice.

Neither James nor Percy heard her. They were watching intently as soldiers came out the door of the monastery carrying gold plate, bejeweled vestments, and precious stones taken from smashed statues. The booty was loaded onto a cart as the soldiers made jokes and boasted about who had taken the most valuable pieces.

Morgan and the others had all been slowly moving closer to the monastery. The villagers eyed the well-dressed newcomers surreptitiously. Morgan thought at least one glance seemed to beg for help. She held Robbie tighter and discovered she was praying. "But why?" she asked herself. "Why am I praying for these men of Rome, Rome which cost me so much—" She cut off her self-questioning abruptly, riveting her attention on the door of the monastery through which a tall blond soldier was emerging. He carried a ruby-encrusted gold chalice in one hand and had a piece of fusty cloth thrown over the other arm.

A gasp went up from both villagers and monks. The old brother who had protested earlier suddenly made a rush for the soldier, crying, "St. Mary Magdalen's veil! No, no!" He grabbed for the soldier's left arm, displaying an unnatural strength in such a feeble-looking body.

Swiftly, the soldier jerked his arm free and struck out at the monk with the chalice. The old man went sprawling on the cobblestone walkway, blood running from his bald head.

Morgan could no longer restrain herself. A scream escaped her lips as she started running for the monastery gates. She was halfway there when a hand on her shoulder made her come to a stumbling stop. James had both her and the baby in a steel grip.

"You fool! Are you mad?"

She looked up at him, then shook her head as if to clear her senses. She leaned limply against her husband, not trusting herself to speak.

The villagers were now watching the noble party with mixed reactions—sympathy for Morgan, hatred for the others. James motioned to Percy. "We'd better leave at once."

Percy assented. James helped Morgan and Robbie back into the carriage. Mary, who had remained inside during the entire episode, was clutching her cloak and looking anxious. "Such commotion! Why did you run up to the monastery?"

Morgan was still shaken. She handed Robbie, now fussing loudly, to Agnes, who began to nurse him. "I don't know," Morgan answered at last in a hollow voice. "I don't know."

The wheels started to grind again. Morgan looked out the little opening toward the monastery. The old monk still lay on the cobblestones. Some of the villagers watched him helplessly; others stared malevolently at the retreating entourage. On the roof, several soldiers were busy with tools. Morgan was puzzled at first, then realized what they were doing to the roof.

"The lead. They even want the lead . . ."

* * *

After the stop at the monastery, Percy had made a sudden decision. He told James he thought they should pause at Snape Hall, the home of Lord Latimer. The name was only vaguely familiar to James, but Percy explained that Latimer was a Neville, a wealthy man, and a supporter of the old faith.

Above the sound of the wheels and the horses' hooves, Morgan could barely hear what James and Percy were saying. She listened as closely as she could, hearing James ask why they were going to pay Lord Latimer a visit.

"I want to know what accounts for the attitude of these villagers," Percy replied. "I'm sure Lord Latimer can tell us."

"If they'd been armed I think they would have attacked those King's Men," James said thoughtfully.

"Yes. That's what I want to find out. How much resistance—armed or otherwise—is there to the King in the North?"

James didn't reply; the two men rode along in silence. Morgan sat back on the carriage seat, trying to relax. Shut away at Belford for so many months, she had given only fleeting thoughts to the strife in the rest of England. Now, with the carriage creaking along the rutted road to Snape Hall, and Mary Percy dozing on the opposite seat, Morgan had time to think. And what she had seen at the little monastery forced her mind into contemplation of recent political and religious happenings.

How much authority did the King really have in church matters? Were all the abbeys and convents and monasteries riddled with sin and perversion? How did the common-folk feel about the uprooting of their old faith? Had all this upheaval been caused by the King's fancy for Anne Boleyn and his desire for an heir, or was it genuine, long-needed reform? But most of all, was it ever right to hurt and maybe even kill a defenseless old man in the name of justice or the King . . . or anything? And how many times, in how many places in England, had that same scene been played out?

Morgan looked down at Robbie, now content and staring solemnly up at his mother. Irrelevantly, the thought came to her that that old monk was someone's son, long, long ago. . . .

Chapter 11

IT WAS TWILIGHT when the little party turned into the road at Snape Hall. Lord Latimer's dwelling stood on the crest of a small hill, surrounded by oak and maple trees. Several servants and a large sheep dog came out to greet the visitors.

James helped Morgan and Robbie alight from the carriage. Robbie was again screaming with hunger, his tiny face all mouth, his little fists waving mightily. Morgan vainly tried to shush him, but her efforts only made him yell even louder.

Lord and Lady Latimer had come to the entranceway, greeting the Percys effusively. Percy, in turn, made the introductions to the Belfords. Lord Latimer was a fairly tall, lean man of indeterminate middle age with thinning dark hair and a close-cropped beard. His wife was pretty, small, and plump, her red hair done up neatly under a linen coif. She was many years younger than her husband, perhaps not much older than Morgan herself.

Morgan apologized for her small son's behavior but Lady Latimer only laughed. "The poor mite is half-starved! Give him to me—just for a moment, anyway. You have a wet-nurse with you?"

Morgan assured her hostess that she did. The party went into the house, where Lady Latimer called for food and drink. Robbie was handed over to Agnes, and the grown-ups settled down to a tasty supper of roast goose with savory stuffing.

After they had finished, Percy began to steer the conversation away from casual talk to serious matters. Noting this, Lady Latimer motioned to Morgan and Mary. The women excused themselves, going to Lady Latimer's sewing room where a small fire was already burning in the grate.

"It's been a long time since I've seen you, Mary," Lady Latimer said, motioning for her guests to sit in two comfortable armchairs.

"I don't often leave Northumberland," Mary answered, warming to her hostess's kindness. "Not that I don't keep busy. We have enormous holdings and the servants number over a hundred at the castle. We have guests, of course, though not a great many since we are so far north. Still, when the weather is fine, a goodly number pause to visit."

As Mary stopped for breath, Lady Latimer smiled at her sweetly and turned to Morgan. "Your estates are even more remote, I understand."

Between the emotional strain at the monastery, the long ride, the filling supper, and Mary Percy's soporific conversation, Morgan was half-asleep. But she rallied at her hostess's comment.

"That's so, but as a rule, there's sufficient activity. My husband's brother . . ." Morgan paused as Francis's image as she had seen him last flashed through her mind, standing tall and unapproachable in the courtyard on the morning of her departure with James. "My husband's brother and his wife and their children usually are with us," she continued in a slightly forced voice. "Your home is very comfortable, Lady Latimer."

"Please, don't call me Lady Latimer! It makes me feel a hundred years old! Just call me Cat . . . and I shall call you . . . I don't know your first name!" Lady Latimer laughed merrily.

"It's Morgan."

"Morgan! What a wonderfully unusual name! I've always felt there were too many Annes and Marys and Catherines about. Catherine always comes to Kate or Cat anyway. Cat Parr—that's what they always called me before I was wed. No romance to it—but then I'm not a very romantic person."

Romantic or not, Morgan was finding herself very relaxed in Cat Parr Latimer's presence. "Have you and Lord Latimer been married long?"

"Seven years. I'd been married at sixteen—to Lord Burough." Catherine pulled her sewing frame in front of her and began to work with precise efficiency. "He was quite old—he died very soon. I was sorry; he was such a kind man. But Lord Latimer is kind, too. I don't think I've known a better man."

"Do you—do you have children?" asked Mary, who was beginning to feel left out of the conversation.

Cat Parr looked up quickly from her needlework. She smiled, a soft, sad smile. "No. No, I've never had a child." She didn't speak again for a moment and Morgan felt embarrassed by Mary's question. But Cat was quick to sense the feelings of others. "I don't mind you asking, Mary. But I've never been blessed with a babe. That's why I wanted so much to hold yours, Morgan. Well. Come look at this tapestry. It's Fair Rosamonde in her arbor. Isn't that a lovely color for her hair?" Morgan agreed with enthusiasm; the talk turned to domestic matters, but before long it was time for the weary party to retire. Morgan thanked her hostess for such a gracious welcome, but Cat only smiled. "You can repay me," she said, patting Morgan's shoulder. "Before you leave tomorrow, I must hold your sweet son, just for a little while."

It was late afternoon when the weary party finally arrived at Greenwich on May 2. As they rode up to the palace entrance, Morgan noted that the pennants from the previous day's tournament drooped from their standards in the tiltyard and that a handful of servants were still busy clearing away the debris from the May Day festivities.

Noting this activity, Mary Percy could not help but remark that if they had left the North a day or two sooner, they might have arrived in time to see the spectacle.

"We discussed that before we left Alnwick," Percy replied caustically. He and his Countess rarely spoke to each other, and though Morgan was by now bored with Mary's constant chatter, she understood the other woman's need to talk.

But the atmosphere at Greenwich was far from festive: The palace seemed deserted, almost ghostly. The usual assortment of pages, guardsmen, and dogs was missing from the entry area. The corridors seemed lifeless, with no sound of courtiers' banter or servants' bustle. A lone halberdier directed the Sinclairs and the Percys to their quarters on the second floor. The group trudged silently up the stairway, their retainers following with the baggage.

"Something's amiss," Morgan declared after the door was closed and Robbie had been taken into the next room with Agnes and Polly. "The weather is fine, yet I see no one outside in the gardens."

"Perhaps they're merely resting up from yesterday's celebration," James said.

"It's eerie," Morgan said, still looking out the window toward the river. "James! Look, the royal barge is just pulling out into the tide."

James joined Morgan at the window as someone rapped on their door. Before James could even ask who it was, the door flew open, and Tom and Ned Seymour burst in.

Tom enfolded Morgan in a bear hug while Ned shook James's hand. Both Seymours seemed tense and yet somehow exhilarated. "What's happening, Tom?" Morgan asked after the preliminary greetings were finished. "Where is everyone?"

But it was Ned who responded. "There has been a tragic turn of events this day," he said gravely. "You saw the barge just now?" As both Morgan and James nodded, Ned continued in his smooth, controlled voice. "That is Anne Boleyn, on her way to the Tower. She was arrested this morning for treason."

Morgan's hand flew to her mouth; even James seemed to reel at the news. "Treason?" he cried. "How can the Queen commit treason?"

Tom was concentrating on the gold braid that banded the cuffs of his dark brown doublet; Ned nervously licked his lips, stared at the ceiling, and finally looked at James and Morgan. "By committing adultery. She has been charged along with five men."

"What?" Morgan shrieked. "Five! Who?"

Ned seemed to be speaking by rote: "Mark Smeaton has already confessed his crime to your uncle, Thomas Cromwell. The others are Will Brereton, Francis Weston, and Harry Norris."

"Sweet Jesu!" Morgan breathed, and found herself leaning against James. Smeaton was but a carpenter's son, and though a fine musician, hardly the sort of young man Anne would have taken into her bed. As for Brereton, Weston, and Norris—they were all decent sorts, especially the kindly, middle-aged Norris.

"Hold on," Morgan said suddenly, jabbing a finger at Ned. "You said five—that only makes four. Who else?"

Net let out a long sigh and actually shuffled his feet. "There are only four charged with adultery. The other charge is incest—between Anne and her brother, George."

The mere idea was so incredible that Morgan could hardly keep from laughing hysterically. There was no doubt that Anne and George were close, but it was the kind of sibling relationship that Morgan herself had envied: a brother and sister who loved each other, who supported each other, who enjoyed each other's company. Even if she could have believed the other charges, this one was so preposterous as to make the rest equally ridiculous.

"By Our Lady," Morgan exclaimed fervently, "I'd as soon believe that of Anne and George as of you and Jane!" To Morgan's surprise, Ned actually flinched at his sister's name. "As for Mark Smeaton, how was this confession elicited?"

"Please, Morgan," said Tom, who finally came to face her, "that's not important. What matters is that he did confess, and implicated the others."

But Morgan knew all too well how her uncle secured information. Sean's face flashed before her eyes, and if Thomas Cromwell had been present, she would not have been able to keep from trying to tear him apart with her bare hands. "He used torture! You know he did; *I* know he did!" Morgan was screaming at Tom, and James had to restrain her.

"Wife, hold on! This is a grave matter. We must curb our tongues! Pray excuse my Countess, gentlemen; she has had a long and arduous journey."

"It didn't addle my wits," Morgan snapped, and shook off James's hand. But the shock of Anne's downfall horrified her. Anne Boleyn, who had vanquished the most powerful men in England, who had steered her course into apparent safe harbor, was now heading up the Thames toward the Tower and a fate which only God could know. If Anne had failed at triumphing over her adversaries, how could a lesser mortal such as Morgan take charge of her own life?

Ned was talking to James, but Morgan missed hearing the words. Apparently, they were discussing Percy, since Ned was making an abrupt bow to Morgan and James was murmuring something about the Earl. As the two men left the room, Tom went to the window, looked out toward the river, frowned, and turned back to Morgan.

"I'm sorry, I'd no idea you would come to court at such a terrible time."

"I'm beginning to think there is never a good time to come to court," Morgan asserted bitterly as she sat down on a large crate which had not yet been unpacked. "I don't believe any of it. The King is just trying to get rid of Anne. By the Saints, it's a wonder you and Ned weren't arrested too!"

Tom's perennial tan seemed to darken. He was standing with his arms folded across his chest, the gold earring winking in the late-afternoon sun, his wide mouth tightly closed in the red beard. Morgan eyed him curiously as it finally dawned on her that both he and Ned had been behaving strangely, even given the horrendous circumstances in which they had greeted her and James. "All right," she said quietly. "What *aren't* you and your gruesome brother telling us?"

"Oh, muffet!" Tom's hands flew out in a gesture of exasperation. "Ned's not gruesome. He can be a prig, but he's a decent sort." Tom paused, aware that he was not addressing Morgan's question and was obviously reluctant to do so. But there was Morgan, looking at him with reproachful topaz eyes and, he judged, about to explode with wrath. "His Grace is going to marry Jane."

"God's teeth!" Morgan breathed, using one of Tom's favorite oaths. "I don't believe it!" But before Tom could speak again, Morgan was on her feet, shaking both fists at his chest. "But I *do!* Of course I do! That's the reason you and Ned always spoke so unkindly of Anne! The reason the King visited Ned's estates and Wolf Hall on progress last year!"

Tom grabbed Morgan's wrists before she could do any real damage. "No, Morgan," he said with unaccustomed sternness. "Jane didn't attract the King's attention until he came to Wolf Hall. I didn't even know about this when I visited you at Belford. As for our hostility toward Anne, Ned and I never felt she was suited to be Queen."

"And Jane is?" Morgan demanded. "Jane, with her prim little mouth and no chin and the taste of an aging mother superior? What will she wear to her coronation—a wimple?"

Tom dropped Morgan's hands and slapped her, hard. Morgan reeled, almost falling over the crate. Eyes flashing fire, she glared at Tom and reached for the first thing at hand, a pair of James's riding boots. They flew past Tom and landed on the hearth. He and Morgan locked furious gazes for several seconds—and then she was in his arms, sobbing against his chest, as he stroked her back and whispered soothing words into her ear.

"Life is a damnable thing, Morgan. Sometimes I think that irony dominates us more than any other element," he said at last, letting go of her as she blew her nose and wiped her eyes. "I never dreamed Jane would capture the King, I swear. God's eyes, I love my sister and she's a kindly creature, but I thought she'd be fortunate to get herself a nice country squire. Yet here we are, with Jane all but on the throne, and with any luck, perhaps she will finally give Henry the son he craves. And if she does, perhaps the rest of us can live in peace for a change."

Exhausted from her emotional tirades Morgan could only nod. Tom put his hand under her chin and looked into her eyes. "I didn't mean to hit you—does it hurt?"

"Of course it does," Morgan replied with a tremulous smile. "But I was being very unkind."

"You were being very angry," Tom said, and bent down to kiss the cheek he had struck. "Now why don't you show me that fine son of yours, muffet?"

Morgan's smile grew more steady. "Of course, if he's awake." She started toward the door to the baby's room but paused in midstep. "Just one thing, Tom. Don't ever call me 'muffet' again."

When James returned over an hour later from conferring with Ned Seymour and Harry Percy, he looked solemn and hardly spoke as he and Morgan ate a late supper in their rooms. But at last Morgan told him she knew about Jane Seymour and he seemed to relax somewhat.

"But do you know about the commission?" he inquired, toying with a dish of clotted cream. Morgan said she did not, and James began to explain. "The commission will investigate the charges against the Queen. I have been appointed to it. So has Percy."

Morgan all but choked on a spoonful of the rich dessert. "You! Oh, James, no! And Percy—he and Anne were once . . ." Morgan's words trailed off as she tried to take in yet another shock.

James set his dish aside and took a long sip of sweet wine imported from the Levant. "Francis ought to try this vintage, though he might find it a bit cloying for his taste."

"Pox on Francis!" Morgan cried angrily, and bit her tongue, for she knew she was not upset with her brother-in-law but with her husband, her uncle, the King, Percy, and all those self-righteous men who were seeking Anne's downfall. "Why, James? Why have you and Percy agreed to do this?"

The pale blue eyes turned cool; the hand that held the wineglass tightened perceptibly. "It is our duty," James replied frostily. "The King has requested us to serve. Percy and I are the only loyal men he can count on in the North. As for Percy's former feelings for Anne, that was a long time ago. I didn't realize until we took this journey how Percy's fortune has dwindled. He needs the favor of the King—he is even seeking a pension. I learned this from him one night when we stayed up late and he got to drinking." James stood up, aloof, yet ill at ease. "I never told you about the talk Percy and I had with Lord Latimer. He told us that those villagers at the monastery were typical of the people in the other northern towns. They're isolated; they haven't kept pace with the times. As their abbeys are being destroyed, they grow resentful and rebellious."

"What of Latimer himself?"

"Oh, he clings to the old faith. He's not a well man, and as tends to happen, he grows conservative. Indeed, he told us these stubborn souls contend that they support the King but think he has fallen into the clutches of evil councillors—like your uncle."

Morgan sat with her chin on her fist and stared into space. She had been so eager to come to court, but now, caught up in the ceaseless political and religious turmoil that followed the King like a long, dark, menacing shadow, Morgan wished she were back at Belford, watching the tides, talking to the tenants, visiting the villagers, seeing Francis stride across the courtyard. . . . She shook her head to dispel the familiar images, which suddenly seemed so comforting. Especially the mental picture of Francis Sinclair.

On the third day of Anne Boleyn's imprisonment in the Tower, Morgan felt edgier than ever. In the early afternoon James came into the apartments to find his wife standing by the window, staring gloomily out at the Thames.

"James," she said, without turning around, "let's go into London. I am so tired of staying here . . . waiting for something to happen."

James had just returned from conferring with Cromwell about what information his matrons had managed to wrench from Anne Boleyn. He had been cooped up with Morgan's uncle for over three hours and was very tired. "Nonsense!" he said, smoothing his pale blond hair into place. "Why don't you read or tend to your sewing?"

She turned to face him. "I don't feel like reading and you know I despise sewing. For me, it's only an excuse for keeping your hands busy while you gossip."

James was pulling off his doublet. "As you will. I'm going to rest a bit and then I have more work to do."

"Work! You call putting nails into a poor woman's coffin work!"

James carefully hung his doublet up in the oak closet. "I shan't argue with you, Morgan. Pray hold your tongue, I'm weary."

Morgan sighed as her husband disappeared into the bedchamber. She stood by the window for another minute and then went to fetch her green lace shawl. She would go for a walk, anything to get outside the palace.

She went down to the riverbank, where robins pecked in the grass, searching for tidbits to feed their young. They scattered at Morgan's approach and she smiled guiltily at their soaring figures.

It was a fine day, the blue sky marred only by an occasional fluff of cloud. On the river, a few barges and wherries moved with the tide. The slight breeze brought a faint foul air off the Thames; the smell of blood, Morgan thought suddenly, and shuddered. Wondering at her own morbid mood, she headed back toward the palace.

At the tiltyard entrance, she saw Richard Griffin walking toward her, the crimson plume on his dark gray bonnet keeping in jaunty rhythm with his step. Morgan's first reaction was to flee. But it would have been more than rude, it would have been cowardly. She stood her ground, watching him break into that charming, gap-toothed smile.

"Welcome, Morgan, Countess of Belford! I heard you were at Greenwich when I arrived this morning." He put out a hand, but Morgan kept hers tucked up under her shawl. "Well? I didn't expect open arms after our last meeting, but a simple 'hello' would not be amiss."

Morgan held her head high and spoke in a low, controlled tone: "At first I thought I hated you for what you did and said when you came to the convent. Now I realize how little I've thought of you at all."

Her candor clearly stung Richard's vanity. The green eyes actually appeared wounded; the smile faded instantly. He took a step forward, tentatively touching her upper arm. "Did you ever realize why I acted as I did? And why I came at all?"

The topaz eyes blinked twice, rapidly. "No," she answered truthfully, "I assumed you were sent by the King or my uncle and that you behaved so wretchedly because . . . because . . . I don't know, because you thought I was a traitor and a fool."

"Oh." The hint of a smile returned to Richard's mouth. "Yes, that's all very reasonable. And very wrong." Before she could respond, Richard put a finger to Morgan's lips. "I was not sent. Surrey was to go, but I told him to let me take his place. I had been very jealous of Sean O'Connor, and as you had spurned me for him, I wanted to be the one to break the news. Surrey thought me a callous knave, but since he's basically a lazy sort, he finally agreed." Richard paused, noting the skeptical expression on Morgan's face. "You see, I knew someone had to save you, not only from your uncle but from yourself. And I wasn't sure the others would realize how you might react."

Morgan considered his words with great care. She wanted to believe him, though she wasn't sure why. He was charming, amusing, attractive—perhaps he was also kind, in his way. Morgan stood very straight, and when she spoke, her words were stilted. "I should be grateful— maybe some day I will be. But," she went on, plucking at the lace fringe on her shawl, "your words were so heartless."

"They had to be." Richard's arm went around her shoulders. "You had to find out about Sean in one swift blow. Holding back would have been far more agonizing. Don't you realize that now?"

Morgan stood close to him, her face almost touching his chest. "I suppose. Yet at the time . . ." But she didn't want to think about that terrible time any more; she had tried so hard to bury that moment of horror and heartbreak in the darkest corner of her mind. "All right. I'll concede that your motives were justified, even generous. Now let's speak of something else."

They did, Richard talking about the visit to Wales from which he'd returned only the previous day and Morgan telling him about her infant son and life at Belford.

"You speak with professed enthusiasm for your new life, but it sounds like a dreary place to me," Richard said, tracing circles with the heel of his boot in the dirt path. "What of your lord? I hear he's on the commission to try poor Anne."

Morgan nodded. "I'm sick at heart about her plight. Yet what can I do?"

"Nothing. None of us can help her. Good God, I'm glad I was in Wales these past few weeks or else I might have gone the way of Norris, Brereton, and the others." He saw her questioning look and grinned. "Nay, I've never bedded with Anne—but neither have they."

It had never occurred to Morgan that Richard Griffin could have been endangered, too. She felt an unexpected surge of relief that he had been spared, and it showed in her topaz eyes.

"Oh, Morgan, I think you don't hate me so much after all!" Richard put his arms around her again. "You are lovelier than ever. That lion's mane of yours gleams in the sun like golden bronze!"

"Twaddle, Richard, let go of me! I'm a wife and mother now!" She pulled away and tried to look stern but ruined the effect by giggling, an uncontrollable outburst which bordered on hysteria. Richard began to look alarmed, but when he moved to take her in his arms once more, she shook her head, quieted down, and finally spoke in gulps. "I'm sorry . . . I'm so upset about the Queen . . . and seeing you reminds me of . . . the past."

Richard appeared sympathetic. "Leave the past in the

past. As for Anne, I only hope the King will get his divorce and leave her in peace. I just wish to God she weren't being supplanted by that sheep, Jane Seymour, along with her insufferable brothers."

His remark made Morgan angry; it also made her realize that her loyalties were once again divided. She had never known Catherine of Aragon, yet sympathized with Henry's first Queen. Then she had served Anne and felt not only loyalty but admiration and respect for the King's second consort. But here she was, distraught at Anne's downfall yet torn by her friendship with the Seymours, especially Tom.

Richard saw her reaction and sighed. "I'm sorry. I forgot that you are on familiar terms with our next Queen and her kin. But I must be honest—both Ned and Tom are steeped in ambition."

Ned, beyond any doubt, thought Morgan, but not the carefree, adventuresome Tom. Her fit of near-hysteria had drained her, however, and she would not argue further with Richard. "It's a pity one must have friends at all," she said sadly. "It seems each friend must be the other's adversary in this venomous world at court." Before Richard could respond, she shook her head, gave him a ghostly smile, and with the shawl trailing behind her on the spring breeze, Morgan walked wearily back into the palace.

Morgan and James were packing again, preparing to move to Westminster, where the King was in residence. But Morgan's orders to Polly and the other servants were absentminded and distracted. George Boleyn, Harry Norris, Will Brereton, Francis Weston, and Mark Smeaton had all been found guilty and sentenced to death. Henry did not want to divorce Anne; he wanted to kill her.

"His own wife!" Morgan cried to James that evening. "Surely you and Percy and Norfolk and the others will vote for clemency!"

James did not reply. His manner was distant, the pale blue eyes unfathomable. "You and Robbie and the rest of our entourage will leave early in the morning for Westminster," he said after a long silence. "I will meet you there after Anne's trial."

Morgan's mouth clamped shut into a hard, tight line. If

her husband's demeanor was any indication, the verdict had already been rendered in the judgment of Anne Boleyn.

Slipping out of Westminster had been easy; getting inside the Tower was another matter. Morgan gazed up at the formidable structure with its many turrets etched against a flawless May sky. She and Polly had engaged a small barge to take them from Westminster to the Tower. As Morgan hesitated, the bargeman began to shuffle impatiently. The weather was good and so was business, with all those fine folk being executed on Tower Hill. A dithering passenger, albeit a Countess, might lose him a fare.

"Madam," he began, as Morgan stared anxiously at the water that lapped at the worn stone steps leading from the river, "like I said, it's sixpence for . . ." But his words were cut off by the boom of a nearby cannon. The barge rocked and Morgan all but fell on top of Polly.

"What's that?" gasped Morgan.

The bargeman shrugged. "Another execution. Weston, maybe, this time." He put out a beefy, callused hand in an importunate gesture.

"Oh, Christ have mercy!" Morgan whispered, and crossed herself. She had not given a thought to arriving while Weston and the others were being butchered on Tower Hill. Her only concern had been to avoid James, who would have forbidden her to attend Anne during the condemned consort's last hours on earth. "Here," Morgan finally said, shaking some coins from a small silk purse and handing them to the bargeman. She didn't wait for his thank-you's but began to mount the slimy stairs with Polly at her heels.

Anne Boleyn was situated in the same suite where she had spent the eve of her coronation some three years earlier. As the door opened, she was sitting in a high-backed chair, the almond-shaped eyes looking straight ahead, the tapering hands folded in her lap. Margaret Wyatt stood next to her, while Madge Shelton, who had been rumored to be engaged to Harry Norris, wept noiselessly in one corner.

But as soon as Anne saw her, Morgan flew across and fell at her former mistress's feet. "Your Grace! Forgive my intrusion, but I wanted to be with you!" She felt Anne's hand rest lightly on her head, then draw away. Morgan looked up, amazed at the calm Anne's face displayed.

"I'm well pleased," Anne replied. "I have great need of friends in my final hours. So many have already gone who did show me great devotion."

"I'm sorry . . . very sorry," Morgan said, and wished her own composure were as great as Anne's. "I'm sorry, too, that my husband was on the commission."

Anne waved a hand in an indifferent gesture. "My own father was on the commission. It matters not; my fate was sealed long ago." The faintest of smiles touched her mouth. "Yet I am surprised that you came. Why?"

Morgan had pulled over a footstool proffered by Margaret Wyatt. "I don't know," she answered truthfully, seating herself and pulling her lawn skirts about her ankles. "You were kind to me, you tried to help me, I felt as if you—as if we—had some sort of common bond."

Anne considered Morgan's words carefully. "But not common destiny, I trust," she said with a wistful smile. "If you don't aim as high, you will not have so far to fall."

"I have no great ambition," Morgan replied, "yet I admired how you overcame obstacles and matched wits with Wolsey and the King and the others . . ." Her voice trailed away as she saw two of Cromwell's matrons pause to listen. "You seemed to know what you wanted—and you made certain you got it."

Anne shook her head and laughed. "Oh, Morgan, see where it led me! Was I so clever after all?" She laughed again and the sound echoed faintly of hysteria. Margaret Wyatt looked alarmed and put a hand on her mistress's shoulder.

"Yes," Morgan declared. "You were. Clever and single-minded and daring. What happens tomorrow . . . cannot taint your victory." She lowered her voice and took the Queen's hand in her own. "You won, Your Grace. In these last few days, you have vanquished your enemies."

Anne Boleyn had requested the privilege of dying not by the axe, but by the sword. Since no such expert executioner resided in London, Cromwell had had to send to St. Omer in France. When Anne stood ready in her short, ermine-trimmed cape and her pearl-encrusted coif, her women grouped around her, and Mary Boleyn threw her arms about her sister. Morgan remained aloof; she had not known Anne as well or as long as they. She decided to occupy herself in some other, more practical manner. Seeking permission from Cromwell's women to leave for a few minutes, she went off down the narrow passageway to search for Master Kingston, the Lord Lieutenant of the Tower. She found him at the end of the corridor, waiting for Anne and her party.

"Master Kingston," she addressed him, "I have a question to put to you. What . . . how is the Queen to be buried?"

Kingston rubbed his beard and thought a moment. "I cannot say, madam. No arrangements have been made."

"Then we must find something, some sort of coffin," Morgan said, keeping her voice as businesslike as possible. Kingston replied that he had none. "None in the Tower?" asked Morgan. "Surely there must be something."

Kingston rubbed his beard some more. Then he nodded. "Yes, I believe there is an arrowcase in the armory. It would do. She . . . she is a very slender young woman. I'll send for it."

Morgan hurried back to the Queen's rooms. Everything was ready and the ladies-in-waiting had becalmed themselves somewhat, although both Madge and Mary Boleyn were still weeping. Presently the guards and Master Kingston appeared and the little procession headed along the passageway, down the narrow steps, and out onto Tower Green.

As many London citizens as could be admitted were crowded near the scaffold. Anne and her women were oblivious to them as they walked along the path and up the steps to the high platform where the ominous block stood.

Anne turned to face the crowd, her voice high but composed. "Good Christian people, I am come hither to die, according to the law, and I will speak nothing against it. I ask mercy of God and my King, for a gentler nor a more merciful prince there never was." She took a deep breath and went on: "I take my leave of you and the world, and I heartily desire you all to pray for me."

Margaret Wyatt removed Anne's cape while Madge Shelton took off the pearl coif and replaced it with a linen cap. Morgan, conscious of the lithe, muscular figure of the masked executioner not three feet behind her, held out the bandage for Anne's eyes. Morgan put the bandage in place, whispered, "God bless you," and stepped back with the other women.

Anne knelt to the block. Morgan averted her eyes, looking up at the Tower walls where a crow sat swinging back and forth. As a shimmer of steel flashed in the sun, he cried out and flew off toward the river.

I'm going to faint, thought Morgan. She turned away as Margaret ran to pick up the head, wrapping it in a white cloth. Morgan suddenly saw Tom Seymour, along with Ned, in the crowd below. He was watching her. He looked as if he were trying to say something, a word of courage, perhaps. Morgan gathered her strength and went back with the other women to take Anne's body away. Blood still gushed from the severed neck as Morgan and Mary Boleyn lifted their pathetic, broken burden into the arrow-case.

With silent tears, the little group made its sad journey to the chapel where they laid Anne next to her brother, George. Morgan left them then, hurrying to a small chamber near the chapel, where she retched violently.

At last she wandered out, weak and white. She was vaguely aware that she should help the other women collect their belongings and Anne's from the Tower suite. Polly would be wondering where she was, and James would be furious by now. But she walked aimlessly along the passageways, oblivious to the guards and serving people. One hand felt the wall, as if for support.

Then, at the end of a short corridor, she saw Tom Seymour. He stood waiting until she was standing in front of him. Wordlessly, he picked her up in his arms and carried her out of the Tower and through the main gate, where his horse stood tethered. They rode in silence to Westminster.

Chapter 12

JAMES FACED MORGAN with such a chilling gaze that her foot faltered in the doorway. Before he could speak, he saw Tom Seymour behind his wife and the narrow shoulders slumped in surprise.

"Your uncle has asked to see you." James was avoiding Tom's eyes but keeping his tone even. "You should have sought permission before going to the Tower. He is mightily vexed."

"Morgan is mightily ill," Tom intervened. He had his hand under her elbow as he guided her to a chair. "As for Cromwell, you may tell him that Morgan had permission from the future Queen of England."

Both James and Morgan stared at Tom; his white lie had caught them offguard, and only now did they both fully realize his new position of authority. Thomas Cromwell might be the King's private secretary, but Tom Seymour was the King's future brother-in-law.

"I think some wine is in order," Tom was saying as he seated himself opposite Morgan and adjusted the links in the gold chain that hung from his broad shoulders.

James seemed momentarily frozen in place, but Tom's assertion of authority made him move for the wine cabinet, where he got out a decanter and three goblets. His hand was none too steady as he poured, and to Morgan, her husband's reaction seemed to signify the changing of the old order: Throughout the court—all over England, in fact—men and women were reexamining their allegiances, reestablishing their alliances, and all because Henry Tudor had chosen another wife.

"Jane wants to see you as soon as you feel up to it," Tom said, after he had taken a hefty drink from his goblet. "She is staying at Sir Nicholas Carew's house."

"Tomorrow?" Morgan asked in a voice that was still shaky.

"Well enough." He downed the remainder of his wine in two swallows and set the goblet on the mantel. Turning to Morgan, he took her hand and kissed it gently. "You were brave today, Morgan. It seems you have inherited your father's courage and daring." Tom bowed briefly to James, gave Morgan a smile that was but a shadow of his familiar grin, and left the room.

The long, hollow silence that followed Tom's departure made Morgan so uneasy that she got up and refilled her goblet. James was standing by an oaken armoire, staring at the floor. At last he spoke and his tone was strained. "I seem to have married a woman with highly placed friends and relations. I trust you will not use them to any disadvantage."

The topaz eyes widened. "Whatever are you talking about, James? I seek nothing, except to perform my duties at Belford in a manner befitting your Countess."

James regarded his wife with a questioning expression. He gave a short laugh and put a hand on her shoulder. "Of course, of course. I was being . . . fanciful. The past few days have been difficult for us all. Perhaps the sooner we go back to Belford, the better."

"I agree," Morgan said, and made an effort to smile. "But I do have one request. I would like to visit Faux Hall as long as we are so near. My family would be dreadfully disappointed if they didn't get to see Robbie."

For once, James did not take an inordinate amount of time to make up his mind. He told Morgan that they would leave for Faux Hall before the month was out and continue from there back to Belford. In the meantime, he would take care of certain matters pertaining to their estates. "I've had little time to do so since we arrived," he added, "and any visit to London must be used well."

Morgan agreed with as much enthusiasm as possible, hoping that her husband's ire had indeed disappeared and that they would resume their amicable if loveless relationship. And for once, Morgan was not distressed because she and James had not found passion in marriage. King Henry and Anne Boleyn had—and now he was about to take another wife and Anne lay dead in an arrowcase inside the Tower's cold walls.

* * *

Jane Seymour would never be a beauty, but Morgan had to admit that the royal bride-to-be exuded a radiance that enhanced her plain appearance. Her clothes were definitely unlike her customary apparel, however, and while scarcely as daring or innovative as Anne Boleyn's had always been, Jane's prim, unadorned grays and blues and browns had given way to rich saffron-colored damask, and the emerald necklace she wore had stones the size of robin's eggs.

Morgan started to curtsey when she entered the sitting room of Sir Nicholas Carew's elegant home, but Jane took her visitor by the arm and laughed. "Not yet, Morgan. I'm still Mistress Seymour."

"When, Jane?" Morgan asked, feeling ill at ease despite Jane's warm welcome.

Jane shrugged her slender shoulders. "I'm not certain. I only came to London three days ago from Wolf Hall. His Grace is tending to the arrangements." She motioned for her guest to sit beside her on a crimson velvet settee. The brilliant background and the saffron gown gave the characteristically subdued Jane a new vibrancy, Morgan thought—or was it Jane's inner excitement? How long, Morgan wondered, had Jane been considering the possibility of a royal diadem? Tom had avowed that his sister had only come to Henry's attention the previous autumn. But Jane was subtle and clever: It was possible that Jane had known who Henry's next wife would be long before he did.

"I offer my heartiest congratulations," Morgan said, and thought the words sounded lame.

Apparently Jane thought so too. A fine line creased her forehead as she regarded Morgan with a questioning look. "Tom told me you went to the Tower. I can't honestly expect you to feel great joy at my good fortune."

Impulsively, Morgan put a hand on Jane's damask-covered arm. "But I do, really. It's just that—that yesterday is still so fresh in my memory. And I did admire Anne, after all."

Jane sighed and suddenly looked more like the serious young woman Morgan remembered. "Of course you did. I did not. I served Catherine of Aragon and I was very fond of her. So much so, in fact, that if Anne had lived a hundred years, I could never have forgiven her for the wounds she inflicted on that saintly soul. No, no," Jane said quickly, seeing Morgan about to rise to Anne's defense. "It wasn't all Anne's fault, it was . . . others' as well, and the circumstances."

It was Henry, Morgan thought, and she wondered if despite her obvious exhilaration, Jane might not feel apprehensive about becoming the King's third wife. "But you must know I wish you well," Morgan said, and this time sounded sincere.

"Yes, I'm sure you do." Jane smiled and again the radiance showed through. "There is other matrimonial news in our family—have you heard?"

"No," Morgan answered, wondering if it could possibly be Tom. But he would have told her, surely. "Who?"

"My sister, Elizabeth, is marrying your uncle's son, Gregory. The date is not yet set, but the betrothal will occur as soon as His Grace and I are wed. Our families will be linked now by kinship as well as friendship."

"I haven't seen Gregory since we were children," Morgan said, and proceeded to tell Jane about Robbie and then about James and Belford and her life in the North. They spoke of Jane's trousseau and who she would choose as her ladies-in-waiting.

"If your cousin Nan wishes, I would like to include her."

"I'm sure she would be delighted," Morgan said. "James and I will talk to her about it—with your permission—when we go to Faux Hall."

"Please do. Of course I shall issue a formal invitation—when it's proper."

Morgan could not suppress a smile. She had no doubt that Jane would be a very "proper" sort of Queen, dealing carefully and kindly with every person and matter that came to her attention, carrying herself regally on state occasions, willing to let her royal husband make all the important decisions, giving as little cause for contention as possible between them. And it suddenly dawned on Morgan why Henry had chosen the prim, solemn Jane as opposed to a younger, livelier, prettier girl: After Anne Boleyn, even after Catherine of Aragon, Henry wanted peace—almost as much as he wanted a son.

"Well, I think he's a stick," Nan declared, tossing another pebble into the fishpond. "Oh, he's pleasant enough, but you've been here four days and I haven't heard James laugh once."

"He's quiet," Morgan asserted, well aware that she had spent a good deal of her time at Faux Hall defending her husband from Nan's outspoken criticisms.

"Quiet! His idea of expressing emotion is blinking! Oh, Morgan, I hope Cromwell doesn't choose a husband for me!"

"Everyone at court is a pawn," Morgan said tersely, and got to her feet. "It's starting to drizzle. I'm going to see Grandmother."

Nan scrambled up and hurried to Morgan's side. "Morgan, I know I shouldn't rattle on about James—it's just that I'd hoped for some other sort of husband for you. I mean, I know you can't be thrilled at . . . No, no, I'm putting it very badly. It's just that you have to live in that barren place and I would like to think you at least had someone you loved to share it with."

Morgan had told Nan she did not love James; it had practically been her cousin's first question and there was no point in lying. Her parents had not asked; either they already knew from the tone of her letters—or they knew Morgan.

Of course Grandmother Isabeau knew, too. The old woman did not give James her usual warm, witty welcome. At first, Morgan thought it was because her grandmother's health had failed considerably in the last two years and that she was almost constantly bedridden. But later Grandmother Isabeau had talked to Morgan alone:

"An unfortunate choice of Cromwell's," she had told her granddaughter bluntly. "You might mold him, but he'll never bend."

Morgan recalled the words as she went up the stairs to her grandmother's room, Nan still at her heels, still apologizing. "See here, Nan," Morgan said with her hand on the latch, "let's not talk about James any more. Then you won't have to be sorry for what you say."

Nan's long, oval face seemed to grow even longer; for the first time, Morgan realized that Nan had changed in the fourteen months since she had seen her cousin. The angular features had softened; the tall, coltish figure had filled out; the big, black eyes were still innocent but more aware.

Nan was no longer a child, and Morgan had to remember that from now on she must not treat her cousin as such.

"Nan," Morgan said with a fond smile, "what you have been saying may be quite right. But it does no one any good to be reminded of what-might-have-beens. James is kind and good, and a fine father."

Nan shifted from one foot to the other, somewhat embarrassed but still not quite willing to surrender her point of view. "I don't know—it just seems that life is too short to waste it in—merely surviving."

"Oh, it's not that grim!" Morgan forced a bright smile as she moved to lift the latch of her grandmother's door. "The child is a delight, and there is much to be done on the estates. When the weather is good, I keep quite busy. And James *is* really pleasant company, which is more than some men are."

But Nan did not look convinced. She made a little face, murmured, "I suppose you are right," and wandered off down the hall. Morgan watched her for a few seconds and tried to fight down the sudden surge of anger she felt rising in her breast.

"It's natural, this resentment," Grandmother Isabeau said five minutes later after Morgan had told her about the exchange with Nan. "You feel cheated by life, and well you should. We all are, *ma petite,* but those who accept the fact without challenging it live dreary lives indeed." Grandmother Isabeau paused to take several deep breaths and allow Morgan to offer her a few sips of water. Despite the summer weather, the old lady had weakened just within the short time Morgan and her family had been at Faux Hall. "You are still a young woman. Who knows what the fates have in store? I recommend what patience you can marshal and a will as hard as sapphires."

Morgan smiled at her grandmother as she dabbed the old woman's chin with a fine linen napkin. "I cannot change James, though, Gran'mère. What are you suggesting?"

"Qui sait?" The fine lines in Isabeau's forehead creased together. "James is thin, almost frail. How many winters will he last in that cold North Country?"

Morgan sat up in shock. "Oh, Gran'mère, I can't wish him dead! He is my husband!"

Grandmother Isabeau gave Morgan's hand a feeble pat.

"Oh, don't be a dreamer, *ma petite!* I realize you are young and kindly disposed, but I am old—and close enough to death myself, I daresay—to know that we all must die. I see James and I see poor health in his frame. I am merely being realistic." She laughed softly and then began to cough; Morgan proffered more water, but Grandmother Isabeau shook her head. "If you care not to face such probabilities and bide your time," the old woman went on when she had composed herself again, "then I would suggest a lover, a hearty, robust sort such as Saint-Maur."

"Tom!" Morgan was even more shocked at that idea than at her grandmother's fatalistic pronouncement about James. "Why, he's been like an older brother to me!"

The corners of Grandmother Isabeau's mouth turned down in a droll expression. "So he has—while you were still a little girl. Ah, I didn't say him precisely, I said someone like him, someone with flair, panache, excitement in his blood." The blue eyes were still bright and they fixed Morgan with a probing stare. "You would prefer the tall one in the orchard?"

"Oh!" Morgan gasped and all but fell off the chair. "You know!"

With an unsteady finger, Grandmother Isabeau pointed toward her casement window. "Above there, on the top story, where my sewing things are kept, is an excellent view. I saw him; I saw you."

Morgan's cheeks were hot; she was both angry and embarrassed. "You couldn't have! The trees were in full blossom! We would have been hidden, even from such a height!"

Grandmother Isabeau laughed again and this time she did not cough. "I did not say I had seen you together, *ma petite.* I said I saw him—and you, later, trying on your new dresses. You were not the same young maid who had left the house an hour before." The thin, old shoulders lifted in a typical French shrug. "And though it must have been a shock to you, poor child that you were, it was quite clear that you did not find him—or his attentions—truly repugnant?"

"I . . ." Morgan stared at the bedpost and felt her heart hammering away in her ears. "I did, though. I loathed him. He was—an animal. I was terrified and worried and . . ."

"Intrigued." Grandmother Isabeau nodded slowly. "As well you should be, if he performed as well as he gave orders to the Madden twins and cared for his horse and—what? The old collie? I liked the way he moved—not with grace as does Saint-Maur, but with purpose and confidence. I almost wished that he could have ridden away with you before Cromwell and his minions sent you off with a lesser sort of man." She paused and sighed deeply; Morgan could hear the ominous rattling noise in the old woman's chest. "Did you ever learn his name, *ma petite?*"

Morgan saw the question in her grandmother's eyes and the love and concern on her tired, wrinkled face. Her first reaction had been to lie, but she knew the truth would give her grandmother a sense of peace. "I did. He is my brother-in-law." She spoke quietly, her eyes fixed on her wedding ring. "He is Robbie's father."

"Ah?" She nodded with satisfaction. "Then you *do* know what I'm talking about. I thought you would. I am disappointed you tried to deceive your poor old gran'mère! You and—what is his name?"

The blue eyes were wide as Morgan murmured, "Francis," in reply.

"Oh, Francis, a fine name, fit for a King, as our French François would agree." She coughed again, sipped at the water, and smoothed the counterpane with the blue-veined hands. "You and Francis must love each other very deeply."

"By Our Lady, we don't love each other at all!" Morgan blurted. "We—we have not even been together since I married James. And he loves his wife, Lucy, very, very much."

"Hmmm. Of course he does. It is well for one's lover to love his wife; it shows a great heart. Oh, *ma petite,* I wish now I were not so close to heaven! I would like to remain here to see how much you and Francis do not love each other!" She laughed in an unnatural, noisesome way, which alarmed Morgan. But Grandmother Isabeau finally shook her head and waved her granddaughter's ministrations away. "More water and I shall float to *le bon Dieu* like an aged, leaky caravel. You will prevail somehow, dear child, and I will wish you well from heaven's gate."

* * *

Grandmother Isabeau died that night in her sleep, after receiving the sacraments from her own confessor, a handsome young priest from Berkhamstead. Sir Edmund told a grieving Morgan that they had found the old woman with a smile on her face.

Chapter 13

MORGAN AND LUCY spent most of July and August out on the terrace at Belford working on another set of baby clothes. The terrace not only afforded spectacular views of the sea, but the cool breeze drove away the summer heat. Lucy's two older children played nearby and the babies sat propped up on cushions where they could finger their toes and make gurgling noises at each other.

As before, Lucy was anxious for news of London and the court. Morgan tried to convince her sister-in-law that the journey had not been an enviable experience. "By the Saints, Lucy," Morgan said with a trace of exasperation, "the executions, the intrigues and scheming, the ruthless ambition—not to mention those poor monks we saw on our way south—I can't imagine you would enjoy such spectacles!"

Lucy flushed slightly and bent to retrieve a skein of yarn, which was rolling toward Robbie. She was almost into her sixth month, and her body was growing cumbersome. Dr. Wimble had permitted her to sit up at least part of the day as long as she did not spend too much time on her feet. "From this distance, it sounds rather . . . exciting. But I understand how you feel," Lucy asserted, as Robbie let out a disappointed cry when the skein was picked up before he could capture it for his own. "Such a sad homecoming, with your grandmother's death."

Morgan avoided Lucy's gaze; Grandmother Isabeau's words about Francis were still fresh in her mind. "In truth, I was glad to have been there when she died. She was a remarkable woman."

"French, you said?" Lucy plucked a long piece of thread from the skein and snapped it off with her small, white teeth. "Didn't you tell me once that she met your grandfa-

227

ther when he . . ." Lucy stopped speaking and beamed with pleasure. "Oh, Francis! You're home! I expected you yesterday."

Francis strode past Morgan, greeting her with a perfunctory hello before he bent to kiss Lucy's lips. He had been gone for a week to Newcastle, buying provisions from Flemish sea captains.

"A certain Vanderhoef proved obstinate," Francis said, as his two older children scrambled for his attention. He hugged and kissed each in turn, then picked up his youngest child. "Either you've grown, small scamp, or your clothes have shrunk. Lucy," he said, turning back to his wife as he bounced little George in his arms, "shouldn't you be back in bed? It's well onto four o'clock."

"Don't fuss, I'm fine," Lucy said with another smile. "Just sitting here doesn't tax me. I feel too weak when I stay abed so much."

But Francis's frown eased only slightly. "I must assume that Dr. Wimble knows his business. And that you do, too." Carefully, he set the baby back down among the pillows. "I must change and wash," he announced in that deep voice, and saluted both women before heading into the castle with his two eldest children at his heels.

"Such a worrywart!" Lucy exclaimed fondly. "To tell the truth, Morgan, I have a cramp in my leg. I get them often these days. Shall we walk just a bit before I retire?"

"I don't know—you really aren't supposed to, are you?" Morgan looked questioningly at Lucy, noting that her almost-constant pallor had given way to a heightened color with Francis's return.

But Lucy was already on her feet. "Peg?" she called, and called twice more before the servingwoman appeared with a basket of fresh-cut iris under her arm. Peg also looked dubious when informed that the two women were going for a short walk, but took up her post watching the babies as Lucy and Morgan headed slowly down the stone stairs to the sea-cliff path.

"A lovely summer day," Lucy declared, gazing out toward the rocky wedge of the Holy Isle. "There, my cramp is already gone. You have not yet been to the isle, have you, Morgan?"

"I keep intending to," Morgan answered, treading cautiously on the pebble-strewn path, which led down to the water's edge. "James was going to go with me last week, but that was when the village chandler burned his hand so badly in hot tallow."

"The chandler is better, though?" Lucy asked, turning to look over her shoulder at Morgan. Suddenly Lucy's face froze and she halted in midstep. "Oh!" she cried, and staggered toward a twisted tree trunk.

"What is it?" Morgan demanded, rushing to her sister-in-law's side. She felt Lucy sway; it took all her strength to keep the other girl from going over the cliff. Morgan dragged her away from the edge, and Lucy collapsed against some rocks, her hands on her stomach.

"The child! Something is wrong . . ."

Morgan looked frantically about her. No one was in sight and it was almost a quarter of a mile back to the castle. "Can you walk?" she asked Lucy, already knowing the answer.

"The pain! Oh, God!" Lucy doubled over and screamed, her brown hair tumbling over her face.

Morgan bent down, shouting over the wind and Lucy's groans. "I must fetch help! Listen, Lucy! I must leave you, but I'll run." Lucy's head nodded slightly as she writhed against the rocks.

Morgan picked up her skirts and raced away, stumbling occasionally over stones, unaware that she had torn her dress on a brier bush. It seemed like an hour before she reached the terrace, only to find it deserted. Peg must have gone indoors with the babies. Morgan hesitated as she heard James's voice calling to a servant. Sure enough, he was at the south entrance, about to mount his bay gelding.

"James!" Morgan called, leaning over the terrace railing. "Get Francis quickly! Lucy is having the baby!"

James looked up, the riding crop falling from his hand. "Where? Where is she?"

"On the sea-cliff path. Francis came back to the castle, but he went to change his clothes. Hurry, James!" But James had already disappeared. Morgan started back, hurrying down the path, but she had only gone half the distance when she heard Francis running behind her, dressed in shirt and hose, his hair still damp.

"James has gone for Dr. Wimble," he called. Morgan nodded, not wanting to waste her breath on words. But within a few yards, Francis had overtaken her, all but

229

pushing her aside. His mouth was set in a grim, hard line, and the look on his face frightened her so much that she averted her eyes, concentrating instead on a prayer to the Virgin for Lucy's safety.

They found Lucy unconscious among the rocks. Massive amounts of blood clotted the dirt. At the edge of her skirt lay a tiny baby boy, the cord still attached. He was dead.

Francis fell to the ground, a strange animal cry wrenched from his throat. He gathered up both Lucy and the dead babe in his arms and sobbed. Morgan covered her face with her hands and turned away, an overwhelming sense of misery and desolation enfolding her.

Somehow, she pulled herself together and turned back to Francis and Lucy. Lucy's eyes flickered open as she tried to talk. "Forgive . . ." was all she could say. Francis kissed her forehead and rubbed his cheek against hers. Then he gathered Lucy up in his arms.

"I will take her back to the castle," he said to Morgan, forcing his voice to stay even. "I want you to take your skirt and wrap the baby in it and bury him—here."

Morgan was aghast. "But Francis—I have nothing to dig with. The ground is hard . . . I can't . . ."

"I want him buried here—overlooking the sea!" He was almost screaming and the look in his eyes was near murderous. "Use your shoes, your hands, the rocks, anything! Just do it or I'll whip you!" He was already moving up the path, with Lucy's brown hair streaming over his arm.

Morgan stood staring at the tiny body for a long time. Afterwards, she had no idea what thoughts had been in her mind unless she had been praying. Finally she grasped the light wool of her black mourning dress at the waist and gave it a fierce tug. She stooped down and tenderly wrapped the baby in the cloth. Then she kissed the little bundle where the curve of the head showed.

"Poor little creature," she said aloud, making the sign of the cross with her thumb, "that much love at least I can give you." She set the sad burden aside, selected a sharp rock, and began to dig a few yards away under a crooked tree whose limbs stretched out toward the Holy Isle.

Lucy was dangerously ill for almost a week. Francis spoke little, but paced their room during the days like an angry lion. He never asked Morgan if she had buried the child; it apparently never occurred to him that she would disobey.

When at last it was certain that Lucy would recover, Dr. Wimble told Francis she must never try to have another child. Francis didn't answer him, but went into the village that night and got very drunk.

Morgan, of course, didn't know until later—when Lucy tearfully told her—what Dr. Wimble had said. But she did know that Francis was gone all that night, and in the morning when Lucy asked to see him, Morgan stood waiting in the entrance hall until he returned.

He rode into the courtyard about nine o'clock. Morgan noticed that he was reeling slightly; she had never seen him drunk. When he came into the hallway she could smell the liquor on his breath and she saw four long scratches on his left cheek. She thought of Lucy, her sweet, pale face propped up against the pillows, and anger overcame her.

"You scurrilous knave! You've been drinking and whoring! While your poor wife cries out for you from her sickbed! If it hadn't been for your filthy lust she wouldn't be there in the first place!"

Francis's gray eyes glittered. His right hand snapped up as if to strike Morgan, but he let it fall back to his side. He shrugged and turned his back on her.

"You have a vicious tongue, Morgan," he said, trying to control both his rage and the slur of his speech.

"You! Criticizing me!" she lashed at him. "I haven't known what to tell poor Lucy. I've been lying to her for almost two hours. And you can't go to see her looking like that. Those scratches—how will you explain them?"

He wheeled around and grabbed Morgan's shoulders in a viselike grip. Francis picked her right up off her feet so that his face was almost touching hers. "I don't have to explain anything, especially to you," he said in a low, furious voice.

She kept looking straight at him but was unable to reply. His eyes seemed to paralyze her and his fingers dug so deep into her shoulders that she thought he must be drawing blood. He kept staring at her until she thought she would scream, but instead, she finally spoke in a firm, level voice. "Put me down, Francis. Now."

To her astonishment, he did just that. Then he strode

away, his booted and spurred feet echoing over the stone floor.

He had gone directly to see Lucy. She told Morgan about his visit later that afternoon. Lucy also told her then about Dr. Wimble's admonition. It distressed Lucy greatly, but more for Francis's sake than her own.

Lucy, however, made no comment about Francis's absence or the condition in which he had returned. Apparently, Morgan decided, Lucy understood her husband very well.

By early October Lucy was feeling recovered and even Francis's droll humor was restored. For the first week or two after his night away from the castle, he spent a great deal of his time walking the sea cliffs, where Morgan was certain he visited the grave of his tiny son. James told her later that Francis had had a cross put on the grave and that Lucy had gone there with her husband one afternoon to pray.

The weather that fall was warm and clear, with the promise of further good crops. Belford's tenants had harvested large quantities of wheat, rye, and beans so far. Indeed, reports from all over England were good that year. It seemed to be a sign of favor for Henry and his new Queen.

Beneath the surface, however, there were new, serious troubles. In early October James received a letter from Percy, who was very ill at his Northumberland ancestral home. He told in detail of a rising in Lincolnshire by supporters of the old faith. Lincoln itself had been taken the day before Percy had written. Encouraged by local priests, nobles and commoners had banded together to demand that the dissolution of the monasteries should stop, that taxes be lessened, and that heresy should cease.

Percy wrote that he was certain the King would refuse the requests. For his own part, he could do nothing; he was too tired and ill. But he begged James and Francis to resist should the disturbances creep northward. "For you and your brother are the only North men I know to be loyal to King and country," Percy concluded.

James had read the letter aloud in the library where Francis had been encamped among his books. Morgan and Lucy were both present, for James thought that they, too, should hear Percy's words.

"I heard murmurings in Bamburgh when I was there day before yesterday," Francis said, crossing his long legs at the ankle. "But if the King reacts firmly, the insurgents will desist."

"Mayhap," James answered. He fingered Percy's letter thoughtfully. "You would be glad to see them put down, Brother?"

"I'd rather not see civil war in England, whatever the cause," Francis replied. He stretched lazily, his long arms appearing to reach almost across the small room. "I would always opt for reason and goodwill to prevail, though such notions make me sound impossibly unrealistic."

It was unrealistic, as all the inhabitants of Belford Castle soon learned when the threat of civil war was brought disturbingly close. In York, Lord Latimer and other Catholic leaders instigated the Pilgrimage of Grace, marching with banners which urged King Henry to reject his evil councillors and embrace the true Mother Church once more. York was turned into an armed camp as the King sent his soldiers north to combat the insurgents.

James was indignant over this bold challenge of his sovereign's policies. Francis, however, defended the pilgrim rebels' right to moral persuasion. After a particularly heated argument at supper one evening, Francis stormed from the table, and as Lucy started to follow him, James deterred her:

"My brother is too impulsive and sentimental," he told Lucy. "You must not pander to his ill humor or reckless opinions. It is one thing for him to speak his mind within the walls of Belford, but it would be foolish and even dangerous if he were encouraged to speak so elsewhere."

Lucy murmured that no doubt James was right. The three remaining members of the Sinclair family finished their supper in awkward silence.

It was Morgan, in fact, who sought out Francis later. While she could sympathize with the pilgrims' motives, she still had contempt for those who staked their lives on religious principles. The lesson of Sean O'Connor was not easily forgotten. But most of all, she disliked the dissension between James and Francis. James was so cold and correct, Francis so obstinate and volatile. And Morgan knew better than anyone how religious differences could wreak havoc.

It was a blustery autumn night when Morgan entered Francis's library to find him seated in his favorite chair, his feet propped up on the desk, a thick tome in his hands. He did not look pleased at the intrusion.

"Don't think me predisposed toward heresy because I was married to your brother in the new rites," Morgan began without preamble as she seated herself across the desk from Francis, "but my own feeling is that once Henry has a son, he will return to the Church of Rome and all this controversy will be put aside. Meanwhile, it's best for all of his subjects to bide and hold our tongues."

"Faugh! We will never go back! At least Henry Tudor will not." Francis scowled at Morgan from under his bushy eyebrows. "You think he would relinquish the power of heading his own church? How little you know of human nature!"

"I know enough to realize that James can be goaded just so far," Morgan warned as a gust of wind rattled the casements. "Don't exacerbate the quarrel further, Francis."

Slowly, he lowered the heavy volume onto the desk. "Don't lecture me, Morgan. I'm not a fool. I don't intend to stand up in the middle of York Minster or Whitehall and bellow my beliefs. But there are matters in life about which no man can remain silent and still retain his honor."

Morgan blinked at Francis, who seemed pompous, dignified, and angry all at the same time. His words confused her; he did not intend to proclaim his convictions, yet he vowed not to keep them within himself, either. "I don't know what you're talking about," she said at last in a sullen tone as rain slipped through the chimney opening and spluttered among the flames.

"I didn't expect you to," Francis asserted, now looking more angry than pompous or dignified. "You sign oaths, acts, and marriage contracts as you would scribble your name on a dressmaker's chit. You never think for one minute what any of it really means."

Morgan leaped to her feet, toppling a small bust of Aristotle onto the worn carpet. "That's not so! I was coerced into each of those signatures!"

Francis snorted. "Coercion or not, I daresay you never thought any of them through, never agonized for more than a few seconds—and probably can't even recall to what you swore your soul away."

"And what if I had? What good would it have done? What good did it do Sean O'Connor?" she blazed.

He had also stood up, looming over her across the four-foot width of the oak desk. "I knew you'd dredge up his name for the sake of this argument. I would like to think that at least O'Connor had an inkling of what he was martyred for, though I suspect he may have been as much anti-English as he was pro-Rome. Heretics and fanatics alike have a way of bending the truth to suit their own needs and ambitions."

"And you?" Morgan waved a finger in his face. "What makes you different from Sean or Henry Tudor—or your brother, for that matter?"

Francis snatched the hand that waggled in front of him and held it fast. "That's difficult to say," he replied evenly. "But for one thing, I'm not steeped in self-deception, as so many are. I won't deceive you either, Morgan. I want you. Now."

Morgan's free hand flew to her mouth; the topaz eyes widened in surprise. It had been such a long time since she and Francis had touched except in the most casual, even accidental manner that she had all but stifled the threat of his desire—and her own response.

"Well?" He was still regarding her steadily, the anger now replaced by a hint of amusement. She was silent, a reaction he took for consent, and he let go of her hand to stride to the door and lock it. When he turned back to her, she was leaning against the desk, offering neither resistance nor invitation. "Well?" he repeated.

"I'm with child, Francis."

It was his turn to look surprised. And then he threw back his head and laughed in that deep guffaw she had not heard for some time. At last he sobered and shook his head. "By God, I'm glad for James! I didn't think he could manage it." He stopped and raised those bushy eyebrows at her again. "It *is* James's?"

"Of course it is, you beast! You think I would betray him?" she shouted, and quickly lowered her voice lest a servant passing through the corridor hear her.

"You have, you know. Your question should have been, 'You think I would betray him with anyone but you?' " He pulled her into his arms and removed the gold-trimmed coif to kiss the top of her head. "I'm merely amazed at James's virility. And genuinely happy for him, too."

"You have a very peculiar way of demonstrating it," Morgan retorted vexedly. "Now let me go; it's getting late."

"It is getting late, but I'm not letting you go. Nay, don't think to put me off with the mother-to-be's lament of abstinence during pregnancy—it may work with James, but I know better. You were already carrying my babe the last time we made love."

"It was so long ago, I'd almost forgotten." Morgan had meant the words to sound mocking, but to her chagrin, the plaintive note in her voice gave her away and Francis gripped her shoulders, forcing her to look up at him.

"It was indeed long ago—but I have not forgotten, and neither have you, you inept little liar." Before Morgan could answer, his mouth was on hers, drawing the very breath from her, blotting out the sound of the wind and the snap of the fire. He lifted her off her feet, kissing her throat, her neck, the curve of her shoulder, and the cleft between her breasts in the square-necked gown. Morgan's hands pulled him even closer, her fingers in his hair, her teeth bared against his ear, her body pressed tight against him. His weight was forcing her down onto the floor in front of the fireplace and she crumpled unresisting onto the old carpet. "Damned hooks," he murmured, "why don't you help for once?"

She did, laughing at his clumsiness, astonished at her own. But it was not long before they were both naked, with the fire casting an amber glow on their bodies and their shadows merging on the library's far wall.

"You are more womanly than when I last saw you thus," Francis declared, holding her rounded breasts in his hands.

"I shall soon be more portly as well," she sighed, letting her eyes roam over his long, lean body and tracing her fingers through the mat of dark blond hair on his chest.

He flicked each nipple with his thumb and grinned at the hard, pink points. "Your eagerness is always so gratifyingly obvious. Do you greet James with equal ardor?"

"You need not know that," Morgan replied. But of course he already knew she did not. "As for you," she murmured, reaching down to clutch his hard manhood with her fingers, "do you want Lucy that much, all the time?"

"Usually." His tone was matter-of-fact, but the mouth that covered her breasts with kisses was impassioned and made her moan with pleasure. His hand moved between her thighs and she felt the flesh throb at his touch. Morgan writhed, arching her body toward him, urging him to probe harder, pressing her legs together to feel the full sensation of those searching fingers. To her astonishment, the fulfillment she'd yearned for came in a startling, sudden frenzy of delight, rendering her limp and gasping on the carpet.

Francis rolled over onto his side and regarded her with amusement. "I didn't realize you were *that* eager," he commented dryly, pushing the sandy hair from his forehead. "I trust your endurance matches your impatience."

Morgan looked at him through a haze of contentment. "I'm sorry—I couldn't help it." She felt her cheeks flush with embarrassment and started to turn away, but Francis moved suddenly, trapping her between his knees.

"Indeed, I'm flattered. But you can pleasure me in more ways than one." He held her chin with his hand and moved the pride of his virility toward her mouth. Morgan stared in surprise and dismay. "Well?" Francis demanded. "Are there parts of me you find undesirable?"

Her cheeks grew even warmer as she fixed her gaze on his face. "No . . . but I never . . . it seems strange . . ."

"Hardly strange at all, since you willingly accept my member in another part of your body. Somehow, such squeamishness doesn't suit you."

She paused for just a moment, transfixed by the nearness of him. But the firm masculine flesh that hovered over her lips *was* part of Francis; it was the source of her firstborn child, the instrument of her contentment. She took him, tentatively at first, and then with more intensity, and felt him all but fill her mouth until she thought she would choke.

And then he withdrew himself to fall on top of her, plunging between her thighs, and from somewhere in the night a brilliance rent the darkness like so many shooting stars blazing across the sky.

* * *

They lay quiet for several moments, savoring the joy they had given each other, reveling in the sudden peace born of their passion. "Francis . . ." Morgan spoke at last, craning her neck to look into his face. The light from the dying fire threw shadows that made the bushy brows seem more pronounced and the long face almost wolfish. She paused, suddenly afraid to go on.

But Francis's voice was not only encouraging, it was surprisingly gentle. "What is is, Morgan?"

"I'm confused . . . I don't understand why . . ." She lowered her eyes and stared at the mat of hair on his chest. "It seems that you make me feel so . . . uncontrolled."

"Uncontrolled?" Francis chuckled. "I would have chosen a different word. But it's quite simple. You are a woman and I am a man."

Morgan propped herself up on one elbow, her rounded breasts almost touching Francis's chest. "God's teeth," she swore, using one of Tom Seymour's favorite oaths, "that's *too* simple. I don't believe it!"

Francis shrugged and brushed her nipples with his forearm. "All right. We are well mated—at least in this sense. There are many ways man and woman can be mated—physically, intellectually, emotionally, spiritually, romantically. Lucy and I are well matched emotionally and spiritually. Perhaps romantically, too. She does not, however, share my intellectual or physical temperament. Still, we have made a good marriage."

The last log sputtered and cracked in two. A smattering of sparks landed on the hearth, glowing red-hot before fading into the darkness. "So," said Morgan slowly, "it is because of the physical differences that you go to whores—and me?"

He saw the bitterness in the topaz eyes and touched her cheek with his hand, forcing her to look at him. "You are no whore. You are a woman, totally female, utterly without pretense or coquettishness when aroused by the right man. You are young and healthy, finely made, but not fragile. And you have an instinctive aptitude for what pleases a man—and yourself."

The calm, succinct explanation rendered Morgan speechless. She blinked several times, then frowned as she pondered Francis's words.

"You are still puzzling why, after the baby was born

dead, I sought out a strumpet when I could have come to you," Francis said in the same reasonable tone. "For one thing, you were also upset. You would have wanted tenderness, but I needed a violent purging of my rage. Even in happier times, Lucy could not abide my unleashed passions, in body or in mind. There are many aspects of lovemaking she finds distasteful. And she is very delicate, even more so now that she has lost the child. We must be very careful that she never becomes pregnant again."

The fire had gone out, and the only light in the room came from the three-tiered candelabrum on Francis's desk. Outside, the wind was blowing out to sea but the rain was pelting the windows with renewed vigor. "I see—I think." Morgan gave a choked little laugh. "How complex—and difficult for you both. I take it Lucy knows about—the whores?"

"Oh, yes." Francis was sitting up now too, his arms encircling his knees. "We never discuss it—but she knows." He was silent for a moment, staring into the darkest corner of the room. "She does not know about you, of course. She must never know that." The gray eyes swerved to fix on Morgan's shadowy face. Francis's voice had sharpened and she heard the unspoken threat.

"I would never tell her—or James," she asserted.

"No, you would not," Francis agreed. He reached for his clothes and stood up. "That's why I stay away from you as much as I do. They must never, never find out what is between us. Come now," he said brusquely, "it's late and it's cold."

They dressed without speaking and Francis was ready first, going to his desk to put away the books and blow out the three candles. Morgan adjusted her coif just as the mantel clock struck eleven. She could barely see Francis in the darkened room, but felt his hand on her arm, guiding her toward the door. They entered the empty hallway and walked to the main staircase together.

"I'm hungry," Francis announced. "I think I'll go forage in the castle kitchen."

Morgan nodded once; she felt she ought to say something to resurrect the closeness she had felt toward Francis such a short time ago. But it was only physical intimacy, she told herself, and there was no need to play on sentiments that did not exist. "Good night," she said at last in a wispy,

239

small voice. But Francis was already striding toward the kitchen and did not seem to hear her.

To her surprise, James was not only awake, but still dressed and pacing their bedchamber. Morgan froze in midstep as he stopped to gaze at her with ice-blue eyes.

"Where in God's name have you been? It's past eleven! You left the supper room over two hours ago!"

Morgan's brain whirled in an effort to offer a credible explanation. But James gave her no opportunity to reply. In a half-dozen quick steps, he was in front of her, his hands on her upper arms. "Well? Am I right? Were you with my brother?"

Oh, Jesu, Morgan thought dazedly—he knows. She jerked away from him and rubbed at the place between her eyebrows with frenzied fingers. "Please, James, I'm so tired— and the new babe makes me queasy, even at night."

James snatched at her hand and pulled her directly in front of him so that they were almost touching. "But not so tired that you can't while away your evenings with Francis! What were you two doing?"

The cold fury in James's face made Morgan tremble. Yet how could he be sure of the truth? She tried to control her shaking limbs and raised her voice: "I went to see him because the two of you worry me! All this quarreling over religion gets on my nerves. I can't stand it, especially right now!"

James let go of her hand and moved back a step or two. "As I suspected," he said, nodding in satisfaction. "And I know what happened next—Francis played on those pro-Papist sympathies you shared with that Irishman, and no doubt my brother has set you against me!"

"Oh, rot!" Morgan cried as much in relief as in anger. "It's because of 'that Irishman,' as you so unkindly call him, that I detest your quarrel with Francis! That's what I tried to tell him." To help compose her churning emotions, she began to remove her coif and pearl necklace. "Naturally he put forth his own case, and naturally we argued. But," she continued, placing the necklace in her jewel casket and speaking in a more normal tone, "neither of us would give in, so we spoke of other things, mainly Lucy and the poor dead babe. Francis is still sorrowing and so afraid for Lucy. Though you must know all that as well as I

240

do. After all, James," she said with a diffident smile, "Francis must envy you a wife who can bear your strong, healthy children without serious complications."

The play on James's masculine vanity worked. His sharp features softened and the blue eyes warmed. "Well, at least he already has three robust youngsters. Yet the prospect of never having more must distress him, of course."

"I would imagine so," Morgan agreed, unfastening her dress and hoping that the candlelight played invitingly on her fruitful body. "Still, I didn't intend to worry you, but you know how Francis can go on once he gets started."

"I certainly do." James paused and watched his wife step free of her garments. "Are you certain we couldn't—that we shouldn't make love tonight?" he asked in a plaintive voice.

Morgan frowned and bit her lip in apparent anxiety. As before, she and James had agreed it would be better to abstain from marital relations during her pregnancy. But she was so relieved that he had not guessed what had really gone on between her and Francis that she weakened in her resolve. "Perhaps we could—but wait until tomorrow night, James. I am a bit queasy and very, very tired after arguing with Francis."

Morgan was safely delivered of another son on April nineteenth in the year 1537. The labor was hard but not long, and she was grateful that her second child had come into the world under happier circumstances than her firstborn. The child was christened Edmund, after Morgan's father. As soon as she could sit up and write, a letter was dispatched to Faux Hall.

One month later, the letter that came back was not from Faux Hall, but from London, and was penned in Nan's rounded hand. It contained shattering news: Morgan's parents had died within a week of each other, Lady Alice passing first, and three days later, on the day of his namesake's birth, Sir Edmund had joined his wife in the final sanctuary of death.

"It was not plague," Nan wrote, "though it was feared so at first. Both your parents succumbed to high fevers and excruciating stomach cramps, and ultimately, delirium.

They have been buried next to Grandmother Isabeau and Grandfather William in the family plot at St. Michael's."

It was two days before Morgan could emerge from her grief to finish reading her cousin's letter. Nan had returned to court, taking Aunt Margaret with her. Faux Hall was too empty now, and though Nan knew how much her mother detested court life, she felt that the serene atmosphere under Jane Seymour's influence might make Aunt Margaret's stay more bearable.

"She is not as well as she might be, having contracted the same disease in a less serious form," Nan wrote. "Naturally, she was mightily distressed over the King's harsh dealings with the participants in the Pilgrimage of Grace. So many were executed, though Lord Latimer was spared." But Nan's letter was not all grim: "The Queen told me she is with child. Now all know it and the King rejoices, treating Jane as if she were the most delicate piece of Venetian glass. Her Grace and I have become quite close, and last March her brother, Harry, came to court for a visit. He is jolly like Tom, dark like Ned, but of such an even disposition and with the ability to make everyone who converses with him feel as if she—or he—is the most important person ever born. He is a widower with two small children, and no doubt lonely beneath that kindly exterior."

Morgan folded the parchment and replaced it in her leather pouch for safekeeping. Nan was in love with a Seymour, or so it appeared. A faint smile played at Morgan's mouth, the first since she'd learned of her parents' death. But for James, the important news was that the Queen was pregnant and that King Henry might get the son and heir he had wanted so desperately.

Morgan smiled encouragement as she watched Robbie toddle on chubby legs along the long gallery at Belford. The July day had started out sunny, but heavy clouds moved in from the North Sea and rain chased both mother and child in from their romp in the orchard. Little Edmund was napping in the nursery and James had gone into the village to settle a quarrel between two tenants who were in conflict over a boundary which ran through their adjoining fields. Still, he ought to be back by now, she thought, as it was past the supper hour and she was growing hungry.

But it was Francis, not James, who came into the gallery, the bushy eyebrows drawn together and his mouth set in a tight line. "Sit, Morgan," he ordered peremptorily, motioning to the settee with its fine-stitched covering made by the Dowager Countess some years earlier.

Morgan obeyed, eyeing him speculatively. Robbie continued to scurry about, chasing a tabby cat one moment, kicking at a ball the next. When Francis remained silent, she finally plucked up the courage to ask what was wrong.

He did not respond at once, but kept his gaze fixed on Robbie's happy, unceasing movements. "Much is wrong," he said at last. "Lucy and I are leaving Belford tomorrow."

Morgan's mouth dropped open. "Why? For how long?"

He sat up straight but still didn't meet her eyes. "Forever, I daresay. I have quarreled with James. It is not a matter that can be mended."

"What do you mean?"

Now he finally faced her. "It started out over these bloody reprisals the King and your uncle instigated against the poor souls who took part in the Pilgrimage of Grace. Until now, I've gone along with many of the new ways, since I felt reform was needed in the Church. But these murders—how many I've lost count—are too much for my stomach. And murder it is, not justice. James disagrees; he thinks it right and proper. He told me he could not shelter a traitor beneath his roof."

Protests came to Morgan's lips but Francis stood up, stalking the gallery, and went on talking. "If he considers me a traitor, I will not stay here to scar his conscience. It is, of course, *his* roof—he never lets me forget that." He looked down to his boot where Robbie was clambering, begging to be picked up. Francis bent over to swing the child high above his head, and Robbie squealed with pleasure.

"Oh, Francis!" Morgan came to stand beside him. "What of Lucy? Where will you go? To Woodstock?"

Francis held Robbie in the crook of his right arm. "As you know, Lucy has always had strong feelings about the old faith. You also know that an uncle of hers died this winter in Carlisle. He was a childless widower, with fond memories of Lucy as a little girl. He left his possessions to her—not much, just a small manor house and a few farms, but we'll make do. Woodstock is too close to London for my tastes just now." He set Robbie on the ground, regarding the little boy with a fond, faint smile. "Grow up strong, wee one."

Morgan's eyes were flooding with tears. Francis started to walk away but she grasped his sleeve. "Francis! You can't leave us, not like this!" She clung to him, both hands holding his arm.

He shook his head. "No tears, for Christ's sake! I can't bear tears! We leave before daybreak, and I wish you'd spare Lucy the pain of farewells. It's better that way."

Morgan covered her face with her hands; she was sobbing aloud now and could only nod. Francis bent down and gently took her hands away. He kissed the tears on her cheek, and was gone.

James was jiggling tiny Edmund on his knee. One look at his wife's red eyes told him what he wanted to know. "You've heard, then?"

"Yes. Francis told me." They said no more, and Morgan went into the bedchamber and fell facedown on the counterpane.

Acceding to Francis's request, Morgan did not see Lucy. But as the first light crept into the western sky, she rose from bed and tiptoed into the hallway and down to a window overlooking the courtyard. Lucy and the children were already there, watching as the servants piled the last items atop the carriage and onto the mules. Francis came out from a side entrance. He helped Lucy and the little ones into the carriage and called for their serving people to mount. Then he swung up onto his gray gelding, and the gates opened wide as the little procession moved out of the castle courtyard.

Chapter 14

NOW THE LONELINESS set in. Gone was Lucy's high, clear laughter, the children's scampering feet, Francis's gruff, booming voice. James never mentioned them; it was understood that their names should never more be heard at Belford Castle.

He knew why his wife was strangely quiet, why she spoke to him in words instead of sentences. But he was certain she would get over it in time. Meanwhile, he could devote even more of his energies to building up Belford and its lands.

It was autumn before Morgan's spirits began to pick up. She must remain friends with James, she reasoned, for there was no other companionship except for the children and the servingwomen. Gregarious by nature, she could no longer endure her self-imposed unsociability.

She would not apologize for her remoteness, of course. Instead, she arranged for an especially tasty supper for herself and her husband, with candles burning in the best gold candlesticks and incense permeating the room.

James was appreciative. He told her so as they finished up the last morsels of the pheasant, and she smiled, the first real smile in months.

"After all," she said, serious again, "we only have each other and the children now."

They both drank more wine than usual. James suggested a walk to clear their heads and Morgan agreed. They ventured down the castle roadway, then up the little hill where they could survey not only the sea but the surrounding countryside. The moon glistened on the waves and they could hear the water lapping on the shore far below. James looked all about him, in every direction.

"I love this land," he said, aware that the wine had

made him expansive. "The crops have been good and I . . ." Something caught his eye, far off on a distant hill. "Look! Bonfires!"

Morgan shuddered. "Not another border raid?"

"No, no—those are signal fires. It must be the Queen. She must have given birth."

The fires seemed to grow brighter as Morgan peered into the darkness. "Does it mean she's had a son?"

"Aye, I wager it does." James lifted a hand in the air and cried out, "God save England! God save the King!" He smiled foolishly at Morgan. "I grow too exuberant." He put his arm around his wife; even though they had continued to sleep in the same bed, they had not touched each other since the day before Francis and Lucy left Belford. "You are cold," he said, feeling her shiver slightly.

Morgan wasn't sure whether it was the night chill that made her tremble or something else. But she nodded. "Yes, perhaps we had better go inside."

They made love that night, more tenderly, if not passionately, than they ever had before. When at last they lay back in bed, Morgan noticed that James hadn't drifted off to sleep as he usually did. Suddenly she sat up, resting on one elbow. "Who did you really wish to marry, James? Did you love her deeply?"

She couldn't see his face very well but she heard the sharp intake of breath. "Why do you ask?"

"I don't know—I've just always wondered," she replied.

He shifted his body beneath the bedclothes and cleared his throat. "She was the daughter of a Newcastle shipbuilder. She had hair as black as a raven's feathers and eyes as blue as an ocean sky. My father forbade us to wed. She was beneath me, he said. The last time I saw her was on my way to London to become betrothed to you." He had kept his voice even, as if he had been discussing how the pear orchards had fared that year.

"I'm sorry," Morgan said simply. She settled back into bed and was silent. Maybe she shouldn't have pried, for he had never inquired into her own past. But then maybe he had never cared enough about her to be curious.

They learned the next morning that Jane Seymour had given birth to a boy who would be called Edward. All England rejoiced. Morgan was delighted for Jane and smiled at the thought of Tom Seymour as uncle to a future King.

Soon other news reached Belford. Queen Jane was dead. She had come down with fever after the christening, and five days later she had died while Henry paced outside her room and wept.

Morgan wept, too, and hurriedly wrote a letter to Tom. "You have been with me in so many of my troubles," she told him, "that only the good Christ knows how much I wish I were with you in yours."

She looked down at the words written in her big, sweeping script. How she did wish she could be with him! Almost two years since she had seen him. "Dear Tom . . . how I miss you!" she whispered into the empty room. Quickly, she folded the letter and applied the seal.

"I look like a Turk!" Nan leaned forward into the mirror, hands on her hips. She turned around to where Morgan was laughing on her bed. "This isn't a wedding headpiece, it's some sort of hideous burnoose! Did I really order this?" She snatched the ornate coif, veil and all, from her head. "I'm tall enough without that!"

Morgan pulled herself to her feet, still laughing at her cousin. "You told the shop owner you wanted one like the Duchess of Suffolk's. I heard you say it."

"Kate Willoughby is a clever wench, but she never did have an ounce of taste." Nan sighed and collapsed into a chair. "Let's drink," she said, snapping her fingers at her serving wench. Nan surveyed the rest of her wedding finery, which was scattered about the room. The ceremony uniting her with Harry Seymour was only two days off. Though now the uncle of a prince, Harry still refused to spend much time at court.

But he had, of course, come to London for little Edward's christening and Jane's funeral. Though his stay was brief, it was long enough to convince him that the dark, dazzling Nan with her vivacious manner would make not only a winsome wife but an excellent stepmother for his two small children. If Harry lacked Tom's dashing good looks and Ned's penetrating mind, he had his own quiet charm and wry sense of humor.

"Well, it won't do," declared Nan, giving the headgear a kick with her satin-shod foot. She accepted a goblet of wine from her serving girl and took a deep draught. "Lord, I'm so glad you came, Morgan! Two years! I was ready to saddle up and come see you."

Morgan was as glad to be back at court as Nan was to have her there. They had arrived ten days earlier, James setting off immediately to handle business affairs while Morgan helped Nan choose her trousseau. The ceremony would be at Wolf Hall in Wiltshire and the wedding party was to leave the next morning.

Aunt Margaret, now supported by a cane, came thumping into the room. "What! You girls drinking again? You'll both be sots before the festivities start." She had grown thinner and more lined, but Morgan had been so glad to see her aunt that she wouldn't have cared if the older woman had looked like a hamper of prunes.

The serving wench proffered a glass of wine to Aunt Margaret, which she accepted readily enough, and sat down on the bed next to Morgan. "You and I must talk," she told her niece. Morgan asked her what about. "Faux Hall is yours, of course," Aunt Margaret said. "I'm going to live with Nan and Harry. My daughter's condescended to take in her doddering mother." She pulled a wry face at Nan, who was kicking off her shoes. "So, I suggest you make arrangements for the maintenance of the place through Thomas Cromwell." She spat out a mouthful of wine. "Faugh! I can barely speak that vulture's name!"

"Have a care, Mother," warned Nan. "There may be a spy under the bed."

"I wish there were," asserted Aunt Margaret, brandishing her cane. She turned to Morgan again. "All my belongings have been moved out. You and James should go to Faux Hall, if you have the time."

Morgan nodded. She knew she'd have to do something about her old home, but the thought of visiting there without her parents waiting in the doorway was hard to bear. "I shall speak to James," she agreed.

Morgan rode beside Tom on the trip to Wolf Hall. James was directly ahead of them with Ned Seymour and Nan. Aunt Margaret traveled in a litter, though the others were mounted on high-spirited horses, ready for a brisk morning canter.

"Good wedding weather," Morgan remarked to Tom as

she surveyed the blue sky with its scudding white clouds. "Is it true the King is looking for another wife?"

"It is being urged upon him, at least by your uncle," Tom answered. He was somewhat subdued since Jane's death. "Henry has mourned Jane to such an extent that his heart doesn't seem to be in it."

"He truly loved her, didn't he?" Morgan tugged on the reins, for her little mare was eager to trot. "I've seen Prince Edward only once, and then he was asleep. He looks so pale."

"Jane's coloring," Tom said. "I thought you might bring your boys to Wolf Hall."

Morgan explained that they would be gone for only a few days and that she had thought it best to leave them at Hampton Court. "They're too young to enjoy a wedding," she added.

"Speaking of weddings, I suppose you heard that Richard Griffin has taken a bride?"

The topaz eyes widened in surprise. "No. Who is the happy lady?"

Tom gave her a sidelong glance before he replied. "He wed two weeks ago with Margaret Howard. They're still on their wedding trip in Wales where he took her to meet his mother."

Morgan shook her head in bemusement. "Strange that I had not heard. I suppose we've all been so excited about Nan's marriage."

Tom slowed his black stallion to a walk to make certain they were out of hearing range of the others. "Did you ever really care for him, Morgan?"

She frowned, ostensibly studying the needlework of her kidskin riding gloves. She could be candid with Tom if with anyone. "I don't know. I felt some sort of response to Richard, but it certainly wasn't love. It's odd, but as much as I cared for Sean, I never really felt that same kind of—desire for him. Does that make sense?"

Tom nodded. "Yes, it does. To me, at any rate. And James?"

"Are you prying?"

He grinned. "I believe I am."

"James is my husband. That's all I have to say about that." And thank God, Morgan thought, he did not mention Francis. . . .

* * *

Nan and Harry Seymour were married on the morning of May seventeenth in the family chapel of Wolf Hall. Aunt Margaret and Morgan cried, Ned and Tom laughed, and everyone except James drank too much. It was a wonderful wedding.

James and Morgan were back at Hampton Court Palace on the twenty-first. It was then that she broached the subject of Faux Hall. James agreed that he should talk to Thomas Cromwell and went to see him that very afternoon.

When he returned, he told Morgan that Cromwell had been most agreeable. He had, in fact, insisted that Morgan not pain herself by going down to her old family home.

"I truly think he means well, Morgan," James said.

"Perhaps," said Morgan. At least the subject had been confronted. But it was still too soon to face the emptiness of Faux Hall.

Chapter 15

MORGAN INVITED what James referred to as "half the countryside" to Belford for Christmas that year. Although he grumbled about all the wine and food it took to serve their guests, he let her have her way. He knew she was determined not to spend the Christmas holidays alone as they had done the previous year.

The long gallery was decorated with pine and yew, red satin bows clung to the holly wreaths, and a ten-foot Yule log burned on the hearth. The servants wore their best and Morgan herself had a new red velvet dress for Christmas Eve.

Since the visitors came from long distances, they would stay several days. Among the guests were Lord and Lady Latimer. It had pained James to have them, but Morgan insisted. And while he vehemently disapproved of Latimer's religious views, he did not want to make Morgan angry. Besides, Latimer was a sick man, sick as much in heart as in body since the failure of the Pilgrimage of Grace. It had cost him dear to travel to Belford over the snowy roads, but Lady Latimer had been as insistent as her hostess that they, too, would have a gay holiday. Since Lord Latimer doted on his redheaded Cat, he accompanied her without complaint.

But Lord Latimer's heart ached more than ever that Christmas of 1538. He had heard recently of another outrage committed by Cromwell's men, a blasphemous deed which made what had gone before seem trifling by comparison: The shrine of St. Thomas à Becket at Canterbury had been desecrated.

While the others sang carols and drank mulled wine, Lord Latimer sat on a window seat with a fur robe over his legs and told Morgan what had happened. She listened

251

with growing shock and disbelief as he reiterated how the soldiers had carried off two large chests of jewels and numerous wagonloads of other booty. Then they had smashed open the tomb and scattered Becket's bones to the four winds.

"It is said," Latimer concluded, "that the King will declare that great saint a rebel."

Morgan's eyes were wider than ever. "Sweet Jesu! And he dead these four hundred years! It's senseless!"

"Aye." Latimer nodded. "But he defied his King in his time and Henry finds that unforgivable, even at this late date."

Morgan shook her head sadly, then turned to her guest. "Why do you tell *me* these things? You must know how my lord feels about these actions."

Latimer pulled the robe up close about him. "Your husband condones them, I know, but I think you do not." He regarded her with shrewd eyes. "As I recall, I once heard a tale of your distress upon seeing a monastery near Snape Hall being dissolved."

"I remember too well. That poor old monk, lying on the cobbles . . ." She blinked quickly, trying to dispel the vision which contrasted so vividly with the merrymaking across the gallery from where she and Lord Latimer sat.

"There is something else you should know, too, my lady," Lord Latimer went on softly. "You remember Margaret Pole, Countess of Salisbury?"

"The old Countess? I met her just once but she's a dear friend of my Aunt Margaret's."

"She has been imprisoned in the Tower."

Morgan could hardly speak. The Countess must be close to seventy. But tall and straight as a halberdier's pike and boasting the courage of a dozen men in her flat bosom.

"She's a Plantagenet, and Henry is out to purge all royal blood except his own from the face of England. The Marquis of Exeter and Lord Montague were put to death earlier this month."

"Dear God—it is no longer what you do but who you are. Is no man safe?"

Lord Latimer took her hand and was about to speak a word of comfort when he saw his wife bustling toward them. "No hand holding in the corners," she clucked merrily, her cheeks rosy from the spiced wine. "You two aren't singing. Come, my lord, I will make you comfortable by the fire. We must be merry for it is almost midnight and the time of Christ's birth draws nigh."

The two women, with the help of a servingman, settled Lord Latimer into an armchair next to the hearth. Morgan stood beside Cat Latimer and raised her voice in an ancient carol. But though her lips sang the joyful words, her heart was heavy.

By March, Morgan was sure she was with child again. She had not yet informed James. She was thinking about telling him that evening at supper, when Polly came hurrying into the nursery where Morgan was playing with her sons.

"My lady," she began breathlessly, "Willie is here with a message for you."

At first Morgan didn't know who Polly was talking about. Then she remembered: Willie was one of Francis's servants. Quickly, she handed Edmund over to Agnes. Robbie wanted to go with his mother but she told him firmly to stay in the nursery until she returned.

She raced along the corridors, Polly at her heels. Dear Lord, had something happened to Francis? Visions of his big gray gelding galloping riderless along the edge of Solway Firth flashed through her mind. Her heart was pounding wildly when she came up to Willie in the entry hall.

"What is it, Willie? Tell me quick!"

He had obviously ridden hard, for he was covered with mud and sweat. His boots had left wet tracks on the stone floor. He fell to his knees, head bowed low. "Master Francis told me to do thus when I saw ye and to bid ye return with me to Carlisle where Mistress Lucy lies near death."

"Lucy!" Morgan felt a strange sense of relief, immediately suffused by shock and fear. She bent down to raise Willie up. "How is she ill?" asked Morgan, with pox and plague in her mind.

"She was with child, in her fourth month, and she lost the babe. That was a week ago." Willie, devoted to both Francis and Lucy, had tears in his eyes.

Morgan was incredulous. "But she was to have no more children! That's insane!" She passed her hand over her forehead. How could Francis have allowed her to become pregnant again, how could he so selfishly have imposed his will upon his wife, how could . . . Morgan turned to ask Polly to bring food and drink for Willie.

"Come into the library," she said, leading the way. She didn't even think about his muddy boots tracking over the fine Moorish carpet which she had laid after Francis left Belford. It had been his room until then—even James acknowledged that.

She was offering Willie a chair when she heard James's footsteps in the hall. He turned the corner and saw Willie, recognizing him at once.

"What are you doing here?" he demanded sharply.

Morgan held up her hand, signaling Willie to be silent. "Lucy is dying," she told her husband. "She has asked for me."

"You will not go." It was a flat statement, giving no quarter for argument.

Morgan faced him directly. "I will go," she said in a voice as calm as her husband's. "I must and I will."

His blue eyes turned to glacier ice. "I forbid it, Morgan." The tone was menacing.

Morgan felt a tingle of fear flicker in her legs, but anger had the upper hand. "It is not Francis who needs me but Lucy. I could not refuse a dying woman. Even you could not be so heartless." She turned her back on him and began talking to Willie in as normal a voice as possible. At last, she heard James walk away, and she sank into a chair opposite Willie as Polly came into the room with the food.

The small caravan rode the rest of the day and all that night, skirting the Cheviot Hills, moving through forests of juniper and mountain ash. For some of the way there were no roads, only sheep trails winding across the heath-covered moors. In spite of the poor footing, they kept a furious pace, causing Morgan frightened concern for the babe she carried. Dear God, she kept praying, please save my child. Was she forfeiting her baby's life in exchange for a grateful smile from a dying woman's lips? Maybe Lucy was already dead. She prayed harder, blinking against the rain and wind. Willie rode up ahead, with Polly and two Belford retainers behind her. She had taken the men with her reluctantly, for she didn't know what James might do to them when he found out they had accompanied their mistress to Carlisle.

Polly was keeping pace, but it was difficult. Morgan tried to shut out everything but what she would find at the manor house. Sinclair House, Willie had called it, renamed by Francis.

It was small, as Francis had said, built of stone among a copse of sycamore trees. Its two stories looked square and sturdy but very bleak in the murky dawn light.

Servants, some of whom Morgan recognized from their service at Belford, somberly met them at the door. She let a servingwoman remove her soggy riding cloak. Morgan had ridden so long and so hard that her whole body ached.

She noted that none of them wore mourning bands. "Where is Master Francis?" she asked.

She was told that he was with his wife; he had not left her side since the miscarriage. A servingwoman held a tray of food but Morgan waved it away. "Take me to them," she ordered.

The room was very dark, with a single taper burning beside the bed. Lucy's face was flushed against the white pillow, a damp cloth across her brow. In the dim light she didn't recognize Morgan until she heard her sister-in-law's voice.

"Lucy!" Morgan ran across the room and fell on her knees beside the bed.

Francis had been at one of the windows, trying to let in a little morning air. His long, quick strides brought him to Morgan's side but he said nothing. Lucy smiled feebly, her lips dry and cracked.

"You did come," she whispered, touching Morgan's shoulder.

Morgan took the thin fingers in her own. Even Lucy's hand was feverish. From behind Morgan, Francis spoke. "I will leave you two for a few moments," he said. Morgan turned to see his big, retreating figure and fury enveloped her.

When he was gone, Lucy bade Morgan to sit upon the bed. "It will not matter," she said in hoarse voice. She asked Morgan for some water. "I thirst so, all the time now." She drank as Morgan held the tumbler. Then Lucy fell back again on the pillows, her brown hair lank and damp. "I know what you think. I saw how you looked at Francis just now. But it was not his fault. I—I deceived him, Morgan."

"Lucy, pray do not tire yourself . . ."

Lucy shook her head. "I deceived him," she went on, as Morgan leaned forward to catch the words. "I knew he wanted another child so much, and I'd so little trouble with the first ones that I thought Dr. Wimble must be mistaken. So I told him it would be all right for us to make love one night . . . when I knew it wasn't. You mustn't blame him. He is a good man, Francis is, in spite . . . in spite of some things." She closed her eyes, exhausted from talking so much. Then she opened them to look at Morgan again. "You heard me?"

"Yes, oh, yes, Lucy." Morgan sat rigidly on the bed, fighting back the tears.

"Francis has been everything I ever wanted in a husband," Lucy said in that weak yet determined voice. "He didn't love me in the beginning, though I always loved him." She paused long enough to let Morgan give her more water. "But he grew to love me and was always kind and humorous and good to me. Too kind, you see . . ." Her words became almost inaudible and Morgan started to tell her to stop wearing herself out.

"No," she breathed, "I must say this; it's important that you understand. I was always frail. My parents never expected me to live beyond childhood. But I did, and part of it was because of the care Francis gave me." She smiled softly at her memories as Morgan tried to picture the two of them in the early days of their married life and felt her own heart turn over.

"But you see," Lucy went on, her voice a little stronger, "there was another, more—oh, dear heaven, how shall I put it?" She frowned and seemed to wither against the pillows. "A more violent side to his nature. Nothing cruel, I don't mean that," she said so quickly that it made her cough, and Morgan proffered more water. "Sometimes he needed someone to . . . to satisfy him in ways I couldn't." The lusterless eyes pleaded with Morgan for understanding.

"It's all right, Lucy," Morgan assured her. "It's all right," Morgan repeated with more intensity. "Francis loves you very much. He often told me so."

"Of course he does." Lucy smiled faintly. "But you have to understand this about him, to accept him as he is, as I have done. Will you, Morgan?"

Morgan was puzzled and confused. And then she had a blinding, frightening insight: Lucy knew, she had always known, and forgiven them both anyway. And now all this selfless woman asked was that Morgan somehow make sure that Francis would have someone who understood and accepted him as his wife had done.

"I—I think I know what you mean," Morgan said in a shaky voice. "I'm not sure how much I can . . . help, but I'll do what I can for Francis. And the children."

"You'll find a way. God will help you find it."

Lucy was still smiling, but now her eyes closed, and Morgan removed the compress and dipped it in cold water. She wrung it out and put it back on Lucy's forehead.

"Go rest," said Lucy.

Morgan hesitated, but decided she would be little good to anyone if she didn't sleep a bit and have something to eat. Besides, there was the child in her womb. She got up slowly and started across the room on tiptoe, but Lucy wasn't asleep yet.

"Thank you, Morgan. God bless you." Morgan turned, but Lucy's eyes remained shut.

Lucy died the next morning, just as the wind quieted down and the first streaks of light edged over the northern Pennines. Francis had kept his long vigil to the end, his shoulders slumped as he sat next to the bed. He stayed with her for an hour after she was gone, holding on to one of her lifeless hands, as if the contact could will her back to him.

Morgan made all the preparations, sending servants for a coffin, getting a priest, thanking the doctor for doing all he could, comforting the three children who were all old enough to know they had lost their mother. They clung to Morgan's skirts, especially the eldest, nine-year-old Mary.

Finally Morgan went back to Lucy's chamber. She put her hand on Francis's arm and spoke gently. "You must eat, Francis. There is no more you can do." He let her lead him away like a big, weary stallion. His eyes were empty, and though Morgan noticed he had added some weight since she had last seen him, his face seemed very gaunt.

They ate in his study as the early spring sun filled the

room with light. They had talked little since Morgan arrived, and even now they exchanged only a few words, mostly about the funeral which Francis said would be that afternoon. When Morgan exclaimed about such haste, he looked at her levelly, a spark of life at last coming back into his gray eyes. "I will not wait. I cannot."

Morgan left the next morning with Polly and the two retainers. Francis had seen them off. He was still numb with grief, but at least he walked upright in his black mourning clothes. He had helped Morgan onto her horse and for a moment his hand lingered on her arm.

"What of James?" he asked.

Morgan shrugged. "I'll deal with him when I arrive at Belford." She tried to act unconcerned, but her heart was afraid. She thought of telling Francis she was with child but did not; the news would only make the wounds of his grief run more freely.

"Well," said Francis with finality, and Morgan knew it was time to be off.

"Farewell, Francis. Take care of the children . . . and yourself."

He looked up at her but made no reply. Then he took her gloved hand and brought it to his lips. It is good-bye again, Morgan thought, mayhap for more long years, and mayhap our debts to each other are at last settled. How very much she wanted to take him in her arms and surrender herself to ease his pain. But there was no desire in the gray eyes, no sign that he wanted her: She saw only emptiness in his expression, as though part of him had been buried with Lucy. She blew a kiss to the three children, who stood in the doorway. Morgan tugged at the reins and did not look back at Sinclair House or its master.

Chapter 16

THE RETURN TO BELFORD was taken at a more leisurely pace, two full days, with a night spent at a monastery in Otterburn. A handful of other travelers had stopped there too, since there was no respectable inn in the little town. In the common room at supper that night, Morgan listened vaguely to the gossip—about King Henry's marital prospects; about the Countess of Salisbury still being held in the Tower; about the pursuit of recalcitrant priests who refused to submit to the new ways; about the possibility of war with France.

But Morgan's thoughts were turned inward. What *would* James do when she returned? She was sure he wouldn't mistreat her physically, not when she told him she was with child. Ironic, how every time things seemed to be going well with them, some situation developed to throw them apart again. She had never expected them to be lovers, but she had hoped they might be friends. Perhaps even that was no longer possible. Stern and conscience-filled, James knew only one way to live: his way. How different it would have been had she married Sean! She, who had always dreamed of the great love, the noble passion that would never diminish through the years. You always want too much, her mother had told her when she was small. But, she would think to herself, better to ask too much of life than to ask too little. Where had all those dreams gone? Why had all the hopes turned to dust? And where was her faith, her old faith, the comfort of her ancestors? How frail we all are, how weak, how in need of God's mercy! She plucked at a piece of meat and caught a bit of conversation next to her.

". . . And they found the priest in his wine cellar and hanged them both on the spot!" It was a fat wool merchant speaking, his round stomach buffeting the trestle table. The horsefaced woman next to him looked happily horrified. The man turned to Morgan, hoping his grisly tale had at last captured her attention. "I have little sympathy for those who hide corrupt priests. What of you, madam?"

Morgan stammered slightly. He looks like an old sow in a fur-trimmed doublet, she thought. "I? Oh, I think little on politics, sir."

He leaned toward her and she felt his wine-soaked breath on her cheek. "What *do* you think of then, pretty lady? Eh?"

She stood up, gathering her skirts about her. "Pigs," she replied. "I think a lot about pigs." And she swept out of the common room, leaving the fat merchant's eyes popping in astonishment.

It was dark by the time they arrived at Belford. A half-dozen lights burned in the castle windows. Morgan dismounted wearily, Polly trailing behind her, complaining of her aches and pains. Morgan let her grumble awhile before announcing she would go straight to bed after looking in on the children. She mounted the circular staircase with dragging feet. James was nowhere about. As well, she thought. I'd rather not face him tonight.

Robbie was delighted to see his mother, but Edmund was asleep. She held her elder son on her lap for a few minutes and told him a brief story about elves in the woods. When she was done he asked for another, about little people on the Holy Isle. She shook her head and said she would tell him that story—his favorite—another time. She kissed him good night, took a last look at Edmund, and made her way to the bedchamber. With luck, she would be asleep before James came in.

But there was something odd about their chamber. She couldn't place it at first. It looked different, but her tired mind wouldn't function. Something missing . . . A noise behind her made her turn with a start. James was at the door.

"From now on we will sleep separately," he said calmly. "I have moved my belongings from here into another chamber."

Morgan had anticipated some kind of retaliation, but

even so, this move shocked her. She couldn't take it in, not just now. "You mean . . . for always?"

"Aye. For always. We are quits, you and I."

He watched her carefully; there was something about his eyes . . . I am so weary, thought Morgan, I cannot argue, I cannot even think properly.

"I see," she said, even though she saw nothing save the soft bed and inviting pillows. He watched her for another moment in silence, then was gone, quietly closing the door behind him.

"We are quits, you and I," he had said. "For always." The words went round and round in Morgan's head as she lay in bed the next morning. She had dreamed wild dreams, of Francis and Lucy and James and renegade priests and fat men and elves in the forest. She sat up and called for Polly.

Distractedly, she ordered Polly to get her some breakfast. Well, she thought, as Polly helped her into a brown overskirt, at least we have the children. The children! I never told him about the babe I carry! That would have to wait, she decided. Maybe there would be an opportunity in the next few days. Maybe he would relent.

But he did not relent, nor did he seek her out. They would eat together or meet in the halls but they spoke little. He was polite but so distant that sometimes he seemed half a world away. Morgan began to wonder if he would keep her prisoner in the castle. No, she reasoned, he would not. He would wish to keep up appearances. That was why they still ate together.

He had not asked about Lucy. Surely he must wonder, she told herself. But he had shut Francis and Lucy out of his life as irrevocably as he had now turned from her. Lucy—and Francis, too—had died long ago as far as James was concerned.

By early June, Morgan could no longer keep silent about the child. She had felt life the day before and was now adding a new panel to one of her older gowns.

She confronted him that afternoon in the library. He was going over the accounts and his thumb was ink-stained. She stood before him, one hand on her breast.

"I'm going to have a child, James."

He looked up, that odd light in his eyes which she had

seen the night she returned from Carlisle. He stared at her for a long moment. Doesn't he comprehend? she asked herself. She was about to repeat her words when he suddenly stood up.

"You carry no child of mine!" he cried, the strange light glittering in his eyes. "Francis! You carry his child!" His arms flailed and the account sheets flew about the room.

Morgan stepped backwards, trying to decide between protest and flight, but he was around the desk and gripping her shoulders in fierce, clutching hands before she could make her move. "You and Francis! I knew it all along! I saw the lust in your eyes for him—and in his for you!" He shook her violently, his teeth bared.

"No! No!" she shrieked, vainly trying to get away. "I was with child when I left! I swear it! Ask Polly!"

He stopped shaking her; his hands loosened their grip. "You swear?" The voice was a whisper. She nodded, trying to get her breath. "You'll swear—on my father's tomb?"

"Yes . . . yes. Anywhere!"

He held her arm, dragging her from the library. They went to the chapel and Morgan fell to her knees beside the old Earl's tomb. She swore that she carried James's child. He watched her intently, his breathing fast and heavy, and seemed satisfied when she was done. But after that, they did not eat their meals together.

In August, Morgan wrote to Nan, begging her to come to Belford for the baby's birth. Nan had had a boy in April. Morgan had hinted in her previous letters that all was not well between herself and her husband, but now she poured out the whole story to her cousin. Nan must know before she arrived just what kind of situation she would find.

It was September first when Nan arrived at Belford. She was accompanied by several servants and the baby, Thomas, named for Tom Seymour. The two young women embraced warmly, laughing as Morgan's bulk got in the way.

"You'll never know how glad I am to have you here," Morgan said. "I don't think I could survive without you."

Nan laughed again, but her eyes revealed deep concern. Morgan was so thin and pale, while she herself bloomed in the happiness of her marriage and new motherhood.

Nan took over the domestic duties at Belford. James didn't interfere, and treated Nan with courtesy.

"Frankly," said Nan the next day, "I find him as usual. Perhaps the birth of the babe will make a difference."

Morgan sighed. "I have grave doubts."

"Well," said Nan, "if it does not, I think you had better get away for a while when you can travel. Come back with me to Wolf Hall for a visit. Mother would love to see you. She's been unwell ever since her old friend, the Countess of Salisbury, was put in the Tower. Surely James wouldn't stop you?"

"He'd probably be glad to see me go," Morgan replied. "Let's talk of other things. How are Tom and Ned?"

Nan told Morgan that she and Harry had fretted much over whether to name their son Edward or Thomas, and had finally chosen to honor the younger uncle. Ned had been unhappy about it, but managed to cover his disappointment. Nan shrugged. "I just like Tom better," she said.

"So do I. In fact, next to you I've missed him more than anyone since I've been at Belford. He's been knighted, I understand."

Nan nodded. "He and Ned have both been showered with lands and honors since becoming uncles to a future King. Tom was offered Mary Howard's hand, you know."

"Oh?" Morgan looked up from her stitching. The Howard women seemed very busy making matches with men Morgan knew well. "She's beautiful, rich, widowed by Henry's bastard son—what more could Tom ask for?"

Nan noted the asperity in Morgan's tone, but decided she would ignore it. "Love, I suppose. And Surrey disapproved. I'm not sure why. He and Tom used to be boon companions."

"Politics seems to divide everyone eventually," Morgan sighed, and wondered why she was pleased that Tom had not married the lovely Howard widow. And so she and Nan talked the days away, and Morgan's spirits rose a bit. Nan, capable and comforting, had brought some life back to Belford.

On September fourteenth Morgan's labor began. Eight long hours later, early in the morning of the fifteenth, a daughter was born. "Tell James," she said to Nan, and fell asleep.

When she awoke Nan was by the bed. She herself looked very pale, and Morgan chastised her for not resting more. "What did James say?" she asked.

Nan seemed disconcerted. "Oh," she answered, getting up to straighten the bedclothes, "he didn't say much. But I believe he had Agnes bring the babe to him." She turned and looked at Morgan, a little color now in her face. "He did say for you to name her."

"Then I shall name her Anne, for you," said Morgan.

Nan bent down and hugged her cousin.

But if Morgan prospered following the birth of her much-wished-for daughter, Nan seemed increasingly nervous and ill at ease. Two weeks after little Anne was born, Morgan exercised her authority as the elder of the two cousins and ordered Nan to come sit by her divan.

"Something is bothering you," she said bluntly. "Ever since the baby was born." A sudden fear overtook her. "Is aught wrong with the babe—something I've not noticed?" She remembered the wild ride to Carlisle.

Nan smiled faintly. "No, no. The babe is perfect. Dr. Wimble said so himself." She sighed and leaned against the silk pillows next to the divan. "I can't stay here until you are ready to travel. I must go within the week."

Morgan sat up, clutching her fur-trimmed robe around her. "But why? Has Harry sent for you?"

Nan shook her head. "I wasn't going to tell you, but perhaps I should. The night the babe was born . . . when I went to tell James . . . he didn't speak for the longest time. Then he came up to me and touched my face with his hand—it was so *cold*, Morgan—and said something I could barely make out about 'hair like a raven's feathers.' " Her voice gained momentum. "I thought he was going to kiss me, really I did, but he dropped his hand and seemed to become himself again and spoke of the babe. Yet ever since that day, he watches me. I even see him on the terrace or at the library window when I take the children for a walk." She shivered. "Maybe I imagine it, but . . ." Her voice trailed off.

Morgan brushed the hair from her forehead. "No. It's not your fancy. You remind him of someone. Of someone he loved very much long ago." She fell back against the divan. "Yes, for your sake, you had best leave as soon as possible."

Somehow, Morgan struggled through the fall and winter and into the spring of 1540. She occupied herself with the household, which she now ran adroitly and with more efficiency than her mother would have ever thought possible. Indeed, she had picked up the reins quite easily when Lucy had moved away and now had fallen with surprising naturalness into the role of chatelaine.

James paid little attention to his daughter and seemed to grow estranged from the boys. Robbie, at four, had a tutor from the village twice a week, and Edmund begged to join him at his studies. Morgan told him he must wait but he was impatient to keep up with his big brother. She spent long hours with all her children, bestowing upon them the love she could offer no one else.

News, as usual, filtered slowly into Belford Castle. Nan wrote in early February insisting that Morgan come to Wolf Hall as soon as the roads were passable. She also wrote that the King's marriage to Anne of Cleves had taken place January sixth. It had been arranged by Cromwell, who sought political alliance with Anne's brother, but rumor had it that Henry was ill pleased with his new bride.

"He calls her his 'Flanders Mare,'" Nan wrote. "Imagine! Some already say her fate may be the same as another Anne's."

Morgan pondered on what effect the marriage might have on her uncle. She wrote back that she would try to come to Wolf Hall in May. Another two years since she had been there or to court. She looked into her mirror. Can it be possible that I am twenty-four years old? In spite of three children, she was as slim as ever, the topaz eyes as limpid, the tawny hair thick and shining. And still James kept away from her.

It was May, the month she had promised to visit Nan. But little Anne was sick. Dr. Wimble said it was only her teeth, but he advised against traveling for a while. Morgan had not approached James about her proposed journey; she would wait until she knew her exact departure date.

It was a beautiful spring. The lilacs and fruit tree blossoms brightened the backdrop of the somber castle walls, and their petals fluttered to earth in pink and lavender drifts. In the woods the wild columbine began to open, and even on the moors the heath seemed more lush, more verdant. Sparrows built their nests in the castle eaves and kestrels nurtured their young in the rock pools along the seashore. Goslings dotted the fields, calves stood up on shaky legs, and lambs bleated for their mothers' milk. The common folk seemed restored by the season, walking with a lighter step from their stone and clay thatched cottages into the fields newly sown with wheat and rye.

James was in Newcastle for a few days, and Morgan was relieved to have him gone. She felt a sense of freedom with him away from the castle and one afternoon she caught herself musing on what it would be like at Belford if James never returned from his trip. Guiltily, Morgan put such thoughts aside, set down the book she had been trying to read, and told Agnes to take charge of the children. She would walk in the orchard for a bit.

She strolled among the fruit trees, wondering how Francis fared with his three motherless children. Perhaps he was wed again by now—unless he was content to keep company with the whores of Carlisle. If only she dared write, but all the servants had been given strict orders never to carry any messages to the younger Sinclair. James had not punished the retainers who had gone to Carlisle with Morgan, but it was understood that no one at Belford would ever communicate with Francis again.

Morgan sadly shook her head. What kind of Christianity pitted brother against brother? Then she saw something next to a big pear tree that drove all else from her mind. A bundle of rags. Perhaps someone had left their belongings. But she was mistaken. With a little cry she realized the bundle was a man. She started to run away, but stopped. Cautiously, she approached the huddled form. She bent down. Was he dead? No, but he didn't seem to be asleep either. Something about him was unnatural.

She put her arm under his head reluctantly, for his clothes were dirty and ragged. He was in his forties, she judged, with close-cropped graying hair and a hawkish face. There was a spot of dried blood at one corner of his thin, straight mouth.

His eyes flickered open and he coughed twice, his emaciated body shaking. Morgan supported him, her heart thumping. What if he were a thief or border raider who had been chased off by some law-abiding citizens? To her surprise, he smiled a little, his dark eyes bright.

"I did die after all and am surely in heaven." He spoke well in a resonant voice with a trace of a Northern accent. Certainly he could not be an outlaw! She relaxed slightly.

"Are you ill, sir?" she asked, aware that her voice sounded weak and small.

He tried to sit up, though he had to let her help him. "Aye, sick of body and soul." He coughed again, so deep that Morgan thought it hurt her, too.

"How did you get here?" she inquired, letting him go as he leaned against the tree.

He smiled again, ruefully. "Such a tale would keep you here all day, my lady."

"I'll send for some of my serving people. You must come to the castle and rest and eat."

"You are the lady of the castle then, the good and beautiful Countess of Belford?"

He sounds like a courtier, though there is mockery in his voice, Morgan thought. Who on earth could he be? She nodded and stood up. "I'll be back shortly."

He held out a hand to stop her. "Nay, nay. You must not. I shall rest here and be on my way. I daresay I swooned a bit, but I feel much better now."

"Nonsense!" said Morgan, her self-assurance restored. "I insist you come to Belford. You're not fit to go on."

He again asserted that he was. But as he started to get up, he fell forward and would have dropped to the ground had she not put out an arm to steady him. He was of medium height, with slightly bowed shoulders. He is so thin, she thought. He cannot have eaten well for months—or else his coughing sickness has wasted him.

"Come, lean on me." She took his arm.

He shook his head, his dark brows drawn together. "Madam, I cannot! Do you know who I am?" She said no. He seemed to be debating whether he should tell her. But her tenacity forced his hand. "I am Father Bernard. You have heard of me?"

Morgan searched her memory, at last recalling something about a priest named Bernard who had defied the King's Men in Lancashire. Nan had spoken of him when she had been at Belford. Father Bernard had refused to turn over his holy relics to the soldiers and had somehow managed to escape. He was said to have fled to France. Or Ireland. Or some place.

"Father Bernard!" Morgan whispered the name.

He smiled wryly. "Now you will call the guards, madam?"

She looked at him carefully. Somehow priests should always be old, bald and chubby, or tall, thin and white-haired. How different this one was!

Morgan made her decision in an instant. Looking back later, she would never know how or why—except that he was another fellow being, ill, alone, hunted and virtually helpless. She could not have denied him any more than she could have stifled her distress for the monk at the Yorkshire monastery or suppressed her compassion for Anne Boleyn on the scaffold.

"Come," she said, and took his arm before he could protest. As he tried to stand, another coughing spasm racked him. He was so thin that she could almost carry him. They stumbled along the path until they came within sight of the castle.

There Father Bernard paused, forcing her to stop, too. "My lady, do you know the penalty for hiding renegade priests?"

"Yes. Do you know who *I* am?" she asked. He replied that he had already said he did. She shook her head. "Did you know that I am Cromwell's niece?"

"No." He frowned, the heavy dark brows again converging. "Then why do you do this for me?"

"I told you. I'm Cromwell's niece. Maybe that's reason enough."

He peered off toward the castle. "I see. Well, if you're so determined, then I would at least suggest for both our sakes that we wait until dark before I go into the castle."

She finally agreed to that. She helped him back to a more secluded part of the orchard and asked if she couldn't bring him something to eat. He said he would wait; Morgan must not take a chance of being seen bringing food outdoors.

Back in her sitting room, Morgan felt shaky. She poured herself a cup of brandy and stood by the window, trying to think how she would hide Father Bernard. She could not tell anyone, not even Polly. The responsibility must be hers alone, for she could not share the guilt and endanger others. What was it that fat merchant at the monastery in Otterburn had said about someone hiding a priest? Something about hanging . . . Morgan clutched the brandy cup tightly.

Now that she ate alone or with the children, it was simple enough to set aside sufficient food for Father Bernard. While Polly was out of the room, she put meat, bread, dates, and a flacon of ale into a hamper. Robbie and Edmund, preoccupied with which of them could stir their gravy the fastest, paid no heed.

After the boys had been sent back to the nursery to play, Morgan slipped into the corridor and hurried up the narrow, winding steps to the tower room. She deposited the hamper and uttered a quick prayer of thanksgiving that James was away. By the time she had arranged the bedding on the tower room floor, the sun had almost disappeared behind the Cheviot Hills.

She waited another twenty minutes, occupying herself by helping Agnes put the boys to bed and making sure Anne was sleeping peacefully. She tried to control her taut nerves by exchanging casual conversation with Polly and Agnes.

It was dark now, with only a sliver of moon rising out over the sea. The wind was up a bit; all was quiet. She headed for a side door, which opened out onto the sea-cliff path. Skirting the edge of the castle, she hurried down the little grade and then up the hill to the orchard.

It was so dark that she wasn't sure at first where she had left Father Bernard. She almost stumbled over him before she realized she had reached the hiding place. He had been able to make out her outline as she approached him, but said nothing. She aided him in getting to his feet as he put an arm around her shoulders to let her support his body with her own.

"Slowly now," she whispered.

They went back the same way she had come. The hardest part was the little grade up to the castle. Father Bernard stumbled once and Morgan braced her knees to keep them both from falling down. They were almost to the side door when he started to cough. Five times the coughs racked him, and Morgan stiffened like a hunted animal, straining to hear if anyone was nearby. But the only noises were the sea and the wind and Father Bernard's heavy breathing.

She opened the door, which seemed to creak loudly. Had it made such a noise when she came out of the castle? It must have, but she hadn't noticed it then.

They ascended the first flight of stairs successfully, but on the third step of the second stairway, Father Bernard sagged against her and she had to clutch at the wall for support. Morgan struggled to lift him, ignoring the sounds they made. God help me, she prayed. And then she heard the voice.

"Who goes there?" It was Matthew, James's steward. He was below them, around the corner in the corridor.

Morgan thought she would faint, but suddenly she heard words coming from her lips. "Someone is lurking near the side door. Go look quick."

"Aye, my lady," she heard him reply.

She didn't wait for his hasty footsteps to move away. With a supreme effort, she lifted Father Bernard and half dragged, half carried him up the remaining steps and down the narrow corridor into the tower room. She eased him onto the pallet, where he lay with his eyes closed, his breathing rapid and hoarse.

"I will be right back," she said, and raced from the room and back down the two flights of stairs to the side door.

Matthew was looking around the castle walls. She called to him: "Is anyone there?"

He shook his head. "It's so dark I can't tell. Should I send some men to search?"

"No, perhaps it was my fancy. I was going to take a walk and I heard a noise when I got to the door. I thought I'd look from one of the windows, but then I heard you."

Matthew was back inside the castle. He regarded his mistress with concern. "You look frightened to death, my lady."

She tried to laugh. "Oh, no. I get nervous sometimes when my lord is gone at nights. It's silly, of course." Morgan thanked Matthew and walked as casually as possible back up the stairs.

* * *

James returned to Belford three days later. He greeted Morgan perfunctorily and retired to the library to record his purchases.

Now that he was back, Morgan wondered if keeping her secret would become more complicated. Perhaps not, since James paid her little heed. But it increased her anxiety to have him inside the castle again. Besides, she reasoned, Father Bernard was already showing signs of improvement. With luck, he might be able to leave Belford in a fortnight. He had told her that he was bound for Bamburgh, where he hoped to find a fishing boat headed for the Continent.

Morgan visited him only at night, long after the castle's other inhabitants were asleep. She brought him not only food, but clean clothes and even some books that Francis had left behind.

He was sitting, as usual, by the turret window. They never dared light a candle, but tonight the moon was full, casting its beams into the little room. They spoke in whispers, though it was doubtful they could have been heard had they shouted.

"How are you feeling?" she asked, as she set the hamper down on the stone floor.

"Better." It was the same reply he had given her every night, and from all appearances, it was true. Morgan thought his face was filling out a bit.

"Your cough?" she asked. Always the same questions, she thought, like one of those African parrots.

"It, too, is better." He smiled. "I've been drinking your elder-flower tea. It helps."

She was about to ask if he needed anything else when he invited her to sit down. "My quarters are not lavish; perhaps you'll accept the pallet?" He still wore his wry smile.

Morgan hesitated, then sank onto the makeshift bed. "My daughter," he began, and Morgan was suddenly aware of him as a priest instead of as a man. "I know how your lord feels about the old faith, for I learned that he drove his own brother out of Belford for disagreeing with him. So why is it that you do this?"

Morgan pleated the folds of her night-robe between her fingers. "I don't know, Father. To atone for what my uncle has done to those who cling to the old ways, to counteract James's attitudes, to do something for a fellow human being in trouble . . ." She looked up at him. "I just don't know. I've thought a lot on it, but I'm still not sure."

He broke off a leg of quail and started to nibble at it. "You follow the new ways here, of course."

"Yes." She stood up, pacing the small chamber. "I have great trouble putting all that's happened into perspective. I fear I don't comprehend all these changes as a religious conflict but rather as one faction of men mistreating another." And she told him about the monastery in York, and before she knew it, she was unleashing the whole story of Sean O'Connor and the bitterness she had felt at first for Rome and her loyalty to Anne Boleyn and all the confusing thoughts which had perplexed her for so long. She even told him about her estrangement from James and the sorry state of their marriage.

When she had finished, he regarded her thoughtfully, draining the last drops from his wine cup. "Mayhap," he said at last, "women are the only true Christians after all. By bringing life into the world, they regard it more preciously. When they see a man abuse his brother or do him unto death, no matter the cause, they think, 'That could be my son.' Women see events in terms of people, not ideas. It is well that they do."

Morgan smiled at him. "How strange it is to hear a priest talk plain, without preaching!"

"Aye, had more of us spoken so to our congregations for these long years, we might not have come to such a pretty pass. We priests and bishops and cardinals are as much to blame as King Henry. The majority of people have become estranged from their religion and care not which way the wind blows. They want security, not salvation." He fingered his pointed chin thoughtfully. "Yet if our errors have given the King and others an excuse, it is still no reason to destroy the old faith. Sometimes the things that happen in life are unavoidable—I don't think this break with the Pope was one of them."

"Then what is the remedy, Father?" Morgan asked.

He shook his head slowly. "There is none, I fear, save that steadfast men and women not deny their faith, that they go on seeking salvation as they have always done and uphold the Holy Father as Christ's vicar on earth."

"You make it sound so simple, but it's not," Morgan countered.

"Oh no, it's simple enough. It's what happens to a man if he does these things in England that complicates the situation." He sighed and slumped against an old wine cask.

Morgan stood up. "You must be tired out, listening to me gabble so. I'll leave you now." She reached down for the hamper, then suddenly sank to her knees. "Bless me, Father," she implored.

He rose and put his hand on her hair. "Go in peace, my daughter," he said.

Morgan had dark circles under her eyes the next morning. She had slept only about three hours, what with waiting until all was quiet and then staying so long in the tower room. Still, she felt better inside, her mind less troubled than it had been for some time. Just talking about her troubles had eased them.

The sound of horses in the courtyard brought her to the window. She looked down and saw at least two dozen riders and their mounts inside the walls, their leader talking to James and Matthew. She shielded her eyes against the morning sun and recognized the green-and-white armbands the newcomers wore. King's Men!

Panic overwhelmed her. Should she go down to the courtyard and find out what they wanted? Would James think it odd? But she was too upset to stay in her room and wait. She grabbed the brandy decanter and took a long draught. Her throat and stomach burned fiercely for a few seconds, but she felt better. She hurried along the corridor and down the main stairway, then slowed her pace and tried to walk as calmly as possible into the courtyard. The bells in the village church tower were striking nine as she reached the group of men.

"I see we have visitors," she said to James. "Shall I order refreshments?"

James paused, his eyes distant. But the leader of the troop bowed. "We breakfasted a short time ago, my lady," he said. "We head now for Bamburgh." He thanked James and mounted his horse. The signal was given and the men trotted out through the castle gate.

"What was that all about?" Morgan asked her husband.

He never seemed to meet her eyes anymore. "They search for a runaway priest, a certain Father Bernard of Lancashire. I told them this was an unlikely place to look for him." James turned away and walked back toward the castle.

Morgan froze in place. She was aware that Matthew was watching her. He spoke: "That may solve our mystery, my lady."

Morgan jumped. "Mystery? What mystery?" She regarded Matthew closely.

He spread his hands. "The sound you heard a week or so ago, when my lord was away. Don't you recall?"

"Oh!" She forced a little laugh. "Of course! Do you really think that might have been the priest?"

He nodded gravely. "Aye, madam, and I told the King's Men so. You see, they found a little silver cross in the orchard. They are sure he came this way."

She stared at him for a long second and then shrugged. "Mayhap. But I daresay he's far from here by now."

Was there a strange, quizzical look in Matthew's eyes? Morgan wasn't certain. But he only said, "Aye, madam, no doubt," and then he, too, headed back toward the castle entrance.

Morgan felt an oppressive need to get outside the castle walls. She put on a pair of old shoes and a light cloak, and set out for the sea-cliff path. She would walk down to the beach, for the tide was far out. There was always much activity this time of year along the shore, with the gulls and rooks and kestrels and other birds seeking food for their young. Sometimes Morgan would kneel down by one of the tide pools and watch the curious little sea animals, living out their lives in that small, watery world.

She walked quickly, noticing the bright colors of the lichens which clung to the rocks. Turning a slight bend, she saw someone ahead of her several hundred feet. Morgan slackened her step and held her hand up to keep the sun out of her eyes. It was James, she was quite certain, but he seemed to be sitting on the ground. She stopped, stepping behind a big rock currant bush. No, he wasn't sitting—he was kneeling down in front of the cross marking the grave of Francis and Lucy's dead baby.

So he is sorry after all for what he has done to Francis, Morgan thought. She wondered if this might be the moment to approach him, to salvage some scrap of their relationship. But just as she was pondering her decision,

James rose and turned to face the sea. Suddenly his arms and legs stuck out in what looked like a wild caricature of a court dance. He was crying out something and Morgan strained to hear his words over the roar of the sea.

It was a chant, almost a song, and at last Morgan picked up a few words: *"Kyrie, eleison . . . Christe, eleison . . . Domine, non sum dignus . . ."*

Morgan clutched at her cloak. The Latin words from the Mass—"Lord, have mercy . . . Christ, have mercy . . . Lord, I am not worthy . . ." What did it mean, coupled with such terrifying gyrations? But she did know, of course. She knew now for certain what she had feared all along: James's mind was twisted, perhaps from guilt over his treatment of Francis or from sorrow for the renunciation of his faith. Whatever the cause, the effects were ghastly and frightening. Morgan gathered up her skirts and started to run. Glancing back over her shoulder before she rounded the bend again, she saw him, still leaping about the edge of the cliff, calling out over the sea: *"Mea culpa, mea maxima culpa . . ."*

Chapter 17

POLLY WAS GRUMBLING to Peg. "What's a bit of fowl and some wine to a rich man like him? I always thought he was a miser. I remember one time, why, he was no more than seventeen, and I had eaten some sweetmeats from the sideboard and . . ."

Morgan, listening outside the door, came into the room where the two women were remaking some of their mistress's gowns. "Tut, tut," she reprimanded as she walked through the door, "is it your master you speak of?"

Peg blushed but Polly held her ground. "Aye, madam. You should have new dresses, not old ones remade. So now his lordship complains because too much food is being eaten. If you please, my lady, I swear he keeps track of every drop of ale."

Morgan shook a finger at Polly. The older servant felt rather free to speak her piece now that James and Morgan were estranged. But her criticism was getting out of hand. "No more of that, Polly. My lord has always kept strict accounts of our stores and purchases, and that's as it should be. Surely you can't complain that you're not getting enough to eat."

Polly put her hand to her little round stomach and chuckled. "Ah, no, madam! It is not me he complains of." She stopped and the chuckle faded.

Fear swept over Morgan. "Well? Who is it then?"

Polly hung her head. "It is you, madam. I overheard him tell Matthew that you were eating enough for two people."

Morgan reached for the brandy decanter, her back to the women so that they could not see how her hands shook. "Faugh! How silly!" She took a great gulp of brandy and set the cup down abruptly. I'm drinking too much of this lately, she thought. But she did feel better. She faced her

276

servingwomen and laughed. "At least eating brings me some pleasure. There is little to savor around here these days." She picked up one of the remodeled gowns from a chair. "Your embroidery is improving, Peg," she said, and they fell to discussing Morgan's wardrobe.

That evening Morgan tried to write a letter to Nan, but her thoughts were distracted. If only she could unburden herself to her cousin—but of course she dared not. A drop of ink fell from her quill onto the parchment. She tried to blot it up quickly but the stain had set. "Pray forgive the appearance of this letter, dear Nan, but I seem to be unnaturally upset. Mayhap it's the weather," she wrote. "I think we are due for a thunderstorm." Morgan cursed and flung down the pen. More inkblots, but at least this time on the desk top. She wiped them away, picked up the quill, and finished off her letter. "Tell me more about the King and Anne of Cleves. Write soon, for even a letter is some small consolation." She sent her love to all the Seymours and signed her name with less of a flourish than usual.

She leaned against the stiff back of the chair. Two weeks since Father Bernard had come to the castle. She had hoped that by now he would be well enough to leave. But though he was definitely stronger, he still coughed blood and his legs were weak.

There was a knock on the door. Morgan leaped from her chair, Nan's letter fluttering to the floor. "Who is it?" she called, a hand at her throat.

"It's me, my lady," answered Peg.

Morgan's shoulders slumped in relief. "Enter," she said.

As Peg came in, Morgan noted at once that her hazel eyes were troubled. What's the wench done, Morgan thought wearily, got herself with child by a groom? She sat down and directed Peg to take the chair opposite her.

"My lady, I should not ha' come," Peg said, her face averted from Morgan's gaze. She was a border lass, some said Matthew's illegitimate daughter. It was he who had sought service for her at the castle the winter before Morgan's marriage. "I should not be sayin' what I'm goin' to say," she said.

Morgan's patience was hard pressed. "Well, you're here and you might as well say something."

Peg raised her head but still couldn't meet her mistress's eyes. "It's about you, my lady." Her fingers fretted at a small mole by her left eye. "It's what Polly said today, about the food." She paused again, her hands now pulling on her white apron.

"Yes? Go on," prodded Morgan. My nerves, she thought, and eyed the brandy decanter covetously.

"Polly didn't tell ye all 'twas said between his lordship and Matthew. No doubt she held back out o' kindness," Peg said, her words coming faster now, "but I think ye should know, seein' all the troubles your ladyship has had t' bear." She stopped again, waiting for more encouragement.

Morgan felt like screaming at the girl but she kept tight control. "So? Out with it, Peg."

"His lordship said ye were eatin' enough for two and then—Polly said—he called out a terrible oath and cried that ye must be wi' child and that ye must ha' a lover in the castle." She buried her face in her hands and started to cry. "Polly and me—we knew it was not so. But I had to tell ye . . . even if ye beat me for it." She sobbed aloud.

Morgan stood up and put her hand over her eyes. Dear God, she thought, what next? She gave Peg's shoulder a kindly pat. "Of course it's not so. Don't upset yourself over such queer talk. His lordship gets undone sometimes, that's all. Now forget about this and go wash your face and get straight to bed."

Peg looked up gratefully at her mistress. "Oh, madam, ye are so kind! How can his lordship speak such things?"

"To bed," Morgan repeated firmly as Peg got up, made a little curtsey, and withdrew.

Morgan leaned against the door. I cannot bear much more of this, she thought. She started for the brandy decanter but stopped short. Instead, she pressed her hands together in a prayerful attitude for a moment and then crossed the room to her writing desk. She picked up her letter to Nan and took quill in hand. "Pray for me," Morgan wrote across the bottom of the page.

That night she made no mention of the day's events to Father Bernard. If he noticed that his food had decreased somewhat, he said nothing. They exchanged only a few words and then she was gone, making her stealthy way down the steps and along the corridor. She was weary, so weary that she was certain she would fall asleep as soon as her head touched the pillow. Quietly she opened her bedchamber door and went in.

James was standing in the middle of the room.

Morgan cried out. She turned to flee, but he was upon her in a second, his hands clutching her arms. "I've ordered every inch of this castle searched." His voice was low, his eyes wild. "We'll find your lover before dawn. And then you will both pay, oh, so very dearly!"

Morgan tried to pull free and knew it was useless. She stared into those wild eyes, the eyes of a stranger. "I have no lover," she said dully.

"Lying bitch!" He released her and struck a sharp blow across her face. She reeled back against the bed. "Lies! You've told me nothing but lies! I knew before and let you dupe me! It's Francis, it's always been Francis, and we'll find him before the sun rises." He opened the door. "Don't try to leave, madam," he ordered, and his voice sounded very normal. "I have posted men outside." He closed the door very quietly behind him.

Afterwards, she thought she must have swooned. She felt as if she were floating, sailing along on a ship of clouds, high over the Cheviot Hills, above the countryside, even as far as London. It seemed like hours, days, weeks. When she awoke, it was still dark. Was it still the same night? she wondered. Did I dream what happened? No, for there was a drop of blood on her shift. He cut my mouth, she thought dumbly, and was scarcely conscious of how her face ached.

Then Morgan heard sounds outside the door. She rose up on one elbow as James came in, breathing hard. He walked to the bed. He acted very composed, for all that there was a sense of elation about him.

"So," he said in a low voice, "I was wrong."

James waited for her to speak, but when he realized she would not, he went on. "This is worse—far worse—than what my brother did. I have no choice. A messenger is already riding to Cromwell."

My wits are useless, she thought stupidly. "Cromwell?" she repeated, trying to get up. There was a pounding in her ears. Am I losing *my* mind? Then it became clear. "What's that noise outside?" she demanded.

"The scaffold," he replied. "For Father Bernard."

"How did you know who he was?" What was the use of denials, of struggle now?

James held out his hand. "This," he said, and he showed her the little silver rosary in his palm, the cross missing.

"You would hang him—without waiting for word from the King?"

"We take the law into our own hands in the North—you ought to know that by now." His hand slapped over the rosary. "If you weren't kin to Cromwell, I'd hang you, too."

Stunned into silence, Morgan watched him leave the room.

He was gone for nearly half an hour and returned just as the sun was starting to come up. The storm had never materialized and it was already obvious that this would be a beautiful, warm May day.

"Come," said James.

Morgan was still lying on the bed in her shift and nightrobe. "Come? Where? I'm not dressed yet."

"Come," he said, more coldly imperious than ever. Morgan knew if she did not obey, he would drag her by force. She got up from the bed, her feet seeking her slippers. He let her precede him from the room. "To the window over the courtyard," he directed her.

She suddenly knew; that she had not guessed before amazed her. When they got to the window she did not even register surprise. The hastily constructed gibbet, the little crowd of castle servants and retainers, a few early risers from the village—and Father Bernard walking among them, his hands tied behind his back.

Matthew escorted the frail priest up the steps. The noose dangled, swaying in the spring breeze. Father Bernard looked to all sides, his gaze untroubled, as several onlookers crossed themselves. He said something but Morgan couldn't hear it through the window. Matthew brought the noose down around the priest's neck and Morgan turned away. That other May, in the Tower with Anne . . . and the spring before that and Sean . . . She closed her eyes tight.

James grabbed her and shoved her against the window. "Look, bitch!" he cried. But her eyes remained shut fast, and only the gasp in unison from the onlookers told her that Father Bernard was dead.

* * *

Edmund was crying. He couldn't understand why he wasn't allowed to see his own mother, not if she were just down the hall in her room. Agnes rocked him in her lap, trying to stop his tears.

James still kept the guards outside Morgan's door. She had been confined for ten days, since the morning of Father Bernard's execution. None of the children were allowed to see her and only Polly had permission to wait on her mistress.

Robbie was lunging at his shadow with a toy sword. He regarded Edmund's snifflings with disdain. But inside, he, too, was upset. He sheathed the sword and turned to Agnes. "Is it true that our mother is going away without us?"

Agnes glanced down at Edmund, who had fallen asleep in her arms. "Aye, Robbie," she answered.

"When?"

"Soon. Mayhap today."

Robbie looked down at his toes, his lower lip protruding sulkily. "But she cannot go," he cried. "She promised to take us to the Holy Isle this summer!"

"It is not her fault," said Agnes shortly, and turned away to hide her own tears.

Morgan's windows looked out to the sea. It was in that direction that she watched now as she had often done during the long days of her confinement. She had almost lost track of time. It must be June by now, she calculated.

Her knees ached from spending so much time at her prie-dieu. For the first time in a long while, she felt as if she were praying not into a vast empty void, but directly to her Creator. She prayed not for mercy for herself but for her children, for the souls of Father Bernard and Sean O'Connor and Thomas More, Anne Boleyn, her parents, and for the welfare of all people who suffered in the world.

"Go in peace," Father Bernard had admonished her on the night of their long talk in the tower room. The words came back to her with great comfort. He must have died at peace, she thought, because he had kept the faith, the old faith I almost lost. But by his counsel and example I will be at peace, too, no matter what happens. Maybe it wasn't just the old faith which I let slip away, but faith itself.

Whatever it was has been restored to me, and if Father Bernard has been the cause of my earthly destruction, I rejoice because he is also the instrument of my eternal salvation.

And then she heard the shouts of men in the courtyard and knew that it was time. Stiffly, she went to the wardrobe and took out the first cloak she saw. I will not weep, I will not ask to see the children, for James would deny me even that. She put the cloak on and sat down on the bed to wait.

James himself came to fetch her. "The King's Men are here," he said, and that was all. She did not answer.

We will never see each other again, Morgan thought, we who were never lovers, rarely friends, and now deadly enemies. She walked ahead of him, thinking how strange it was to be outside her room at last. There would be the fresh air and the ride to London, one last look at the green, lush land she loved so well. Morgan blinked against the sun as she saw nearly a dozen men in Tudor livery waiting on horseback. Morgan blinked again, this time in disbelief: Their leader was Tom Seymour.

She wanted to cry out, for this final irony was too much. Tom held the warrant, which he read aloud to Morgan. She didn't look at him, didn't even listen to the words. So formal, his voice sounded, not at all like Tom. When he finished, she turned toward him, watching not his face but his big hands as they rolled up the parchment.

Morgan looked straight through James as he helped her mount. She only half listened as he talked to Tom. "I have done my rightful duty, Sir Thomas," he said.

Tom nodded. "You have indeed, my lord. Master Cromwell has praised you well."

"A man cannot do too much for his country and King, is that not so, Sir Thomas?"

Morgan looked more closely now at James. He sounded like a schoolboy seeking reassurance from his tutor. Was there just a flicker of doubt in his voice? She turned her gaze to Tom; a muscle moved along his jawline.

"Aye," Tom said, "you are a true defender of your King." He raised his hand, then motioned for Morgan to ride next to him. Peg and Polly were weeping, Matthew looked worried, and some of the others seemed openly afraid. Morgan looked away as Tom led the horsemen out of the courtyard and down the hill to the village.

Morgan never looked back, even though she could have seen the castle from nearly a mile away. She was still so shocked that Tom would be in charge of her arrest that she could only stare straight ahead, like a wooden image. They spoke not at all until both castle and village had been put behind them.

"You are in my personal care," Tom finally said, speaking in what seemed an unnaturally loud and severe voice. "Any attempt to escape will be dealt with by me, and I'm short on mercy, as my men will tell you."

She threw him a sidelong glance. Had the whole world gone mad? Tom, even Tom, after her blood! But she would not weep, not now, no matter what else happened.

Late in the afternoon Tom announced they would spend the night at Alnwick. His second-in-command, Will Herbert, commented that he thought they could get to Morpeth before nightfall.

Tom gave him an angry look. "You question my orders?" Herbert backed off, protesting that he only meant his words as a suggestion.

The inn was small and crowded. Tom told the innkeeper his men could stay in two rooms. He and the woman would require a third. Morgan looked up at him in surprise. Surely locking her in a room by herself was secure enough. Anger flared, for the first time in days.

"At least I could have brought a servingwoman with me. I'll not share a room with you, of all men!" She struck out at him blindly. "False friend! Traitor!"

He snatched her wrists with his hands. "God's teeth! The kitten scratches!" Incredibly, his eyes glinted with humor.

"You fiend! To mock me so at a time like this!" She tried to wrench free but failed.

He picked her up, as easily as lifting a sack of apples, and tossed her over his shoulder. Giving orders to his men to go to the lodgings the innkeeper was readying for them, he mounted the stairs two at a time.

The innkeeper's wife was at the top of the stairs, her round eyes startled. But she was accustomed to not asking questions of her guests; she showed Tom to the room and left. He dumped Morgan on the bed, then returned to the door and slid the bolt.

"You beast! How could you?" Now the tears were flowing free. "Horrible enough for my uncle and my husband to turn on me—but you!" She pounded the straw mattress with her fists.

Tom was standing by the bed, his arms folded across his chest. "When you are through ranting, we can have a civil talk." She looked up between gulping sobs. The amusement was still in his eyes.

"What do you mean?" she asked.

He sat down next to her, his arm around her shoulders. "God's beard, Morgan, do you really think I'd lead you to your death?" He watched her face, a composite of distress and noncomprehension. "If you will calm yourself, I'll tell you why I came to Belford. Oh, here!" He handed her a big handkerchief.

She blew her nose loudly and wiped her eyes, trying to compose herself. He waited patiently for at least two full minutes before he began.

"Your wretched husband sent word to Cromwell about how you had hidden Father Bernard. Cromwell could hardly pass up your latest misdeed, and I swear at this point he'd put his mother in the Tower if he thought it would save his own neck. You see, even though the King recently made your uncle Earl of Essex, he's in mortal danger. The marriage with Anne of Cleves is a fiasco and Henry blames Cromwell."

Morgan's eyes were enormous; she could scarcely believe what she was hearing. "I didn't know," she said. "I've heard little news lately and Nan has to be careful in her letters . . ." She dabbed at her eyes with the handkerchief again.

Tom stretched out his long legs, then started to pull off his boots. "Aye, it's so. Our problem is that we don't know how long he can hold on. It may be that Henry will keep him in power until he can secure a divorce for the King. In any case, we must fight for time; every hour away from London may mean that Cromwell—instead of you—goes to the Tower. That's why I decided to stay here tonight and not try for Morpeth."

Morgan sank back on the bed, a weak smile on her lips.

"And I thought . . . All the things I called you! Can you forgive me?"

He kicked the boots away and leaned over her. His blue eyes twinkled even more merrily. "I think so."

"But how did you come to take command?" she asked, resuming a partial sitting position.

Tom was removing his leather doublet. "I'd been alarmed about you for some time. Nan had come back from Belford and confided to me about James's odd behavior and your estrangement. Then, when James's message about you and Father Bernard came to Cromwell, Ned happened to be with him. Ned told me at once and I went to see Cromwell and volunteered to lead the party to Belford. I told him it was a personal matter, hinted about some great affront done me at your hands, and of course he is only too eager to please a Seymour—or any other man who has the King's ear these days."

She sighed deeply and smiled, her big, familiar smile. "I know I'm still not safe. But just to have hope! Oh, Tom! I'm so grateful! Why have you been so good to me?"

It had not been meant exactly as a question, but Tom took it for such and the twinkle faded from his eyes. He leaned toward her and ran his hand against her cheek. "Don't you know?"

The topaz eyes were huge again, the lips still parted slightly. He bent down and kissed her gently. "Am I so difficult to read? I love you, Morgan."

She clung to him, her head awhirl. "You!" she breathed. "You and all your women!" And she laughed aloud and took his face between her hands. Her eyes turned serious. "Tom."

"So, you believe me?" He was grinning, the white teeth flashing at her, the candlelight catching the golden glints in his red hair.

"I don't know. I don't care. I suppose we've always loved each other, in our own way, but more as brother and sister. Yet . . ." She paused, tracing his jawline through the thick beard. "No man but Sean ever said he loved me."

"And I have never told any other woman I loved her. Or meant it, at any rate." The grin turned sheepish. "Will you fight me like a tigress if I try to make love to you?"

The big eyes regarded Tom steadily. "No." Morgan wasn't at all sure if she loved Tom, at least in the romantic sense. But she had been alone for so long and no man had ever both loved *and* made love to her. Despite Tom's optimism about saving her from the block, she was still too close to death to deny herself—and him—the joy they might offer each other.

He was already adroitly unlacing her soft chamois riding jacket. With expert hands, he slipped the silk bodice from her shoulders and cupped the full, white breasts. "I thought you'd look like this," he said appreciatively. "You are a most lovely and inviting woman."

Morgan watched with delight as his strong fingers moved in circular motions around her breasts and finally touched her nipples. He pinched each one experimentally and she sighed as she saw them turn taut beneath his fingers. It was not just Francis who could arouse her, she thought with involuntary satisfaction, and pulled Tom's head down into the valley between her breasts.

Morgan's skirt and undergarments were off in the next few seconds and Tom's clothes lay in a heap beside the bed. He spread her legs and gazed with pleasure at the tawny triangle that crowned her womanhood.

"Childbearing has done little harm to your body," he declared, and fell facedown to kiss her stomach and the curling hair and the insides of her thighs. She felt his tongue probe upwards, sending fiery flames throughout her entire being. Morgan's hands were in his hair and her legs wound around his back.

"Oh, Tom," she gasped, "now, please!"

He lifted his head, giving her a quick, bemused glance. Then he was straddling her, thrusting inside her body, moving in rapid, throbbing intensity until they both groaned with ecstasy. He did not withdraw from her for a long time, and she lay beneath him, listening to the steady beat of his heart. At last he moved away and they were quiet, so quiet that Morgan thought Tom must have gone to sleep. But eventually he hugged her tight, and when he spoke, his words were unusually sober: "You did not learn to love like that from James, I'll wager."

The denial should have rushed to Morgan's lips—but it did not. She could lie to James, to Richard Griffin, even to the King himself—but not to Tom Seymour. "Does it matter?"

The moon was up, full and silver, floating in a cloudless

spring sky above the River Aln. Morgan could make out every nuance of Tom's face a scant six inches from her own. He appeared to be struggling with himself, knowing he had long ago lost count of the women he had bedded, and yet unable to accept the possibility that Morgan had dallied with another man outside of wedlock. "No." He hugged her close and kissed the tip of her nose. "What matters is the future, not the past."

Morgan gazed at him in wonder and gratitude. Did she love Tom? Perhaps. But she wanted to be certain, and Grandmother Isabeau had told Morgan that she should know when real love was there. And surely, locked in Tom's embrace, she had to believe that this was the man she was destined to love forever.

Chapter 18

THEY STAYED IN NEWCASTLE the following night, Darlington the next, then York. During the day, Tom treated her rudely, casting frequent aspersions on her loyalty to King and country. Morgan seldom replied but rode with eyes staring straight ahead, trying to look defeated but dignified. It was not that difficult to keep up the pretense, for when she thought what might befall them if they got to London too soon, or if Henry changed his mind about Cromwell, she became overwhelmed by fear.

Tom figured they had three, maybe four days before they reached London. It was the sixth of June; he wished he could find out what had gone on while he'd been away from London. Most of the gossip he had heard at the inns along the way didn't tell him much more than he already knew. There was talk about the new treason bill Cromwell had introduced into Parliament. It was said that the chancellor was going to arrest at least five more bishops.

They reached the forests of Nottingham by midafternoon. As they stopped by a stream to water the horses, Will came up to Tom. "Think we can make Newark this evening?" he asked.

Tom cupped water in his hands and drank. "We stop at Tuxford."

Will eyed Tom quizzically. "Tom," he said, for they were friends as well as companions-in-arms, "this slow pace causes the men to spend too much time at inns drinking and wenching and dicing."

Tom stood up, grinning. "I've never heard you complain about that sort of amusement before, Will. Is your wife turning you into a homebody?"

Will smiled back, looking a bit foolish. Morgan watched from her saddle as Will pulled Tom away from the others.

"I've heard it said," Will told Tom in a low voice, "that you keep the Countess with you at nights for sport, not guarding. For my own part, I know that you were friends with her and her father as well. It makes even me suspicious, Tom."

Tom threw back his red head and laughed. "Oh, Will, be suspicious then! But don't let me catch you peering under the door tonight!"

Tom was troubled at the inn in Tuxford, but he kept it from Morgan. He knew his men both feared and respected him; there would be no direct challenge from them.

After Morgan and Tom had made love and lay back among the pillows, she asked what Will had said that afternoon. He shrugged the question off, mumbling something about the men doing too much wenching. "Go to sleep, sweetheart," he ordered, flinging an arm across her body. But Morgan had overheard most of the conversation and remained awake for a long time.

They stopped in Stamford next—only one more night now, and two short days. He decided that Stevenage would be their last stop.

Stevenage was a tiny village with only one inn, and that was full. Next would be Hatfield, but that was so close, too close to London. If they went that far and no farther, Tom knew Will's suspicions would be confirmed.

"Will you gamble with me?" Tom asked Morgan in a low voice as they rode out of Stevenage. She nodded. "Then we must make for London."

She stared at him, her heart beating rapidly. "But I thought . . ."

"We will arrive close to midnight. I will take you to Seymour Place. In the morning we will see what steps must be taken next."

The dejected pose came all too easily now. She clutched at the reins and bit her lip. London! Was it possible that she had ever longed to see that city again? Now the very word set her trembling with fear. Tom turned in the saddle. "We'll make straight for London. Move along!"

Will Herbert smiled, his concern ebbing.

The city—with its lights still burning, traffic still moving in the narrow streets. The bells of St. Paul's chimed the midnight hour as they rode through King's Cross. Then they turned, not toward the Tower or Whitehall where Cromwell dwelt, but in the direction of the Inns of Court where Seymour Place was situated.

"Where do we ride?" Herbert asked.

"To my place," Tom replied.

"Sir Thomas . . ." began Will.

"You heard me. Think I would wake the diligent Cromwell at this late hour? He may do much of his thinking in bed, but he sleeps there, too. We will remain at Seymour Place until I dispose of the prisoner tomorrow."

Tom lodged Morgan in a room next to his and posted guards outside. He had already explained that he dared not come to her that night. Alone in her bed, she tossed and turned, unable to sleep. Without him, the night held more terror than the day. And suddenly her guilt of sin overwhelmed her. Adultery, she thought, what an ugly word! Holding him close, delighting in his kisses, feeling his big body against hers, she had no sense of shame or guilt. But now, conscience was at work. Adultery might be regarded lightly at court, but for Morgan, raised in the strict environment of Faux Hall, it was sin, plain and simple. It was also confusing. She had not felt this way with Francis. Why was it different with Tom?

I love him, I must love him, whereas I don't love Francis. Else why should I feel so happy with Tom, so content, so oblivious even to the danger we share? She rolled over again and began to pray.

Tom came to her room early that morning. He took her hands and kissed her cheek. "I have sent word to Cromwell that you are here," he told her, and saw the terror in her eyes. "Now we must wait."

The guards stayed outside the door. After he left, a servingwoman came in with food and clean clothes. Morgan listlessly went through the garments, noting a low-cut red dress among them. In spite of her apprehension, she was faintly amused. For whom had Tom bought that piece of frippery—or who had hastily left it behind? But it fit reasonably well and she was grateful to discard the chamois riding habit she had worn for the last week.

Tom had been out of the house for several hours. Morgan paced the room, nibbled without appetite at some cold pheasant and continued to wait. She sat on the bed, trying to conjure up scenes with the council, with Henry, with Cromwell. Her shrewd, cunning uncle—surely he could not fall into the same trap that he had set for so many others! The King was aware that Cromwell was virtually indispensable in running the government. Certainly Cromwell, at the height of his power, could save himself. Despite the June warmth, Morgan shivered, rubbing her hands together. They were cold as ice water, though her cheeks were hot.

She got up again, wandering to the window for what seemed like the hundredth time. The view was always the same—a peddler pushing his cart, a carriage rattling by, young boys running and shouting to one another, lawyers and their clerks heading for the Inns of Court.

It was almost suppertime when she heard heavy footsteps in the hall. She jumped up from the bed where she'd been trying to nap. Was it to be now? The door opened to reveal Tom Seymour, with Ned and Will Herbert behind him.

"Cromwell's been arrested. You're free!" said Tom. Morgan stood dumbfounded as Tom hurried to take her in his arms.

After supper, with Ned and Will Herbert as Tom's guests, Morgan learned of the turn of events which had saved her life. Cromwell had received Tom's message at ten that morning. But there were more pressing matters on his mind; he was putting together warrants for the five bishops he deemed "too conservative," trying to build a wall of security around himself with the misdeeds of others.

After dinner Cromwell had rushed to the privy council meeting where Ned had joined the others. Tom had waited in the music room, helping Margaret Howard Griffin's young cousin, Katherine, tune her lute. Ned told him later what had happened—how, in the middle of the session, the captain of the King's guard had stomped into the room and held out a warrant for the "villain minister's" arrest. Norfolk had leaped from his seat and flung himself upon Cromwell, wrenching the cross of St. George from his neck. Norfolk, that proud Howard, had at last seen the fall of the upstart Cromwell. Screaming with anger, the disgraced chancellor was taken to the Tower by barge.

"I should feel sorry for him out of Christian charity, but I cannot," Morgan declared, turning the stem of her wine goblet in her hands. "Yet I don't understand how I was freed so rapidly."

Tom poured Scots whiskey for himself and Ned. Will declined, saying he'd have no traffic with the imported liquor, but would stick to brandy.

Tom leaned back in his chair and waved a hand toward Ned. "My good brother came hurrying to the music room with the news. He'd hardly got the story out when the King came in with neither music—nor Cromwell—on his mind."

"You mean he's courting this Katherine Howard?" asked Morgan incredulously. "But he's married to Anne of Cleves!"

Tom smirked at her. "You still don't know our monarch very well. Do you want to hear what took place or not?"

"Yes, yes, of course," said Morgan hastily.

"Actually, there's not much more to tell. I informed the King that I had you here under arrest at your uncle's request and asked if the charges would be dropped now, and he just kept grinning at Katherine and then waved his hand and said, 'Oh, by the Mass! That pretty wench! Certainly, certainly!' And he added something not fit for your ears, so Ned and I left him to his light o' love."

"Howards!" snorted Ned contemptuously. "They seek the reins again."

Morgan, ignoring Ned's remark, wriggled with pleasure and relief. "Free! I still can't take it in!"

Ned frowned slightly and cleared his throat. "There is still one matter which my brother has not touched upon." Morgan looked at him questioningly. "Your uncle confiscated Faux Hall, a property he has long coveted."

Even that bit of news couldn't shake Morgan. "Ah, I should have guessed! He was always envious of my mother's side of the family and my father's possessions." She remembered how anxious he had been to relieve her of any responsibility for her family home after her parents died. "Surely it will revert to me now."

Ned still frowned. "Mayhap. But the rumor is that a week ago Cromwell turned Faux Hall over to the King as a gift to placate him. And 'tis said that the King, in turn, has presented it to Katherine Howard as a wooing present."

Morgan slapped her hand on the table. "Oh, faugh! Who is this chit, anyway?"

Will Herbert supplied the information: She was Norfolk's eighteen-year-old niece, plump and pretty as a Persian cat. She was one of Anne of Cleves's ladies and the Howards were pushing her into Henry's aging arms.

"Well," said Morgan, "I'll not think about it now. I'm not going to think of anything tonight, not even about getting back to Belford and the children."

Tom eyed her from over the rim of his whiskey tumbler. "You would go back to Belford?"

"I must. I am going to take the children away from James. I fear for their safety, especially Anne's."

"You set another dangerous task for yourself," Tom warned her. "I will go back with you."

She stayed in London less than a fortnight. She visited the court but spent most of her days and all of her nights with Tom at Seymour Place. Occasionally she felt shame and cursed herself as a wanton woman. But mostly she experienced sheer joy from being with Tom and glorying in their mutual passion. At Whitehall one afternoon, several ladies vied with each other for Tom's attentions while Morgan was cornered by John Dudley's tiresome political opinions. Morgan had looked over Dudley's shoulder and had seen Tom give her a long, slow wink. Her blood had begun to race with desire and the pride of possession. Let those featherheaded wenches flirt themselves into a fit, she'd thought—Tom belongs to me. And in that moment, she was absolutely sure that she loved him.

She saw Richard and Margaret Griffin briefly, observed the King from a distance, chatted with the Earl of Surrey, and caught a glimpse of the rangy, fair-haired Anne of Cleves. Two days before she and Tom had decided to leave for Belford, Nan came to London and met Morgan at Seymour Place. Nan was far gone with her second child, and Morgan chided her for making the trip in the summer heat.

"Nonsense! I'm healthy as a plow horse!" She added, however, that her mother was not. "She's ailed ever since the Countess of Salisbury's arrest," Nan said, pulling off her short gloves. "Gloves in this kind of weather!" She tossed them on a table.

They talked for three hours straight, Morgan spilling out the whole horrendous tale with Nan exclaiming and shaking her head. When at last Morgan had brought her up to date, Nan regarded her cousin seriously.

"I have heard some things, too, even at Wolf Hall," she said. Morgan asked her what they might be. Nan answered her evenly: "That you are Tom's mistress."

Morgan got up and walked to the sideboard where she extracted two wilted roses from a bouquet. "It's true, Nan," she replied, throwing the roses into the grate.

Nan was silent for a few seconds. "Strange," she mused, "I remember when he used to come visit your father, when we were very young, how I thought you should marry him. Instead, I married a Seymour." She folded her hands across her big stomach. "How long ago that seems."

"Yes," said Morgan, and stared at the Seymour coat-of-arms above the mantelpiece.

Henry Tudor made one thing clear: He had had enough of Wolseys and Cromwells. From now on, he would run his kingdom by himself.

"Ned pouts," Tom reported to Morgan one warm June evening. He grinned and brushed her lips with a kiss. "Should I feel sorry for my poor brother?"

"He's Earl of Hertford. He has all sorts of lands and perquisites," Morgan replied, nestling her head against Tom's chest. "In fact, you have grown quite wealthy since becoming uncle to a prince. I expect there will be more preferments for you both as Edward grows older."

"Hmmmm." He fondled her body under the thin silken peignoir. "It's you I prefer, sweetheart."

"Such a welcome declaration," Morgan sighed, moving his hand to the soft yet firm flesh of her belly, "since I prefer you to whatever else the world might offer. Oh, Tom," she exclaimed, guiding his fingers between her thighs, "I marvel that it took so long for me to realize I love you!"

Tom lifted the peignoir's flowing skirts to reveal the lush nakedness of her lower body. "I was slow to discover the truth, too," he declared, his sea-blue eyes savoring the slim legs, the curve of hip and thigh, and the tantalizing triangle which drew his lips like a magnet.

"When, Tom?" she breathed, as he dropped on his knees to kiss the mound of her womanhood. "You never told me."

But Tom was too engrossed to reply at once. His tongue was probing her eager flesh as she stood with legs spread apart and clutched at his hair. At last they both tumbled onto the divan and he pulled the peignoir all the way off, then hurriedly removed his own clothes.

"At Belford, when I was blown ashore." He tossed the last of his garments onto the adjacent footstool. "There you were, bulging like an overripe melon, clumsy and none too happy—or so it seemed to me—and yet I found myself totally smitten."

Morgan laughed aloud, delighted at the absurdity of his description, enchanted by the ardor with which he kissed the hollow of her neck, the crevice between her breasts, the curve of her waist. It was perfect, this love of theirs: Sean had wooed her, Richard had stirred her senses, James had married her—but Tom offered not only his heart but his body, to bring contentment of the flesh and peace to her soul.

And then there was Francis. Even as Tom's hands explored her buttocks and she covered his chest with biting kisses, Francis's lanky image flashed before her. But there was no love there, only an animal attraction which had served their lustful urges well. Nor was Francis Tom's equal in any number of ways—he lacked Tom's finesse, his grace, his sense of romantic passion. Tom might be part pirate with the reputation of a rake, but he was also a gentleman, schooled in the ways of the court, well versed in words a woman wanted to hear.

But all Morgan wished to hear at that moment was the cry of her own delicious pleasure as Tom held her tight and brought them both to an exquisite, blinding joy. She felt the sudden, shattering surge of his explosion inside her as it mingled with the release of her own desire in the most intimate recesses of her body.

Moments later, as they clung together on the narrow divan, she expressed her feelings about the miracle of their love.

"Perfect?" Tom repeated with a dubiously raised eyebrow. "Wonderful, I'll concede—but not perfect."

"Why not?" Morgan looked puzzled as she shifted her body to see him more clearly.

"Because," he replied, pulling her closer, "we are lovers, not man and wife. I've waited too long for love not to want to make it a permanent arrangement."

"But that's not possible!" she breathed. "Are you suggesting an annulment or divorce?"

"It's a possibility." Tom released Morgan and stood up, going to the wardrobe to get his dressing gown. "You could find grounds somehow. James is clearly unstable; he would have had you killed. There must be a way, and once we get to Belford and secure the children's safekeeping, we'll come back to London and figure out what we can do."

Morgan's eyes widened as she scanned Tom's face. "You're serious! You would marry me! I can hardly believe that!"

"Try, sweetheart. God's teeth, don't you know how much I love you?"

The return to Belford was made in six days of hard riding. Now that Morgan had left London behind she was desperately anxious to see her children again. Over a month had gone by since she had clasped them in her arms.

But she wished she would not have to see James at all; the mere thought of encountering him again after all he had done filled her with revulsion. He would have to be dealt with, however, and Morgan was extremely grateful that Tom was at her side to help shoulder the responsibility.

On the day before they left London, June twenty-ninth, Commons had passed an Act of Attainder condemning Cromwell as a heretic and a traitor. Tom told Morgan that Henry would let his former chancellor live long enough to obtain him a divorce from Anne of Cleves, who would meet with a far better fate than the other Anne had. "There is talk of pension and special titles and privileges," he said. "And she takes it well, having neither ambition nor great vanity."

The July sun beat down on the towers and roofs of Belford Castle. Tom called to his half-dozen retainers to follow him through the gates. They had stopped to eat in the village, in case the lord of the castle was inhospitable. Morgan had been welcomed warmly by the townspeople, who were amazed and delighted to see their Countess again.

Tom had warned her at least once a day on the trip north

that James would undoubtedly resist her plans. That was why he had brought his men along, though he knew that if James wanted to create a conflict a small army would be needed to fend off the supporters of Belford. It was an uncertain situation, but there was no telling Morgan she couldn't have her way and take the children under her care. She had sent a letter ahead, saying her request was sanctioned by the King, which indeed it was, since Henry was still in an expansive mood.

"He'd never rally the people of Belford against me," Morgan kept telling Tom. "Besides, he cares nothing for the children. He doesn't even believe Anne is his daughter." She was convinced he'd relinquish them without protest as long as she promised to raise them well and let them visit their father when he wished it. She would put it in writing if necessary.

The courtyard was empty. It was very quiet, ominously quiet, Tom thought. As they dismounted, he ordered his men to stay with the horses. Tom opened the great castle door and ushered Morgan inside. James stood alone in the hallway.

I don't even think enough of him for hate, thought Morgan, and to her surprise, James smiled. "Welcome, welcome," he said. "We were expecting you."

His voice sounded so odd, not at all as Morgan remembered it. "We've come for the children," she said abruptly, as Matthew came quietly into the hallway. She acknowledged him with a curt nod.

"I heard you were in the village," James said, as if she had not spoken. "Yes, I was waiting for you."

"The children," Morgan said impatiently. "Have Agnes bring them at once. They are ready to travel, I assume?"

"Travel?" He seemed vague. "Oh, they are traveling already!" He smiled and nodded.

Morgan felt panicky. "What do you mean?" She advanced on him, her fists clenched.

"You promised them a trip, don't you remember?" His eyes glinted. "They have gone without you, madam, to the Holy Isle." And he laughed, a high wild shriek, which seemed to cut into the very stones of Belford.

Morgan screamed and started at him, but Tom pulled her back and turned to Matthew. "Where are the children? Quickly, or I'll have you on the rack!"

Matthew spread his hands. "I—I'm not sure," he stammered. "I did see his lordship with them on the sea-cliff path a bit ago . . ."

Tom called to his men. "Come," he commanded Matthew, "show us the way."

Morgan herself led them, racing out of the castle and along the path, her skirts in her hand. Unseeing, she sped headlong, oblivious to everything but her terror and fear. And suddenly, she stopped, for halfway between the shore and the Holy Isle she spied a little boat with three tiny figures in it. Buffeted by the waves, it pitched and plunged in the sea. She screamed and Tom grabbed her arm.

"Wait, do you hear?" He shook her. She nodded, unable to speak. He turned to Matthew. "I see other boats on the beach. How do we get to them?"

"There's a path just a few yards from here, where the cliff drops down. Believe me, my lord, I had no idea . . ."

"Enough," said Tom, and Matthew and the retainers followed him down to the beach.

Morgan clung to a tree, her eyes fixed on the little boat, which still bobbed and tossed and turned on the waves. Were the children moving? Anne, not even a year old! James must have carried her down the path and put her into the boat with her brothers. How could he? How could he have done such a thing? But of course she knew that James was completely, hopelessly mad.

It seemed like hours before Tom, Matthew, and two of the retainers had shoved a boat into the sea and climbed in. Tom was at the oars, pulling mightily. The other four men took a second boat and followed their master into the water.

Morgan knelt on shaky knees in the dirt, praying, her hands clasped so tight that the nails dug into the skin and drew blood. The boat with the children mounted a great wave and slid out of sight. Morgan gasped and leaned forward. Suddenly it appeared again, and she counted the three little heads, still aboard.

And then Tom's boat was next to them. He climbed into the children's craft as someone—it seemed to be Matthew—handed him an extra set of oars. Tom brought the boat around quickly and started for the shore.

Morgan couldn't wait any longer. She jumped up and plunged down toward the beach, the sand flying from her feet. She was waiting at the edge of the water as Tom let the oars rest in their oarlocks and got out of the boat.

She waded straight into the sea and grasped the bow of the boat. "My babies!" she cried, and picked up Anne in her arms.

"Why did we have to come back?" Robbie was asking. "You promised!"

She held him, too, and Edmund. And then she handed them over to Tom and ran back up the hill, not even hearing Tom's voice shouting at her to wait.

She had never felt so full of strength. Fury and fear, followed by her children's rescue, had given her a sense of great power, an almost supernatural energy. Yet she moved slowly into the entrance hall. Yes, he was still there; she was sure of it. He was alone, just staring ahead.

He heard her and turned. "They are gone, are they not, madam, gone to the Holy Isle?" Still that ghastly smile.

She was on him in an instant, her fingers tearing at his throat. He struggled to break free but her hold was fierce. He gasped for air, his eyes beginning to bulge. And then he could breath again as Tom held Morgan fast, her grip at last broken. James recognized the naked murder in her eyes. He took in air gratefully and then his own anger flared.

"Whore! Slut! Bitch!" His face went purple, even more so than it had with her fingers around his neck. He took a step forward and fell to the stone floor.

Dr. Wimble mopped his forehead with a handkerchief. Why did people always have to get sick on the hottest day of the year? He stepped outside the chamber where James lay, and faced Morgan and Tom Seymour.

"He is conscious now," he told them, "but I regret to tell you that he cannot move or speak."

"Will he recover?" Morgan asked.

The doctor shook his head. "I have seen other cases like this, madam. Although some of the patients have lived for months, even years, they seldom get back the use of their limbs or their full speech. In some cases only one side of the body is affected and on occasion they will recover to the point—"

Morgan silenced him with her hand. "You mean he will be like this forever . . . until he dies?"

Dr. Wimble nodded sadly. "I fear so, madam. And such a young man." He shook his head again.

After the doctor left, Morgan led Tom into her chambers. The furniture was covered and dust was everywhere. It seemed that no one—not even the loyal Polly and Peg—had expected their Countess to return.

"We should have gone into the library," Morgan said, as she lifted the covers from two of the chairs. They both sat down. "You must know, I am sure," she began, "that I cannot return to London with you."

Tom's eyebrows pulled together. "Morgan, you don't mean that. After all that James has done to you, it would be ridiculous to stay here, isolated and alone, watching over him. It might be months, even years, as Wimble said. You have a good sleep tonight, and we'll talk about it in the morning." He started to get up.

"No, Tom, I mean it."

His blue eyes were openly incredulous. "Morgan," he said, leaning toward her. "That's absurd! There are servants to take care of him here. Pack your things and get the children ready and I'll take you back to London. I'll even find a house for you there."

"No." She stared at her hands in her lap.

He knelt in front of her, his own hands pressing against her thighs. "You would not part from me now, surely?"

She looked at him straight on, the topaz eyes unwavering. "Yes. That is why I must stay. What has happened to James and to me is like a judgment. I've sinned with you. I sinned with—another man. I yearned over Sean's memory. I even thought about Richard. No wonder James and I were never truly happy!"

"Muffet . . . !" He squeezed her knees, still unconvinced.

"No more 'muffet,' I told you so long ago. I have not been a good or faithful wife. Now I will do my penance. I will not leave him. As long as he lives, you and I must deny our love."

His arms went around her waist and he shook her hard. "Morgan, Morgan! That's asking too much—of me and of yourself. James tried to kill you! You don't owe him anything! If you must talk of owing, then it's to me that you owe your life and it's you I claim as my reward."

"You already have claimed me," she replied with a soft

smile. "Please . . . don't make it any more difficult than it is. You know I love you," she said, and was sure she spoke from the heart.

Tom still gripped her about the waist as he fathomed the determined and unhappy expression in her big eyes. He leaned closer, his hands moving to undo the hooks on her dress. "Would you be cruel enough to deny either of us what we both want so much?" he breathed.

She jumped up and out of his grasp, knocking the chair over behind her. "Yes!" Her hands covered her face.

He stood up, his face dark. "By God's most precious soul," he murmured, as if to himself, "I've waited so long for you. I never had to play the monk with a woman before. Now I finally declare my love, and then . . ." He cut himself off and gave one of the drapes a shake. Dust flew about the room. He grinned at her but it wasn't quite real. "Well. I'm not a patient man, but I'll do my best."

She smiled back, trying to stop her tears. "You'll not be lonely while you do," she said. "I know that." But I will be, she thought. I will be unbearably lonely for his great smile and I shall hunger for his touch during those weeks and months that lie ahead.

She had refused to sleep with him, asserting that making love under her husband's roof would be unthinkable. But Tom's urgent caresses and fierce kisses had won her over. They came together that night with almost savage passion and scarcely slept at all.

Tom left with his men the next day. Before leaving, he talked with Morgan about how to run the castle and its lands but she assured him there would be no problem. She was used to being in charge of the domestic life at Belford, and Matthew was expert at caring for the surrounding properties and farms. It would mean that she would have to keep the accounts, but Matthew could help with that, too. The tenants were friendly, and the villagers, she had heard from Polly, now regarded her as a heroine.

"So you see, all will be well," she asserted, standing with him in the entrance hall.

"I hope so," he replied, glancing out to see if his men had their horses saddled up. They did, and he knew it was time to leave. "One thing—I suggest you write to Francis and tell him what has happened. He will hear rumors, of course, but I think you should tell him yourself."

Morgan considered for a moment. "Yes, mayhap I should."

Tom leaned down and put his hand under her chin. He kissed her gently on the mouth. "I love you, Morgan." And then he left her, his boots resounding sharply on the stone floor.

PART THREE

1540–1549

Chapter 19

A WEEK LATER, Francis Sinclair rode into Belford's courtyard. He had never again thought to see the stark strength of its walls, the entryway, the little balcony overlooking the courtyard, the rose window of the small chapel. He stood for a moment, his hands still on the reins of his horse. It is all the same, he thought, but those of us who have lived here are much changed.

"Master Francis!" It was Polly, at one of the side entrances. She waddled as fast as she could to Francis and fell to her knees, grasping his hand. "Oh, Master Francis, it is so good to see you back within these walls!"

He lifted her to her feet, brushing aside her effusive comments. "You seem rotund and well fed as ever, Polly. Where is your mistress?"

"In the wine cellar, checking the stores. She is so capable for such a pretty little thing! Why, just yesterday she even found some errors in the account books which the Earl had made in his . . . his sickness. She has had all the walls scrubbed within and without, and the windows cleaned and new rushes laid and . . ."

He half listened to Polly rattle on as she led him down the winding stairway to the wine cellar. At the door, she called to Morgan: "It's Master Francis come home!"

Morgan flung open the door, a smudge of dirt on one cheek and her dress patched with dust. Her tawny hair was done up on her head and loose strands flew in several directions.

She started forward as if to hug Francis, but offered her hand instead. "I never thought you'd actually come!" She smiled up at him, surveying his face in the dim light. He is so tall, she thought, and his hair seems darker. "Oh!"

cried, "I'm such a mess! Come upstairs and I'll clean up while Polly gets you something to eat."

He followed her up from the cellar, commenting that Polly might also send a groom to care for his mount. Francis headed straight for the library and Morgan soon joined him, her face clean and her dress free from dust. Even the stray locks of hair were back in place.

"How is he, Morgan?" Francis asked without preamble.

Morgan settled herself on the window seat. "The same as when I wrote. He neither moves nor speaks. Dr. Wimble says it is quite hopeless."

"If it were not, I wouldn't have come. Does he know or understand anything?"

She shook her head. "He eats and sleeps and the rest of the time just stares straight ahead. I have no love or hate for him, Francis, but there is much pity."

"If he knew I was here . . ." Francis shook his head. Polly came in with food for Francis and a decanter of brandy. She gave him another fond look, sighed contentedly, and left the room.

Francis began to eat. "I have heard most of what has happened to you," he said between mouthfuls. "You have suffered a great deal."

Morgan shrugged. "Everybody suffers, at one time or another." She told him what he didn't already know, especially of the day she had come back to Belford. Francis listened without comment, but occasionally he frowned.

"And still you stay with him," Francis said at last.

"I told you, I pity him. Besides . . ." She hesitated, not sure whether she should speak. "I have been a false wife."

Francis looked up at her, letting the carving knife slip to the table. "So? I was a false brother. At least you did your penance while he could still be a husband to you. I did not. But I don't owe him my soul; I owe that only to God."

"That's true," Morgan said slowly, pushing aside the plate of trifle she had scarcely touched. "But it wasn't only you."

"Oh?" Francis's features tightened. "Perhaps it shouldn't, but that comes as a surprise." He picked up a pheasant leg and chewed with noisy gusto.

"Don't misunderstand," Morgan said hastily. "I haven't been . . . promiscuous. In fact, it happened after James had me arrested." She saw the skeptical look in the gray eyes. "I fell in love," she added defensively.

"Ah," Francis added with mock solemnity. "Congratulations. To both you and Sir Thomas."

Morgan's hand flew to her breast. "How did you know?"

Francis wiped his face and hands on a napkin. "Who else but your gallant, rakish savior? Spreading your legs for Seymour was an extremely generous act of gratitude, made even more touching by your sudden discovery of true love." He paused to take a hefty drink from his wine goblet. "But now you must forsake his ardor and tend your helpless husband. By the Mass, I'm well-nigh moved to tears!"

The rage, which had started out as astonishment, unleashed itself in a flurry of flying tableware which bounced off Francis's shoulder. "Whoreson! How dare you make me out as such a conniving wanton! You! Of all people!" She grasped the brandy decanter, but Francis leaped up and clamped a hand on her wrist.

"Becalm yourself," he commanded in a steely voice which held an echo of James's chilly tones. "Perhaps I spoke too bluntly. But you do have a habit of hurtling into situations you never think about beforehand. As an impulsive sort myself, I understand the dangers well."

Morgan's heart was still pounding wildly with emotion, but her anger had begun to fade as Francis grew more reasonable. She set the decanter down carefully as he let go of her wrist. "We love each other," she declared, attempting to look dignified. "We would have sought an annulment and married had James not fallen ill."

Francis said nothing. He sat in silence finishing his brandy and eating at least two dozen fresh raspberries. Morgan watched him covertly; it occurred to her that she no longer felt the overwhelming need for his kisses or the surging power of his body in hers. As he pushed away the now-empty silver fruit bowl, her eyes strayed to his hands. And from somewhere in the very depths of her being, she felt a jarring sensation which made her knees go weak. Oh, sweet Virgin, she thought, I am *not* yet free of him, despite Tom!

Francis appeared to be paying her no heed. A manservant called Simeon, who was almost stone-deaf, had come to remove the dishes. Simeon looked quizzical as he bent to retrieve the three forks, two spoons, and the napkin ring Morgan had hurled at Francis.

"Awkward," bellowed Francis, and Morgan jumped, but Simeon still did not hear.

After Simeon had poured brandy and left them, Morgan decided it was time to put the conversation on more neutral ground. She inquired about Francis's children, who were thriving; she asked how Francis liked the house at Carlisle and was informed that it suited him well, especially since he'd enlarged the tiny library; she queried him about his neighbors but was told they were few and far between, which bothered Francis not at all. At last she asked the question she had put off:

"Have you considered marrying again?"

He avoided her eyes, looking instead at the arrangement of iris and lilies on the trestle table. "No." His face was in shadow as the sun began to fade behind the western hills. "It is too soon for me." He took one final sip of brandy and stood up. "Come—I wish to see Robbie, and the other two as well."

Francis spent four days at Belford, consulting Matthew, speaking with the retainers, going over the improvements Morgan had already effected, and riding out among the fields and farms and orchards. He did not see James. Even though he had been assured by both Morgan and Dr. Wimble that James would never recognize him—or anybody else—he avoided his brother's sickroom.

Nan had given birth to a daughter on July twenty-eighth. She wrote a long letter to Morgan, filling in the details. The new babe would be named Margaret, for Nan's mother. Two other, more momentous events had taken place that same day, Nan wrote. Thomas Cromwell had been beheaded and Katherine Howard had become the King's fifth wife.

Morgan did not dwell on either her uncle's death or King Henry's youthful bride. She was too engrossed in the running of Belford, riding out at least once a week to supervise the tenants, with Matthew always at her side. She spent an hour each day checking provisions, going over the ledgers, and toting up the accounts. She kept tight rein on the castle servants, even tighter than when James was well.

She visited James every day while he was having his noon meal. Sometimes she would feed him herself, but usually Cedric, his body servant, served him. He lay propped up among the pillows, unseeing, unhearing. He was thinner now, and looked at least ten years older. Morgan gave orders to Cedric to bathe and shave his master every day. She dedicated herself to taking the greatest care of her husband.

Dr. Wimble came every Thursday. At the end of August, he told her that in truth his visits were useless. "I can only see whether he grows worse, but as I have told you, I cannot make him better."

"I know," Morgan replied, leaning wearily against one of the library bookshelves.

"In fact," Dr. Wimble went on, observing her carefully, "I worry more about you than I do about him. You are very pale and too thin. You must not work so hard, and try to eat more."

"I will," Morgan promised.

It was that exchange with Dr. Wimble that forced her mind to accept what she had been trying to deny: She was pregnant again, pregnant with Tom's child. At first she had so lost count of the days that her physical state went unnoticed. Then she told herself that it was only the terrible strain she had been under and the subsequent hard work. But now she had to face the reality of her condition.

She debated whether or not to write to Tom. She had had another letter from Nan saying that Tom had gone to Vienna to enlist support for England against the French and Scottish alliance. He would not return for several months.

The rest of the world might not guess that the babe she carried was not her husband's, but the inhabitants of Belford would know the truth. She thought of Polly's face, imagining her shock and distress. She thought of Matthew and wondered if he could continue to respect and obey her. And she thought of Francis and could not even fathom his reaction.

At the end of the second week in September a visitor came to Belford Castle. Peg brought the news to Morgan, who was with Agnes in the nursery watching Anne crawl across the floor.

"She'll be walking soon," Agnes was saying as Peg entered the room and curtsied.

"There is a lady to see you, madam," she said. "I *think* she is a lady, at least from her speech, but her clothes are patched and old."

Morgan headed for the hallway, biting her lip and trying to think who the newcomer could be. Because of James's strong leaning toward the new ways, they had not been friendly with the more conservative families of the North.

Peg told Morgan the visitor was in the library, warming herself. It had been a cool, foggy morning, although the noon sun was beginning to penetrate the clouds.

Mary Percy, the widowed Countess of Northumberland, had lost the freshness of youth and stood with the air of one who has come to a fork in the road and has no idea which turn to take—and little interest in reaching her destination.

"Good day, madam," said Morgan. "It's been years since we've met."

Mary moved away from the fire. "I was uncertain about coming to Belford," she replied. "You knew my lord is dead?"

Morgan had heard that Percy had died, but she had taken little notice since he had been ill so long. She had not given a thought to his widow.

"My condolences, madam." But Morgan was puzzled. "Would you care for something to eat or drink?"

To Morgan's astonishment, the Countess took quick steps across the room and fell to her knees. "My lady, I beseech you! I am penniless, alone, homeless! I know your sympathies were not on the side of my husband, but I beg you to let me stay at Belford."

Morgan looked down at the bowed head, partially covered by a frayed woolen veil. There were some gray hairs among the brown. Morgan's mind raced: What had befallen the widow of the great lord of the North? Something James had said about Percy being on a pension, his vast fortune gone . . .

"Pray rise, madam. We are equals," Morgan said somewhat stiffly. "Tell me what has brought you to such a state."

310

At the time of Percy's death, Mary explained in faltering tones, almost all his property had been confiscated by the King to pay his debts. For the last three months, Mary had been living in abandoned servants' quarters near Alnwick Castle. She had barely enough to eat. Although she had written repeatedly to her Talbot relations, their only help was in the form of advice: Have patience and wait for better times.

"It has become clear that better times are not coming and I am well out of patience," Mary declared bitterly. "I had heard your own lord was ill and you were the only person close by who might be sympathetic. The others all opposed my husband's religious views and his persecution of Lord Dacre. At least you were not here at that time, and I had to seek help somewhere . . ." Her voice grew very small.

Morgan thoughtfully eyed the other woman for a long moment. She could find no reason to refuse her. At least it would be someone of her own class to have as a companion.

"Do you have any servants with you?"

Mary's eyes lighted up. "Oh, madam, do you mean I can stay?"

Morgan smiled in spite of herself. "Yes, of course. We will become a household of women, but I see no harm in that."

Mary would have fallen to her knees in gratitude but Morgan restrained her. There were tears in the Northumberland Countess's eyes. "You are as kind as you are fair!" she cried, pulling out a tattered handkerchief and wiping her eyes.

Mary Percy had only a servingwoman and two elderly retainers. The others had been dismissed or had run away. Morgan put Mary into Lucy and Francis's old rooms, and felt a pang for the past as she watched Polly and Peg ready the musty chamber.

After two weeks at Belford, Mary began to look better, her face less pinched, her eyes no longer dull. Polly and the Countess's servingwoman hurriedly made over some of Morgan's dresses. Morgan watched wryly, thinking that soon she would have to put the serving wenches to work adding fabric to her own clothes.

It was the first day of October when Morgan woke up to bright fall sunshine and saw blood on the bedsheets. Startled and frightened, she picked up the bell to ring for Polly, but thought better of it. She decided to spend the day in bed, however, complaining of a mild stomach upset.

By afternoon she seemed recovered and got up to dress. Peg came in to help her, and as she slipped the gown over Morgan's head, she felt her mistress sway.

"Madam! You'd best get back to bed. You're still unwell." Morgan mumbled agreement but shook off Peg's helping hand.

She slept most of the rest of the day and all through the night until it was almost dawn. She woke up in great pain, and suddenly knew that she was losing her child. Sick and dizzy, Morgan felt a terrible thirst and tried to raise herself to reach for the water tumbler by the bed. But the pains overcame her and she fell back against the pillow, helpless and moaning.

Only Polly and Dr. Wimble knew she had lost a babe. The rest of the household was told that Morgan was still suffering from stomach trouble but there was nothing seriously wrong. She stayed in bed for a week, with Polly clucking over her, concern suffusing any other feelings she might have.

Morgan recovered fairly quickly and Dr. Wimble was pleased with her progress. On the day before he told her she might try to get up for a little while, she spoke to Polly. "Pray try not to think too ill of me, Polly," she said.

Polly patted her hand. "Never, madam. You have suffered much at his hands," she said, waving in the direction of James's room. "There is nothing you could do, no sin you could commit, that I could truly blame you for after all your troubles."

When she had left, Morgan stretched out in the bed and tried to sleep. It was still hard to believe that she had lost her child, Tom's child. She would not write him now. Some day, perhaps, when they met again face-to-face, she would tell him. She felt an overpowering sadness, not just for the babe's sake but because the tiny being had been her last tangible link with Tom, and now it was gone.

Cedric was shaving James. "He is so thin, madam, that if the razor slips I fear it will go straight through to the bone."

Morgan, sitting with her embroidery in her lap, looked sadly at her husband. Over a year now he had lain thus, not moving, not speaking. Dr. Wimble was as pessimistic as ever, saying it was only a matter of time before death would claim James's body as it had already claimed his mind.

He looked at least sixty. The veins stood out everywhere, startlingly blue in the white skin. Much of his pale blond hair had fallen out and his beard was sparse—so sparse that Cedric only shaved him twice a week.

Morgan still came in every day, taking time out from her numerous duties around the castle estates. She spent the rest of her free time with the children, for she had to be both mother and father to them now. Robbie was fair and outgoing, quick at book learning as well as at sports. Edmund was somewhat withdrawn, and clung to his mother's skirts more than Morgan felt necessary. It was too soon to tell much about little Anne, but she seemed a happy child, walking everywhere and beginning to talk in phrases.

Morgan surveyed her handiwork in the embroidery ring with distress. "I shall never learn to sew properly, not if I spend my life practicing." She sighed and got up. "I must check with Matthew. He's going to Newcastle next week to get our provisions for the winter." Cedric bowed as she left the room.

Another winter, she thought, as she made her way down the wide central staircase. The previous winter had been cheerless enough, with big drifts of snow piled against the castle walls during most of January and February. She had tried to bring some gaiety to the household at Christmas with carols and a great wassail bowl, but somehow the season failed to lift her own spirits and she feared that her feelings were transmitted to the others.

As she descended to the entrance hall, she saw Matthew speaking to a messenger clad in green-and-white Tudor livery. She paused with her hand on the stair rail and called out, "What is it, Matthew? What brings a royal messenger to Belford?"

Matthew explained what the visitor had already told him. The King was on a royal progress through the North. He and the court would be pleased to visit Belford Castle before turning south and making their leisurely way back to London. The messenger proffered the official letter to Morgan and she read it three times.

"We will be deeply honored," she said.

Morgan was certain Tom would be among the courtiers. She could already see him, riding through the castle gates, waving to her as she stood in the entryway. Her spirits rose to almost fever pitch, and though neither Mary nor the servants knew the real reason, they were pleased to see Morgan so happy again.

She set the servants to readying the castle, polishing the silver, preparing the long-closed guest rooms, sorting the linens that had been stored away. She worked herself and the household into a frenzy. Matthew was dispatched to Newcastle to purchase enough food not only to last the winter but to feed the King and his party as well.

Morgan spent hours going over a plan of activities. She would arrange a ball, a hunt, perhaps a small tournament in the castle courtyard. This late in the year they would probably stay no longer than two or three days. Some of the courtiers and many of the retainers would have to be quartered in the village.

She got out her best dresses, unworn in almost two years. They must be hopelessly out of style, but at least she would look presentable. Mary Percy's wardrobe was pressed and tended by Peg. Gazing critically at their gowns, Morgan wished she had thought to tell Matthew to buy cloth as well as provisions.

The King and his courtiers arrived on September twenty-third, a fitful autumn day of rain and sun. As the huge party came over the castle bridge and filled the courtyard, Morgan looked for Tom. But he was not there. A terrible disappointment overwhelmed Morgan until she told herself that perhaps he was in the village, seeing to the quartering of the retainers. Yes, no doubt that was where he was; soon he'd ride up, laughing and apologizing for his tardiness.

Morgan forced a wide smile of welcome for the royal party. To her surprise, the King had to be helped from his horse. He seemed enormous, even larger than when she had last seen him a little over a year ago. But he walked unaided, if with a slight limp, and he peered at her closely as she curtsied before him in the doorway of the castle.

"I am the most honored woman in Christendom," she declared as he gave her his hand.

"You're too thin," he said by way of blunt greeting. "I liked you better with more meat. Like this one." He pulled Katherine Howard forward by the hand and she giggled so hard her bosom bounced.

Morgan curtsied again, observing the new Queen for the first time. She looked much as both Nan and Tom had described—plump, small, and vivacious. She was dressed extravagantly, even in her riding costume, which glittered with jewels. "What a wild land is this North Country!" Katherine exclaimed.

Morgan forced a gracious smile. "We have some aspects of civilization, Your Grace. I hope you will enjoy our small efforts." She ushered the King and Queen inside and the courtiers followed. Morgan watched the colorful aggregation, thinking how long it had been since she had been a part of it. Then she saw Richard Griffin, with Margaret on his arm. He made an exaggerated bow, which Morgan acknowledged with a curt nod.

Somehow she successfully settled over four hundred people inside the castle within the next hour. The rest of the great company moved into the village. Morgan's own apartments were turned over to the King. She moved Mary out of Francis and Lucy's old rooms so that Katherine Howard could stay there.

Morgan took time to ask the King if all pleased him.

"Yes," he replied, "this is a remarkably comfortable place, considering the outward appearances." He was allowing one of his men of the bedchamber, Thomas Culpeper, to help him ease onto the bed. "Your lord—he is bedridden, I hear?"

"Yes, Your Grace."

Henry nodded and spoke no further of James. Illness was both repulsive and frightening to him. An ulcer, Surrey had whispered to Morgan as they had gone up the great staircase.

The supper was lavish, with several kinds of fowl, boar, and even a big stag, which one of the servingmen had shot that afternoon. There were pastries and sweetmeats and wines and a sugar cake in the form of Belford Castle. All was going very well, Morgan decided, but she could not help but count the money that had gone into making it a success.

As hostess, she sat to the left of the King, with Katherine Howard on his other side. On Morgan's own left was Surrey, restored to influence now that his kin was Queen. Once again Morgan scanned the gathering for Tom Seymour. Ned was present with his wife, but there was no sign of Tom.

Just as the court musicians began to play and the tables were being pushed back to make room for dancing, the double doors swung open and Francis Sinclair strode in. Morgan almost jumped to her feet, so startled was she to see him. It had been over a year since his visit to Belford and there had been no communication between them since that time.

He approached the dais of the King and fell on his knees. "Francis Sinclair," said Henry, "it has been long years since we have laid eyes on you."

"It is seven years since I have been to London," said Francis, standing now before his King. "I am a true provincial."

"A shame," Henry remarked, his shrewd eyes taking in every detail of Francis's rumpled yet imposing appearance. "I could have put a man like you to good use in my service." He frowned, then waved a pudgy hand. "Eat, good Francis, there must be a few crumbs the rest of us have left!" Katherine giggled at her husband's humor and he caressed her throat with his hand. "Sweetheart," murmured Henry fondly.

Morgan greeted Francis and had a chair brought for him next to Mary Percy. She introduced Francis to Mary, made certain he had a large quince pie and plenty of beef, and then let Ned Seymour escort her onto the floor. They made casual conversation, but finally Morgan could no longer hold back her question:

"Is Tom abroad again?" She tried to keep her voice casual, but Ned was no fool.

"Aye, Morgan, he is in Vienna. He will be gone some months."

She turned her face away so he could not see the bitter disappointment in her eyes. "You both seem as busy as ever with the King's business," she said, trying to steer their talk into impersonal channels.

Ned held out his hand to lead her in a circle step. "We do," he replied, and glanced in the direction of Surrey, who was talking to the King, "in spite of some who would keep us from it."

The dance was done. Ned was escorting Morgan back to her place next to the King. "About my brother, Morgan," he said rapidly in a low voice, "you know why he stays away. Write to him, tell him your future together is hopeless. Perhaps he'll have the sense to come home."

Astonished, Morgan looked up at him. She would have spoken but they were already before the royal dais. "I return our lovely hostess, Your Grace," Ned said, bowing. He turned to Surrey. "Do you dance as smoothly as you speak, my lord?"

Surrey forced a smile and took Morgan's arm. "I will try, my good Ned, I will try."

Morgan was very tired. She had been complimented by the guests and praised by the King, but her head ached and all she could think of was sleep. She had only exchanged a few words with Francis but had not talked to Richard Griffin at all. She sipped at a last cup of wine and put her feet up on a stool that Peg had pulled out for her.

Cursing the fate that had sent Tom abroad, she recalled Ned's words. He knew about their liaison and blamed her for Tom's self-imposed exile. Competitive as the Seymour brothers were, there was sufficient bond between them to cause Ned concern. Should she write and tell him that though James deteriorated, he showed no indication of dying soon? Maybe Ned was right—but Morgan could not yet follow his advice.

She leaned back in the chair, rubbing her neck muscles. Mary's servingwoman was brushing her mistress's hair; Mary babbled animatedly about the evening's events while Morgan listened halfheartedly. She understood that for Mary this was a new and exciting adventure. Indeed, she had never seen the other woman so exhilarated.

"All those gowns!" Mary exclaimed. "And the men, why, they dress as elegantly as the women! I never ate so much in my life. I thought my seams would burst." She motioned to her serving wench to put down the brush. "Your brother-in-law," she said, turning toward Morgan, "you say he is widowed?"

Morgan threw Mary a sharp glance. "Yes," she answered shortly, "he is."

Mary leaned back in her chair, stretching her arms luxuriously. "He is so tall and speaks so well! Three children he has?"

Morgan stood up abruptly. "Yes, three. He cares for them very well by himself." She gathered her night-robe around her and tied it at the waist. "I must go make sure everything is secure for the night. Pray excuse me."

As she walked along the corridor she wondered just what there was to check. It scarcely mattered—she had an overpowering urge to be alone for a few minutes. Too many people after so little company for so long, she reasoned.

At the end of the hall, two halberdiers were posted outside the King's door. No one else was about, although laughter and voices trickled out into the corridor. Morgan turned a corner, wondering if she should look in on James. Suddenly a shadowy form moved at the end of the hallway. Morgan caught her breath and stood very still. Someone was there, standing by the head of the back stairs. The figure disappeared down the steps, and Morgan moved forward until she heard a noise. She withdrew quickly into a doorway, belatedly conscious that she was directly across from the Queen's chambers.

More noise; soft footsteps came closer. Morgan held her breath. Then she saw them, a man and a woman. She smiled in the darkness—two lovers meeting secretly, she thought, and hoped they would hurry along to their trysting place, for it was growing chilly in the hallway. But they stopped only a few yards from her, at the Queen's door.

The woman rapped softly on the Queen's door. It opened a crack to reveal the Queen herself. The scrap of light fell on the man's face and Morgan saw it was Thomas Culpeper. He stepped inside hastily and the door closed behind him.

Morgan leaned against the door, too shocked to move. Could that little scene mean what she thought it meant? Katherine Howard—sweet, pert, pretty—and the most foolish woman in England! Still stunned, Morgan headed back to her temporary quarters.

The royal party hunted the next morning after Mass. Through the Belford woods and orchards they rode, a gay group laughing in the autumn sun. Morgan tried to join in their high spirits but she was deeply distressed. She glanced ahead, where Katherine Howard rode next to Henry, her plumed hunting cap sitting rakishly on her auburn hair. She laughed merrily at her husband's jests and the little plume bounced.

"And how is our hostess this morning?" Morgan turned in surprise, for it was Richard Griffin who spoke, touching his dark green serge bonnet in salute.

"Richard! You startled me," she said. "I'm glad to see you again."

His eyes were as mocking as ever. "Are you now?" He patted his stallion's black neck. "Do you think you can survive our monarch's gracious visit?"

Morgan smiled somewhat cynically. "I can, if our supplies can."

"I hear we leave tomorrow. We still have many other places to visit; I doubt that we will be in London before the end of October." He ignored Surrey and Thomas Wyatt as they called out that they had spotted a big stag. "I hope the progress pays off in the dividends His Grace expects."

"How so, Richard?"

"This is no ordinary progress," he explained. "Henry has not been north since the Pilgrimage of Grace. He comes to test the loyalty of his subjects. And I must say, he has been welcomed most warmly. Despite all that has happened, his people still hold him close."

Morgan looked beyond the other riders to Henry's big back. "He has always looked like a King," she said.

"Yes," said Richard, "and acted as a King must act."

With the weather holding, the miniature tournament was held that afternoon after a ten-course dinner. Surrey emerged the winner, unseating Ned Seymour in the final round. Ned took the loss with apparent humor, but Morgan noted that later he seemed in a dark mood.

In the evening there was another great supper, with more music and dancing. The King heaped flattery and gratitude upon Morgan, who again sat by Henry. This time Culpeper was at her left. Eyeing him surreptitiously, she observed that he was a handsome young man with dark hair and brown eyes. His conversation was charming, if superficial. At the other end of the table, Mary Percy was chatting animatedly with Francis Sinclair. Why, thought Morgan, she's making a regular fool out of herself over him! And she must be at least four years older than he is! Morgan turned to Henry: "Shall we have the tables moved back for the dancing, Your Grace?" Henry nodded and Morgan gave the signal. The courtiers moved out onto the floor to enjoy their last night at Belford.

"Well?" asked Morgan, facing Francis with her fists on her hips. "Are you all undone by the Countess of Northumberland's charms?"

Francis surveyed her from under his bushy eyebrows. The courtiers had departed two hours earlier, laughing and chattering in spite of the misty rain.

He sat down on a padded bench and put one leg over his other knee. "She's a very good lady," he said with reproach in his voice. And then he changed the subject. "Do you know why I joined the progress here?"

"No," she answered, though she had wondered, knowing of his distaste for court life and the nobility's exaggerated manners.

He waved his big hand at her. "Oh, sit! You're stalking the room like a tigress on the prowl." She obeyed, settling into a chair across the hearth from him. "I have written a book, a treatise on theology. I have tried to set forth some of the rights and wrongs in the Church and what might be done—or undone, at this point—to improve the situation."

"You tread upon dangerous ground," said Morgan. "I think it most unwise."

He rubbed the back of his head and regarded her with benevolent amusement. "Ah, what discretion from the lips of a woman who hides priests, and consorts with Irish Papists!" He paid no heed to her angry stare but continued speaking. "I realize one must go carefully. And that's why I came here—to see the King. I have submitted the book to him, for his eyes first. If he thinks I have been mistaken or incautious, he can suppress what I have written."

"Your discretion amazes me," Morgan murmured caustically.

"Discretion has never been my byword, but I'm not a fool. I think we head for calmer times under the Howard influence."

"Then what of the Countess of Salisbury finally being executed and the hanging of Lord Dacre?" Both events had taken place just before the King started on his progress.

"Henry still seeks balance—and that is the key, balance between the two factions. Such is the aim of my treatise, to create a Church in which the best of the old ways and the best of the new can exist together." He stood up and stretched. "I'll bore you no longer with my theological and literary pretensions. Aren't we going to eat before I leave? I never travel well on an empty stomach."

Francis returned for Christmas, bringing his children, who were at first shy with Morgan. But she fussed over them until they were once again on familiar terms. Little Mary, in particular, stayed near her aunt as much as she could.

Francis brought not only gifts but news garnered from his stopping places on the way to Belford. Katherine Howard had been discovered, and her three lovers, Culpeper, Henry Mannock and Francis Derham, had already been put to death.

"What of the Queen?" asked Mary Percy at supper that night.

"She is confined at Syon until Parliament meets in mid-January," Francis told her. He looked closely at Morgan, who was chewing on a slice of roasted boar. "You seem amazingly unruffled by the news."

She shrugged. "Anybody could see how that silly chit would end. A shame for the Howards to have another setback, though." And she attacked a second slice of boar with unusual aggression, as Francis eyed her with rising annoyance.

"Well, *I* am surprised," said Mary, and she smiled sweetly at Francis. "More whiskey, my lord?"

"Oh, by the Mass," he expostulated, "don't call me 'my lord!' I neither deserve the title nor do I cater to courtly manners." He let her refill his drinking cup. "That's a most becoming dress you have on, though. I have manners enough to tell you that."

Mary glowed. "In truth, Francis, your manners are at least genuine." She edged a bit closer to his chair. "Tell me more about your trip to Belford."

Morgan got up, almost tipping over her chair. "I'm going

to look in on James and the children if you two don't mind." She withdrew swiftly from the dining room, her skirts snapping around her ankles.

Morgan and Francis were arguing vehemently: It had started over a line from William Dunbar's poetry, moved on to the merits of the tutor Morgan had hired for the children, and from there to Francis's manner of running Sinclair House. Afterwards, neither could recall exactly upon which points they had disagreed, but the final explosion came over Morgan's gibe about the infatuated Mary Percy.

"Go ahead and marry the brainless ninny," Morgan railed. "At least it would get her off my hands!"

"I told you, I'm not marrying anyone yet! You, of all people, dispensing matrimonial advice!" He lurched around on his heel, knocking over a pewter goblet, which toppled to the floor from the plate rail.

"You dare say such a thing to me!" Morgan flew at him, her hands clawing at his arm so that he was forced to face her. "You, who were so faithless to poor Lucy!"

The gray eyes turned cold, reminding her sharply of James at his sternest. "And are you any better than I?" he demanded in a voice as chill as the hoarfrost that covered the mullioned windows.

Morgan's hand fell away like a lifeless bird. On impulse, she flung herself against him, her head buried in his white shirt. "I'm sorry, Francis, my nerves are strung out! I get so lonely, even with Mary here." Sheepishly, she looked up at him; her head didn't even come to his shoulder. "I even miss quarreling with you."

The chilling aura vanished. Francis held her close for a long moment, each savoring the physical contact so long denied them. It was very quiet in the library and they seemed to be breathing in unison. Finally, he moved back a step but kept her in the circle of his arms.

"You are waiting for Seymour, I gather?" he asked in a voice that was more gruff than usual.

Morgan's eyes widened. "I—no, that is, I can't wait for another man while my husband still lives."

He let go of her and began pacing the library. "But if James dies—and he will some day, he cannot go on forever like this—you will marry Seymour?"

Morgan's hands gripped the back of a heavy Spanish

chair she'd recently had Matthew purchase in Newcastle. "I don't like thinking about the future in those terms. It's as if I were wishing James's life away."

Francis's fist banged on the mantel, jarring the little clock and the pewter candlesticks. "Don't talk sentimental drivel! James's life *is* over—else I would never have crossed the threshold of Belford Castle again. For once you must think seriously about what you want to do with your life. Do you want to spend it with Seymour?"

Chin thrust upwards, hands clenched on the chair, Morgan gave him a crisp, defiant reply: "I do. I love him."

The look they exchanged was long and challenging. Francis stood by the fireplace, his tall silhouette outlined by the last fading winter light of the afternoon. Morgan remained motionless, waiting for him to stalk out of the room and slam the door.

But instead, he took four long, quick strides and gathered Morgan into his arms. They crashed to the floor, knocking over the leather bellows that stood by the hearth. His face was a scant inch from hers, the gray eyes angry as the wintry North Sea that pounded the cliffs outside the castle.

"Seymour plunders women the way he plunders ships," Francis growled, pulling off her coif and grabbing a handful of tawny hair. "As soon as he gets you pregnant with his heir, he'll be bedding half the women at court again."

Morgan wriggled beneath his weight, wanting to land a blow or at least claw him with her nails. But they had fallen in such a way that her arms were trapped beneath his chest. "You—of all men—have no right to criticize Tom!" she railed, squirming in vain and wondering why on earth she had ever thought she missed quarreling with her infuriating brother-in-law.

"Paugh!" Francis snorted. "Don't make unfair comparisons! My philandering was to spare Lucy, not to hurt her. Tom has made a career of seduction, and will hardly mend his ways just because he takes a wife!"

"You don't even know him! Get off of me, I can't breathe!" In truth, Morgan felt crushed beneath him, her neck stiff, her hands growing numb.

"You bear his weight without complaining, I imagine," retorted Francis archly, "and he is heavier, if not taller, than I. But," he continued, the hand that grasped her hair giving the thick strands a head-jolting tug, "do you find my touch any less exciting?"

Morgan was about to reply that she found his touch and everything about Francis repulsive, when he covered her mouth with his, almost suffocating her with a long, fierce kiss. She resisted, trying desperately to quell any response, but the hand in her hair had moved to her throat and down to the square-cut neckline of her bodice. His tongue forced her lips apart, but still she would not respond; he had eased his body from hers just enough to pull the fabric of her gown off of her shoulders and bare her to the waist. She felt his hand move across her breasts, back and forth, taunting the pink tips into peaks of rigid fire.

But Morgan resolved to resist him—or at least not to let him know that he could still arouse her. He had stopped kissing her and was staring boldly into the topaz eyes, challenging her to deny him. Morgan returned his stare without a word, hoping that her frozen expression gave him all the answer he needed.

But Francis was as determined as she; with one swift, violent tug, he ripped the overskirt and petticoat apart at the waist and thrust his hand between her legs. Morgan tried to keep her thighs tightly closed but she was no match for his brute strength. His fingers tore through the thin undergarment to ply the tender flesh and make her bite at the inside of her mouth in an effort to keep from crying aloud.

"You feel nothing?" Francis jeered, watching her implacable features swiftly turn to torment.

"No!" Morgan cried. "Nothing but loathing!" She saw a fleeting look of anger, followed by disbelief and finally obstinacy, cross Francis's face. The brief lapse in his physical concentration gave her the opportunity she needed. Morgan jerked her entire body so quickly that she almost banged her head on the fireplace tiles, but it was just enough to escape his grasp. She hoped she could get her hands on the fire tongs, but her feet were tangled in the torn overskirt and petticoat. As she stumbled, Francis stood up and caught her easily. He grabbed her around the waist and threw her down into the heavy Spanish armchair.

"Your intentions appear to be dangerous, if not lethal," he declared, holding her by the upper arms and leaning over her. "You would resort to violence to prove your lack of desire, you feign indifference and hostility, you spit words of hatred and rejection—and every inch of your body is screaming for me to take you. What is the difference between now and the times we've devoured each other before?"

"I told you! There's Tom now—and your brother a-dying upstairs!" Morgan was on the verge of tears, not just of fury, but of humiliation, sitting all but naked in her torn undergarment with Francis looming over her like the shadow of some dark angel in a forgotten churchyard.

He let go of her arms and stood up straight. "Still as self-deluded as ever," he remarked in an oddly nonchalant manner. "And willful." He sighed, shrugged, and pushed the sandy hair off his forehead. "As you wish." He started for the door, stopped, and gave Morgan a slanted, wicked grin. "I can't resist," he said.

Morgan felt the pent-up emotions in her body churn from head to toe, waiting for release. She took in a sharp, deep breath, thinking that if she had not triumphed over her own desires, at least she had bested Francis briefly—and now he could offer her the outlet she needed so desperately to ease her tumultuous feelings.

But Francis moved not toward her, but to the pile of her torn and crumpled clothing. Still grinning, he snatched up her garments, threw her a quick, mocking salute with one hand—and left the library.

Morgan sat stupefied in the chair, mouth open, hands clutching the arms carved into lions' heads. She wanted to scream, cry, rage—anything to rid herself of the mental and physical frustration. But she felt totally impotent, defeated, and miserable. Francis Sinclair was no gentleman; he was a beast, a churl, a blackguard, and probably the most wretched man she had ever met. He must leave Belford at once. She should never have allowed him to return. And she would never, ever speak to him again.

But her opinions and vows were secondary to her need to flee the library without anyone seeing her in such a disreputable state. It was getting cold, too, as night settled in around the castle and the wind picked up off the North Sea. Morgan looked around the room; only the heavy damask drapes might offer cover. There was no bell cord in the library to summon servants. Francis had never wanted them intruding on him when it was his private sanctuary, and Morgan had never bothered to install a bell cord after his departure. Nor would she, on second thought, have called for Polly or Peg in any event. It was bad enough that Polly knew of her liaison with Tom Seymour and the subsequent miscarriage. But it would strain even the faithful servingwoman's loyalty to discover her Countess in such a scandalous situation.

Slowly, Morgan stood up, discovering that she was shaking and that her legs were extremely wobbly. She moved to the nearest of the two tall, mullioned windows and examined the drapes. They were old and sun-faded; she should have had new ones hung when she had the carpet laid. Still, their sorry state gave her an excuse to pull one of them down. She'd order Matthew to purchase new cloth on his trip next week to Newcastle.

But the drape did not give. Like everything else at Belford, the drapes exemplified the care and efficiency of the late Earl and his elder son. Morgan cursed them both for their thoroughness as she pulled the Spanish armchair over to the window and climbed up on it to see if she could reach the hooks that held the fabric in place.

She could not. They were at least a foot out of her range. She cursed aloud and gave them a fierce, wrenching tug with both hands. Still, the heavy damask would not yield. Morgan began screaming then, calling out every oath she'd ever learned from her father and Tom Seymour, raging at the drapes, at Francis, at the North Sea itself as it roared back in apparent mockery.

"Do you want Matthew to find you like this?" It was Francis, lounging in the door, the dress and petticoats still over one arm. "You are a sight," he said dryly, strolling into the library and over to where she stood on the chair, still clinging to the drape. "I don't believe I've ever seen a woman—let alone a Countess—in such a dire situation."

"I hate you! I hate you!" she shrieked, and reached out to grab at his hair.

He tossed her clothes onto the floor and chuckled. "This is amusing in many ways. I so seldom have the opportunity to look up to anyone."

Morgan told herself that if she'd been armed she would have killed him on the spot. But she was shaking harder than ever. The cold air coming in between the cracks in the window embrasure had turned her flesh to goose bumps and her teeth had begun to chatter.

Francis's head came just to her breasts. His arms went around her waist and his tongue flicked her nipples. As his hands strayed to her buttocks and squeezed them firmly, he started pulling down the torn undergarment with his teeth until it slipped to her ankles. Morgan was too overwrought to struggle, too depleted to care which of them won this battle in the unceasing war that seemed to rage between them. Unresisting, she let him pull her down into the chair and remained motionless as he undid his breeches.

"I did intend to leave you thus, you know," he said quietly. "I thought it might teach you a well-deserved lesson. Then it occurred to me that I was being a mite unfair—and perhaps you've learned something as it is."

Morgan stared at him woodenly. All she wanted was to be warm and comforted, even if it meant the invasion of her body by this most ungallant and infuriating of men. She put her arms around him as he wedged himself between her open thighs. With her back pressed against the hard carved woodwork of the chair, Morgan felt his thrust with even more than the usual intensity. She gasped, nails digging into his shoulders, a sudden surge not merely of warmth but of fire taking over her entire body. They moved together in the chair, rocking back and forth in a cadence of consummation, until their mutual cries of completeness seemed to mingle and fade into the night.

The sea had grown quiet and a soft snow was falling over the castle battlements. Morgan lay beside Francis in her own bed, his arm flung across her back, his deep, regular breathing assuring her that he was asleep.

After they had made love—or whatever it was they did together, Morgan thought in bemused bewilderment—they had left the library immediately before the servants began to wonder what had happened to her ladyship. Francis would have gone to his own room, but Morgan had looked so forlorn and upset that he'd changed his mind. He ordered her directly to bed, heated wine with a red-hot poker from the fireplace, made sure she had not taken a chill—and then discovered he was perishing from hunger.

To Morgan's horror, he called for Polly and asked her to bring beef and bread and cheese.

"Oh, Francis! What will poor Polly think?" Morgan asked, clutching the bedsheets around her chin.

"Whatever Polly has been thinking about me for thirty years, more or less." Francis looked into his wine cup and made a face. "Belford's cellars have suffered mightily since I left."

"Truly, Francis, we don't want the servants and the villagers and the tenants and half of Northumberland to know what's happened!"

He sat down on the bed and pulled at a strand of the tawny hair. "I told you long ago, our servants have always been both loyal and discreet. You have won over all of Belford during your years as Countess. I am told that after you were led away to London to be put on trial even the most ardent Protestants wept. Of course," he went on in a more casual tone, "I'm not sure if it was because you are so kind or because James was so cold. It matters not, in any event, and besides, who would criticize a brother-in-law—even one who was cast out—for comforting his poor, lonely, long-suffering sister-in-law?" He touched the outline of her breasts under the sheet. "And you were comforted mightily, if I may say so. Why in God's name did you fight it so? You know how little I like expending great amounts of energy."

Morgan started to give him an angry retort, saw the droll expression in his eyes, and threw up her hands in exasperation. Of course the sheet fell to her waist; Francis grinned, fell down beside her, and was covering her with kisses when Polly knocked.

"Food," Francis announced, getting up at once. Morgan watched him lope to the door and just shook her head, wondering which of them was the most crazed—James, Francis, or herself.

Morgan had discovered she was hungry, too, and let Francis slice off pieces of beef for her. As she sat among the pillows, chewing on the rare meat and watching him break off a chunk of bread, she marveled at the peculiar relationship which had grown up between them over the years. Propinquity and lust made easy bedfellows. It was a simple and convenient way to explain what they meant to each other. It also didn't seem to be a complete or satisfactory answer. In less than two hours, she had veered from wanting to murder Francis to sitting in bed with him eating supper. Her mercurial range of emotions did not seem to trouble Francis in the least.

"There's too much marbling in the meat," he commented, popping a piece of Flemish cheese into his mouth. "Whose cows were these?"

"Crimmin's, I think. Or Baxter's." She leaned over to pick up a thick piece of brown crust. "Crimmin still drinks too much."

"His cows eat too much," Francis replied, with his mouth full. "And Baxter believes every old wives' tale he hears about farming. Does he still think that bulls should only mate when the wind is coming from the north?"

Morgan giggled and all but choked on the crust. "I never heard that one. I do know he thinks the touch of a redheaded woman with green eyes will cure colic in calves."

Francis snorted. "And him with four blond daughters and a towheaded wife. He must still rely on Marjorie Beck."

"Marjorie won't go near his calves anymore since one stepped on her and broke her toe. The last I heard, he'd had to send to Bamburgh for the cooper's sister."

"Did it work?" Francis poured more wine for both of them.

"I guess so, but the wench seduced his oldest son and stole one of his daughter's bracelets."

Francis laughed and shook his head; Morgan laughed, too, and suddenly recalled how seriously James had taken his duties as lord of the manor. He had never seen any humor in his tenants' eccentricities, never been amused by their vagaries. But, she reminded herself, Belford was *his* manor, not Francis's.

"What now?" asked Francis, noting the change in Morgan's expression. "Have you decided to do me in after all?"

"I was thinking of James," she said. "Do you remember the girl he loved?"

Francis eyed the empty plate with dissatisfaction. "I should have had Polly bring sweets. I would like a sweet very much right now." He paused, apparently considering whether or not to summon Polly again. Then he shrugged and put the heavy pewter plate on a side table. "Oh, yes,

Joan the Unworthy. Or so our sire thought. A pleasant young thing, with dark hair and a flat bosom."

"James never stopped loving her, you know."

"Hmmmm." Francis was undressing and yawning extravagantly. "A good excuse for never loving anyone else." He went to the window and looked out. "It's snowing harder. I may have to spend the rest of the winter here." He blew out the three candles on the side table and climbed into bed. "Don't think me crass, Morgan. I have a difficult time trying to think charitably about my brother. Did his madness overtake him by some decree of fate or did he seek that path of his own volition?"

"No one wants to be mad," Morgan said in genuine shock.

"True in itself. But we make choices and travel the paths we have charted for ourselves. I've often wondered if such were the case with James." He stretched out beside her and grunted. "Your bed is too short. My feet stick out."

"Then you're too tall." Morgan sighed in exasperation and shook her head. She was too exhausted to argue any more with Francis; she couldn't dwell any longer on her husband's aberration; she didn't even want to think about Tom tonight, as she always did when lying alone in the darkness. But she wasn't alone now, she thought, she was with Francis, and remorse overcame her. Certainly Tom wasn't living like a monk in Vienna or wherever he was, but that was different with a man. Still, she reasoned, as Francis dropped off to sleep beside her, this perplexing, vexing brother-in-law of hers had behaved most cruelly and her submission had come about only as a result of her humiliation and desperation.

Yet it was not just the physical surrender which disturbed her as she lay under his arm. It was the time they had spent together afterwards—her reliance on him to take care of her, the shared supper and conversation and laughter, and the absence of any apology from him for his boorishness, coupled with the unspoken acknowledgment that his contrition wasn't necessary. All of that bothered Morgan far more than letting Francis possess her body.

She turned just enough to look at his face in repose: He looks so *young* when he's asleep, she thought, though Francis was now well over thirty. She smiled as she watched a muscle twitch on his forehead. Such a strange man, she told herself, for good or for ill, unlike any other she had ever met. Confused, weary, and actually sore from their physical encounter, Morgan finally closed her eyes and slept.

Francis stayed until the day after New Year's. The snow had lasted only a day or so, but there would be more, and Francis felt it best to take advantage of the break in the weather.

He and Morgan did not sleep together again. "I have decided it would be too risky," he had announced the morning after their tumultuous scene in the library. "You might get pregnant, and that wouldn't do under the circumstances. I don't think we could convince anyone that James had had a temporary miraculous cure."

Morgan had been angered by his arbitrary decision: How dare he assume she would have consented? Perhaps he had already impregnated her. And why did he always have to be so arrogant? But for once she had decided not to argue; indeed, though she still ached all over, she felt more lighthearted that morning than she had for some time. It was illusory, of course, Morgan told herself, the fleeting sense of physical comfort, the sharing of her burdens with someone who knew Belford as well as she did, the reassuring presence of a man to lean on, even for a short time. And, she thought with a pang, the opportunity for Robbie to be with his father. It didn't matter that Robbie had no idea Francis was his real sire. Neither he nor the other two children had had a father or an uncle in their midst for far too long. They visited James occasionally, but Morgan knew her children were upset at the sight of the inert, wizened man in the big bed, and she wondered if she should let them see him at all.

"They may resent it when they are grown if you do not," Francis had counseled on the morning of his departure. "When they are old enough to understand, they will appreciate having been permitted those visits, no matter how strange and even frightening they find them now. Nor do we know precisely what James actually comprehends. And that's why I don't visit him myself. He would not want me to."

Morgan conceded that Francis was probably right in all respects. She was helping bundle up his children against the cold when Mary Percy appeared, looking nervous and ill at ease.

"It seems a pity to take the little ones back to Carlisle when it might snow at any moment," she declared, looking up diffidently at Francis.

"It's clear as a bell," he asserted, watching his own Mary cling to Morgan's skirts. "I can't leave my home untended for too long."

Mary Percy plucked at the edge of her oversleeve. "I suppose. Still, it's so good for your youngsters to be with their cousins."

"True." Francis surveyed his little band, noted they were muffled to the eyes and ready for travel, and glanced down into the courtyard where his two servingmen waited by the small baggage cart. "Easter, or perhaps in summer, we will return." He smiled with what Morgan would have called determined kindness and kissed Mary Percy's hand. She flushed and wished him a safe journey.

A few minutes later, Morgan stood with her own children in the courtyard, watching the little party trot out over the drawbridge as a few scattered clouds blew in from the north to blemish the flawless blue sky. She waved until they moved out of sight. Turning, she noticed that all three of the children were sniffling and sobbing quietly into their woolen scarves. Morgan was about to reproach them for such unseemly tears—until she realized that she was crying, too.

Chapter 20

KATHERINE HOWARD went to the block on February thirteenth, 1542. Katherine died with more dignity than she had lived, and like her cousin, Anne Boleyn, begged the people to pray for her soul.

Morgan learned of Katherine's beheading in a letter from Nan. She reflected not so much on the tragic death of the young Queen, but on what it might mean to her. What had become of Katherine's properties, namely Faux Hall? Certainly they would revert back to the crown; would Henry consider returning her family home to its rightful owner? Surely it must have been one of the smaller properties Katherine had had in her possession.

Morgan pulled out a piece of paper and began a letter to Nan, telling her cousin she would be in London before the end of April.

"But Morgan," Mary protested when she heard the news of the proposed trip, "you invited Francis and the children here for Eastertide!" Then a sudden thought seemed to strike her. "Of course, I will be happy to act as hostess in your stead."

Morgan flicked her tongue over her lips. "Nonsense, Mary! You're coming with me."

Mary's expression changed from anticipation to distress. "Oh, court life terrifies me! I'd much rather stay here!"

Morgan masked her face with kindness and concern. She patted the other woman's arm. "Mary, please come, I have a plan. You must see the King and beg him to return at least some of your lands. We will both go as petitioners to seek what is rightfully ours. Surely you've not lost your will to fight?"

Mary had, but she wouldn't admit it to Morgan. She

frowned and fussed but at last gave in. Even after relenting, she still pestered Morgan about her decision.

"I thought you had sworn never to leave your lord as long as he lived," she said.

"I did. But I'm doing this for Faux Hall, the home that should be my own."

Mary sighed. "As a Talbot and the Earl of Shrewsbury's daughter, I should have been a wealthy heiress, but my father . . ." She paused, her lips trembling. "I was forced on Harry Percy, given no dowry at all, only my family name to appease Harry for not marrying Anne Boleyn. Why did James marry you, Morgan? Were you deeply in love?"

The envious catch in Mary's voice unnerved Morgan. "My marriage was no love match, either," she replied evenly. "There were political considerations—the union was arranged by my uncle, Cromwell."

"Oh." Mary looked away, embarrassed. "I'm sorry."

So am I, thought Morgan, but she said nothing out loud.

Tulips, hyacinth, primrose, narcissus, violets, pansies, daffodils, peonies, and lobelia heralded another spring at Greenwich Palace. The rich, fresh tapestry of nature's colors, the heady scent of damp earth and a thousand flowers, and the warmth of a friendly sun gave Morgan courage as she moved purposefully down the garden path toward her King.

Of course she was nervous, and it wasn't helping much to have Mary Percy twittering apprehensively behind her. "He'll refuse us," she said. "Maybe he won't even see us," she protested. "I think I should have stayed at Belford," she moaned.

Morgan was about to tell Mary to please hush when she saw the King, surrounded by a group of courtiers. At least Morgan assumed it was the King, since the others wore an obviously deferential manner. But something was wrong; Morgan slowed her step, puzzling over what was amiss with the tableau only a few yards away. Henry himself, she realized with a start: He was heavier than ever, but no longer tall and hearty. Instead, he leaned on a walking stick and looked far older than his years. She was reminded of James. While her husband had wasted away and become totally inert, Henry Tudor bulged with almost obscene weight and his vitality was shockingly diminished.

Mary Percy let out a gasp. "His Grace looks so—old! Yet he can't be more than fifty!"

"I know," Morgan replied in a whisper. "I heard he took Katherine's death very hard, but I wasn't prepared for this." She paused, wondering if indeed this was the time to approach their monarch. Henry and the dozen courtiers who accompanied him all looked distressingly solemn.

But one of them also looked very familiar. Richard Griffin stood just slightly apart from the rest, his broad-shouldered form attired completely in black, a mourning band on his arm. He turned just as Morgan hesitated and they stared at each other. Richard's solemn expression broke into a grin and he beckoned to Morgan and her companion.

"There's no turning back now," Morgan said in a low voice. "The King has seen us, too." She took Mary's hand, pulling the other woman along and all but shoving her in front of the King.

Mary immediately dropped to her knees, hands clasped together. "Your Grace," she began in a shaky voice, "I come to beg a favor of you . . ." Mary faltered under Henry's curious yet impatient gaze and had to be prompted by Morgan. "A favor of your generous, kindly nature," Mary continued. "I am the widowed Countess of Northumberland, left penniless and alone in the world. I seek only a small portion of my late husband's holdings so that I may live independently and . . ." Again she stopped, obviously on the verge of tears. Morgan was both concerned for Mary's distress and exasperated at her lack of courage. She was about to intercede and finish the speech herself when King Henry's voice boomed out in the old familiar cadence:

"How can your ladyship desire any living of your husband's lands, seeing your father gave no money to your husband in marriage with your ladyship, or what think you that I should do?"

Mary glanced quickly at Morgan, who made an encouraging gesture, but no words came forth. The widowed Countess simply stared at Henry with sad, pleading eyes. "What it please Your Grace," she said at last.

Henry scanned the petition she had handed him.

"Madam," he said, "I marvel greatly that my lord, your father, being so great a wise man as he was, would see no direction taken in this matter in his time." He paused and his eye caught Morgan's. She was sure she detected the hint of a twinkle. "Howbeit," he went on, "we will be contented to refer the matter to our council."

Mary kissed his hand, her eyes damp with tears. "I beseech Your Grace to be good and gracious to me," she pleaded with a weak smile.

He nodded. "We will." Then he turned directly to Morgan. "Do you petition, too, madam, or only sponsor others?"

She dropped to her knees in the place Mary had left vacant. "I have one small favor to ask of Your Grace." She turned the great topaz eyes up to him. "I pray that Faux Hall may be restored to me for my sake and that of my children. It is the only possession in this world that is truly my own."

"Faux Hall?" Henry looked momentarily puzzled, his forefinger tapping his chin. His little eyes brightened. "Ah, yes! Near Aylesbury, of course! What's your forfeit, madam?"

Morgan's eyes flashed. "Forfeit? It is lawfully mine, Your Grace, taken from me by my late uncle. I almost forfeited life itself in that exchange."

She clamped down on her tongue to stop the flow of angry words. Had she gone too far? She spotted Richard then, standing directly behind Henry. He was still grinning at her.

And Henry was grinning, too, and giving her his hand. "Oh, come up here, Morgan Todd Sinclair, so that we may see you better. Have your home by the river and our best wishes with it. You must promise one thing, though—to stay awhile at court and brighten our lives. There is not much spring here this year."

Morgan did stay on, though she felt guilty about leaving her children and husband. At least this time the young ones were safe, with Agnes and Peg to care for them. She had, after all, accomplished what she had set out to do—Faux Hall was hers again, to hold for Edmund until he came of age.

Mary was enjoying London and life at court, but occasionally would express a desire to return north. Now that some of her properties had been restored, she would move out of Belford, and Morgan sighed with guilty relief. Morgan pointed out to Mary that she was free to leave whenever she chose, but Mary said she would wait until they could make the trip together. The Countess of Northumberland was not used to traveling great distances with only her retainers.

Nan had come to London in early May. She was still touched with sorrow, for that winter her mother had died. "The Countess of Salisbury's execution upset her terribly," Nan told Morgan. "Perhaps she found that blow to a cherished friend—and to the old faith—too much to endure."

Morgan was saddened by her aunt's passing; the older generation of her family was now laid to rest. She and Nan spent a great deal of time talking and reminiscing, but Morgan would not admit, even to Nan, that she was waiting for Tom Seymour. He was still gone, but was rumored to be returning to England to help fortify strategic points along the east coast, lest the long-talked-about war with France actually materialize. Indeed, now there was even talk of war with Scotland.

The last days of May brought heavy clouds and rain to England. Morgan sat in a window seat at Greenwich, trying to concentrate on Francis's book. It had been published just before Morgan had arrived at court. Those two theological antagonists, Cranmer and Gardiner, were having difficulty deciding which side to take. The King had praised the book; should they not do likewise? Yet neither wanted to agree with the other about anything. The courtiers, meantime, jested about the predicament in which Francis Sinclair's treatise had flung the longtime religious adversaries.

"Your brother-in-law has made a name for himself with that little volume," said Richard Griffin. He was dressed in a black riding costume and the dampness clung to his clothes.

Morgan offered the other half of the window seat to him. "This weather," she said, as he eased himself down next to her, "sends my spirits plummeting."

"It does for a fact," Richard replied. He was subdued these days, which was fitting in a man who had recently lost his wife, but, Morgan felt, this was not quite the entire explanation.

She set the book down beside her. "You seem downcast yourself," she told him. "You must still mourn Margaret deeply."

He carefully scrutinized the touch of silver braid on his cuff. "It was very tragic, yes. She had always been so healthy. But six months ago, she began to sicken, her appetite dwindled, and she grew very weak." The green eyes looked away and he frowned. "There was pain before the end, but not unbearable, thank God."

"I'm so sorry. Margaret was a kindly creature. And very beautiful. It's a shame you could not have had more years together."

"So true." Richard, however, did not appear overwhelmed with grief. Saddened, Morgan thought, but not sorrowful. His next words, however, helped explain his attitude. "His Grace and I did not have good fortune with our Howard wives."

Something inside Morgan winced. Richard had never loved Margaret. He had married her for the family name and influence. Now Margaret was dead and so was Katherine, and Richard's link to the King was buried with them.

"What a pity you didn't marry a Seymour," Morgan remarked archly, and bit her tongue. It had been a doubly cruel comment, cutting both Richard and herself.

But Richard displayed no irritation. Instead, his hand brushed the artful drape of her lavender oversleeve. "And you? Your cousin married a Seymour. I assume you remain on intimate terms with the family?"

Morgan flinched. She tried to keep her voice level. "I see Ned occasionally. But of course Tom isn't at court. I've not seen him in almost two years." Two years! It seemed incredible when she said the words aloud.

"Well, it doesn't sound as if you were swimming in their stream these days. If you had been I would not speak my piece." He glanced up and down the length of the gallery to make sure they could not be overheard. The only other people present were practicing on lutes and virginals at the far end of the long room. Richard grinned at Morgan, a trace of the old mockery showing through. "I can talk to you, Morgan, even if I can't make love to you." He leaned closer. "Or can I?"

She made a face at him. "You cannot. Pray, talk instead."

He straightened up. "As you will. Alas, I'm not certain what to say. Except that since the Howard influence has faded, the Seymours and their hangers-on grasp for more power than is good for them—or for England."

Annoyance crept over Morgan but she stifled it. "Surely that is for the King to decide."

"Oh—by the Mass, you know how our King can be . . ." His tone was impatient but his customary discretion prevailed and he went on more reasonably. "Nor does their nephew's status as royal heir give them any right to exercise power on their own," he asserted earnestly. "Now Ned has his title, Lord Hertford. Ned brandishes it as a peacock does his tail. The man grows too arrogant."

Morgan couldn't help but agree with Richard's appraisal of Ned. Ned *was* becoming more arrogant; she had noticed that herself. "You distress yourself too much over politics these days," she said with a smile. "I think I liked you better when you were just another frivolous courtier."

He looked at her closely. "Did you? I never had much indication that was so, even then." He stood up and bowed very low. "I'd like to see about an inch less of that dress and an inch more of you—at the bosom." He walked rapidly down the gallery and out through the big doors.

Morgan and Mary started back for the North the first week of June, just before the court moved to Windsor. The women and their small entourage made their way out of the city and onto the Great North Road on a clear, bright spring morning, taking the same route Morgan had traveled two years before with Tom Seymour at her side.

There was still no word of Tom at court. Now that she was leaving, Morgan told herself it was just as well that she had not see him. If she had, if they had been together, alone, she knew she could not have resisted the lure of his arms or the touch of his lips.

It took them ten days to get to Northumberland. She and Mary would part at Morpeth, with Mary going on to her old home nearby and Morgan continuing north to Belford. Mary was full of plans for renovating her properties, even Alnwick Castle. Both women had sought advice on overseeing their restored possessions, and Morgan had asked Nan and Harry if they would see to the care of Faux Hall.

It was miserably hot under the late afternoon sun. The party had stopped to water the horses and drink some ale in Morpeth. The time for parting had come and Mary was loath to say good-bye.

"You have done so much for me," she began, her eyes moist.

Morgan admonished her with a long finger. "I cannot bear any sentimental speeches from you, Mary. You have repaid me a thousandfold with your friendship. But you must visit us sometime."

"I promise," said Mary. "And we'll get together for holidays. I want to give a big banquet and ball for as many people as will come." She paused and studied her horse's reins. "Do you think I should invite Francis?"

Morgan shrugged. "Invite anyone you like." She moved uncomfortably in the saddle, her clothes sticking to her body. "You had best be off before we all melt. My best wishes and prayers go with you, Mary."

Mary leaned from her horse and hugged Morgan. "Bless you, dear friend, bless you!" She resettled herself on her mount and flicked her reins. Twice she turned to wave as Morgan and her serving people watched them trot down the road beside the River Wansbeck. Morgan was sorry that Mary would no longer be at Belford for companionship, but she was oddly unmoved at their parting. Instead, she felt a sense of relief; ashamed, she prayed for Mary's good fortune in her new life.

They spent the night at the town of Alnwick and arrived at Belford the next day shortly before noon. Morgan had been anxious to finish the journey before the hot afternoon sun began to beat down.

"Thank the good Lord we're back," said Polly, as they dismounted in the castle courtyard. "My poor bottom feels as if I'd been sitting on a rock pile for six months!"

Morgan laughed. "The next thing I know, you'll be asking for a litter to travel in."

Matthew and Peg came out to greet them. Matthew had optimistic news about the crops; Peg chattered happily about how well behaved the children had been. Agnes brought the young ones into the entrance hall to greet their mother and they squealed delightedly under her hugs and kisses.

At last, Morgan turned to Matthew. "How is my lord?" she asked.

He turned his palms upwards. "The same, madam. Always the same."

It was true, Morgan noted, when she went to see James after supervising the unpacking. He was almost like a skeleton now, so thin and frail. She wondered if he suffered, but Dr. Wimble assured her he did not. As she watched him, his wasted body almost swallowed up in the big bed, she felt a terrible guilt. She had never prayed for his recovery, not once, for in her heart she admitted to herself what she would admit to no one else: She did not want him to get well.

"I am wicked," she said, and Cedric looked sharply at her.

"Madam?" he asked, unsure of what he had heard.

"I am going to the chapel now. I go to pray for my lord."

Matthew was running hard, taking big, gasping breaths. He had just come back from the village where he had gone by foot to pick up a new pair of shoes for his mistress and spend an hour or two at his favorite inn. He stopped in the entrance hall to get his wind, and saw Polly on the stairway.

"Where is my lady?" he asked.

Polly surveyed his excited state. "You're all undone, Steward Matthew. Her ladyship is in the kitchens."

Hurrying in that direction, he almost collided with Morgan as she came through the door.

"Careful, man," she reproached him. "You go too fast! Why, whatever is wrong, Matthew?"

The words came tumbling out. "There's been an English raid on Teviotdale. I heard about it at the Golden Eagle. They burned homes and villages, but the Scots ambushed them. One of the prisoners is Master Francis!"

Morgan was incredulous. "What? Francis wouldn't be among them—he's no soldier. Come into the kitchen, Matthew, and have some ale."

Matthew obeyed silently, one hand mopping his forehead and bald spot. He fell onto a stool and readily accepted a mug of ale from one of the kitchen wenches.

Morgan pushed back some loose strands of hair that clung to her cheeks. It was almost unbearably hot in the kitchens on this August day. "Now, tell me—slowly—exactly what you heard."

A line of foam was on Matthew's upper lip. He took another big gulp of ale and finally caught his breath. "I went to the inn for a little drink and talk. Some merchants came in who were traveling from Scotland. They were agitated and anxious to tell their tale. Four days ago, Sir Robert Bowes—he's Warden of the Middle Marches—swooped down on Teviotdale and put the torch to much Scots property. They started back to England in triumph, but some two thousand light horsemen were waiting for them at Haddon Rigg. Many of the English escaped, but they captured Bowes and Master Francis."

Still unconvinced that her brother-in-law could have been among the raiders, Morgan clucked at Matthew. "Much of the story may be true, but I cannot believe that Francis would be among the raiders. What made these merchants think it was he?"

Matthew held out his mug to the serving wench, who refilled it promptly. "One of the merchants told about a nobleman—a great, tall man with fair hair—who put down four Scots in hand-to-hand fighting before he was taken. Right off, I thought of Master Francis. I asked him if that was the name and the merchant said it was. He remembered because he said it was a Scots name as well as an English one and he had been confused at first as to which side the nobleman fought on."

Morgan blinked rapidly as acceptance of the report sank in. She stared unseeing at the great open fireplace where chickens were turning on a spit. Once more, fear nagged at her.

"I must write to Sinclair House for verification that Francis did go with Bowes and his men." She turned to Matthew. "I do believe you, Matthew, but I must know for certain. If it is true, we must ransom Francis at once." She gave brief, final orders to the kitchen help and started for the door.

Matthew called after her, "Madam, my lady," and she stopped, noting the shamefaced expression he wore.

"Yes?"

"In all the excitement, madam . . . I forgot your shoes."

A smile flickered on Morgan's lips for an instant, and then she hurried out of the kitchens to get paper and pen.

A few days later, King Henry declared war on Scotland. Ammunition and supplies had already been sent north to the border towns of Wark, Norham, Carlisle and Berwick. Soon, the royal armies would be on the march.

Nervously, Morgan listened to the news of the battle preparations. Berwick and Norham were only half a day's ride from Belford. It was possible that Belford itself might be attacked by the Scots. She gave orders to Matthew to fortify the castle and to make sure that sufficient men were recruited for its defense. Unlike the border raid of six years before, there was time now to make ready.

A week after she had written to Sinclair House, a letter came back in the youthful but precise handwriting of Francis's daughter, Mary. "I write to you in my father's absence," she began, and Morgan knew that the tale about Francis's capture was true. Mary tried to explain why her father had gone with Sir Robert Bowes: "Sir Robert came here in July to beg my father to go with him, saying it would be revenge for all the evil things the Scots had done to us in their raids. My father became very angry and told Sir Robert about the raid at Belford, which I, too, remember. He told me all this later, before he departed, and said things about honor and justice. We are very lonesome without him, My Lady Aunt, and wish he would soon be free."

Morgan scanned the letter again and then summoned Matthew. "Send six men to Sinclair House," she ordered. "I want Francis's children brought here. They will be safer in a castle than a manor house so close to the border."

It was now mid-September and the King's armies had still not come north. Francis's children were elated at being reunited with their aunt, though young Mary, in particular, fretted constantly about her father's wellbeing. Morgan tried to reassure her that he would soon be back, safe and sound. But her heart was afraid, and the fear mounted when she received no reply from Scotland to her offer to ransom her brother-in-law.

Then, in early October, a rumor reached Belford that an English army was on the road from York to Berwick. Morgan rounded up the children and took them up to the little hill next to the castle. It was a hazy day with no wind. Morgan raised her hand over her eyes and looked to the south. She could see nothing but quiet fields and orchards, red-gold trees, and the rolling moors. They waited for almost half an hour, the four boys chasing each other among the trees, the two girls staying close to Morgan. Suddenly Mary pointed toward the horizon.

"Look, My Lady Aunt! I see something move!"

At first, movement was all they could see; then forms began to take shape. Morgan knew it was a column of men, a huge column filling up the road and rolling like a human wave in the direction of Belford.

The boys were very excited. Robbie watched them intently and asked his mother if she thought they would stop at Belford. "Mayhap," she replied, "though I would rather they did not. If they feast on our provisions it will leave us little if we have to withstand a siege."

They stayed on the hill until the men got so close that they disappeared into the village. There were foot and horse soldiers, with swords and lances glinting in the uncertain October sun. Morgan wondered who their leaders were, and if Tom Seymour might be one of them.

She directed the children to follow her back inside the castle. They were about to sit down to dinner when Polly came in to announce that "some great nobles and their men" were in the courtyard. Morgan told the children to eat without her and hurried outside.

At least a hundred men were gathered inside the gates. At their head were the Duke of Norfolk and Ned Seymour. A Howard and a Seymour, thought Morgan, and wished that it were Tom instead of Ned.

Norfolk bowed, his aging figure no longer agile under the chain mail. "We would like to quarter some of our men at Belford, my lady," he said. "The rest will stay in the village. We will continue our march in the morning."

Morgan frowned. "My lord, we are not provisioned for large numbers of men. I don't wish to be inhospitable, but I fear we cannot handle a great force, even for one night."

Norfolk's heavy brows drew together but it was Ned who spoke: "Our men have had a rugged march. Supplies have been held up at sea. Tomorrow night we should be in Berwick, but I have grave doubts about the state of our men's morale if we do not have at least one good meal and some real English ale before we reach our destination."

Morgan eyed the horsemen carefully. They looked tired and dirty and in ill humor. If they were discontent, the foot soldiers must be near mutiny. And then Morgan thought of Francis, lying in a filthy, vermin-infested Scots prison. She looked straight at Ned and then at Norfolk.

"Bring them in, my lords, as many as can come. We will offer you all we can afford to give."

Norfolk grunted his satisfaction and gave the signal to his men. Ned smiled, that peculiar thin smile so characteristic of him, so different from Tom's big, expansive grin. "I will tell the King how generous you have been," he said. He walked beside her into the castle.

"You needn't praise me to the King," she answered. "If you repay me, it will be by seeing that Francis Sinclair is ransomed. I will provide the funds."

Ned was taking off his helmet. He brushed the dark hair back into place. "I cannot do that, Morgan." She stared at him in puzzlement. "The Scots refuse to ransom those prisoners," he explained. "They remain in detention—or worse —until this war is over."

The soldiers ate and drank so much that Morgan thought they could march clear to John o'Groat's, let alone Berwick. They acted ravenous, chewing loudly on meat and fowl, quaffing down big tankards of ale, keeping the servants running to bring more. She watched them from the door of the big dining hall and then went in to take a look at the men who were eating in the gallery where trestle tables had been hastily set up. They would sleep in these rooms, too, and then eat again in the morning before continuing north.

The four boys were thrilled to have soldiers in the castle. She let them watch, too, and after supper, introduced Ned to them. He told them about his own two boys and patiently answered their questions about army life and going to war.

Morgan tried to keep her voice level when she inquired about Tom. Ned responded curtly, saying he had been recalled to England at last. The frosty gaze indicated that it was no thanks to her that Tom was finally coming home.

* * *

While the household had watched the army ride away, Morgan consulted with Matthew about procuring more supplies. He would go to Alnwick immediately to seek additional provisions.

After he and three retainers had left, Morgan went up to look in on James. But all the time she watched his vacant eyes and sunken cheeks, she thought of Francis. No ransom, she thought with a shiver, and wondered if he were getting enough to eat. The ultimate fear she suppressed. Francis could not die, not when his brother was already half-dead. Surely one day soon she would see that great loping figure stride through the entrance of Belford Castle.

But the news from the border was not good. On the march into Berwick, the bridge across the Tweed had collapsed and five men were drowned. A raid was made on Kelso, but with little effect. Norfolk was discovering that his old bones, which had fought so well so often for England, were no longer fit for battle. He wanted to relinquish his command to Ned Seymour, regardless of the familial rivalry.

The autumn chill was turning into winter cold. In late November King James gave orders for his Scots to attack. But there was dissension in their ranks over leadership, and as they hesitated, quarreling among themselves, the English rushed forward. First came the cavalry and then the foot soldiers, trapping the Scots between Solway Moss and the River Esk.

It was a disaster for Scotland; King James, now as sick of heart as he was of body, watched helplessly. Many of his finest nobles were killed or drowned during the encounter. Several earls and barons, along with two hundred lairds, were captured by the English. Ned wrote triumphantly to King Henry that "there are now in your hands men who, with good order, may make the peace, or the conquest, of Scotland." And on that optimistic note, Ned asked to be recalled.

The victory brought some cheer to Belford that Christmas. Mary Percy came for the holiday, fretting constantly about Francis's imprisonment. Her worries hardened Morgan, who asserted on several occasions that anyone as big and stubborn as Francis could certainly take care of himself. The brave words, however, did not lift her own spirits.

The day after Twelfth Night, Mary and her entourage returned home. By the next morning Matthew brought news from the village that the ailing King of Scots was dead, dying shortly after his wife gave birth to a daughter. She was their only child and would be named Mary. Fate had dealt a double blow to Scotland; in London, Henry could begin another wily round of politics. He could also turn his attention to war with France.

Morgan relaxed at last, certain that Francis would be released any day. Of course he would probably head for Carlisle, but when he found out his children were at Belford he would come there. Morgan would have a big feast to welcome him. She sighed with relief, thinking how good it was not to have to worry about a possible siege.

But January slipped into February, bringing more cold and snow. Morgan's temper sharpened along with her nerves, and she found she was snapping too frequently and for little reason at both the children and the servants. To make it up to the young ones, she had Matthew rig up a sled. Piling them amid the furs and wrapping them so that only their eyes showed, she herself drove them around the grounds of Belford Castle.

They had just returned from one of those excursions when Polly met Morgan at the door. It had been snowing in big, wet flakes, and Morgan had to wipe the moisture from her eyelashes before she could focus on Polly.

"My lady, I have terrible news!" Polly cried, twisting her hands in her apron.

Morgan clutched at her breast. Francis! Oh, God, not after all this time! She put her other hand out as if to clutch Polly for support, and the servingwoman's words seemed to come from far away:

"My Lord James—Cedric says he is dead!"

Morgan stared at Polly. She had a hideous desire to laugh wildly, loudly, to bring down the castle with laughter. Am I mad? she asked herself. No, merely relieved. But relieved because James was finally at peace—or because Francis was apparently still alive? She wasn't sure, and so she just stood there, oblivious to the children, who had come into the castle and were looking curiously at the two women.

Morgan gathered her strength, telling Polly to get the children out of their heavy clothes and give them a treat.

347

Polly was more composed, too, as she unwound a long scarf from Anne's head. Morgan left them and hurried upstairs.

Two lone tapers burned upon the altar in the chapel. The musky smell of incense hung in the air. Everyone was gone now, everyone but Morgan, who knelt by the new tomb, trying to pray for her husband's soul. Death had come so suddenly, so unexpectedly, for all that she knew it could come any time, indeed, that it was long overdue. Yet there had been occasions when she was sure James would go on forever, living out long, empty years in that same bed, maybe even outliving her in final irony.

Now it was over, what had actually ended almost three years ago, what had really finished even before that, on the day in March when she had returned from her forbidden trip to Sinclair House.

She crossed herself, brushed back the black veil, and got to her feet. Behind her, the chapel door scraped on the floor. She turned quickly and saw Francis Sinclair, his big form looming in the dimness.

"Francis!" It was a shouted whisper, echoing among the hand-carved pews.

He came forward, thinner and tired, with a bushy blond beard which greatly altered his appearance. His heavy tread was unusually loud in the chapel's stillness. He seemed totally unaware of Morgan's presence, passing right by her and dropping on his knees at his brother's tomb.

Morgan withdrew to the door of the chapel but stayed inside. She watched Francis as he knelt motionless for long minutes. He was dressed in riding clothes, and even though he had lost weight, the garments were too tight. She guessed that he had borrowed them, mayhap stolen them somewhere between his Scots prison and Belford.

His shoulders heaved a great sigh and he stood up. He came down the short aisle, still not speaking. She watched him warily as he opened the door for her and let her precede him into the courtyard.

"You are safe," she said, and her voice sounded strangely small.

"Aye." He stood looking up at the castle, his hands on his hips.

She bit her lip, wishing he would speak. He wore his familiar stormy look, which had come between them so often—a look that brooked no interference, accepted no kindness.

"You will take the children back to Carlisle?" she finally asked.

He continued to look off, beyond the castle towers and to the heavy gray snow clouds. "I will take them today, unless we have a blizzard."

Morgan set her jaw and made a sudden decision of her own. "That's just as well, since I plan to leave for London."

Francis swung his head around to stare at her. "London? In this weather?"

"Well," she amended hastily and in annoyance, "I mean as soon as the roads are passable. It's almost March now. I'll go in another month or so."

He folded his arms across his chest, apparently unaware that Morgan was freezing from the cold. His coarse wool cape flapped about him as the wind picked up. "You are that eager to get to Seymour—and your lord dead only three days!"

"As if he would have cared what I did!" she flared at him. "Or you for that matter! I'm getting out of this wild country and I hope I never come back!"

"Yes, yes," he said impatiently, "get away, run away, do what you will. But if you're going to abandon Belford, I must insist that you leave its care to me, for all that my brother would have hated you to do so."

"Have its care. Live here. I'd give you the cursed place except that it belongs to the children now." She tried to keep from shivering outright as the snowflakes began to fall.

"We won't move here, I told you that before. But if you really decide to go to London," he said with a challenging look, "I will see that Matthew and the others take good care of it in your absence."

"Thank you," she said, and knew she sounded ungrateful.

Francis took another look at the sky. "I think we had better leave at once. If it gets worse along the way, we can stop at the Countess of Northumberland's until the weather is better." He started toward the castle entryway as Morgan watched him, cold and shivering, her anger rising steadily.

"She'll be thrilled to see you," Morgan called after him. "Her whey-face and all."

He stopped and turned back, his head cocked to one side. "Do you think Seymour will like you in black—or will you keep your clothes on long enough for him to notice?" He stamped on into the castle.

Morgan clenched her fists and kept her lips clamped shut as a horde of vile oaths hovered on the tip of her tongue. Surely no man was ever more infuriating! Or callous. Or cruel. He had no right to criticize her, not after her miserable marriage to his brother, not after the way Francis himself had mistreated her on so many occasions. She sighed wearily as she made her way across the courtyard and through a side entrance, hoping she wouldn't see Francis alone again before he left.

But why did it matter so much? And why did the thought of his possible courtship of Mary Percy upset her? Useless questions, she told herself, as useless as the energy they expended in quarreling with one another. The answers didn't matter; all that mattered, Morgan told herself with determination, was joining Tom in London and finding happiness in his arms.

Chapter 21

A GENTLE MIST hung over London, dampening the flowers and trees around Whitehall. The smell of wood smoke lingered in the air as the city's residents fought off the early spring chills.

Morgan glanced out the window of her apartment before putting on a black silk gown over her petticoats. The dress was cut square and low at the neck, too low perhaps for a widow of less than two months. She stood quite still as Polly put the pearl-trimmed black coif over her tawny hair. She would need a little color—perhaps some lip rouge would suffice. She dabbed into a cosmetic jar before looking in the mirror. A touch on her cheeks, too—and she smiled in satisfaction at her image.

She and the children, Polly, Peg and Agnes, and a half-dozen retainers had arrived at Whitehall the night before. Tired from the trip, Morgan had gone straight to bed, but now after a full night's sleep she was refreshed and even exhilarated. Tom was at court. She had heard that he was at Whitehall from one of the pages, and within hours, maybe minutes, she would see him again.

Excitedly, she pondered what she would say. It would depend upon the circumstances under which they met, of course. Perhaps in the palace gardens, maybe in the gallery, or then again, not until supper that night. Should she act indifferent to tease him a little, or be candid about her feelings? She smiled to herself as she applied a touch of perfume along her throat. After three years of waiting, these last hours of anticipation were as difficult as they were exciting.

I'm free! she thought, hugging herself and twirling around the room like a delighted child. I'm free of James and Belford, free of Uncle Thomas, free at last to love someone who loves me. She started to laugh aloud but checked herself for fear that Polly or Peg would think she had gone daft.

Morgan decided to walk down to the gallery; it was too damp to stroll in the garden.

As usual, there was a group of courtiers gathered in the gallery. Morgan scanned the faces quickly but Tom's wasn't among them. She noted Ned, however, and Sir William Paget, the new secretary of state, but the others, both men and women, were unfamiliar. How quickly people came and went at court! It seemed that every time she came to London, there were new faces to replace those who had left the court or died—or been executed.

Feeling buoyant and self-assured, she approached the group with a smile. Ned took her hand and made a little bow. "How good to see you at court again, my lady, even though you are in the sad state of mourning."

Morgan felt a touch of reproach in his voice and bowed her head slightly. "Yes, my lord, but truly, it is well that death released James from such a terrible void."

Ned nodded gravely, outwardly sympathetic. He introduced her around and the courtiers resumed their gossip. The talk was, as it had been for these past months, channeled in two directions: the war in France and the King's next matrimonial venture. Both topics afforded much speculation.

Soon Will Herbert joined them, happy to see Morgan and full of opinions about a possible new bride for the King. "She will be English," he asserted. "After Catherine of Aragon and Anne of Cleves, he will not seek another foreign wife."

"You seem so certain," said Ned. "Is it possible, Will, that you might have some idea who this lady will be?"

Will smiled, a secret kind of smile. "I? Oh, no! How should I?"

Ned eyed him carefully. "Well, since you disclaim all knowledge, I see someone coming to join us who might have further information." He lifted his hand. "Greetings, Brother."

Morgan looked up and saw Tom Seymour, as dashing as she had remembered him and more handsome than ever. He was grinning at Ned, but then he saw Morgan and the grin died on his lips. "Morgan," he said with unwonted gravity, "I didn't know you were at court!" He took her hand and kissed it. Why, she thought, he is quite undone! I've never seen him so disconcerted. She was so happy she could burst, but she maintained perfect decorum.

"You are very tan for so early in the spring, my lord. Have you been to sea again?"

"Briefly, a week or so ago." He turned to Ned. "Well, what good gossip have we under way?" And they were off on another round of pleasant conjecture, this time about the French King's next moves.

Morgan kept waiting for Tom to give her a wink, a smile, some kind of sign. But he kept talking to the others as if she were not present. She knew little about the latest war on the Continent so she kept silent. As she listened with diminishing interest, she was suddenly conscious of being an outsider. Observing the women's gowns, she was aware of her own, made at Belford before leaving for court, and that it was at least a season out of style.

It was time for dinner. The group moved out of the gallery and toward the dining hall. Surely Tom would give her his arm, but instead he escorted Anne Herbert, Will's wife. Puzzled, Morgan let Will lead her to a place at the table.

During the meal she sat between Will and Surrey. Directly opposite her was Lady Latimer, also attired in black mourning.

"Cat!" she exclaimed as they sat down. "It's been years!" They leaned across the table and exchanged a kiss on the cheek. "You're in mourning—I've not heard . . ."

"My husband," she answered. "He was ill for such a long time, like your own, you know. I have already heard about your loss. I'm sorry."

The two women exchanged condolences. Cat asked if Morgan had met her sister, Anne Herbert, and Morgan said they had just been introduced in the gallery. Cat was most interested in Morgan's children, plying her with questions and insisting that she would come to visit them soon. They chatted throughout the meal, with Morgan grateful for the diversion. She kept telling herself, however, that as soon as dinner was over, Tom would seek her out, perhaps ask her to accompany him for a walk in the gardens now that the mist had evaporated.

But he did not. He rose with only a general word of farewell for the company and left the hall alone. Morgan watched him walk away, then leaned toward Ned, who was sitting next to Lady Latimer.

"Pray could I have a word with you when you are finished, good Ned?" she asked.

He hesitated but finally answered, "Yes, my lady, of course. I am finished now."

They withdrew to an antechamber off the dining hall. Morgan came straight to the point. "Your brother—is he afraid to approach me in public?"

Ned paced the floor with quick steps before answering. He sighed. "How shall I phrase it?" For a man who was considered articulate in political affairs, Ned seemed tongue-tied with more personal matters. "Tom loved you very much," he allowed, ignoring her stunned reaction to his use of the past tense. "He stayed away a long time, waiting for your freedom. But last fall, when he returned to court briefly, he met someone else. Her gentle demeanor captivated him, and her . . ." Ned's usual composure failed him as he nervously fingered the glittering symbol of the Garter which he wore against his dark doublet. "He fell in love with her, Morgan, and in so doing, fell out of love with you."

The words had the stunning effect of a physical blow. Morgan actually felt herself reel. She leaned against a little table, mouth open and eyes wide. "I don't believe it!" she gasped. "He said he would wait . . ."

"He did. I told you that," Ned asserted, now meeting her shocked gaze head on. "I know he did. But you cannot expect a man like Tom to wait forever, not when he had already waited so long for real love." He saw the depths of her distress and put his hands on her shoulders. "He did love you, I swear it, but he knew that James could live for five, ten years, maybe more, and that you had sworn to be faithful to him. Tom is human, Morgan, more so than most men. You asked too much of him, I fear."

Morgan looked up at him blankly. "Who is she?" Her voice was hoarse and shaky.

Ned put his arms down straight at his sides. "I cannot tell you."

"You must!" she cried. "You must tell me who she is! The conniving slut! Scheming harlot . . ."

He raised a hand as if to silence her by force, but she held her tongue of her own accord.

"Very well, I will tell you, lest you misunderstand his feelings. She is no slut, I assure you. But you must swear on your mother's soul never to repeat what I confide in you, not just for Tom's sake and hers, but for yourself. The knowledge is dangerous."

Morgan stared at him. She couldn't understand what he was getting at. "I swear. Who is it then?"

"The Lady Latimer," he replied.

Morgan's hand flew to her face. "Cat! But that's incredible!" Cat, kind and sweet, small and square, nowhere near Morgan's peer in looks or wit! Morgan started to laugh hysterically.

Ned took another step forward. "None of that! I warn you!" He was menacing. Again, Morgan controlled herself.

"But what is the danger? She is a widow now, too." She simply couldn't fathom all this.

"Exactly," Ned said evenly. "And she is soon to end that lonely state by becoming the King's next wife."

Morgan spent the rest of the day in her rooms and most of that time in bed. She couldn't confide in anyone, though she wished Nan were with her. She pushed away a half-finished bowl of soup. Polly fussed at her, convinced that her mistress's malaise was caused by working too hard for so long and that the trip to London had been too much.

"If you kept in bed for a week, you wouldn't harm yourself any, my lady," Polly asserted.

Morgan paid no attention. She wanted to be alone to cry, to weep far into the night, to pour out her grief for her lost love. At first she had blamed him, but Ned's words came back to her and she wondered if it really had been Tom's fault. Perhaps Ned was right. Had she asked too much of him? Maybe neither Tom nor any other man could have been expected to give what she demanded.

I have lived on the promise of a dream for so long, she thought, mayhap the reality would not have been so sweet. It matters little for I will never find out. And he will never know about the babe we almost had, for now I cannot tell him.

She avoided Tom in the following days at Whitehall.

When they did see one another their words were cordial, but they never seemed to look directly at each other. He knows that I know—Ned must have told him, she thought. But if he wanted to explain or make amends, she never gave him a chance. That would be borrowing pain, and she had had enough already.

Instead, she began to fling herself into court life, mourning gown or not. She was determined to become part of it again, to be in the center rather than on the periphery. She had new clothes made, the most splendid black gowns she and the dressmakers could dream up. She got out all the jewels and furs she already owned—a substantial amount, in spite of James's thrift—and pondered how to use them to best advantage. She studied new books and verses and songs with great care. She picked up every snatch of gossip she heard to tuck away for future conversational use. She sang and danced and laughed and talked with the other courtiers far into the night. And often, she would fall into bed exhausted, too exhausted to allow time for the tears which were always so close to the surface.

I have been through a lot, she lectured herself. I can survive this, too. I will not eke out my days living on faded hope. I will start again, somehow, somewhere.

But it was not easy. Part of the problem was with Morgan herself, part with the court. Life within the royal palace was not as gay and vibrant as it had been ten years ago. Henry was older and had sustained the shock of being married to at least one unfaithful wife. Though many of his courtiers had individual wit and daring, they were not given the opportunity to shine in the King's circle as their predecessors had.

I don't truly feel part of this, Morgan thought one day as she sat with William Paget and John Dudley watching an archery competition in the palace gardens. After a few weeks she felt as if the only reward she had received from her efforts to join in with life at court had been the deadening of her inner senses.

"Surrey's form is excellent as always," Paget commented, nodding in the direction of the contestants.

"Indeed," answered Dudley, "but Will Herbert has greater accuracy." He turned to Morgan. "Wouldn't you agree, madam?"

"What? Oh, yes, Will always hits near the mark." I

don't much care if Will hits Archbishop Cranmer in the backside, Morgan told herself, and wondered how she could politely take leave of Dudley and Paget.

"A shame Thomas Wyatt's son isn't taking part today," Paget was saying. "Have you ever noticed his wrist motion? He doesn't just *shoot* the arrow, he *springs* it free. Last fall at Hampton Court . . ."

Morgan was gratefully distracted by a small terrier nuzzling at her ankles. She reached down to scratch behind his ears as he panted with pleasure. When she looked up again, Richard Griffin was coming toward her, waving his hand.

"A poor cur gets more attention from you than some humans," he said, squeezing in on the bench between her and Dudley. "If I came crawling on hands and knees, with pitiful eye and wagging tail, would you be so kind to me?"

"I'd have to see that happen first—particularly the wagging tail," Morgan replied, unable to keep from smiling and thankful for Richard's intrusion. Rogue he might be, but boring he was not. She settled back and listened as he drew Paget and Dudley into somewhat reluctant conversation.

In June the royal entourage packed up and moved to Hampton Court for the summer. On the second day in residence, Cat Parr, the Lady Latimer, came to see Morgan and the children.

"I was going to come sooner, but I have been so busy!" she exclaimed, rolling her golden eyes.

Morgan surveyed the sturdy, compact little figure. She had charm and goodness, there was no question of that. She was even pretty in a solid, English manner. But Morgan could not accept the attraction Cat held for Tom Seymour. And strangely, she could not feel resentment toward Cat, not even jealousy. For Cat herself was not going to wed Tom, but the King, and everyone knew that now.

"Will it be a great state wedding?" Morgan inquired as Cat put an agreeable Anne on her lap.

"No, no," Cat replied quickly. "His Grace and I—we have both been wed too often for that. I thought we should be married here, in my chamber, as simply as possible."

Morgan wondered how Cat felt about marrying the King

when her heart was with Tom. But if she dared not ask, neither could she resist a bit of probing: "How does it feel to become Queen of England, Cat?"

Cat chucked Anne under the chin and smiled wryly at Morgan. "I don't know yet. Though I suspect your query is really, 'How does it feel to marry a man who has had five wives?'" Morgan flushed slightly at Cat's shrewdness, but the other woman didn't seem to notice. "It's different now, with Henry older and . . . and more settled. It's a little like marrying Moses."

Morgan laughed at Cat's candor. Maybe it is this honesty, this forthrightness, which had delighted Tom so much. But the thought of Cat lying in Tom's arms, moaning under his kisses, stifled her laughter. How much does she know about me? Morgan asked herself. One thing was certain—Tom wouldn't tell her. Tom wasn't like that.

"Best of all, though," Cat said, "I will be able to have Henry's children at court with me—little Edward, Mary, even Elizabeth. They need a mother so desperately." She looked down at Anne's small head. "Almost as much as I need children."

Cat's eyes traveled to Edmund and Robbie, squabbling over their toys in a corner of the nursery. "Mayhap you'll have some of your own now," said Morgan encouragingly, though she doubted Henry's ability to produce further offspring.

"Mayhap," said Cat, but there was little optimism in her voice.

She envies *me*, Morgan realized, because I have had babes. If she knew I almost had Tom's! She thrust the thought aside and the two women began to talk of Cat's trousseau.

King Henry and Catherine Parr were wed on July twelfth, 1543. It was a brief ceremony, as Cat had planned. There was a wedding feast afterward in the Great Hall, and no bridegroom seemed happier than Henry the Eighth. The whole court turned out, but with one exception, Morgan noted: Tom Seymour was not among them. He had left a few days earlier for France before going on to the Low Countries.

* * *

"She is making him happy," Richard Griffin said, referring to Cat and the King, who led the hunting party through the park at Windsor. "She is one of those rare women who truly know how to please a man."

Intended or not, Morgan felt a sting of reproach. "With two previous husbands, she's had considerable practice," Morgan snapped, and wished she hadn't.

They were riding a little way apart from the others. Richard pulled up on the reins and laughed aloud. "Don't tell me you were planning on a crown for that wild head of yours!"

Morgan's first impulse was to roar angrily at him, but instead she scoffed. "You are most exasperating."

He reined his horse closer to hers. "I tease too much," he said seriously. "Perhaps I only meant that the King and his new Queen set a good example for their subjects. An example which you and I could follow, Morgan."

Uncomprehending, she looked up at him. There was no mockery or humor in his eyes now. "What do you mean, Richard?"

"Well," he said with an exaggerated sigh, "if I can't get you in bed illicitly, I'll have to try a more honorable approach. I'm asking you to marry me."

"Oh!" Morgan let the reins slip from her fingers but quickly retrieved them. She looked at him closely; he had seldom seemed so sincere. "It's so soon," she ventured.

"Soon?" Richard made a deprecating gesture with his hand. "Margaret has been dead for a year and a half and James might as well have been dead for the last three. Why, Cat Parr was only a widow for five months before wedding with the King. The question is, do you *want* to marry me?"

I don't know the answer, thought Morgan. Hastily, she considered the alternatives, knowing them by rote after months of conjecture. There was the prospect of perennial widowhood, which appealed very little to her warm blood; there were other eligible men at court, but they were dissipated, dull, or in the market for a fresh young bride; and then there was the faint hope that with Cat Parr married to the King, Tom might one day turn back to Morgan. He had already demonstrated that he wasn't one to play a waiting game. But that was the sort of dream she had foresworn—nor could she really believe in it. If nothing else, her pride would not permit her to consider it any longer. And had she not always found Richard amusing if irritating company? Hadn't his touch fired her blood as Tom's had done? Reluctance was pushed aside as she felt her hands go slack on the reins. "Very well, Richard," she said in a low, even voice, "I will marry you."

"I believe I am as happy as I had hoped," Morgan wrote to Nan, wondering if her words lacked conviction. She brushed the end of the quill against her cheek, pondering the misgivings she could not suppress. What kind of father would Richard make for her three children? Would he remain as courtly and ardent once they were wed or would he tire of her quickly? Would Richard become entangled in political ploys against the Seymours and their supporters? Why did she often feel a stab of regret for her hasty decision?

She put the quill down and nibbled her forefinger. It was useless to worry over such things, save perhaps about Richard's attitude toward the children. So, she demanded of herself, why this feeling of reluctance? She should be delighted that this time she could choose her own husband instead of submitting to her uncle and her parents as she had done before. Was it Tom's image that stifled her enthusiasm? No, it must not be—much better to bury his memory with Sean's. And if it were not Tom who bothered her so, then what was it? Only her fantasies, she assured herself, and she picked up her quill again.

"Yes," she wrote very swiftly, "I am very happy indeed and know that Richard and I will find great joy together."

Morgan and Richard were wed New Year's Day at Greenwich in a ceremony conducted by Bishop Gardiner, who had performed the ceremony for the King and Cat Parr. Gardiner was more conservative than his archenemy, Cranmer, and Morgan preferred that he officiate. Richard readily agreed, for the Howard influence was still upon him.

At last, after ten long years, Morgan finally lay in Richard's arms, experiencing the delights of his long-practiced lovemaking. How different from James, she thought, even different from Tom, and certainly not like Francis. Richard was artful and almost poetic. She chided herself for making intimate comparisons, and with deliberation she swept her mind clean of any thoughts at all and succumbed blissfully to Richard's ardor. It was a new year and a whole new life for Morgan Todd Sinclair, of late the Countess of Belford, and now Lady Griffin.

Chapter 22

LIKE VESSELS of Burgundy wine, the rubies shimmered in the candlelight as Morgan excitedly fastened the necklace clasp. "They're too lovely," she cried, beaming at her reflection in the mirror. She whirled around to where Richard was standing and hugged him close, half laughing and half crying with pleasure. "Thank you, oh, thank you, dear heart!"

He laughed, too, satisfied that his birthday gift had been an immense success. "Rubies are your perfect jewel," he said. "Pearls are too tame, emeralds too dark, diamonds too colorless. Only rubies glow with a life and fire to match your spirit."

Morgan looked up at him with an arch smile. "You speak as smoothly as ever, even after two months of marriage, good husband," she said. "On whom else have you practiced that speech?"

He kissed her nose. "No one. I swear it. How could I? I've never been able to afford rubies before. Margaret kept me on an allowance."

Bursting into laughter, Morgan broke away from him. "You are impossible! You could bend Margaret any way you wanted." She went to the mirror again, tilting her head to this side and that, feeling the coolness of the jewels against her skin.

"But not her uncle, Norfolk," Richard said lightly. "I fear he's always mistrusted me—at least he did where the Howard money was concerned." He came up behind Morgan and put his arms around her, cupping her breasts in his hands. "But let's not talk about Howards and money and other mundane matters." He slipped one of his hands inside her dress as his lips pressed the back of her neck. "In fact, let's not talk at all."

She leaned against him, sighing contentedly. "Oh, must I take off the necklace already?"

"No, no," he whispered, his hands already at work on the fastenings of her gown, "just everything else. You may keep the necklace on."

Richard laid her on the bed, smiling in appreciation at the white, voluptuous body. The rubies took on a life of their own in the reflected candlelight. He leaned down to kiss her eyelids, tracing the outline of her jaw from ear to chin.

"You are more fair than when you were a young girl," he said, and plaited the long, tawny hair between his fingers. "Fine jewels become you, so do your elegant gowns—but your adornments are not what make you so desirable."

"Then you could have saved the money you spent on the necklace," Morgan replied, kneading his shoulders with her hands.

"Nay, I like to show you off in splendor. I want it said that my wife is the most dazzling woman at court." He unclasped the necklace to lay it across her breasts, the two largest rubies each lying on her nipples. "You see? The gems are beautiful, but what lies beneath them is beyond price."

The gold setting of the stones was cold on her flesh and Morgan shivered. "I have no wish to compete for attention with the other ladies," she declared. "Why does it matter, as long as everyone knows I belong to you?"

He moved the necklace down between her thighs and brushed the tawny hair over the rubies and gold. A look of supreme elation crossed his face before he answered. "It matters. Such things do, for me."

Morgan frowned, but her expression changed swiftly as Richard took one of the rubies and rubbed it against the soft, intimate flesh of her womanhood. She began to writhe with pleasure as his other hand fondled her buttocks. After a few moments, he held the moistened necklace up to her face. "You see—you have baptised it with your own desire."

Morgan smiled at him, but inwardly she marveled at the paradox of passion and possession which was so much a part of her husband. Still, her senses were too stirred for coherent thought and the hands that now parted her legs left her bereft of any emotion except the need for consummation. Morgan and Richard moved together in a steadily increasing rhythm of intensity until they both lay gasping and replete—and unaware that the ruby necklace had fallen onto the floor beside the bed.

Henry was going to war again. He had new armor made, built with ample space for his enormous stomach. The battle attire was so huge that two average-sized men could have worn it. Yet neither his girth nor his age would keep Henry from the field in France.

He would sail for Calais with thirty thousand troops, leaving Catherine Parr behind as regent, as he had left another Queen Catherine over thirty years before during a different war across the Channel. Henry was also leaving behind a burned and ravaged Edinburgh, for the Scots had had to be taught another lesson and Ned Seymour had been designated as their tutor.

With Henry would go Richard, and Morgan wept over the parting. She plied him with words of caution and pleas to take care. He laughed and kissed her lips, her throat, her forehead. It was his first real war and he was eager for battle.

"An earldom is all I want out of this," he told her on the July morning of his departure. "Would you not like to be a countess again?"

She took one of his hands in both of hers and squeezed it hard. "No, no, I don't care about that. Nor do I like to see you so concerned about it, either."

But Morgan knew that he would not rest until he achieved an earl's coronet. She only hoped that he would not gamble too hazardously or risk his life too recklessly in the attempt. They had been so happy together in their first half year of marriage that Morgan could not bear to think of anything happening to her husband.

The English already had a foothold on the Continent—Calais. But Henry wanted another, a possession that would be as much of a blow to French pride as to French strategy. He was after Boulogne, and only its capture would satisfy him.

With so many noblemen at war, it was a quiet summer at court. In August, Morgan packed up the children and servants to head for Wolf Hall. She had not seen Nan and her family—now increased by the birth of twin boys the previous year—since the wedding. Nan had stood up for her cousin, happy and relieved that Morgan at last seemed settled.

Morgan stayed the month, enjoying the long visits with Nan but anxious to get back to London where she had more immediate news of the war's progress. She had received only one letter so far from Richard. He had said that little had been accomplished. The English were having difficulties getting supplies, and the midsummer rains were drenching the armies.

"My earldom is obscured by all this water," he wrote. "At the moment I would give up war making for lovemaking with you, sweet wife."

Morgan had kept the letter, bringing it with her to Wolf Hall, where she would reread it every night before she went to bed. She wished he would write more often, but he had warned her that he was a poor correspondent, and the lack of letters proved it.

It was early September; Morgan gave orders to organize their belongings for the return to London. Nan begged her to stay on until Richard returned from France. "You might at least consider visiting your former brother-in-law before you return to court."

Morgan looked at Nan in surprise. "Go to Carlisle? Why, what on earth would I do that for?"

It was Nan's turn to look puzzled. "Carlisle? But Francis is not there now. He is in Woodstock. I thought you knew. The King wished to reward Francis, not only for his religious treatise, but for his valor in the raid on Teviotdale. He gave him additional land for his manor at Woodstock and Francis decided to move there so he could be close to the books at Oxford."

"Well." Morgan sat down abruptly on a big trunk, which Polly had been packing. She shrugged. "Carlisle, Woodstock, it makes no difference. I have no plans to visit Francis. I'm sure he has left Belford in good hands with Matthew."

Nan eyed her cousin curiously but decided to drop the subject. "Come," she said, "I will help you get your gowns ready."

Morgan did decide to make a visit on her way back to

London, but it was not to Woodstock that she ordered her party but to Faux Hall. After so many years, she had finally gathered the courage to face her old home without the presence of her parents. Nan had assured her it was in good repair and that she and Harry made a trip there at least every three months. Morgan thanked them both, confiding that she wanted Faux Hall not for herself but for Edmund. Robbie, as her firstborn, would inherit Belford, but she would keep her old family home for her younger boy.

It was twilight as Morgan, the children and servants reined up at the gravel drive to Faux Hall. Morgan stared straight ahead at the house, unchanged by the years that had altered her own life so much. Solid but graceful among the trees, with the broad sweep of lawn flanking the front, the house was comfortably the same.

Yet inside she knew it would be vastly different. Even now, only three windows were lighted by candles. There would be no fire roaring on the dining room hearth, no roving musicians in the gallery, no big meals being prepared in the kitchen. Most of all, there would not be the quick tread of her mother's footsteps or the sound of her father's deep drawling voice.

"Your house, Mama," said Anne, riding pillion behind one of the servants. "You lived there when you were little like me?"

Morgan nodded slowly. "Yes. I was little like you then." She urged her horse forward.

They were met at the door by Clemence, the elderly serving woman who had come from France with Grandmother Isabeau. She was so bent and lined that Morgan hardly recognized her. But Clemence knew Morgan immediately.

"My lady! You've come back!" She held out her old arms stiffly and Morgan hugged her. "You should have warned us—we've nothing ready for you! Are you here to stay?"

Morgan smiled but shook her head. "No, Clemence, only to spend the night. I had to see Faux Hall again. I've waited too long as it is."

"So you have," said Clemence with some reproach. "Oh, I wish I had known that you were coming."

The other servants had gathered in the hall. Morgan recognized only two of them—Clemence's Welsh husband, Arthur, and the stableboy, Hal. His twin, Davy, had moved with Bess to Aylesbury some years ago. Hal had never married and had remained at Faux Hall where the stables were his domain.

"We only have three horses," Clemence explained. She went on to tell how several of the servants had succumbed to the same epidemic that had taken Morgan's parents. Others had died since or had left the service of Faux Hall and Nan had hired new people, just enough to maintain the house and grounds. Morgan already knew much of this but she listened patiently.

"We've closed up so many rooms—put away much of the furniture, all of your father's books and charts, the table services. I'm afraid it will not look the same to you now," Clemence said with a sad little smile.

Morgan patted Clemence's gnarled hand. "I expected that," she replied. "I'll do my exploring in the morning when the sun is shining. It will be easier then."

Clemence nodded. "So it will." Then she brightened, her watery blue eyes vivid. "Your room is untouched, though. I always thought you might come back. I'll have one of the women prepare it."

"Oh, fine," Morgan said. "We'll put the children next door, in Nan's old room. I assume that's in order?"

Clemence said it was, since Nan and Harry spent the night there when they came to Faux Hall. Morgan stood up, having finished the hasty meal the kitchen help had prepared. "I'll retire since we're all in need of a good night's sleep. We'll ride back to London tomorrow."

For the first time, Morgan noticed the troubled look creep into Clemence's face. They were alone now, Agnes having taken the children off to bed. "Is something wrong?" Morgan asked.

With great effort, Clemence pulled herself up from the chair. She rubbed her wrinkled cheek with her hand and gave Morgan a quick, almost furtive look.

"Well?" asked Morgan.

Clemence was unused to Morgan's being in a position of authority. The sharpened tone of Morgan's voice startled the old woman. She lowered her eyes and folded her hands across her big, drooping bosom. "You know I am not a fanciful person, my lady," she began in a voice that was nearly a mumble.

"What?" Morgan frowned, wondering if Clemence's mind was wandering with age.

But Clemence looked up, her usual alert self again. "I'm not fanciful, my lady, for all my years," she said in a firmer tone. "But there's something you should know, though you may laugh when I tell you." Morgan was still frowning, but more from curiosity than concern. Clemence continued: "There are ghosts in this house."

"Ghosts?" Now Morgan was certain that Clemence had given in to senility. "Nonsense, Clemence!"

Clemence nodded. "I said you wouldn't believe me. But I myself have heard the noises. And so have the others. Ask Hal."

Morgan considered that Hal might be humoring the old woman. "What about Arthur?" she demanded.

Clemence looked sheepish. "He *says* he's never heard the noises. But I don't believe him. Besides, he grows deaf."

Morgan tapped her fingernails on the table. She didn't want to hurt Clemence's feelings. She smiled gently. "Well, there certainly may be something making noises around here—the wind, or the trees, or *something*—but it's not ghosts, I assure you." She stood up again and took Clemence's arm. "If I hear anything tonight, I'll let you know." Morgan gave Clemence another hug. "You sleep well and let me worry about the ghosts."

Clemence started to protest, to try to convince Morgan again, but then merely sighed, smiled feebly, and handed Morgan a taper to light her way to bed.

Morgan undressed slowly by the window, watching the trees sway in the soft breeze, smelling the crisp night air of early autumn, and catching a glimpse of the river in the distance. She looked around the room—it *was* the same, or nearly so. She smiled to herself as bittersweet memories began to come back: her father, reading the works of Chaucer and Malory aloud after dinner; her mother, overseeing the basting of a dozen ducklings for a holiday dinner; Nan, taking her first precarious steps across the dining room floor; Aunt Margaret, missing stitches in her usually sure-handed needlework as she railed about Martin Luther's latest heresies; and Grandmother Isabeau, so worldly wise, so perceptive, and always in such subtle control of the entire family.

I will not cry, she promised herself. I will go to bed and

pray for Richard's safety. Then I will go to sleep. To her surprise, she did just that. But later, from somewhere, something awakened her. At first it was a muffled, thudding sound, which only partially penetrated her sleep. Then, there were louder but more infrequent noises. Fully awake, she sat up, her senses alert. The sounds stopped altogether. Morgan continued to listen, and just as she decided it had been either the wind or her imagination, she heard another thump. The noise was coming from the floor above her, the top floor of Faux Hall. Nothing was up there now but the storeroom, Clemence had said.

But there was something up there now, Morgan was sure of that. Another thump, not so loud this time. Morgan sat on the edge of the bed, curiosity mingled with fear. Ghosts? Certainly there was no such thing! Yet there was little wind; mice or even rats wouldn't be so loud; and a stray dog would bark, a cat would cry.

She would have to get some of the servants to go with her, no matter how frightened they purported to be. She would not wake Polly or Agnes, though—rousing them would mean alarming the children. Just as Morgan got out of bed and reached for her dressing gown, she heard another sound, this time a scraping noise, like a chair being pulled across the floor.

Morgan hurried out of the room, along the hall, and down the stairs, cautious about making any noise herself. She stopped at the first door of the servants' quarters, wondering who would answer her knock. It was Hal, sleepy-eyed and puzzled at the sight of the Lady Morgan in her dressing gown.

"My lady?" He looked as if he thought he were having some sort of strange dream.

"There's a noise up on the third floor," Morgan said, keeping her voice brusque and unafraid. "You must come with me to see what it is so we can get this ghost matter straightened out once and for all. Who shares this room with you?"

"Only Donald," Hal replied, referring to the kitchen boy.

"Well, then, wake Donald and tell him to come along."

Hal hesitated, then went back inside the room. Morgan heard him shaking Donald and calling his name. Presently, both young men came to the door.

"Come with me," Morgan commanded, starting toward the stairs. "It may be foolish but we'd best arm ourselves."

She mounted the stairs noiselessly as Hal and Donald followed. Even in the darkness she had no trouble finding her father's armory. The key dangled on a chain. She inserted it in the lock, turned it, and pulled the door open. There was a slight squeak as the rusty hinges moved. She peered into the cabinet; she already knew what she wanted. Her hand moved over the assortment of weapons until she felt the cold carved hilt of her father's Italian dagger. Then she grasped two pikestaffs and handed them to Hal and Donald. She said nothing but could hear the sharp intake of breath as each of the young men took hold of his weapon.

The stairs made no answering sound as her slippers and the men's bare feet ascended them. At the top, they heard a crackling noise, then a rustling sound. They slipped along the narrow passageway, pausing outside the first door on the right. There was no sound there, no sound anywhere now. Cautiously, Morgan tried the handle, but it was locked. Her mouth was dry. She licked her lips and clutched at the dagger. The spiraled steel hilt dug into her palm. Hal and Donald shuffled nervously behind her. The handle of the second door opened easily. The room was dark as Morgan stepped inside. She gasped as she saw weird shapes and forms cluttering the room.

"Jesus!" whispered Hal.

But as Morgan's eyes grew accustomed to the darkness she began to make out the silhouettes: It was the unused family furniture, covered with protective cloths.

Sighing with relief, Morgan started for the door. She was motioning for Hal and Donald to come along when there was another sound, this time more thumping, almost like footsteps. Morgan leaned against the door, torn between going out into the hall to face whatever was there, or staying in the room where they might be trapped. Slowly, she lifted the latch and eased the door open. There was nothing in the passageway. She stepped out of the room and continued on, less assured and more nervous. Behind her, Hal and Donald seemed to be barely moving. She waved her arm, urging them to keep going.

She was at the third door, and it yielded as easily as the second. Again she moved inside, this time leaving the door open to provide a little moonlight from the windows flanking the balcony. At first glance she saw the history books and naval charts, the prized possessions of her father. Then she turned and saw the huge form lurking over her.

"Hal!" she screamed. "Help!" But Hal and Donald screamed, too, and fled terror-stricken down the hall.

Morgan screamed again as a sense of helplessness overcame her. She plunged frantically with the dagger into the swaying, menacing shape, down into the great threatening form. The dagger stabbed freely through some sort of substance and then nothing. The form still loomed and Morgan screamed again, lashing out impotently with her weapon.

The arms that grabbed her from behind twisted her right wrist until the dagger fell. It clattered harmlessly to the floor as Morgan gasped for air. No sound came out of her throat, though she continued to thrash her arms and legs. Then the hands lifted her off the ground and she was swung high into the air. I'm going to die, she thought wildly, I'm going to die! She closed her eyes tight.

And suddenly she became aware that someone was talking to her, half-angrily, half-humorously, someone with a voice that was very familiar. She opened her eyes slowly, realizing that her head was against her captor's shoulder. She craned her neck, peering into the dimness, and then the face and voice became instantly recognizable.

"Francis!" She goggled at him and was both relieved and furious. "What . . . ?"

He was laughing so hard, in his low rumbling laugh, that he could scarcely hold on to her. "Oh, God! I've got to put you down!" He settled her into an armchair and collapsed on the floor next to her. He could hardly speak for laughing. "You were . . . so . . . funny!" He finally got the words out.

"Funny!" Morgan shrieked at him, trembling from fury and relief. "Funny! Oh!" She was at him with her hands, grabbing at his hair. "I'll make you bald for that!" she yelled.

He grabbed her wrists tight and pushed her back into the chair. "Stop that!" he ordered, finally overcoming his mirth. "Will you let me explain?"

"You'd better," she said between clenched teeth, eyes wild.

He settled himself back on the floor, his hands gripping his knees. "I live at Woodstock now." Morgan nodded impatiently. "I've been helping John Leland, who has been scouring all England to compile works for the King's new library at Whitehall. I remembered you telling me about your father's wondrous collection of books and old charts. I was going to write and ask permission to look at them but"—and he looked at her with his sardonic gaze—"I hesitated to disturb you in your new pleasures. I came here one evening, found Arthur down by the well, and told him who I was and what I wanted. I said—since I hadn't written you—that I would appreciate it if he would keep my visits to himself. I give him a few coins from time to time, and he makes sure the door by the trellis is always open."

Explanation or not, she was still in a rage. "You bribed *my* servant to get into *my* house to go through *my* father's possessions! You are the most contemptible person I've ever met!" She saw he was watching not her eyes or her face, but was staring openly and almost indifferently at her bosom. She looked down and saw her dressing gown open, her nightdress pulled away to reveal almost all of her breasts. She yanked the dressing gown across her chest and blushed furiously.

"I *have* seen your breasts before," Francis drawled. "Or have you forgotten?"

She jumped up. "Wretched churl! You should have stayed in the North with the rest of the Philistines! You . . ." Sounds in the passageway made her stop.

They both turned as light began to fill the corridor. Francis, with Morgan following him, went to the door and looked out: The servants, led by Hal and Donald, were advancing tremulously down the hall, armed with more pikestaffs, swords, daggers, and even a pitchfork. A most disturbed-looking Arthur was doddering at Hal's side.

The sight of them set Francis to laughing again, and this time Morgan laughed, too. The little brigade, squeezed in between the walls, stopped and stared at their mistress and the tall, blond stranger beside her. Arthur looked decidedly disconcerted as his glance passed between Morgan and Francis and back again.

Hal was the first to speak, his words hampered by a stammer: "We were s-so t-terrified. We th-thought the g-ghost had attacked you, m-my lady!"

Morgan smiled at his consternation. "Well, if he had," she said dryly, "I would have been a ghost myself by now."

Hal stared down at his bare feet. "We th-thought we needed . . . more help. It . . . it took us awhile to get our arms together . . . and our courage together again, my lady."

Morgan went up to him and put her hand on his broad shoulder. "You are to be commended for coming back at all. As for ghosts, perhaps Arthur can explain." She gave Arthur a firm but not unaffectionate look. "Go back downstairs, all of you, and try to calm the womenfolk."

They trooped off obediently, their weapons clattering on the stairway. As she turned back toward the room, Morgan saw what she had attacked—Francis's cloak, hung on a peg by the door. She could also see now that there was a blanket over the window so that Francis's candle could not be seen from outside. Morgan waved her hand in the direction of the charts and books piled on a table by the window. "You want these things?" Her anger had subsided now.

Francis furrowed his brow at her. "You'd give them to me?"

She shrugged. "They aren't doing any good just collecting dust. Except for the ghosts, of course." A little smile tugged at her mouth.

Francis smiled back, his familiar, sardonic smile. He was clean-shaven again and he had put on some weight. "And I thought I would cause less trouble by coming here unknown."

Morgan bent down and picked up her father's dagger. She tucked it into the folds of her dressing gown and looked up at Francis. "You are daft, Francis." She started out of the little room. "Don't you know you have never been light treaded?"

He snorted. "Indeed," he said, and began to gather together the books and rolled-up naval charts. His voice had made her pause. "You are wed again, I hear. But not to Seymour. What happened?"

She turned and faced him with a glacial expression. "What does it matter to you?"

He shrugged, but there was tension in his tall frame. "Obviously, it should not. I'm just curious about the course your heart takes. A year ago, you were hell-bent on having

Seymour. Now you are Lady Griffin. But of course this time you finally found true love."

The sarcasm riled Morgan visibly. "I found a man who wanted to marry me and take care of me. An attractive, charming man, too, with wit and flair. We are very happy."

"Assuredly." Francis bent down to pick up a piece of parchment that had fallen from the desk. "I assume he is a good stepfather. I do, after all, have a stake in how my son is raised."

Morgan had given little thought to how Francis might react to having a man other than his own brother take on the responsibility of being a father to Robbie. It had been so long since her children had had any real father at all, and while Richard did not spend a great deal of time with her young ones, his presence added a much-needed figure of masculine authority.

"He is kind and good-humored with all the children," she said in a voice that sounded defensive. "Naturally, since he has never had young ones of his own, being a father is new to him."

Francis raised a sandy eyebrow. "So it is. He had no children by his first wife. Nor, now that I think of it, do I recall ever having heard of him siring bastards." He paused and let his eyes move down the sheet of parchment, apparently absorbed in what had been inscribed so many years ago. Morgan watched him with curiosity, suddenly aware that she had grown quite chilly in her nightclothes and bare feet.

At last he looked up. "I had considered making love to you. I think I will not. It occurs to me that your handsome Richard may be incapable of giving you babes. If I were to get you with child, there could be no greater irony than to see my own son supplanted by his brother. Or sister," he added, almost as an afterthought.

"You blackguard!" Morgan shouted, and immediately lowered her voice lest the servants hear her. "Does it ever occur to you that I don't want you to touch me? Did you ever think Margaret was barren? Or that Richard is very discreet about his illegitimate offspring?"

"Or that pigs fly?" Francis rolled up the parchment and stashed it among a dozen other rolls in an ancient oak cask. "Now begone, it's nigh on to midnight and I have at least an hour's work to do before I ride to Woodstock."

Morgan wanted to make a stinging retort, to have the last word and phrase it so that Francis could not mistake her contempt for his arrogant, arbitrary behavior. But he was scratching away with his quill, acting as if she had already left the room. Still she hesitated as a small voice from somewhere deep inside asked a compelling question: *Why do you wait? So that he will change his mind and fling himself upon you?* Nonsense, Morgan told herself; as much as she missed Richard and his lovemaking, she scarcely needed impassioned consolation from Francis. Noiselessly, she turned on her heel and left the room.

But she did not go back to sleep that night. Some time after one o'clock she heard the sound of Francis's horse trotting down the drive of Faux Hall. Morgan sighed with annoyance at the mere thought of her brother-in-law's brazen intrusion into her old home—and his equally brazen words with her. He must be wrong about Richard. Margaret obviously had not been a healthy woman. And while Morgan had wondered why she didn't become pregnant during the first six months of their marriage, she assumed it was her fault, since she was older now and had lost the last babe she had carried. Nor did her unfruitful state perturb her a great deal; she would like to give Richard a son and heir, but he did not seem obsessed with the idea as were most men. It was unusual, she had to admit, but then her own father had never appeared overly disappointed because he had only sired a daughter.

She turned over and sighed again. Damn Francis, he certainly could stir up her emotions. That blunt attitude, the total candor, the probing questions—not even Tom had ever spoken so frankly to her. Why, she demanded of herself, did she permit Francis to behave so outrageously in word *and* deed? And why in God's name had she hesitated while he turned back to his work in the recesses of the attic?

Because I want him, came that relentless voice once more. Because I have always wanted him. Because I *can* talk to him, as he can talk to me. Because I love him and always have, perhaps from that first time out there in the orchard.

Morgan sat up, her fist rubbing at the place between her eyebrows. Who was really talking to her, her own conscience—or Grandmother Isabeau? Her grandmother's presence seemed to hover in the house, as unsettling as any ghost the servants had conjured up. But not frightening—no, comforting, loving—and knowing.

And Grandmother Isabeau *had* known, even if Morgan had not. Why did I not? she asked herself. Grandmother had warned her that love could be deluding. But Morgan didn't want to know, she couldn't know, not when she thought she loved Sean, not when she was going to marry Francis's brother, not when Francis already had a loving wife, not while she took the heady plunge into passion with Tom Seymour, not while she thought Tom had broken her heart and she needed the balm of a new marriage to ease the pain. And not when she believed that her love could never be returned by Francis. For she was convinced that he did not love her. He had never professed his feelings. He had merely stated that they were well mated in the physical sense. He had loved Lucy deeply. And certainly there was no hint of romance or sentiment in his rough wooing of Morgan's body.

Morgan slapped at the counterpane in anger and frustration. She couldn't possibly love Francis, wretched boor that he was. It was just that she and Richard had been separated too long, that finding Francis instead of an ethereal spectre had been a shock, that she was undone by being in her old home without her loved ones. To think that she loved Francis! She shook her head several times, as if to rid her brain of such a foolish notion. Of course she did not love him and never had—nor, she told herself, did he love her.

Morgan and the children arrived in London after dark the following night, settling themselves into their rooms at Whitehall. Morgan sought out Wriothesley, the new chancellor, and badgered him for news of the war. He had not heard much in the last few days, he admitted, save that Boulogne was still the primary objective of the King's drive into France.

A week after Morgan returned to court, Richard's second letter arrived. He had news of victory, which had already been rumored about the city.

"Our forces threw wild fire into Boulogne, right in the midst of a thunderstorm. A week to the day later I stood beside the King and Surrey and we watched as the castle fell. I have never seen His Grace so pleased or elated. Perhaps my earldom is at hand."

Morgan smiled at the single sheet of paper. He had closed by saying that soon they would be in each other's arms, making up for the lost weeks while he had been away.

For all of Henry Tudor's matrimonial misadventures, his suppression of the old faith, his persecutions and executions, he was still "Bluff King Hal" to his people. Riding in triumph through the streets of London, he waved to the crowds, his great bulk swaying precariously atop the splendidly caparisoned horse. A few yards behind the King rode Richard Griffin, a set smile on his tanned face.

Morgan was waiting at Whitehall. She had heard that Richard would be among those returning with the King. As the procession moved through the gates, she leaned from the balcony, trying to find her husband among the victorious warriors.

"There!" cried Mary Howard, the widowed Duchess of Richmond. "See him, in the bright green!"

Morgan peered down among the men until her eye caught the brilliant color of Richard's doublet. At that moment, he looked up and waved at her. She waved back, beaming, then left the balcony and raced downstairs to meet him.

She was lying naked in his arms as his hand caressed the length of her hip and thigh. They had been making love for over an hour and were both replete. But in spite of her joy at being reunited with Richard, Morgan sensed that he was troubled. She knew he had not yet been granted his earldom; if he had, he would have told her at once.

"You are disturbed, my husband," she ventured, trying to read his face in the dim light. "Do you want to tell me why?"

The mocking smile, with a touch of bitterness, came to his face. "My earldom appears to be not forthcoming," he said, and the smile faded as he lay back on the pillow. "The

King already rewarded several others after the capture of Boulogne but I was not among them. He still considers me a Howard, and for all that Norfolk and Surrey and myself are deemed fit to fight his wars, Henry will not repay us in kind."

Morgan put her arm across his chest, her head against his shoulder. "Don't fret, dear heart. In time, I am sure, he will recognize you for what you are—not a Howard by birth but one of his loyal men."

Richard sighed. "Perhaps," he said, but his tone displayed no conviction. Then he laughed and tickled her side. "I'm turning as grumpy as Bishop Gardiner these days. Just being in France must sour a Welshman's good humor."

"Nonsense," said Morgan, though she knew it was true. He was older, of course, and he had more responsibilities now with her and the children—that was undoubtedly why he was less exuberant, less animated. Having reassured herself for the time being, Morgan slept. But Richard remained awake for a long while, staring up at the canopy over their bed.

Chapter 23

THE NEW YEAR OF 1545 brought still more wrangling between Henry and the Emperor. Charles was suing for perpetual peace, but Henry wanted none of it. In the North, the Scots were again taking the field with the added threat of an alliance with France. And on the seas, the danger of a French invasion menaced the English coast.

Morgan knew that Tom was stationed at Dover, guarding the Channel. Officially now one of the Queen's ladies, Morgan watched Cat Parr's face closely whenever news of the navy was reported. Cat would force her face to keep composed, her voice to show interest—but nothing more. Yet for all the Queen's discretion, Morgan could see a glint of fear in the other woman's eyes whenever Tom's name was mentioned. She still loves him, Morgan thought. But do I? Or did I ever really love him? Or did I only need him at that time, in a way that I have never needed anyone so desperately before or since?

But now she had convinced herself Richard was all she needed. Sometimes it seemed as if the slightest touch across the supper table, a glimpse of her silk-stockinged legs as she lifted her skirts to climb the stairs, or even a glance during a pause in their conversation was sufficient to sweep them both into a flare of mutual passion. Occasionally, he would chide her for the years of pleasure she had denied them.

"I'd have been but a meek young girl," she told him once as he covered her breasts with strands of her long, tawny hair. "You would have tired of me quickly."

"Not so," he responded, smiling at her shiver of excitement. "I would have taught you all you would have needed to hold me. Yet," he added, the smile fading slightly as her hands stroked his body, "I often marvel that you learned so much so well from that stick, James."

Morgan abruptly jerked her knees up, catching Richard off-balance and sending him sprawling on his back. She fell on top of him, burying her face in the hollow of his neck. Her aggressive ardor delighted him; he had no idea that she couldn't let him see the expression on her face, lest he read more than she would have him know.

The following month Richard accompanied Henry and a contingent of nobles to Portsmouth, where the King dined aboard the fleet's flagship. They were draining their wine goblets when a lookout excitedly reported that French ships were on the horizon. Certain that the time for invasion had come, the King and his party hurriedly made for shore. They watched from the beach as the French fleet maneuvered menacingly, but came no farther.

Henry smiled with self-confidence. "Craven French!" he cried, beaming so widely that his little eyes were all but hidden in the folds of his face.

And then disaster struck. A sharp breeze had come up, and as the *Mary Rose,* named for Henry's sister, started to turn with the wind, she took on water through the open gunwales and sank. Over four hundred men, including the vice admiral of the fleet, Sir George Carew, were drowned. Had it been other than the flagship—and one named for a Tudor princess at that—the loss might not have caused such tribulation. But the country's dependence on its fleet was such that the news rocked London, even though the calamity was a worse blow to morale than it was to English naval strength.

Henry returned to Hampton Court in a glum mood, while Richard and several of the other nobles remained in Portsmouth to await the French navy's next move. Tom Seymour was ordered to join the main fleet, replacing George Carew as vice admiral. But the long-expected attack never materialized. By the middle of the month, the French—low on water and with much sickness among their men—turned back for Le Havre.

Richard returned to Morgan more downcast than when he had left. "I never even had a chance to take part," he lamented, as she rubbed his tense neck muscles. "Damn Seymour, if only the French *had* landed! We could have repulsed them easily and I would have made my mark. But no, his reputation for seamanship scared those wretched Frenchies off! Am I never to be free of Seymour meddling?"

Morgan soothed him with words and caresses. Thank God he had never seemed to realize how close she and Tom had been! Richard settled down in her arms and seemed succored by their lovemaking.

Their mutual passion seemed to bind them closer together that winter, though Richard often appeared distracted and frequently went out alone. Morgan made no comment, sensing that Richard's frustrated ambition made it necessary for him to spend some time in solitude. She filled the hours by sharing them with her children, always a source of comfort.

It was hard to believe that Robbie would be ten on his next birthday. He was getting so tall, so bright, so outgoing. He and the other children got on well with their stepfather, although Morgan sometimes wished Francis could see Robbie growing up. None of them really remembered James at all.

It was Richard who made the first move regarding the future of the children. One night at supper, he mentioned casually that it was time to consider a bride for Robbie.

Morgan was astonished. "Nonsense, Richard! It's not as if he were a prince. Surely we can wait a few years."

Richard eyed his empty plate thoughtfully. "Waiting narrows the choice. And I've already given some consideration to the matter."

"You have?" Morgan asked, her topaz eyes wide. "Anyone in particular?"

Richard didn't meet her stare, but answered matter-of-factly. "My first choice is Henry Grey's daughter, Jane. She's near to Robbie in age and would make a fine alliance."

"Oh, no, Richard!" Morgan exclaimed. "Why, she's the granddaughter of the King's sister! I've even heard speculation that if anything happened to little Edward, and Mary and Elizabeth were still considered bastards, Lady Jane could claim the throne. No, no, that's aspiring too high." Morgan shook her head, convinced that the idea was absurd, even dangerous.

Richard pushed back his chair and stood up, walking around the room. "Robbie is already Count of Belford. He has extensive lands in the North—though sometimes I think you forget that," he said accusingly. Morgan started to protest, but Richard went on: "Let us be realistic. Henry is old in body, if not in years. Edward is a sickly child. You've said yourself how the Queen worries over him. And Mary and Elizabeth have been declared bastards. So if the crown should pass to Jane, can you honestly say you would not like to see your son sitting on the throne by her side?"

"You're talking about a chain of improbabilities," Morgan said, getting up and going to Richard's side. She put her hand on his arm. "And even if it were likely, that's the very reason I wouldn't want Robbie mixed up with the Greys. I've had done with intrigue and danger."

He leaned down and kissed her gently on the lips. "Don't make such hasty decisions. Think about it for a while. All right?"

Morgan looked at him uncertainly. He was humoring her, she was sure; his mind was already made up. For the first time, looking into his eyes, she plumbed the depth of his ambition and was afraid.

Cat Parr had narrowly escaped the executioner's axe. Hounded by her old adversary, Bishop Gardiner, she had been implicated in the arrest of Anne Askew, an outspoken Protestant woman who had condemned the Mass. Anne Askew was put to death, but not before she had almost dragged Cat with her.

But either through her own personal wiles or the mellowing of the King, Cat was spared. She promised Henry she would debate no more with him on matters of religion but would follow his counsel in all things. "We are perfect friends again," Henry told her, and settled back to let her minister to him in his deteriorating health.

But the hairsbreadth escape had unnerved Cat Parr. Outwardly she was calm as ever, but alone with her sister, Anne Herbert, and Morgan, she often seemed distraught.

"If only I could have given him a child," she exclaimed one day, big tears standing in her eyes. "Now surely it is too late!" Anne patted her sister's shoulder as Morgan turned away, sympathizing with the Queen.

Henry, however, seemed content. He had at last made

peace with the French. Boulogne would be returned to France—but it would cost a staggering two million crowns. The court relaxed and set out to enjoy what remained of summer.

In the new atmosphere, Richard began to make his move. Morgan watched him talk confidentially with Surrey and John Dudley. With growing anxiety she sensed that they were engaged in a dangerous struggle with the Seymours. Nor was she the only one who was aware of what was afoot. Ned Seymour, seated next to her at dinner one day, leaned toward her:

"Your husband is busy at politics these days," he whispered.

She looked at him warily, wondering if he was warning her. She feigned indifference. "He's always gossiping with someone. You know how he likes to keep up on the latest scandals."

Ned sat back, his eyes fixed on Richard and Dudley. Morgan shifted nervously in her chair and turned to Kate Willoughby to discuss the newest dance steps introduced at court.

Tom Seymour was in London, but Morgan saw little of him. As always, their encounters were proper and polite, but never alone. He seemed to prefer to stay aloof from court life at the moment, and Morgan knew that his decision was wise, lest he give himself away in the presence of the Queen.

If Morgan had not been jealous of Cat Parr before, she was beginning to feel a creeping envy. For Tom had not married though now he was nearing forty. He had not waited for Morgan; was he going to wait for Cat? She glanced at the King, grotesquely huge and now unable to move without being lifted from his chair. Perhaps Tom would not have to wait so long after all, she thought bitterly.

"Your meal doesn't seem to have agreed with you, judging by the look on your face."

Morgan whirled around. Francis Sinclair was settling himself into the chair Ned Seymour had just vacated.

"When did you come to court?" she asked, as he motioned for the serving people to bring him food and whiskey.

"Just now," he answered laconically.

She could hardly believe it was he, after all this time. "What for? It's been years since you've been to court."

He began to eat with such vigor that Morgan moved away a bit, lest some of the debris land on her new blue silk gown. "The King has founded a new college at Cambridge. I come to beg him to do the same at Oxford," he explained. "Since reverting to the crown, Oxford has foundered sadly. I want to help restore it to its former glory." The tone was self-deprecating but Morgan knew his intentions were genuine.

"Why you?" she asked, as Kate Willoughby leaned forward to catch their conversation.

"Because I am interested," he answered shortly, and looked beyond Morgan to Kate. "Pray, good sister-in-law, introduce me to your dinner companion. I've not had the pleasure of meeting her."

The dark-haired Kate, widow to the Duke of Suffolk, dimpled prettily. Morgan made the introductions, then remarked pointedly, "I thought you would be wed by now to the Countess of Northumberland."

Francis shrugged as he took a big bite of pheasant leg. "I never asked her." He shot a sidelong glance at Morgan. "Not all of us run off and get married as soon as the coffin is shut on our last spouse."

"You . . ." Morgan sputtered, and thought better of it. Kate was still hanging over her elbow. "You must meet my husband when he is free," Morgan amended, her voice now calm.

"I met him—many years ago," Francis said indifferently.

"Why, you're the one who wrote the book about religion!" Kate suddenly exclaimed. "It's excellently done. I've read it twice."

Francis nodded, polishing off another pheasant leg. "Good, I appreciate a woman who reads."

Morgan tugged at Francis's arm. "I want to talk to you—right away, alone."

He looked at her with a mixture of amusement and curiosity. "Talk—or rant?"

"Talk." Morgan was sharp and insistent. "About Belford—and something else."

Francis selected half a dozen sweetmeats from a tray before him. "In a few moments. Let me finish my meal in peace."

Finally, after what seemed an interminable conversation with Kate, he rose and grasped Morgan by the hand. "Come along," he said, as if he were the one issuing the request. They started from the dining hall but paused as the King was being moved in his chair conveyance by four servingmen. His gross body seemed to overlap the chair and the servants wobbled unsteadily in their progress out of the hall.

"God's beard!" Francis breathed in amazement. "Can't he walk?"

"No," replied Morgan. "One leg is useless."

Francis shook his head. "I hope I'm not too late with my suit for the college."

They went out into the gardens where the afternoon sun was beating down on the flowers and hedges of Hampton Court. Morgan began the conversation, asking Francis about Belford. He said all was well there, and that he had visited the castle in the spring. Satisfied, Morgan moved on to her second—and most important—topic.

"I must ask a great favor," she said slowly, as they stopped near a shallow pool surrounded by marigolds. She looked up at him, wondering what effect her pleading topaz gaze would have on this unpredictable brother-in-law of hers. None, she decided, and came directly to the point: "I want you to take the children to Woodstock for a while."

Francis drew back, the thick eyebrows pulled together in a frown. "Why? Do you and Richard want more freedom in which to exercise your passion?" His humor was heavy-handed and forced.

Again, Morgan suppressed her anger. "Don't be absurd. It's because of Richard that I ask this."

"Why?" he repeated, and the frown deepened.

Morgan hesitated, nervously twisting her hands together. But she knew she would have to be candid with him. "He wants to use them—at least Robbie—to further his own ambitions. They are my children and Robbie is your son. I want them away from court for a while. Perhaps he will get over the idea."

Francis was silent for a full minute. He stood staring at the gravel path, rocking slightly on his heels. "Christ!" he swore at last. "I won't permit his intrigues on behalf of any Sinclair offspring. When do you want them to go?"

Morgan smiled in relief, then sobered quickly. "Right away. As soon as you are ready."

Francis was surprised at her haste but agreed. Morgan thanked him so profusely that he finally put up his big hand in front of her face. "Enough, enough. Robbie is my own, after all. And you can show your gratitude by championing my cause with the King regarding Oxford." Morgan promised that she would try.

She decided not to say anything to Richard about the children's journey to Woodstock until Francis was ready to leave. As it turned out, there was no need to mention it at all as her husband was dispatched by the King to go into the city for a few days. Before he returned, Francis had already left with the children, who were delighted to join their uncle on an outing.

Francis was half-pleased with his mission at court: He had not convinced the King that a new college should be founded at Oxford, but Henry had agreed to set up a foundation which would help sustain the university in the future.

The day after Francis and the children headed for Woodstock, Richard arrived from London. It wasn't until suppertime that he noticed the young ones' absence. He asked Morgan where they were.

"I let them go back with Francis for a visit to their cousins," she replied nonchalantly. "They haven't seen each other for so long."

Richard's eyes narrowed as he surveyed his wife. She was selecting a gown from the wardrobe with studied calculation, hoping he would ask no more questions.

"You should have consulted with me!" he flared, shouting at her for the first time since they had been married.

Morgan turned in surprise, a red damask gown over her right arm. "Why, Richard, you weren't even here!" She gave him a wifely smile of reproach. "I could hardly have consulted with you when you were ten miles away."

Angrily, he advanced on her. "You did this on purpose!" He was still shouting. "You did this to thwart me! Is it not bad enough to be unsure of the King's feelings and have the Seymours at my back without you blocking my way?"

Morgan laid the red dress on the bed. "Don't be ridiculous," she said with infuriating calm. "This has nothing to do with your plans and plots."

"Plots! How dare you!" He raised his hand but seemed to gain control of himself and dropped his arm to his side. "Write to Francis and have him send the children back immediately." His voice was more normal, but still angry.

Morgan set her feet apart and looked at him sharply. "I will do no such thing. They were promised the visit," she replied firmly.

"Don't countermand my orders!" he shouted. He grabbed her shoulders and shook her hard. "You do what I say! Do you hear?"

Now she was furious, too. "They are *my* children! I will do as I please with them!" She threw the words at him between clenched teeth.

He stared at her, his hands still on her shoulders. He knew he was balked, at least for the moment. He released her so abruptly that she fell back on the bed. "I'm going out," he mumbled, heading for the door.

Her eyes flashed at his back. "Where *do* you go, Richard? To the stews?"

He stood stock-still, then turned around slowly. A hint of his mocking smile played around the corners of his mouth. "Yes. Where else would I go?"

"Oh!" She flung a pillow at him, and then another. Both missed. "Unfaithful beast! I thought you loved me!" she cried, and reached for the vase on the stand beside the bed.

He threw himself across the room and grabbed her wrist. The vase dropped from her hand and smashed to the floor. He looked down into her face and spoke slowly. "Why, good wife, there was never talk of love between us."

She stared up at him, vainly trying to pull her wrist away. "No," she answered quietly. "There was not."

He let go of her arm and she lay back on the bed, staring blankly up at him. Her coif had come off and the thick tawny hair fell in waves on the counterpane. The curve of her bosom rose and fell slowly. Richard dropped down beside her on the bed.

"Love is for poets like Surrey," he said. "We have something else." His arms went around her, his mouth came down hard on hers, and his fingers worked expertly to unfasten her dress. She closed her eyes and moaned softly as he took quick possession of her body.

The matter of the children was left unresolved. Richard knew, as did Morgan, that sooner or later they would have to return to court. He did not bring up the subject again and their relationship appeared to resume its normal pattern.

But the quarrel had left its mark on Morgan. Somehow, she had deluded herself into thinking that Richard loved her in his way, that perhaps she loved him. It seemed too base, too crass, that two married people should found their partnership on lust alone. But she must have recognized it all along, for his words had come as no real shock. In truth, she felt more upset about not having guessed where Richard spent his time away from her. No, even that was not so. Perhaps she *had* guessed and wouldn't admit that to herself either—which was why the words had come so easily to her tongue when she had queried him.

Why he was unfaithful was what bothered her most. Surely, if the only thing that bound them together was their mutual passion for each other's bodies, then shouldn't that tie him to her exclusively? Or was it because she was barren, at least for him? Morgan shook her head to dispel the disturbing thoughts.

The children came home at the end of October. To Morgan's surprise, Richard displayed little interest in their arrival. The change in his attitude caused her relief, but it was soon replaced by anxiety. Was he plotting something else? Was a new plan in the wind? But he revealed nothing to her and she did not pry.

Nan and Harry Seymour arrived at court on December tenth. They greeted Morgan warmly but managed tactfully to avoid Richard. Nan was expecting her fifth child in the spring and already appeared quite large. She laughed when Morgan suggested another set of twins and even Harry shook his head in mock horror.

The three of them sat comfortably together in the gallery. Morgan forgot about her worries for a while as Harry told of visiting Faux Hall on his way to London. The three of them laughed again over Morgan's encounter with the "ghost." They had just stifled their last chuckles when Kate Willoughby came running up to them.

"Have you heard?" she asked breathlessly. "Surrey has been arrested for treason!"

Nan and Will stared at Kate, and Morgan gasped, her heart beating much too fast. "What did he do?" she finally managed to ask.

"I don't know yet. I just heard that he has been taken to the Tower." She shook her dark head. "They say more arrests will follow—mayhap even the Duke of Norfolk himself!"

Morgan sat back on the window seat, her terror mounting. If the King went so far as to arrest his old comrade-in-arms, Norfolk, then no one was safe.

Morgan rubbed fretfully at her forehead. "Jesu, where will all this madness end?" She saw Nan and Harry exchange conspiratorial glances and was puzzled. Then Nan nodded almost imperceptibly and Harry stood up, touching Morgan's sable oversleeve.

"I think we ought to tell Richard," Harry said mildly. "Isn't he quite the one for the latest news of the court?"

Morgan was still perplexed, but she stood up, too. "Of course, though I'm not sure where he is." Pray God not with any of the Howards, she thought, and let Harry lead her from the gallery after he'd insisted that Nan needn't trouble herself to come along, and that she and Kate Willoughby should take their ease and mull over this most recent shocking occurrence.

But Harry did not head for Morgan's quarters. Instead, he guided Morgan into an empty antechamber just off the gallery. Once the door was closed, he turned to her and made a wry face. "You know how little I like politics," he said with a self-deprecating laugh. "But they can't be avoided when you come to court." He cleared his throat and shifted his weight from one foot to the other. "I'd—we—hoped you wouldn't have to find out, but now that Surrey has been arrested, Nan and I can't remain silent."

"What is it?" Morgan demanded in a voice sharpened by fear.

Harry had the same candor as Tom. His words came out in a blunt, factual manner: "Richard is deeply implicated in this plot with Surrey and Norfolk. You realize that I, as a Seymour, as well as Tom and Ned, would be the last to find out exactly what they have in mind. But your husband and the others have been conspiring to make Mary Howard the King's mistress. They also want to use her to unite our families through a marriage with Tom."

Morgan felt dizzy. She moved slowly to a leather-covered bench and sat down. "Putting Mary into the King's bed smacks of . . . treason," she said at last, and the final word came out in a whisper.

Harry sighed and nodded solemnly. "That and other things, since Mary is the King's bastard son's widow. As for marrying Tom, that idea was put forth years ago and nothing came of it. Nor would Tom consider such an alliance at all."

Thank God for *that*, Morgan thought fleetingly, and cursed the Howards and their women, who constantly seemed to be aspiring to the royal bedchamber, with or without benefit of holy matrimony.

Morgan forced herself to stand up. She looked at Harry and took a deep breath. "I must find Richard. They'll arrest him, I'm sure of it." She started toward the door, but turned back to brush Harry's cheek with her lips. "God bless you for telling me. There are some families who would never break silence when their own interests were involved. I'm so grateful the Seymours aren't like that."

The wry expression was on his face once more. "I'd be proud to think you are right, Morgan. But we Seymours are not all alike." He saw her staring at him and gave her shoulder a gentle nudge. "Go to your Richard. And never reveal where you learned of these dangerous designs."

There had been no bravado, no mockery, no argument when Morgan told Richard about Surrey. Within the hour he was packed, saddled up, and ready to ride to Belford. "You must go north," Morgan had asserted. "We can say an emergency summoned you to take care of my property."

Sighing with relief, Morgan watched him from the bedchamber window as he rode out of Whitehall and into the streets of London. Then she thanked God that the warning from Harry Seymour had been in time.

Norfolk was arrested later that same day. The charges not only involved trying to put Mary Howard in the King's bed, but the Howards' presumptuous use of the arms of England on their family shield. Such royal pretensions,

Henry felt, must be snuffed out at once, regardless of his longtime friendship with Norfolk or the services rendered by Surrey.

Nan brought the news to Morgan late that evening. "Do you think the King will put them to death?" Morgan asked.

Nan didn't know. Nor did she inquire after Richard's whereabouts. "You still look tired," she told Morgan. "You had best get a good night's sleep."

Morgan agreed and Nan left her, heading for her temporary quarters at the other end of the palace. Morgan checked first on the children, who were sleeping quietly in the nursery with a snoring Agnes, then returned to the bedchamber and fell into a restless slumber.

The room was still dark when Morgan was awakened by a rap on the outer door. She sat up with a start, at first not recalling the events of the previous day. She looked down at Richard's side of the bed and its emptiness stirred her memory. The knocking sounded again and she leaped out of bed, picked up her night-robe, and went to the door.

"Who is it?" she asked breathlessly.

"It is I, Ned," the deep voice responded.

Tremulously, Morgan unlatched the door. Ned stood before her, a velvet cap with an osprey feather held in his hands and two King's Men behind him.

"Where is Richard?" he inquired, the dark brows closing together.

Morgan looked past Ned to the King's Men. They were armed. One held a torch, which cast a glittering orange light into the room. Blinking in the unaccustomed brightness, Morgan summoned up her shaky playacting skills.

"He is not here, my lord. He left for Belford yesterday."

Ned scowled. Morgan could feel his shrewd eyes piercing through her defenses. He motioned for the men to stay in the corridor as he stepped inside the room and closed the door.

"Why did he leave?" he queried, wishing that Tom had been sent instead. Tom knew Morgan so well, he could read her thoughts.

Morgan busied herself with a taper, glad for an excuse not to meet Ned's penetrating gaze. "Some problems arose there with my properties and we thought it best not to bother Francis," Morgan answered casually. She set the taper down on a table and turned back to Ned, her courage somewhat fortified. "What's going on, Ned?"

Ned sat down wearily in an armchair and Morgan seated herself opposite him. "I'm not sure how much you know," he said candidly, "or even how much Richard knows. But I am well aware that I can't send men after him in the snow."

Morgan opened her mouth in feigned amazement. She kept her hands tucked into her robe, lest he see how they shook. "Were you going to arrest him?"

"Aye." Ned nodded, his hand rubbing his dark, forked beard. "Mayhap it is just as well that he is not here. We have those we want most."

"We?" asked Morgan, with a tinge of sarcasm.

Ned was momentarily flustered. "I refer to the King and his loyal supporters. I hope your husband has not done something foolish." He stood up but made no move to leave. "Hear me, Morgan. Richard may be spared this time, but tell him—and this might as well come from the King's lips as mine—that if he ever intrigues or meddles again to the detriment of the royal person, his next journey will be not to Belford but to the block."

Unsure of how far she could commit herself, Morgan answered simply, "I will tell him, Ned. You have my word."

A glimmer of a smile touched Ned's mouth. "Very well." He bowed. "I'm sorry to have disturbed your sleep, Morgan."

Morgan waited a full week before writing to Richard at Belford. She phrased her letter in careful, innocuous wording, lest it be intercepted between London and Northumberland. She would leave the decision about Richard's return up to him.

The Christmas holidays seemed markedly cheerless. But Morgan put on a gay front for the children and celebrated with Nan and Harry and their brood. On Twelfth Night a great ball was held at Whitehall. Henry watched from the dais, seldom smiling, his gross body looking like a pitiful, dilapidated ruin. As Morgan changed partners, she gave him a compassionate look, then turned away quickly before he could notice her expression. She reached out for the hand of her new partner. It was Tom Seymour.

Morgan was startled into a misstep. Except for his brief

greeting upon her return to court, it was the first time they had touched since their parting at Belford. Somehow, by chance or by design, they had never even danced together.

He had seen her approaching and was prepared. "You are as fair as ever," he said lightly, "if somewhat preoccupied."

"I was thinking of the King," she answered, forcing her voice to keep steady.

"You don't have to play the nervous maid with me, Morgan," he said in a low voice. "We have talked—and touched —before this."

"I know." She also knew their encounter would be brief; there was something she was compelled to say. "Thank you, Tom—for seeing that Richard was spared."

He tried to look surprised, but it was unconvincing. "I know you must have talked to Ned before he came that night," she went on, "and I wanted to express my gratitude."

They made their final turn together. "I have never been a man to wallow in regret, but I remember what we had together. Fate may have treated us unkindly, but by God's blood, I hope we will never treat each other so." And though he smiled, there was a strange, far-off light in his blue eyes. Tom released her hand as she stepped forward to take up the dance with Will Herbert.

The next day Surrey and Norfolk were both indicted for treason. A few days later at Guildhall, Surrey was tried and convicted. He was sentenced to be beheaded on Tower Hill. His father's trial dragged on.

At noon on January twenty-seventh, Richard rode into Whitehall. It was a cold, bleak winter day with the wind whipping up from the Thames. But if it was dreary outside, it was gloomier yet within the palace. By now, everyone from the Queen to the lowliest groom knew that the King was dying.

After a somewhat perfunctory embrace, Morgan told Richard about their sovereign's condition. "He is deathly ill, though it is said he will not admit it."

Richard sat down beside the fire to pull off his boots. He had ridden all the way down from Sheffield that morning and was very weary. He stared at the darting flames for a long while before he spoke: "I should be relieved, mayhap, but I am not," he said somberly. "For all his faults, Henry was a good ruler. If—when—he dies, I fear for England, for I know who will grab first for power. Edward is so young. A protector must govern in his stead."

Morgan knew, too; indeed, everyone knew how Ned and Tom Seymour, and Dudley as well, could hardly wait to take the reins out of Henry's dying hands. She took the opportunity to give Richard the warning that Ned had ordered her to deliver. He listened quietly, but only shrugged when she was done.

"We will see what happens now, how long England will be happy with Seymours and Dudleys in the saddle." He stood up and came to her side, his arm slipping around her waist, his fingers caressing her breast. "We'll worry no more about politics," he said with a change of tone. "I've been too long out of your arms."

Morgan looked closely into the green eyes, trying to plumb the depths of her husband's emotions. Despite the weariness, there was an unmistakable spark of desire, and the fingers that pulled at the fabric of her gown were urgent. But for the first time since she and Richard had been married, Morgan felt no responding chord, not even when his mouth crushed hers in a demanding kiss. She did not resist him, however, and when he picked her up in his arms and carried her to their bed, she forced herself to match his enthusiastic, sensuous passion. And when he finally possessed her, she was both relieved and surprised to discover that she had found fulfillment in his embrace.

That evening, Richard and Morgan joined the other courtiers in the long gallery to keep the death vigil. Shortly before midnight Will Herbert brought the news that Archbishop Cranmer had arrived from Croydon. He was with the King, but Henry could no longer speak. Though the hour was late, no one ventured to leave the gallery. Ned Seymour appeared at intervals to exchange a hurried word with Tom or Dudley or Paget. Ned had already assumed an air of authority, even while Henry still lived. A few of the courtiers eyed him with open distaste and made sniggering remarks behind their hands. But they knew that by morning, perhaps within the hour, Ned Seymour would command new deference as the uncle of a King.

"Vulture," said Richard bitingly, as Ned went past them and out of the gallery. Morgan looked at her husband warningly but said nothing.

It was two in the morning. Morgan dozed on the window seat, her head on Richard's shoulder. William Paget came back into the gallery. One look at his grave face told the courtiers what they had to know.

"The King is dead," said Paget. "Long live the King!"

Chapter 24

AS A DARK JANUARY DAWN broke over England to welcome the new reign, Ned Seymour rode rapidly to Hatfield to tell nine-year-old Edward that he was now King. Whitehall was plunged into mourning, with preparations made for the removal of Henry's body to Windsor, where he would be buried in the chapel next to Jane Seymour—the only Queen to give him a son.

His people, many of whom could not remember a time when he hadn't been their King, mourned him not just from a sense of loss, but because their new sovereign was only a child. England had been safe from civil strife while Henry ruled; with a boy King on the throne and a council in charge, the country's future was uncertain. Henry's awesome will, his quest for material security for his people, his assertion of England's power in Europe, and his mere physical presence had given the English a sense of pride in themselves and their country. His arrogance, his enormous ego, his terrorism directed at those who defied him, even the break with the Church of Rome were now overlooked by the majority of the people because he had brought them peace and prosperity. As the old reign ended and the new reign began, a sense of uneasiness crept over England.

Two days after the funeral, Ned rode back into London with the boy King at his side. Fair, sickly Edward raised his small hand to his subjects as they cheered him on his way. Ned looked satisfied, even smug. He was now lord protector of England.

If Henry's death had put power into Ned's patient if eager hands, it had also saved Norfolk's life. Condemned to die on January twenty-eighth, the old Duke had managed to miss the block by hours.

After Edward's coronation, Richard seemed content to watch the new council members struggle among themselves for supremacy. He seldom mentioned politics though one of his remarks evoked an uneasy response from Morgan.

"I think our new Duke," he said one night at supper in their chambers, referring to Ned's self-requested title of Duke of Somerset, "has made his brother unhappy."

"How so?" queried Morgan, passing her plate to Polly for more meat.

"I fear Tom is angry because Ned did not share the protectorate with him. In fact, I hear the entire council is upset because they did not each get an equal measure of power."

"Once things are settled, mayhap such discontentedness will disappear," Morgan replied, and hoped it would be so. After all, she reasoned, Tom had done very well for himself. He was not only lord admiral, but Baron Seymour of Sudeley. There was even a rumor that he had asked the council for permission to marry the Princess Elizabeth, though Morgan discounted this as absurd. But Cat—did he still care for her? Would he be reckless enough to seek her hand now that she was a royal widow?

Morgan tried not to think about Tom's rumored intrigues. As for Richard, his only apparent interest these days was the purchase of a house in Chelsea. For some time now, Morgan had tried to convince him they should buy a place of their own where they could have more privacy. She also felt that the move would lessen her husband's opportunities for plotting and give them a more settled life. She had brought the subject up again shortly after Henry's death, since she was no longer required to attend Cat Parr, who had moved to Chelsea.

Richard agreed at last and in mid-March they moved into their new home. It was small by the standards of Belford or even Faux Hall, but recently built and very comfortable. Morgan set about decorating and furnishing the rooms.

The proximity of Cat Parr, only a half mile away, permitted the Dowager Queen and Morgan to exchange frequent visits. As spring warmed into summer, Morgan noted that Cat was increasingly excitable, almost exhilarated. Though Cat tried to act natural, Morgan knew her sufficiently well to pick up the nuances of anticipation and excitement.

It was on a stifling July day that Morgan found out the cause for Cat's state of mind. Morgan had gone to pay her a visit before leaving for Wolf Hall with the children. Nan had given birth to another boy in April—dutifully naming him Edward in honor of both the King and his protector—but had been slow to recover. The two women decided it would be more convenient for Morgan to visit Wolf Hall than for Nan to attempt the hot, fatiguing journey to the city.

"I'll be gone a month or so," Morgan told Cat, who was offering her some sweetmeats on a tray. Morgan took one and rolled it around on her tongue. "I don't think Richard will join us, though—you know how he is about any kind of Seymour."

Cat dimpled delightfully, her cheeks pink as a kitten's paws. "Oh, Morgan, I shouldn't say this, but since you mention the name yourself—and since you will be gone when we make the announcement—I will tell you now."

Morgan swallowed the sweetmeat so fast that she choked. She already knew what Cat was going to say. Cat rushed up to pat her on the back, but Morgan had recovered.

Cat stood by Morgan's chair and beamed. "Tom and I are wed—we have been since May."

"You have wed *already?*" Morgan was shocked. She stared at Cat, who glowed like a first-time bride.

"Oh, I grant it may seem hasty to some," Cat said quickly, "but we have written to the King and I am sure he will be pleased that his uncle and stepmother are married. You mustn't say anything until the announcement is official, but I wanted you to know before you left London."

He *had* waited, Morgan thought dully. Waited four years for Cat Parr, waited patiently for the Queen when he had not waited for her.

"What is it, Morgan? Do you think we acted wrongly?" Cat asked in an anxious voice.

Morgan forced a smile. "No, no, you deserve much happiness, Cat. And I am very happy for you. Truly I am." She rose and kissed the other woman's smooth cheek. "I wish you both well. Always."

* * *

Morgan said nothing to Nan about Cat and Tom's marriage, but by August, word had reached Wolf Hall. Nan made no comment, but Harry was outspoken about Tom's rash marriage.

"That brother of mine will go too far some day," he said, shaking his head. "And Ned, too. I dislike the depths of their intrigues."

Morgan, Nan and Harry were seated outside the manor house in the shade of two big oak trees. Nearby, the children played boisterously. Nan pulled a face at her husband. "You think you could convince those two mulish brothers of yours to act otherwise?"

Harry tugged up a handful of grass and studied it thoughtfully. "No, I won't even try. It wouldn't be so bad if they could at least agree between themselves."

Nan stretched out her long legs and yawned. "Well, I'll not worry about them any more than I ever have." She turned to Morgan. "Are the Princess Elizabeth and Lady Jane Grey still living with Cat and Tom?"

Morgan nodded. "They both consider Cat a second mother. And she treats them like her own dear daughters. It's a happy arrangement, since Cat never had children of her own."

But Harry disagreed. "They should not be living with Cat and Tom," he said determinedly. "Ned doesn't approve either."

"They have to live someplace," Morgan retorted. "It's better than having Elizabeth stuck away at Hatfield or Enfield as she was for so many years."

Harry started to reply but Nan held up both hands. "No more wrangling! This is getting to sound like Whitehall," she declared firmly. Dutifully, Harry changed the subject.

The subject was not abandoned so easily in other quarters, however. Behind bejeweled hands, across the supper table, between silken pillows, the whispers grew: The Princess Elizabeth was infatuated with her stepfather. He had made advances. He had come into her bedroom in his dressing gown. She blushed and stammered whenever his name was mentioned.

Richard brought the rumors to Morgan, repeating them with a malicious smirk. She dismissed his words with a sharp laugh. "Stories like that are bound to crop up with a fourteen-year-old girl under the same roof as a newly married couple. Especially," she added slowly, "when the husband has a reputation with women such as Tom Seymour's."

Richard appeared to be closely examining his favorite tennis racquet, which he had decided needed restringing. "Oh, I don't know. Such stories are not circulated about Jane Grey. Yet she also remains under Seymour's roof."

"Jane is different," Morgan countered. "She's such a quiet little thing, a genuine scholar." Bending down to pick up her favorite cat, Erasmus, she added, "You are merely envious because Tom has both chicks in his coop, Richard."

"So you think I'm thwarted in my plans for Robbie then?" He gave the racquet a couple of experimental swings, one of them coming dangerously close to Morgan's head.

"Take care!" She moved a few steps out of range, the big cat cradled in her arms. "I had assumed you'd abandoned such folly."

Richard eyed his wife thoughtfully but said nothing.

There was a somber note about the court that fall and winter. Morgan and Richard spent little time in any of the royal establishments, preferring to give small parties at home. Their guests came readily, glad to take leave of a court where a ten-year-old boy presided under the rigid influence of his self-righteous uncle.

One of the Griffins' visitors in the New Year was Francis Sinclair, down from Woodstock to make an appeal to King Edward and Ned for their continuing support of Oxford. Francis had been elated when the late King had finally founded two new colleges shortly before his death —Christ Church at Oxford and Trinity at Cambridge. Francis was further pleased when Ned had agreed to maintain the universities as long as they remained free of what he considered "insidious Papist teachings."

"Ned would guard our souls as well as our government," Francis commented dryly as he recounted his exchange with the lord protector.

It was the first real meeting in almost fifteen years between Morgan's former brother-in-law and her husband. They treated each other politely but it was plain that their differences were greater than their similarities, and that neither really approved of the other. Francis, sensing the lack of warmth beneath Richard's hospitality, said he would only stay for the day. He spent much of it with the children, and Morgan was pleased to see how quickly all four of them became reacquainted. She noted that Robbie in particular seemed delighted to visit with Francis. But perhaps that was because he was the eldest, and not because he had any instinctive filial feeling for the man he called his uncle.

After the youngsters were put to bed, the three grownups shared a late supper in the private dining room Morgan had furnished in varying shades of blue. "Ned wants to turn us into psalm-singing Protestants like the Scots are fast becoming," said Richard, toying with his venison pasty. "He grows more austere by the week and would have the rest of us follow suit."

"The man's a fool," Francis asserted, spearing half a pullet from the sideboard as Richard eyed him with distaste. "Any man who seeks unlimited power is unbalanced, as far as I'm concerned."

Richard's lips pressed tightly together and a deep crease appeared between his brows. Morgan feared he would say something rude to Francis so she quickly intervened: "Don't fill up completely with this course, Francis. There's blancmange and cheese still to come."

Francis regarded Morgan with amusement. "Eating blancmange is like eating a thick fog. I prefer something with more substance."

Morgan swung a rabbit haunch in Francis's direction. "Really, you can say the most tactless things to your hostess! I had it made specially—you used to eat tubs of it at Belford."

"I did that to please Lucy. I've never touched it since."

"Hunh. I never thought you did anything to please anyone—except yourself."

"I don't, very often. But occasionally I have a lapse." Francis polished off the pullet and pushed his chair back, sighing extravagantly and easing his long legs out so far that his boots appeared on the other side of the table.

Richard had risen. "One thing I'll wager you can't resist is a bottle of French wine I have secreted down in the cellar. Only I know where it is hidden, so if you'll both excuse me?"

Morgan said, "Of course," and Francis gave an indolent nod. After Richard was out of earshot, Francis began to laugh in a low rumble.

"I swear, Morgan, your Richard expects me to grind the meat bones beneath my heel into the carpets and clean the plates with my tongue."

She lifted her chin and threw him a mocking, humorous glance. "Well?"

He snorted, but his mouth turned up in amusement. "Am I always to be the rude country knave in your eyes then, too?" he asked, and there was an unexpected seriousness in his voice.

Morgan sat with her elbows on the table, rubbing the place between her brows and shaking her head. "Oh, Francis, you are—just you—and it's occurred to me that you may be the only true gentleman I know." She let her hands drop and eyed him intently, almost as if seeing him for the first time. Morgan gave him a faint smile, then lowered the thick lashes and stared at her wedding ring.

Francis shifted in his chair, which seemed to teeter dangerously under his weight. "Hmmm. That sounds like a grudging compliment." When she did not respond or look up, he placed both palms on the edge of the table and studied his own hands carefully before he spoke again: "Don't tell me you have finally tired of the courtier's life and the dashing Richard?"

As ever, Francis's candor put Morgan off. Yet she felt compelled to be honest with him, felt a need to reveal her own deepest thoughts. But before she could speak, Richard was bounding into the room, brandishing a dusty, dark bottle in one hand.

"A treasure, this one," he glowed, setting the bottle down on the table in front of Francis and Morgan. "I managed to wheedle an entire case out of a niggardly Frenchman when I was in Boulogne. This is the last of it, so we must savor each drop."

"Indeed," said Francis in a subdued voice, and the quizzical glance he gave her made Morgan feel suddenly sad and empty as she watched her husband fill the wine goblets and propose a toast to better days.

* * *

Cat Parr carefully folded Morgan's embroidered cape over her arm. "What a dreary day," she complained. "It always seems twice as gloomy when it rains in the summer."

Morgan smiled. "You feel discomfort because of the babe's weight."

Cat beamed. She was pregnant at last, soon to bear the child of the man she loved. Though she grumbled about the weather, her splendid happiness showed clearly in her eyes. "True enough," conceded Cat, settling her bulk into a chair by the window. "But I will be out of the city in a few days. Tom wants the babe born at Sudeley Castle. We leave next week."

"That is well," Morgan replied, and was relieved to think that she felt no envy toward Cat for bearing Tom a child. Better for Cat to give him a legitimate heir than for Morgan to have borne him a bastard. Somehow, it seemed so easy to rationalize the sorrows and misdeeds of the past.

"How is Elizabeth?" Morgan asked, and was surprised to see Cat flush slightly.

"I have a letter from her which arrived this morning," Cat answered, the flush fading. "She is sickly at the moment but says it is only a passing indisposition."

Morgan nodded sympathetically, deciding to move on to another topic. Elizabeth was at Cheshunt, having left the Dowager Queen's household in May. Sent away, the rumors ran, after being found in Tom's arms one morning by Cat Parr. Again, Morgan preferred to discount the whispers as malicious, politically inspired gossip.

They were discussing names for the prospective baby when Tom came in. He kissed Cat's cheek tenderly and bowed to Morgan. His manner toward her these days was friendly, if not the same open expansiveness he had displayed in years gone by.

"And how is the future father?" Morgan inquired with a bright smile.

To her surprise, Tom frowned. "I would be happier if I had not just heard certain reports," he said.

Both Morgan and Cat looked questioningly at him. "What reports?" queried Morgan.

Tom shook out his wet cloak and hung it on a peg. "Mind you, I would not mention this if we were not old friends," he began, "but I have heard that your husband is meddling again, this time in a plot to wed Robbie to Jane Grey."

Morgan laughed aloud, but the sound was hollow. "Oh, that! Why, he mentioned it once to me himself, but it was—well, a long time ago! I was sure he'd forgotten all about it."

Tom turned on her sharply. "He has not forgotten. He has never forgotten. He knows that some people favor Jane as heiress to the throne. Even now he is getting efforts under way to convince the Greys that they should remove Jane from this household and take her back with them." He pounded his fist so hard that the table legs trembled. "I will not have it! He was warned about his intrigues, he damned near went to the Tower because of them, and yet he will not give up. This time he goes too far!"

Morgan could not reply. She was too shaken, for she knew Tom was right. Her earlier suspicions were justified.

Cat had gotten up and gone to her husband's side. "Becalm yourself, sweet Tom. Your temper upsets me so!"

He smiled down at her and patted her bottom. "I apologize to you—and to Morgan. But," he said, turning toward Morgan, "I am warning him through you. He must cease his plotting at once." He helped Cat back to her chair and sat down between the two women. His single gold earring glinted as he looked first at Cat and then at Morgan. "Now," he said, his usual good humor surfacing once more in the blue eyes, "let's talk of more pleasant matters."

Richard was before his mirror, fretting at his image. "That fool of a barber! See how close he cut my hair! Or am I getting . . ." He paused at the fearful word. *"Bald?"*

In any other circumstances, Morgan would have laughed and hugged him in doubtful reassurance. Richard *was* beginning to lose his hair, but that was a minor tragedy compared with what faced her now. She had just returned from her visit with Cat and Tom. Her temper and her fear had both mounted as she made the short journey home through the rain.

"I warned you, Richard, not to meddle with my children," she said in a barely controlled voice. He turned from the mirror, his face suddenly white under his tan. Morgan didn't wait for his reply. "Robbie is *my* son. He will choose his own bride. I'll not see him forced into a marriage as I was with James. If anyone besides me has any say in this matter, it will be Francis."

"Francis!" Richard exploded. "What right does your ex-brother-in-law have to have a say about my stepson?"

Morgan angrily brushed the raindrops from her velvet hood and wondered vaguely why she'd worn it in the damp weather in the first place. "He *is* Robbie's godfather," she replied defensively, and wished she had not mentioned Francis's name at all.

Quickly, Richard calculated how to handle his obstinate wife. He decided on a firm stand. "You are married to me," he said calmly. "The husband rules in all matters. Surely you understand that?"

They were on the brink of a serious, perhaps disastrous quarrel. Morgan had hoped this moment would never come, but she was prepared. She stared at the floor, then spoke very quietly: "So. If you persist in this matter, I will have no choice but to take the children and go away. I will leave you, Richard, before I see you involve Robbie in what is bound to become a dangerous, even a deadly situation. I will do this as much to save you as him."

They looked straight at each other for a long time, and both became aware of something ugly in the other's eyes. "I will not let you go," Richard breathed at last.

"You cannot stop me," Morgan said, just as softly. "If you try, I will go to Ned and tell him." She started for the door to summon Polly. Richard reached for her arm, but she ducked away. He advanced again, trapping her between a table and the wall.

"You will not go!" The threat was naked in his voice, though the tone was still low.

Something shiny next to the fruit bowl on the table caught Morgan's eye. It was a small but very sharp knife for paring apples. She snatched it up and held it out before her. "I will," she said evenly, and Richard drew back, his eyes incredulous. He could take the knife from her easily, but he would have lost the battle. It was the war that was not over, and they both knew it. He looked at Morgan long and hard, and the first hint of hate glinted in his eyes. "We are not done yet," he said, and strode rapidly from the room.

The next morning, under a warm July sun, Morgan, the

children, and some of the servants set out for Wolf Hall. Nan and Harry were surprised to see Morgan but even more astonished to hear her tale. She swore them to willing secrecy. They were equally upset over Richard's plot, and Harry was frank to admit his deep concern.

"This is a shocking thing," he said. "That Grey child will be the death of someone one of these days, mark my words."

Tired and distraught, Morgan could only nod numbly in agreement.

It wasn't until she had had two nights of deep sleep that the enormity of what she had done struck Morgan. The breach in her marriage seemed too deep to mend; hatred had come too close to the surface for both of them. And though their mutual passion had taken them to soaring heights of physical joy, it had also brought them to the depths of disaster. There had been much lust between them but never any love, and without love there could be no forgiveness.

"I have failed at two marriages," Morgan said despondently to Nan. "Is it ill fortune that dogs me or is it something within myself?"

Nan, unphilosophical but eminently practical, gave a short laugh. "You married the wrong men, that's all. The first time, it was not your doing, but the second was. You should have used better judgment, if you want my opinion. Which you probably don't," Nan added.

Morgan couldn't help but smile at Nan. "It's easy for you to speak like that. You and Harry have always been so happy."

"We loved each other when we wed. We still do," said Nan. "Why shouldn't it be easy to be happy when you love? I don't give a whit about marriages of convenience or politically motivated unions. They breed more than aristocratic children—they also breed adultery and intrigue and hatred. That's not right; it's not what God intended." She had become unusually heated, her black eyes snapping with the passion of her convictions.

Morgan smiled wryly. "You should have spoken thus to Uncle Thomas and my parents a long time ago."

Nan rearranged the cushion behind her back. "But I didn't know—then."

* * *

The warm, drowsy days of summer drifted by at Wolf Hall. Eating a picnic lunch in a meadow of clover or riding out through the shady Wiltshire woods, Morgan could almost forget about Richard and the bitterness his image brought to mind. Still, at night, she would turn in her sleep and put out a searching arm before she realized he was no longer at her side. The slow, painful realization would overcome her, but she would thrust her heartache aside and try to sleep again.

Morgan knew she would have to start making plans for the future. She could not impose forever on Nan and Harry. Faux Hall was both too close to Richard and, at the same time, too far from court. She lingered over the thought of Belford, surprised that she would even think of returning there. No, she could not—would not—go back to Belford alone, not after all that had happened within its walls.

She sighed, convinced that she would never feel at home anywhere again. Trying not to dwell on the empty void of the future, she glanced at the pages of the book she had hardly begun to read, but immediately was distracted. A rider was coming up the road into Wolf Hall: It was Tom.

She stood up, shaking the loose grass from her skirts. "Tom!" she called. "Welcome!"

His horse was lathered and his own face damp with perspiration. His blue eyes looked tired and empty; there were new lines etched around his mouth. Morgan stared at him as he dismounted without even greeting her.

"Tom! What is it?"

He looked at her dully. "You have not heard?" he asked as Nan and Harry came running out to meet him. He looked at all of them, his dark face unnaturally pale. "Cat is dead."

The others gasped in shock. Harry went forward, his arm going around his brother's shoulders. "God help you, Tom," he said in a shaking voice.

Finally, when they had led Tom into the house and brought him food which he scarcely touched and wine which he only sipped at, the whole story came out. In the last week of August, a daughter had been born to them. Cat seemed to rally from her labor at first, but by the next day she was suffering from fever. "Like Jane's, after Edward was born," Tom said.

Cat's mind began to wander in delirium. Five days later she was dead. Tom had her buried in the chapel at Sudeley Castle as Jane Grey wept big, silent tears over the Dowager Queen's tomb.

"Why didn't you send word to us?" Nan asked, clutching Tom's hand tightly in her own.

"I could think of nothing but her loss," he replied quietly.

"What of the babe?" Morgan inquired.

Tom told them that the child did well, and was being cared for by Cat's sister, Anne Herbert. "And now, as if my troubles were not enough, the Greys want to take Jane from my household," he complained.

Morgan threw him an inquiring glance. He noticed it and for the first time the flicker of a smile came to his face. "Yes, I daresay that Richard is involved. But I'll win the day yet. I intend to promise the Greys marriage between Jane and the King."

Harry raised his eyebrow in the manner he had in common with Tom and Ned. "On what authority do you make that offer, good brother?"

"My own," said Tom shortly, and Harry, out of respect for Tom's grief, was silent.

Tom agreed to stay the night. He slept in the room next to Morgan's, and she could hear him tossing and turning restlessly in his bed. She was almost asleep when other noises came to her ears. Men's voices, heavy footsteps, a commotion belowstairs. She was putting on her slippers and night-robe when she heard Nan call her name.

"Morgan, can you come out?"

Morgan opened her door quickly. She saw Nan's white face and behind her stood Richard, his sword drawn. The green eyes were hard and cold, his face rigidly determined. "I have come for Robbie, madam," he said low and fierce.

Morgan was breathing very hard, trying to think of the best way to counter Richard's intentions. Nan spoke up rapidly: "He has men here. They have Harry and the servants downstairs." She looked hard at Morgan.

Harry. The servants. Morgan's mind raced. Then Richard didn't know Tom was at Wolf Hall. Nan and Harry had shrewdly kept that fact from him. Morgan had to play for time.

She gestured toward the room. "Oh, come in, Richard, and stop acting like a child. If you intend to kidnap my son you can at least tell me where you're taking him." Her voice was more exasperated than angry.

Warily, he hesitated, then called to one of the men he had posted at the top of the stairs. "Take Mistress Seymour back to her husband," he ordered. Nan turned away and walked hurriedly down the hall to where her guard waited.

Fortunately the children were in the nursery with the Seymour brood in the other wing of the house. Morgan sat down on the bed, pondering her next move.

"Well? What do you plan to do with my son, good husband?" Sarcasm caressed each word.

Richard still held his sword unsheathed, but some of the wariness had gone out of his eyes. "Take him to be with the Lady Jane Grey, his future spouse," he replied.

Morgan stared at him. "You mean you've kidnapped the Lady Jane too?"

He smiled, the old mocking smile, but it held a new note of menace. "Not yet, dear wife, not yet. Though I must confess that's my next move."

But Morgan had a move of her own. She jumped from the bed, shouting, "You would kidnap my son and the Lady Jane, Richard Griffin! Preposterous! Sheath your sword and leave at once!"

He kept smiling. "Save your hysterics, madam. They no longer amuse me."

She advanced on him, carefully backing him in the direction of the door. "Kidnapper! Child stealer! Put that sword away! Get out! Get out!"

The smile faded fast. He brandished the sword at her. "I won't use this, Morgan, unless I must. I want no trouble from you."

"Richard Griffin, you're a monster! I won't let you take my child!" Her voice felt hoarse, her lungs weak.

He moved toward her, his face vicious. He reached out and grabbed her by the hair as the door flew open. Tom Seymour, clad in shirt and hose, charged into the room, his own sword in hand. Richard turned quickly as Morgan fell to the floor.

"Fight with men, not women," Tom shouted, lifting his sword.

"Whoreson!" snarled Richard. He lunged with his weapon, barely missing Tom's left side.

Morgan rolled out of the way and picked herself up, leaning against the wall. The blades flashed in the dim light, like silver snakes in a deadly dance. Tom thrust and nicked Richard's doublet. He thrust again, a clean miss this time. Richard wheeled back and around, parrying Tom's efforts to land a wounding blow.

The sound of swords echoed in the room, a deafening clatter in Morgan's ears. Now Richard was on the offensive, backing Tom toward the opposite wall. They were almost on top of each other as Richard brought his arm back to make a final, fatal lunge.

But in the fraction of a second as Richard sought sure balance, Tom's knee came up, hard and punishing, into his opponent's groin. Richard fell backwards, his head crashing onto the stone hearth.

Morgan could not move. As if from another world, she watched Tom bend over Richard's motionless body. Something red and wet was spreading across the gray stones and into the edge of the rug. Tom straightened up.

"He's dead." He threw his own sword on the floor and wiped the sweat from his face with his sleeve.

Slowly, her legs heavy and unsteady, Morgan moved across the room. She dropped to her knees beside Richard and lifted his limp, lifeless hand in hers. She looked up at Tom, who was regarding her with sad, pitying eyes.

"Did I do this to him?" she asked hoarsely.

Tom put his hand in her hair. "No, muffet," he answered. "He did it to himself."

Chapter 25

ONCE MORE ATTIRED in the black folds of mourning, Morgan accompanied Richard's body back to London. Tom, Nan, and Harry rode with her. The children stayed behind at Wolf Hall.

In the aftermath of Richard's death, Tom had gone down to confront his adversary's men. He had warned them that unless they left the house at once and in peace, they could all expect to die by royal command. Recognizing Tom, and devoid of courage without their leader, the men plodded out of Wolf Hall and rode away. They had not had much stomach for the job in the first place, it seemed: Nan told Morgan she had heard one of them muttering, "Child stealing's not a man's work anyway," as he went out the door.

Whatever the men believed was of no importance to either Tom or Morgan. To the rest of the world it would be announced as an accident, suffered in a fall. In essence that was the truth, and further details would only besmirch Richard's memory and add fuel to the fires of gossip surrounding Tom.

Morgan was stricken more with guilt than sorrow over Richard's death. As with James, she kept asking herself if there had not been some point at which she could have turned the tide of their marriage and saved him from his fate. She cursed herself over and over, wondering if she were bewitched, like her namesake, Morgan le Fay. Two marriages without love; two husbands lost in violence and enmity. Twice she'd been forced to rescue her children from the clutches of her mates; twice she had lost the men she was sure she should have wed. "You just married the wrong men—that's all," Nan had said, and had made it sound so simple. Maybe it was. But fate had not given Morgan simple choices. It seemed to her that she had been given none at all, that her destiny had been designed by others. Now, however, she seemed to be free to make her own choices. She had thought she'd been free before when James died. But it was not so; she'd still been tied to Tom, and Richard had only been an illusion.

But Nan didn't try to hide her disapproval about selling the house in Chelsea. "I think you're daft. You've finally got it decorated and fixed up the way you wanted it. It's a charming house."

"Charming—and empty," Morgan replied with finality. Like Richard himself, she added to herself. Nan agreed to keep the children at Wolf Hall while Morgan stayed in London to settle Richard's affairs.

Morgan arrived at Wolf Hall during a swirling snowstorm. The flakes fell so thick and fast that she could not even see the house until she was directly in front of it. She ran to the door as the servants struggled with the baggage cart.

Nan and the children were hanging holly wreaths in the entrance hall. "I never thought you would try to get through in this," Nan exclaimed as she kissed her cousin's cold cheek.

The children clamored around their mother, little Anne hugging her tight. She surveyed them with a loving smile. They had never been separated for this long. "I swear you have grown a foot in these three months," Morgan told Robbie as she tousled his fair hair. He would be thirteen on his next birthday and already she was sure he would be as tall as his father.

Edmund, still the quieter of the two boys, approached Morgan somewhat shyly. "We have been making Christmas presents for you, my mother," he said. "Aunt Nan says we must save them until Twelfth Night. But I wanted you to know."

Touched, Morgan clasped him close. I have my children, she thought, and that is a great blessing.

"I brought presents, too, but some of them you may open now," she told the children. Polly brought the gifts, which she had dutifully unpacked for Morgan. The Sinclair and

Seymour children went to work tearing apart the boxes and packages as Morgan and Nan watched in amusement.

The snowstorm had stopped by Christmas Day, leaving the world around Wolf Hall under a white layer of peace. A sleigh ride followed the rich dinner, with children and adults all raising their voices in the old carols as the horses' bells jingled out over the snow.

They had just returned to the house when Tom Seymour unexpectedly rode in. He, too, was laden with gifts, and distributed them with much teasing and merriment. It was a good Christmas, with laughter and songs and spiced wine and candles glittering everywhere.

After supper, when the children had been put to bed, the four grown-ups sat around a big fire and finished off the wassail bowl. Tom announced he would leave at dawn, for he had business in London the following day.

"I must confer with our nephew, too," he said, looking at Harry. "The child is without pocket money. Ned keeps him poor to hold him in line. I intend to correct that situation."

Harry held up a warning finger. "I don't want to hear another word about politics. We've had a fine, peaceful Christmas. Let us keep it that way."

Tom raised his eyebrow at Harry and grinned. "You worry overmuch, good brother. You think I am incapable of prudence?"

Harry did not answer, but glanced out into the dark December night. "There's more snow in store for us yet. I'd wager on it."

Nan touched her husband's arm. "Tomorrow we must put out suet and crumbs for the birds. The children are afraid they won't get their Yuletide supper."

"They always do," Harry replied, smiling fondly at his wife. "In twelve years, we haven't lost a bird yet."

Morgan and Tom watched their kinfolk with a mixture of affection and envy. But they did not look at each other.

Later, as Nan and Harry were giving instructions to the servants, Morgan and Tom sat alone by the hearth. Tom finished off his last goblet of wine and stood up, stretching his arms. "It's to bed for me, Morgan. If Harry is right about the snow, I'll have to ride hard tomorrow."

Morgan stood up, too, facing Tom. "Don't go," she said suddenly in a low voice.

He stared at her, uncertain as to what she meant.

"You become too involved, Tom," she went on earnestly. "I know, I saw it happen with Richard. Stay here awhile and think it all out. Decide if your schemes are worth the price."

He laughed. "They are certainly worth the reward," he asserted. He shook his head at her. "Nay, Morgan, I know what I do. I am no fool. Do you really think that I, who enjoy life so much, would throw it away like an old cloak?" She gave no answer, and he went on more seriously. "I'm doing this for Edward's sake, for Jane's, and for Elizabeth's good, as well as for myself. Do you really think Ned is capable of understanding other people's needs and desires? He knows only one thing—how to exercise power. And that's not enough." He was grim, his eyes burning hard, like a man driven beyond caution and good sense. He reminded her of Richard and she inwardly winced at the thought of how ambition could corrupt good men.

Morgan took a step backwards. "Tom, tell me—is it true about the Lady Elizabeth? That you would wed with her?"

Tom ran a hand through his thick red hair. "God's eyes, rumors run like rats across England these days!" But he shifted his stance uncomfortably and seemed suddenly to become absorbed with a small inlaid chess piece he'd picked up from Harry's treasured mother-of-pearl and ebony board.

"You've never lied to me, Tom," Morgan persisted. "Don't start now."

He set the pawn down so recklessly that several other pieces toppled over. "She's a delightful young woman," he said defensively, with anger flickering behind his eyes. "The late King suggested we'd make a good match, so why shouldn't I court her?"

"She's scarcely more than a child! Tom, don't you see what will happen? Ned will never allow it!" She had come to stand directly before him and her hands went involuntarily to his shoulders as if she could shake sense into him.

"So Ned should have it all his way then, the way he's always tried to do with me?" The anger was no longer damped down but flaring throughout his big body. "By the Virgin, Morgan, I'm no Richard, making petty plots and blundering my way to a wretched death!"

Morgan let her hands fall to her sides. "But you are,

Tom," she said softly and with great sadness. "That's exactly what you are."

Her words stung him. As long as he had known her she had always admired him, sought his counsel, needed his help, and eventually become his mistress. Despite her obstinacy and strong will, he had always felt in command. But this was a new side of her, a more mature, perceptive woman than he had ever glimpsed before. And for a moment, he was back in time, wanting her above all other women, needing the soft body and the rich laugh and the passionate ardor which matched his own.

His arms were around her before either of them knew what was happening. "Morgan . . . Morgan . . ." His mouth was buried in her hair and his hands gripped her back as if he were hanging on to life itself. Then he was kissing her, feeling the eager response of her lips. But when he paused to pick her up in his arms, she sprang back, tears in her eyes.

"No, Tom. We can't go back. We'd be together tonight and then you'd be gone again, off wooing Elizabeth and leaving me alone and empty. I can't go through that again."

He stepped toward her but she backed farther away. "You sent me away, Morgan, don't you remember?"

"Oh, yes. I nearly died from loneliness. Tom, did you know we had a child, a babe I lost, there at Belford, all alone?"

Tom's dark, weather-beaten skin went pale. He was silent for several moments, too stunned to speak. "No . . ." he breathed at last. "No, I never guessed . . . Oh, Morgan . . ."

Morgan brushed away a tear that had found its way down her cheek. "We had so much to give each other—and the world took it away from us. We couldn't help that. I've learned to mistrust the world—and what it can do to me—and you. Don't let it destroy you, Tom. Save yourself while there's still time."

He moved toward her slowly and this time she did not back off from him. His lips touched her forehead. "I will try," he said, and his voice had a strange, choked sound. "And I will think of you. Always."

He left her then, by the window, where she stared out

with vacant eyes as the first flakes of a new snow began to fall.

The snow came down steadily for the first three weeks of January. Morgan waited restlessly for the storms to cease, as the roads were impossible for travel. She had to return to London to arrange for the transfer of her household belongings. From there, she would go with the children to Faux Hall.

"It is the only place I *can* go, at least for a while. Maybe later I may feel like buying another house in London," she told Nan, "but for now I am done with that city."

"You're welcome to stay here," Nan assured her. Morgan smiled her thanks but said she wanted a place of her own, a home where she could live her own life and raise the children in peace, as Nan herself was doing at Wolf Hall.

But even that enviable peace could be shattered. On January twenty-first Harry received a message from Ned. It was terse and shocking, though not completely unexpected.

"Tom has been arrested," Harry said shortly, crumpling the letter in his fist. "He is in the Tower."

Nan was the first to break the awful silence that followed. She rushed to her husband. "You can help him, Harry. You can plead with Ned to spare him. My God!" she cried, her hands to her head. "His own brother!"

"I can do nothing," Harry said bitterly, and threw Ned's message onto the fire. "Tom forced his hand—the council, if not Ned, would demand punishment. It is Ned and Tom's quarrel, it always was, and I can do no more to stop them now than I could to prevent this from happening in the first place." He sat down wearily, suddenly looking years older. Nan went to him, throwing herself on the floor beside him, her head in his lap, her hands clinging to his knees.

Morgan stood quietly in the middle of the room. Somehow, it had to end like this for Tom; it was inevitable. He would follow Thomas More and Anne Boleyn and Katherine Howard and Surrey and Margaret Pole and all the others to the block; she was sure of it. She walked across the room and took her cloak from the wardrobe.

"I'm going to the chapel to pray," she said. "For Tom—for all of us."

* * *

The details of Tom's arrest had poured out quickly. Little Edward had caused the final break between the Seymour brothers. Tom, possessing the keys to the young King's bedroom, had come by night to visit his nephew. But before Tom could gain entry into the bedchamber, Edward's favorite spaniel had let out a warning bark. Panicked, Tom had shot the dog to prevent further alarm, but the sound of the pistol had sent the guards running. The council, and Ned, too, feared a kidnap plot, and on January eighteenth, Tom had been arrested. John Dudley had helped draw up the charges against Tom, which included illegally storing arms, maintaining a secret army, and attempting to overthrow the protectorate.

Tom displayed as much bravado in prison as out of it. He refused to answer the charges or sign any of the articles brought before him. "They cannot kill me," he vowed, "and if they do, I cannot die but once."

Morgan heard the words from a brokenhearted Harry Seymour and left at once for London.

If Thomas Cromwell had worked in plain clothes and drab surroundings, Ned Seymour's tastes were almost as austere. The room he maintained at Whitehall as lord protector was just off the council chambers. The furnishings were solid and serviceable, the wall hangings heavy to keep out the February draughts, and the only ornamentation was a Holbein portrait of King Edward as a small child.

As Morgan sat across the desk from Ned she was reminded of those long-ago interviews with her uncle. She had argued violently with herself over the wisdom of coming to Ned, one part of her acknowledging Harry's conviction that pleas for mercy would do no good, the other part arguing that Tom had once saved her life and she owed him at least an attempt to do the same.

"Tom has requested an open trial," Morgan asserted, trying to keep any emotion out of her voice. "Surely his request is not unreasonable?"

Ned's dark brows came together in the familiar scowl. "It's not. And I would grant it if I could. But even though I am the lord protector, I can't make such decisions alone."

Ned was no longer riding his authority like an omnipotent charger. Sufficient time had passed to erode the euphoria of his early days as protector. Many on the council delighted in Tom's downfall and were wary of his popular appeal with Londoners. An open trial might produce leniency. Even Ned's wife had warned him that mercy for Tom might prove his own undoing.

"You know Tom better than any of us," Morgan pointed out. "Do you truly believe he meant treason?"

Ned sighed, his hands betraying his inner turmoil by the shredding of some discarded paper on the desk. "I don't know. I just don't know. But thirty-five counts have been drawn up against him. I see no way he can be acquitted."

"His worst crime is fraternal jealousy, it seems to me. Yet that's not included in the charges." Morgan could not control the asperity in her voice.

Ned looked uncomfortable. "It would not be seemly to make such a charge."

"Then how do you condemn a man for foolhardiness?" Morgan demanded.

Ned shook his head and gripped the edge of his desk. "Please, Morgan. You know as well as I—oh, Christ, I can do nothing to stem the inevitable!" For the first time since she had known Ned, she saw his haughty reserve crumble as he put his face into his hands.

"So." The word was soft, final. She rose from the chair and stood for a moment, looking at the anguished lord protector. Then she went out into the empty council chamber and paused at the head of the long oak table. "God help you both," she whispered into the echoes. "You will not be satisfied until you have each destroyed the other."

The Tower cannons boomed out the doleful death knell. The sound seemed to shake the walls of Whitehall, to rock the very floor on which Morgan stood. Tom was dead, almost two months to the day since his arrest, and a trembling King Edward had signed his uncle's death warrant.

Dudley strutted while Ned mourned. Princess Elizabeth remained under house arrest at Hatfield while the council probed relentlessly to implicate her in Tom's intrigues. Harry and Nan Seymour remained at Wolf Hall, overcome with grief.

My eyes are dry, Morgan thought. Have I finally used up my last reserves of grief? Sean . . . James . . . Richard . . .

and now Tom . . . all gone now, snatched away before their time by varying passions of love, hate, religion, and politics. And had any one of them left the world a better place than they had found it? No, thought Morgan, only Father Bernard, who had left her a legacy of faith.

I still cling to that, the old faith of my youth, she told herself, and with it and the children, I shall be sustained in the years to come. It would not be easy. The time had come for Morgan to bring her beliefs out of the shadows. She had to discover what she believed, not what others told her she should believe. Sean's fanaticism about the old faith had brought him death. James's ready acceptance of the new faith had left him with doubts that may have helped unhinge his mind. Richard had followed the King's dictates, but Richard would have followed anyone or anything that promised personal aggrandizement. Tom had only been concerned about religion to the extent that God gave him calm seas and favorable winds. Francis recognized the need for reform—but not for the Reformation.

And it was with Francis that Morgan found herself in agreement. A house in need of repair does not have to be demolished; a church that is flawed by its human members needs Christian concern, not kingly commands. Henry the Eighth, who had defended the Church of Rome from Martin Luther's critical attacks, had turned like a spoiled child on a stern parent and devastated the Catholic faith when the Pope would not grant his annulment from Catherine of Aragon.

Never mind, thought Morgan, as she folded a heavy damask overskirt and placed it carefully in a trunk. Never mind that the Pope had been embroiled in politics at the time or that Henry's grounds were as good if not better than others who had gotten annulments at the drop of a papal bribe. In anger and in greed, Henry had shattered and plundered the old faith, heedless of the consequences, indifferent to the souls of his subjects. Francis might put forth logical arguments by the score to prove why he kept the old faith, but Morgan needed only one reason: Henry's church belonged to Henry, and not to God.

So on the last day of March, Morgan was ready to turn her back on London and its court. There, where men killed each other for the prize of power, where they swept aside centuries of religious truth, where no one was safe from his own conscience, there she would no longer stay.

Morgan looked around the room at the piles of boxes, the heavy trunks, the sealed crates, which were ready for transport from her temporary quarters at Whitehall to Faux Hall. Agnes and Polly and Peg were getting the children ready in the next room, piling them into hoods and cloaks and boots.

Morgan turned back to the window for a last look at the Thames. It was raining, a wet, miserable morning. It would be a muddy journey but she was determined to leave London at once.

From behind her the door scraped open. Morgan remained motionless, staring out as the rain plummeted into the swelling river. There was no further sound in the room, and suddenly Morgan knew who was in the doorway. She didn't need to turn; she already knew he was there, she somehow had known all along who it would be, filling up the door as he always did, his heavy cloak flowing out behind him, his big boots planted on the stone floor.

"Hello, Francis," she said quietly, and at last turned to face him.

He had one hand raised, his arm leaning against the casement. The other was on his hip, and his uneven smile was wry. He did not bother with preliminary conversation. "Moving?" he asked.

"Obviously," she replied. There was a sudden bite in her tone.

He stepped inside the room and closed the door. "You would not mourn for a man you lost long ago, surely?"

She shook her head. "No, I have feared for some time that Tom courted death. I did my mourning before this."

Francis surveyed the luggage and boxes, his boots making wet prints on the floor as he moved idly about the room. "Where do you go?" he inquired in an almost offhand tone.

"To Faux Hall." The words were crisp, all but bitten off by Morgan, who seemed totally absorbed in putting on her kidskin riding gloves.

Francis's thick brows drew close together in feigned surprise. "Oh? I think not." He came to stand before her, his arms folded across his chest. "I don't think you're going there at all."

"Where am I going then?" she demanded, irritation quivering in her voice.

"To Belford," he answered calmly. "Where you—and I—belong."

She was stunned. "What are you talking about? Why should I go to Belford, especially with you?"

Francis seemed to be frowning at the band of velvet trim on Morgan's riding coif. "It would seem convenient for us to live together if we are going to be married."

"Married!" Morgan all but shouted the word, and it echoed back at her from the past, from an almost-forgotten day when she had said it to Francis after he had told her he was a married man. "Married," she repeated, but this time in a hushed voice. "You—and I?"

"Yes, you are beginning to show promise in applying the spoken word to the thought process," he said with a hint of amusement. "It seems quite obvious, after all. Or did you expect me to come on bended knee and lavish flowery speeches at your hem?"

She was looking up at him in amazement, her heart racing, her mind confused. "You . . . are quite serious?"

Francis was growing exasperated as well as impatient. "Certainly. I would have wed you six years ago if you hadn't flown off into that vapid Welshman's bed. I thought I behaved most decently, waiting a proper length of time after James died. And of course I couldn't be sure that you wouldn't marry Seymour if he were willing. But though Seymour was not," he went on, oblivious to the look of pain that passed across Morgan's face, "you still had to plunge headlong into disaster and marry the wrong man all over again."

She had stepped back a few paces, almost stumbling over one of the heavy trunks. "No," she said flatly. "No, no. I will not wed again. Not after all that has happened. Think, Francis—I've not done well at marriage."

He snorted loudly. "Nonsense! You're talking drivel. You were forced into one marriage and fell into the other. Besides," he said, challenging her with his gray-eyed stare, "you love me. You always have. You looked at me with love, even while your body spoke with lust. It is, after all, an ideal combination for a happy marriage."

"Marriage! Love! I don't even know what love is!" Morgan rubbed at the place between her brows with frantic gloved hands.

"Oh, yes, you do. It's making love—and loving afterwards. Do you remember talking of cows, Morgan?"

"Cows?" She blinked. "Oh—of course, after you were so horrid in the library."

He nodded, and took one gloved hand in his. "And horrid or not, you gave yourself to me—not just your body, but your thoughts, your laughter, your trust. That's love, Morgan, not some dreamy-eyed ideal or romantic passion."

Morgan felt his fingers tighten on hers; she was very agitated and her gaze moved haphazardly around the room. Grandmother Isabeau had told her she might not know love when it came. And she hadn't, not until she had confronted Francis in the attic at Faux Hall, and even then she had fought the discovery—and hidden it from herself. But why? she asked again as she had then. Because he had never declared his love for her? Morgan stopped the restless, wandering glances and looked directly up at Francis. "And you?" She finally dared give the words life. "Do you love me?"

The gray eyes flickered almost imperceptibly, and for the briefest instant Francis's face softened into a vulnerability Morgan had never seen before. The sudden change jolted her to the very core, but it passed before he answered her: "Of course I do. I've always loved you."

Morgan felt overcome by two seemingly disparate emotions, happiness and humility. Francis's declaration overwhelmed her with joy, and at the same time it made her feel unworthy. She, who had spent her youth denying her love for Francis, considering him a rude North Country brute, a clumsy ruffian, a carnal animal, had never really considered his feelings. She had not once dwelt upon the pain and sacrifice he had borne, the fortitude he had shown all these years in waiting for her to become his wife. Slowly, she looked up at him again, noting the hint of gray in the sandy hair, the lines of laughter and sorrow around his eyes, the touch of dignity the years had bestowed on him. They had given each other their bodies, but because they had been married to other people, they had not dared to give each other their hearts. Now there was no longer any need to keep the deepest of their secrets hidden.

"Oh, Jesu," Morgan whispered, "I've been adroit at only one thing all my life—self-delusion."

To her astonishment, Francis laughed. "Well, you didn't delude me. At least not all the time, though I had grave cause for concern with Seymour. Richard, too, for a short time. Still, for a woman who never seemed to stop and think, I couldn't expect much else."

"Why didn't you stop me?" she cried, throwing herself against his chest.

"I couldn't. I wasn't there when you fell into their arms. And," he added, feeling the curve of her waist under the heavy riding cloak, "you had to learn for yourself, after all."

"I have. I did. Oh, Francis!" She pressed against him, her coif not quite reaching his chin. "I swore years ago I'd chart my own course—and yet when I could, I steered into the shoals! Why?"

"Because you had no navigator to guide you," he answered, and felt Morgan stiffen suddenly in his arms. "Not that you couldn't have managed on your own, but so often you were, as most of us are, blindly willful. And you, like anyone else, would have steered a keener course with a navigator who cared where you were heading. Now that you realize that, we will do well together."

Morgan looked up and smiled. But she could not resist one last testing remark: "And you will watch your son grow up as Earl of Belford?"

She felt him shrug. "Robbie would be Earl of Belford whether I marry you or not. The question is, do I acknowledge him as my own and let Edmund supplant him as rightful heir?"

That had never occurred to Morgan. She traced Francis's jawline with her finger and looked thoughtful. "No. Perhaps someday we can tell Robbie the truth. But I want no more strife between brothers in my world."

"Then we will not tell him ever. I will be a father to him —and the others. That's all that matters." He took her chin in his hand and kissed her lips; it was a slightly clumsy, surprisingly tender kiss. How long it had been since they had kissed, Morgan thought, and wished they could make love there, among the trunks and packing crates. But that was not possible; the children and Polly and Peg were probably impatient and tired of waiting for the journey to begin.

Francis, as ever, seemed to be reading her mind. "Oh, come along," he said almost gruffly, as he let go of her and gave her behind a swift swat. "It's going to be a long, tiresome ride in this damnable rain."

Morgan gave him a sharp glance, started to say something in tart reply, but smiled instead. "I don't know what I've missed more, Francis—making love to you—or arguing with you."

He said something that sounded like "Hfrumph," grabbed her arm, and hurried her out into the hallway where he began to shout for Polly and Peg. "Load the wagons at once," he ordered as the two women stared at him in surprise. "Where are those lazy retainers? Tell them to get moving. We're going home—to Belford."

Outside, the rain still poured down as London's citizens murmured about floods and the men in the countryside fretted over their crops. The skies glowered, casting dreary shadows over the land. But down in the fields, the first daffodils began to open, pushing their way out from under old stone fences, taking hold even in the rockiest of soil, raising their bright faces to challenge the last storm of winter.

Bestselling Author
__MARY DAHEIM__

In the Splendor of Royal Courts—
Passion Reigns in...

DESTINY'S PAWN 86884-9/$3.50
The spellbinding story of a beautiful young woman who is swept up in the intrigues of the royal court of Henry VIII, and forced into marrying a conceited Earl, before she can fulfill her destiny's passion with the one man who truly loves her.

LOVE'S PIRATE 83840-0/$3.95
A rousing tale of a lovely young woman left penniless by her father's death, who promises a dashing young pirate her silence about his true identity in exchange for the security of marriage. Despite their duties at court and painful separations, both are stunned by the passion that bargain releases.

Buy these books at your local bookstore or use this coupon for ordering:

Avon Books, Dept BP, Box 767, Rte 2, Dresden, TN 38225
Please send me the book(s) I have checked above. I am enclosing $_____
(please add $1.00 to cover postage and handling for each book ordered to a maximum of three dollars). *Send check or money order—no cash or C.O.D.'s please.* Prices and numbers are subject to change without notice. Please allow six to eight weeks for delivery.

Name _____

Address _____

City _____ State/Zip _____

Daheim 4-84